A SPECIAL BREED

A Nevada cowboy is called a buckaroo. He is like a wild horse. A buckaroo will leave bed, board, wife, possessions, his good sense, and any instinct of self-preservation to go after the wild horse or the wild cow.

The buckaroo believes mustang blood is necessary in stock that is to thrive in Nevada. A human must have some of it too, if he is to make a living in Nevada. The buckaroo believes in the saying *"Mejor saber el terreno, que ser el mejor vaquero"*—better to know the country than know all there is to know about cowboying. The point being, it is possible to know terrain, never possible to know all about cowboying.

THE OUTFIT

J. P. S. BROWN

BANTAM BOOKS
NEW YORK • TORONTO • LONDON • SYDNEY • AUCKLAND

THE OUTFIT

A Bantam Book / published by arrangement with the author

PRINTING HISTORY
Dial Press edition published in 1971
Bantam edition / February 1990

ISBN 0-553-28169-0

Published simultaneously in the United States and Canada

*Bantam Books are published by Bantam Books, a division
of Bantam Doubleday Dell Publishing Group, Inc. Its trademark, consisting of the words "Bantam Books" and the
portrayal of a rooster, is Registered in U.S. Patent and
Trademark Office and in other countries. Marca Registrada.
Bantam Books, 666 Fifth Avenue, New York, New York 10103.*

PRINTED IN THE UNITED STATES OF AMERICA

KRI   0 9 8 7 6 5 4 3 2 1

Table of Contents

Chapter 1

THE OUTFIT

In the time of our great-grandfathers, an outfit was a group of men who packed the gear to husband a herd of cattle to market. An outfit made cattle livestock. An outfit rode into a country horseback, set a price on cattle, either bought the cattle or contracted to drive them to market, defended the stock on the trail, gave it value when it arrived where people could buy it, and sold it for its certain value. Later, the ranches became known as outfits. A ranch is an outfit because it is equipped to husband the bovine from birth to market. A cowboy's gear became known as an outfit and is its smallest entity. In some countries a manchild might be called a "little outfit" by his father, who was also born to an outfit. He is an outfit too because he was born with all the equipment and potential for the husbandry of cattle. He is born a cowboy and it is an irrefutable fact that cowboys are born and not made.

Bert Sorrells had never stopped to look at this part of Nevada before, although he had been through it many times. This was a part of the state everybody crossed as fast as they could. When he turned off the highway onto the dirt road that led to the headquarters of the ranch called the Famous Outfit, he stopped the old car he

1

called Carlotta and got out to stretch and look around.

The only manufactured lines in the country were the pavement stretching north and south and a telephone line crossing east and west. Sorrells saw a flat, dry country covered with short brush and joshua trees. He saw blue mountains high and sounding every side of it. The sky was open. The country had stillness until someone hurried a machine along the highway making a muted rush through the heavy thermal air. Sorrells sighed. He saw no fences. He saw no cattle, but he saw cow chips drying to dust. He climbed back onto Carlotta's torn cushions and started her up and went on through the fine dust.

The road headed straight toward mountains in the west and made long dips over ground Sorrells had not been able to see from the highway. He began to see cattle. He saw mother cows with unbranded calves. The cattle were in good shape. He stopped Carlotta again and studied the ground. The feed was shadscale, heavy with maturing seed; white and black sage; and a seldom spot of coarse grass, green at the stem and dry on top. This was August and when Sorrells kicked the ground no moisture showed. These were not cattle a man would have to wait on or fetch and carry for. These made their own living.

The road turned north into the mountains. At the summit of these mountains, on a high windy pass covered with tall sage and piñon, the road ended at the man-made improvements known as Headquarters of the Famous Outfit, Ethel, Nevada.

Sorrells drove by an acre of corrals made of eight-inch steel posts filled with concrete and painted with aluminum paint; an iron and tin aluminum-painted barn and saddle house; a white, board bunkhouse. He saw tractors, trucks, pickups, jeeps. He saw heavy equipment with its paint worn off from use, blades worn and shiny, bodies greasy, dusty. All were parked beside an open shed four times larger than the barn. In the shed he saw black portable welders, torches, compressors, hoists, jacks, steel plates and slabs, and cupboards he imagined were full of fittings, nuts, bolts, spark plugs, springs, shocks.

No men were about. The day was Sunday. All the conglomerate of steel and chipped paint and grease had reverted to its normal lameness as it stood in the attitude in which it had been abandoned on Saturday. It probably would assume useful form on Monday when it would be fired up again and moved toward more improvements over the country. Sorrells saw no flesh and blood of horses or cattle at headquarters that day.

He drove to a square, cinder block house surrounded by a chain link fence. In front of this house an Arizona licensed car was parked. Sorrells recognized the car and stopped Carlotta beside it. He got out. The only shade tree at headquarters had been fenced outside the chain link fence of the cinder block house. He wondered how this place could ever be home for anyone. It evidently had once been a community. Streets were still plainly marked by old false fronts of buildings that were now broken, baked boards filled with bent, rusty nails. The new improvements the Outfit had made of steel, aluminum paint, and cinder block might stay much longer than the wooden community had, but they made headquarters of the Outfit look like a prison stockade.

Sorrells leaned back and let out a squall that started high and ended low. The front door of the cinder block house boomed and shook as if something heavy had bounced off it and then it was jerked open and Roy Cunningham came through it. He was grinning. His wife, Maudy Jane, was behind him, smiling.

"What do you think you are doing out there, Wild Man? Come in," Cunningham said. Sorrells shook hands with him. Cunningham was a half a head taller than Sorrells and Sorrells was six feet two. Maudy Jane was small, thin and wiry from making a living with Cunningham on dry and starved-out ranches.

"You'll stay with us tonight," Cunningham said. "We'll find you a place in the bunkhouse when all the crew is back from town tomorrow. I hardly know the men and don't know how they are set up. Whatever accommodations we find for you will be better than that old flea-bitten blanket you used in Mexico for a bed." Sorrells grinned, ducked his head and didn't answer.

The three friends ate most of a ten-pound beef roast herded along by onions and potatoes and mired in thin, dark

brown gravy. After supper they sat in the living room smoking and talking. Cunningham had been on the Outfit one week.
He had taken over as manager for a corporation owned by a
Hollywood comedian and his son. This ranch was only one of
the many businesses Famous Enterprises ran. Famous had
owned the Outfit three years. The ranch had not been decently
managed since Famous had taken it over. No real cowman had
been in charge since Famous had bought it from an old pair of
wolves called the Parker Brothers, who had run its one thousand sections and two thousand head for thirty years before they
had even owned a truck. They had husbanded their cattle on
horseback and had led packhorses loaded with their beds and
provisions, making a different home in the open each night.

"I've had a sinking spell ever since you told me on the
phone that this outfit is a thousand sections," Bert Sorrells
said. "We're going to be making those big circles."

"Oh, we've got three fences to help us," Cunningham
laughed. "We've got a section horse pasture and a small
pasture for weaning heifers here at headquarters and the
owner told me we're supposed to have a fence running north
and south that cuts the Outfit in two. I haven't seen the big
fence and I've been all over the ranch in the pickup."

"That fence will be a lot of help. It makes two five
hundred section pastures."

"If it gets in our way we've plenty of machinery and
operators to roll it up with."

"How many mechanics have you got?"

"Two who act as mechanics and water men and two hay
haulers."

"How many cowboys?"

"Five with you and me but I'm going to fire one."

"You're going to keep four cowpunchers to gather a
thousand sections? You figure on furnishing lanterns instead
of cots?"

"Hell, I'd hire five more if I could get them. You seen
any cowpunchers who wanted to work lately at this kind of pay?"

"Which brings us to the matter of wages. How much
does it pay, I mean, if it does?"

"Two hundred and fifty dollars a month and your room
and board."

Sorrells didn't have anything to say about that.

"When we finish rounding up, I'll know my crew and the front office will know me, and I'll get you more money," Cunningham said.

"How long do you figure it'll take us to gather the cattle?"

"The front office figures a month. I figure it is going to take us until Christmastime."

"What kind of horses have we got?"

"We're damn near afoot. We've got three head apiece. They all look stout, but I don't know how good they are."

"Why all the mechanics and machinery?" Sorrells asked.

"Famous Enterprises is fixing the place up so it'll pay."

"Didn't it pay when the Parkers had it?"

"Sure it did, but they were wolfing it. They only sold cattle when they needed a saddle blanket or a bill of groceries. Famous wants to increase the head count by a thousand head within the next five years."

"How many are they running now?"

"The last tally was fourteen hundred."

"How many cattle did they sell last year?"

"Two hundred twenty-two steers. Two hundred fifteen heifers."

Sorrells thought about this and lit a cigarette. "How much money do the mechanics make?" he asked.

"Two hundred and seventy-five a month and found."

"They ain't very good mechanics are they?"

"What good mechanic would work for that?"

"They're better thought of than the cowpunchers."

"You want to drive a cat?"

"No."

"I'll let you midnight on one of the cats and I'll fire a wino operator."

Sorrells turned darker in the face. "My saddle don't fit on one of them things," he said.

Cunningham laughed, but he studied Sorrells while he did it. Maudy brought them coffee and cake.

"Let's get our deal straight now before we start," Sorrells said.

"Get what straight?" Cunningham said.

"I'm hiring on to cowboy. If this outfit requires me

getting grease on me, or fixing fence, or hauling hay, or climbing on a windmill, or doing anything without it being horseback, then we haven't got a deal."

"Hell, Bert. You've owned your own outfit. You've been through the very problems I'm going to have. I was hoping you would help me with other work besides cowboying."

"Let me tell you something, Roy," Sorrells said. "I lost my outfit in Mexico two years ago. Ever since then I've let somebody else worry about the market and the trading and the machinery. My saddle never has fit on any creature but a horse."

"Bert, did you ever stop to think that maybe that's why you went broke? In this day and age a cowman has to know and do a lot more than just ride a horse after an old cow. Most managers require a hand to be ready to do anything that has to be done on a ranch, from shoeing a horse to building a dam to fixing a carburetor."

"Do you require that I ride a caterpillar, Roy?"

"No, but there are plenty of cowpunchers around who can, Bert."

"Cowpunchers, Roy?"

"Well, after a fashion."

"You bet, 'after a fashion.' You show me a man who is a good cat operator and I'll show you one making five dollars an hour which don't give him time to be a cowpuncher. Show me one who will work for two hundred seventy-five dollars a month and I'll show you one who is too sorry to make it as a caterpillar driver or a cowpuncher either one."

"Well, no. Most of these operators are winos and they ain't the cowmen you are, or is Dobie Porter or Wilson Burns, our other two cowboys, but they can sit a horse and stop a hole and they have been doubling as cowboys here."

"I figure a cowpuncher, if he's a good one, doesn't have time to do anything else. If you are going to have tractor drivers cowboying part time on horses we are trying to get along with, count me out."

"That's what Dobie said. I feel the same way. The four of us can probably handle the cowboying anyway until we can hire another cowpuncher or two."

"You put a mechanic on a horse and it's going to be just like you had two good men ride away."

"O.K. then, Bert. No mechanics will be cowboying from now on. Maybe when I tell them, they'll quit and I can hire some good men."

"Hell, they can still wear big hats and boots in town. Nobody in town has to know they ain't cowboying."

Cunningham and Maudy laughed at Sorrells. He grinned and laid down his cup. The cup was moist from the sweat of his hand. He couldn't take a job these days without first explaining he wouldn't stand for hauling hay or building pipeline. He was always nervous until he knew an outfit would take him on as a cowpuncher and require no other duties of him.

He stood up. "Where's my bed?" he asked. Cunningham got out of his easy chair and walked down a cinder block corridor. He stopped at a door and opened it for Sorrells. Sorrells stepped into a cinder block room with steel bordered windows, a steel locker closet, a cot, and a steel bedside table. Sorrells sat on the cot, lit a cigarette, and started pulling off his boots. Cunningham was still standing there. Maudy came in with a clean towel. Cunningham put his arm over her shoulder.

"This is the best job I've ever had in my life, Bert," he said. "I'm going to keep it."

Sorrells dropped a boot and looked up at him. "I thought you liked the feedlot. You were there eleven years. You made good money and you knew the business."

"Me and Maudy got tired of town. We were tired of the rat race."

"I know."

"We couldn't hold on to our money. We couldn't see where we were going and we were going like hell. We didn't have any peace. That's why I want this job."

"You can run this outfit lefthanded, Roy. Relax. You have the job."

"We sure do. Don't we, Maudy?" Cunningham said, squeezing his wife.

Maudy looked up at him and smiled. Sorrells looked down at the socks he wanted to take off so he could get to bed. He started unbuttoning his shirt and looked at Cunningham again.

"Well, good night, Bert," Cunningham said and started out.

"Good night."

"Sweet dreams," Maudy said. She turned back. "Bert?"

"Yes, Maudy Jane."

"Do you ever hear from Bonnie?"

"Not for a year and a half. Since before I saw you last."

"I wonder how she is. I always just loved that girl."

"She's probably doing all right. I would have heard if she wasn't."

"Where do you suppose she is?"

"She was in Vegas the last I heard. She liked Vegas."

"She never liked the ranch, did she?"

"No she didn't, but that don't make a bad feller out of her," Sorrells said and smiled.

"Maybe some day she'll come back to you. That could happen, you know."

"Hell, Maudy. I don't care. She's got her business and I've got mine."

"I'm going to hope for you both, like I always have. I pray for you."

"I know you do, Maudy Jane. Good night."

"Good night and sweet dreams, Bert," Maudy said, and went out.

Now if *that* isn't something, Bert Sorrells said to himself. He put his cigarette out on the steel table top. Wouldn't I be smart to look the Maniac up again. Old Maudy wants me to have troubles again. He undressed, put out the light, and got into the bed.

Old Maudy would be happiest if I was "coming home" every night. That Bonnie. "Now Bert, don't go to the saloon and get drunk. You come home when you are finished with your business. You are going to take me to Phoenix tomorrow so I can do some shopping. I need some things." Dear old Bonnie.

"I want to go to town, Bert. To the show. To the dance. Anyplace where there are people. Just so I can get away from here for a while."

"We went to town yesterday. It's seventy miles to town."

"To the grocery store! To the feed store!"

"To the goddam beauty parlor."

"I want to have some fun. I need a little fun once in a while."

"I know you do, Bonnie. So go on. I'm going to bed. I've got work to do."

"You don't have to work *all* the time. You can have a little *fun* once in a while."

"I *want* to work. I like it. I need to sleep so I can do it."

"You told me you had never been tired in your life."

"I'm not tired. Just sleepy."

"If you're not tired then take me to the dance."

Bert had climbed into their bed and shut his eyes.

"Wild Man," Bonnie had said. "Some wild man you are. I don't know where you got that reputation."

Bert had kept his eyes shut and just looked at the bright red of the light on his eyelids. After awhile he heard the car start up and he thought, she won't go. She's just going to make fumes and smoke. Then the bedroom door had opened. The car was still running.

"Well, are you going to take me to the dance or aren't you?" she had demanded.

He had looked at the bright red eyelids and tried to keep from laughing.

"All right. *Now* see," he heard her say and the bright red had turned into many bursting white lights and she had run out and slammed the door. He sat up in bed looking at the pieces of the wedding present she had hit him between the eyes with. Then he heard the car drive away. Later, while he was icing his swelling eyes, a neighbor had driven in and told him Bonnie was out of gas on the highway. The neighbor had refused to give her any gas and had left her sulking in the car. The neighbor had come in to see what was going on. The neighbors had all known the Sorrellses. The Sorrellses had been born, raised, married, and Bert Sorrells had expected they would grow old and die in that country.

Sorrells had gone for her and found her sitting quietly in the car. She had smiled at him. He had taken her home and they had been happy for a while that time. Sorrells smiled to himself in the cinder block dark.

Chapter 2

THE CREW

A remuda is the herd of horses being used by the cowboys on an outfit. A horse takes on his identity as a flesh and blood unit of an outfit when he begins the work of men and becomes a member of a remuda. The ideal remuda is composed of geldings only. Studs and mares fulminate trouble in a remuda because of the demands of their state as procreators in which their efficiency and trustworthiness to man can be stopped by natural forces such as phases of the moon. For geldings, the bachelor horses, man had arranged a life of work. Geldings have been altered to respond placidly to a society of horses doing man's work. In Spanish, remuda also means a change of horses, a relay, a relief. The Mexican saying is "el caballo revolcado es caballo remudado"—a horse that has a good place to roll is a relieved and rested horse.

Cunningham called Sorrells early, and Maudy fixed coffee and bacon, hotcakes, and eggs. They loafed and talked, smoked, and drank coffee until just before daylight, as most cowmen do. They got up hours before daylight just to be sure they wouldn't go to work sleepy. This habit was one of the many foolhardy habits American cowmen have developed since the time of the first Texas cowboys. Get up early. Eat a heavy breakfast. Then sit around and drink a gallon of coffee and smoke and talk until just before it is light enough to do anything efficiently. Then fumble around in the dark saddling a horse, start riding just before dawn when the sun is chasing cold night air through your bones, and at first light be far away from bed and board with all the kinks of comfort gone from the body.

On this morning, Sorrells and Cunningham walked to the bunkhouse at a quarter after five. The light in the bunkhouse kitchen was on, but the big room where the men slept was still dark for sleeping. When Cunningham turned on the light, most of the sleepers sat up and got out of their beds. Cunningham walked up to one of the men who was still asleep, his mouth open, his eyes half open.

"Hey! Hey!" Cunningham shouted. "Roll out, it's burning daylight."

The sleeper rolled so his face was away from Cunningham. His eyes closed. His mouth closed. He had a sparse and feathery mustache that fluffed with his breath and rolled as he chewed his morning mouth. Cunningham pumped down on his shoulder, bouncing him against the cot springs. The eyes came open and looked at Cunningham.

"Up," Cunningham barked. "Right now, or roll your bed and get the hell off the place."

"Don' feel goo'," Feathers said.

"Up! Or out!" Cunningham said and walked on to the kitchen.

Two men were finishing their breakfast at the kitchen table. Cunningham introduced them to Sorrells as Dobie Porter and Wilson Burns. Sorrells and Cunningham sat and drank coffee with them.

Dobie Porter was an old man. He had been a cowboy sixty of his seventy years. He knew nearly every cowboy that had ever amounted to anything, good or bad, that Sorrells knew. While they were talking, Sorrells suddenly remembered a story he had once heard about Dobie Porter. A prison sentence. A knifing. A load of stolen cattle in an auction. Sorrells would think about it later. Porter's face was burned a russet brown from his eyes to his collar. His head was pale and bald from the line his hat made just above his eyes. He had a short, hooked nose, false teeth, and wore thick, tinted glasses. When he rose to take his plates to the sink, Sorrells saw he was very short with wide horseman's hips and bow legs. Like all cowboys his age, he walked with a stiff roll, as though every bone in his body had been broken at least once and when the breaks had healed, the joints in his bones had calcified too. His feet were so small Sorrells was sure he could have worn the boots of a twelve-year-old girl. His Levis had wide cuffs turned up at the bottom.

Porter's talk was an unceasing monotone. Fourteen years ago he had partnered with the Parkers on the Outfit. Now he was back again as a hired cowboy. He knew the location and name of every spring, every draw and canyon. The county maintained a good network of roads to mining claims on the ranch. Porter knew the roads.

Wilson Burns was a Paiute Indian. He was brown and heavy, with thick hands and wide feet and a wide face. His hair hung to his shoulders. It was combed wet and water from it was running down the sides of his smooth face. Wilson looked like a two-hundred-pound Mongol tribesman. He smiled when Cunningham introduced him. Sorrells learned that he had been born and raised on the Outfit. His father had been born on the homestead that was the site of the headquarters. He had worked for the Outfit before and had been back for a month now. He knew the ranch. He and his father still had mining claims on it. They had run wild horses on it.

A man dressed in a new, black hat and a pair of shiny boots came into the bunkhouse. He had on gabardine trousers, a new shirt, and a bolo tie. He didn't say a word to anyone, but went to the stove and poured himself a cup of coffee. Sorrells saw Cunningham swell up. If man had hackles on the back of his neck, Cunningham would have been showing them now.

Porter introduced the man as Duane Jones. Duane turned early morning, staring eyes on Sorrells and nodded.

"Did you make out all right in town, Duane?" Cunningham asked him.

"Sure, why?" Duane said and turned his back on Cunningham.

"I just wondered if you got everything done. It must

have been important and hard to do. You left Thursday afternoon without telling anybody."

"I told Jack."

"Jack didn't tell me."

"Well, I can't help that."

"I can. You're fired."

Duane felt obliged to face Cunningham now. "Now wait a minute," he said, his eyes coming awake. "You can't fire me. I had to go to the doctor."

"I have fired you."

"Hell, Roy. I was sick. Don't that mean anything?"

"You weren't too sick to shill in the hotel casino in Keno every night since Thursday."

"I need that extra money to pay the doctor. I can't get by on the two fifty this outfit pays."

"Well, you won't have to worry about that anymore. You're fired, Duane. Here's your check." Cunningham took a check out of his shirt pocket and handed it to Duane. He took it and looked at it.

"I've got more than this coming," he said.

"Look on the detachable part. I took out the money you owed the company for tires and gasoline. It's itemized."

"You hit me awful hard with this, Roy."

"You got the tires and gas wholesale. That's the best I can do for you.

"You shouldn't fire a man for being sick."

"You and I both know you aren't fired for being sick," Cunningham said.

Duane walked out of the bunkhouse. Another man met him at the door, talked to him, and came into the kitchen. He carried a small, blue satchel with white lettering on it that said, "Icelandic Airways." His clothes and skin were wrinkled and black with the grime of roads and machines and nights out of bed. He wore a faded red baseball cap, a loud Hawaiian sportshirt too large for him, a pair of green slacks too tight and too short for him, an old pair of runover dress shoes, and a pair of sagging socks that did not match. His thin hair grew long and stringy to his neck. He looked at Sorrells because Sorrells had been watching his progress through the bunkhouse. He said, "Mr. Cunningham?" and took off his cap. His skull was balding and sooty on top. He smiled.

"That's the man you want," Sorrells said, nodding toward Cunningham.

"Mr. Cunningham?" the man said again to Roy.

"Speak," said Cunningham. He put his hands behind him and leaned against the stove.

"My name is Coburn," the man said. He did not offer his hand. Sorrells knew the man was sure Cunningham wouldn't want to take it. "I need a job. Mr. Jones brought me out from town. He said you were hiring."

"What can you do?" Cunningham asked.

"I'm a welder, but I've done most everything there is to do with tools."

"Where have you worked?"

"I'm from Texas, but I've worked in every state of the Union and some in the foreign countries. I worked here last year and the year before that."

"Why did you leave?"

"I left when it turned cold. I don't like the cold. I go south when it turns cold."

"Will you stay on if I hire you?"

"I'll stay until the snow flies."

"I don't know. I need someone steady. I've got enough transient help."

"I won't try to fool you, Mr. Cunningham, I'm leaving here when it turns cold."

"I don't know." Cunningham studied the man. He looked at Sorrells. Sorrells looked away. "What have you done around here?" Cunningham asked.

"I made that stock rack on the truck. I put those gates on the corrals last year."

"Are you the one who did that work?"

"Yes sir, Mr. Cunningham."

"Is your name Tom?"

"Yes sir."

"You're hired."

"Thank you, sir."

"Where's your bed?"

"All I've got in the world is right here in this satchel. I'll have to get along until payday."

"I'll advance you some money for bedding."

"I'll get along."

"Where can he sleep, Dobie?" Cunningham asked Porter.

"I don't know," Porter said. "He can't bunk with me. Sorrells will be sleeping in there. That was the only bunk open."

"I'll stay in that old toilet behind the bunkhouse. I always stay in there. I fix it up right nice for myself."

"That place is too small for a man," Cunningham said.

"It has always been my place," Tom said.

"Come on, we'll look at it," Cunningham said. They walked out.

"Bum!" Porter snorted. "Another wino bum! This outfit didn't have enough of them alkys. No! He had to hire one more. Well, by damn, he ain't bunking with us, Bert. I don't care where he parks him but I ain't bunking with him."

"Where am I bunking?" Sorrells asked.

"The only empty bunk is in the room with me."

Sorrells brought in his bed and grip. Porter was in the room they would share. The floor was littered with ropes, scraps of leather, spurs, boots, dirty socks, dirty Levis, manure, hay, dust, and dead flies. Suits of long underwear, half-soiled trousers and shirts, a new hat, a new rope, hung from nails in the wall. A table between the cots was covered with salves, ointments, linaments, a glass full of dirty water, a can of Fasteeth, a used bar of soap, a dirty towel, a sacking needle, and waxed twine.

"The next thing you know they'll have a bum like that working horseback," Porter said.

"Have you drawed your string of horses, Dobie?" Sorrells asked.

"I brought an old horse of mine and a colt I bought recently and I drew two of the company horses. I took gentle horses. They need to be short and gentle for me to be able to get on anymore, I'm so stiff."

"I guess I'd better draw mine."

"Roy set two head aside for you. He said you would need big horses."

"Let's go see them," Sorrells said. When they walked through the bunkhouse, Feathers was still sitting on the edge of his cot with his tattooed arms sagging between his legs, his long hair hanging over his face. Another mechanic was standing before a mirror combing his blond, almost white hair. He lifted his eyebrows at himself.

Wilson had opened the gate from the horse pasture and the remuda of horses was streaming into an alley that ran through the corrals. Porter walked into a small corral where a buckskin horse stood.

"Buck!" Porter said. "Good morning, Buck." Buck looked at Porter. Porter hung a canvas nosebag on him and stood close to him while he ate, rubbing him.

Wilson was hanging morrals on the horses as they followed him into a corral. They crowded around him. While the horses were eating, Sorrells stood with Wilson and looked them over. Wilson pointed out two big sorrel horses Cunningham had saved for Sorrells. One, called Big Red, was wide and muscular, a solid sorrel with no white marks on him. The other, called Roller, was tall and rawboned, with a head he held very high and one white-stockinged hind foot. Roller watched the men out of eyes that showed terror. Both of his front legs were badly scarred around the pastern. One hind leg was scarred and the hoof was misshapen from scar. Sorrells chose another tall, long, rawboned horse for his mount, a bald-faced brown with two stockinged hind legs.

"What about them?" Sorrells asked Wilson.

"Well, if I were you I'd pass old Roller by," Wilson said.

"Why?"

"He's nervous."

"What about Big Red?"

"He's lazy."

"And the bald-face horse?"

"They call him Baldy."

"What about him?"

"He's no worse than any of them, except I figure someone has run a lot of wild horses on him and spoiled him. The farther he goes the harder he is to handle. He's chargy. He'll run into a barn or over a fence when he's hot if you don't get him turned."

"That's nice."

"Oh, they're a fine bunch of horses," Wilson smiled. "The son of the Outfit would call yours spirited. At least Roller and Baldy are. Big Red just don't care."

"Who's the son of the Outfit, Wilson?"

"We call Bobby Lang the son of the Outfit. He's son to Archie Lang, the comedian. The funny feller. They own the Outfit. Didn't you know?"

"Yes, I did. What kind of owners are they?"

"I don't know Archie. Bobby's kind of a nice feller. He's here a lot. I don't think Archie has ever been here."

"What kind of string did you draw?"

"I drew the top horses. Front Office, Bobby's own personal horse, is in my string. So is Brandy, Bobby's wife's horse. Then I've got that little sorrel, Rabbit."

"Wilson?"

"What?"

"You're all fixed up."

Wilson laughed. "I'm wondering how Bobby and his wife are going to take it the first time they want to go horseback riding and I've already got their horses rode down. Old Rabbit's the only one of the horses that can do anything. He was born on the 61 Ranch near here. I broke him when he was a colt."

"Where did they get these horses? How did they put them together, Wilson?"

"A man from the front office bought them in the auctions. Front Office and Brandy were sent up from Southern California. I heard Bobby say he paid fifteen hundred dollars for Brandy and Front Office."

Sorrells laughed. "*That's* a helluva deal. Some chickenfeed horses plus some pets makes us horseback."

"You watch old Roller, Bert."

"What's the hole in him?"

"He'll panic. He'll go clear out of his head for any number of reasons. Just don't go to sleep on him. You can't trust him. I'd turn him out if I were you."

"He's good enough for me. I'll probably get along with him if I can keep him out of the wire."

"He's crazy about a rope too. He's had forty different

kinds of riders on him in his career. Not one of them knew how to handle him and they were all afraid of him. The good hands never would fool with him."

"Why were they afraid of him?"

"He killed an Okie the first time he was saddled after he healed from the wire cuts. The old horse has got plenty of steam, but I was surprised to see him here when I got back. I thought he'd been dog chowed long ago. He really doesn't deserve another chance."

"Aw, the last chance comes soon enough for all of us. I ain't going to be the one to deny him another chance," Sorrells said.

Chapter 3

MEXICAN SADDLE

All a cowboy needs in order to get a job are his bed and saddle, a pair of spurs, a pair of leggings, a good pair of boots, a good hat, a good brush jacket, a warm jacket, gloves, bridles, various bits and hackamores for different horses in his string, saddle blankets and slicker, beside all the clothing he periodically gets torn off his back and butt. His outfit, if it is complete and satisfies him, only costs about a thousand dollars and takes him as few as ten years to accumulate. His outfit is perishable and expendable in his work of assuming life and death responsibility over hundreds of thousands of dollars worth of cattle, and he never looks well dressed and he never has any money except for his other most vital essentials, whiskey and cigarettes.

Sorrells had brought two saddles to the Outfit with him. One was a good used stock saddle. The other was a Mexican saddle of the old skeleton style. A friend had given him the saddle in Mexico. He liked to use it in mountains or in hot weather. It was light, had a good seat, and was easy on a horse's back. It had a horn six inches in diameter. It had no swells; no leather over the naked tree; a short cantle; very short, round skirts; and no fenders on the stirrup leathers. The leather in both saddles

was good and well tallowed, but the Mexican saddle was
lightest, so Sorrells decided to use it the first day he saddled
a horse for the Outfit.

He caught Roller. He put a horsehair bosal on him and
led him to the saddle house. Roller led as though in fear that
if he didn't follow close on Sorrells' heels, Sorrells would kill
him. He almost ran over Sorrells when he led him through a
gate. Big tears ran out of his eyes when Sorrells stood him at
the hitch rail outside the saddle house. He trembled when
Sorrells saddled him. Sorrells bridled him and turned him
around. Roller moved on three feet of lead rope as though the
owls had hold of him. Sorrells threw the stirrups over the seat
of the Mexican saddle and tied them behind the cantle. He
loaded Roller in the stock truck with Porter's Buck, Wilson's
Front Office, and Cunningham's Blue, and climbed into the
truck with Wilson.

Wilson drove south off the summit at Ethel in the still,
August dark. He turned east when the first glow of dawn
began. Before first light, he caught up to Roy Cunningham's
pickup at a place called Flatcar Springs, where a set of
rundown pens with a loading chute was located. Cunningham
left the pickup there and he and Porter got into the cab of the
stock truck. Wilson drove further east. At first light the four
men unloaded their horses, tightened their cinches, and
mounted. They would make a drive along both sides of the
road through a long, wide, draw flanked by mountains toward
Flatcar. Sorrells and Porter took one side of the road. They
would throw the cattle they found to Cunningham and Wilson
on the road.

For all his fear and bad reputation, Roller moved and
handled out in the open better than any horse Sorrells had
ever ridden. This horse did not tire a man. He moved across
country without wavering in his direction as surely as though
he were on a bridle path. At a lope he floated over brush and
rock. He reined at a touch. He moved effortlessly.

Porter took the outside circle. Sorrells took the country
near the road. He watched Porter ride away to higher range.
The old man rode slowly, watching the ground every now and
then for tracks. He had to be quiet now awhile unless he
talked to himself. He might be old and stiff on the ground,

but his foot looked young in the stirrup and he sat Buck like he was part of him.

Sorrells gave Porter time to get ahead of him so any cattle Porter started toward the road would come to Sorrells' front. Then he started Roller toward Flatcar Springs. He kept on top of the ridges. He rode to the high points to see the country, to watch for Porter, and to watch the road.

The ridges held sparse piñon and juniper trees. The draw had joshua, white sage, and some green grass. Sorrells stopped Roller on the point of a ridge over a wash thick with juniper and piñon. He let Roller breathe. Roller stood quietly. He did not draw a long breath. He watched.

The biggest buck deer Sorrells had ever seen moved across the wash below him. He was fat as butter. His great antlers were polished. He stayed ahead of the horseman for half an hour and then went into a wash, changed direction, and was gone.

Sorrells picked up a bunch of cattle. They were trotty. He held them until they quieted. He pushed them on and a bunch came to him from Porter's direction. He held the two bunches together and pushed them down to the road when he saw Cunningham driving cattle there.

When the herd was nearing the pens, Wilson came off a hill on the run with two cows, two big, long-eared calves, and one three-year-old maverick heifer. Porter and Sorrells got out ahead of Wilson's bunch and turned it into the herd. Wilson's cattle went right on through the herd. Cunningham turned them back into the herd again. This time they stayed, but the maverick heifer didn't like it. She moved to the outside of the herd. She watched for a hole between the horsemen. The men had trouble penning the herd and she broke out and ran away. No one followed her. When the herd had been penned, the first man free was Bert Sorrells on Roller, the outlaw. He went after the heifer. He took down a tallowed reata he liked to use. Roller overtook the heifer. Sorrells let him rate her a moment and then laid a nice loop that settled around her horns. He jerked the slack out of the loop, took a dally around the horn of the Mexican saddle, and sat down on Roller to let the dally burn out on the horn. He had fifty feet of reata and he figured all was well, but instead of slowing down behind the heifer, Roller ducked off and ran away with her. Sorrells could not hold that dally with the heifer going one way and Roller caroming the other. He unwound his dally and dropped his coils when the reata flayed his hand. The heifer went on about her original business with Sorrells' reata snaking in the brush behind her. Wilson pounded by on Front Office and caught her with his nylon. Front Office planted his front feet into the ground and tried to duck off too, but the nylon held on Wilson's horn. Front Office was almost jerked down. Wilson's saddle rose high behind but held the heifer.

Wilson led the heifer to the pens and corralled her with the rest of the cattle. Sorrells' reata wound in the hooves of the herd. Cunningham heeled the heifer and Wilson took the reata off. He coiled it and handed it to Sorrells. The reata was dusty, manury, and wet with urine.

Sorrells was ashamed he had been disarmed by the heifer his first day out. If he started blaming Roller now he would never get any work done on him. He would have to prove to be more horseman or he would be helpless on the horse. He did not cuss the horse so Porter, Wilson, and Cunningham could hear him. He only privately made some very certain promises to Roller. "Roller, I'm going to make you wish you were in a can of dog food," he told him.

Porter, Wilson, and Cunningham did not say anything to him about losing his reata. They ignored the fact he would have had hell getting it back if he had been alone with just old Roller to help him. They talked about themes far removed from reatas. Sorrells looked at his roping hand and it was skinned from his index finger across each second joint to his little finger, the exact area of his hand he needed to make a hand as a roper for the Outfit.

The men watered their horses at noon and ate vienna sausages and canned tomatoes at the pickup. They built a fire and made coffee. Cunningham and Wilson went in the pickup to bring back the stock truck. Porter and Sorrells put branding irons on the fire and tightened their cinches. They had the heifer and several baby calves to brand, vaccinate, and earmark.

They led Roller and Buck into the corral and mounted. Porter took down his rope and walked Buck into the herd.

The maverick heifer stood and faced him a moment. Porter gave his loop a short, overhead flip and it landed neatly around her horns. He walked Buck after her when she turned and crowded her way into the herd. He took up his coils until he was close to her and then he turned Buck away and dragged her out of the herd on a short rope.

Sorrells rode to heel her. He was leaning over Roller's shoulder to stand a loop in front of her hind legs when Roller fell back and reared. He bashed Sorrells in the mouth with the top of his head. Sorrells leaned back with blood in his mouth and rammed his spurs into Roller. He pointed him toward an empty corner of the corral, gave him a slack rein, and poured the steel into his shoulders and barrel. Roller would not buck, but as soon as Sorrells rode him back to the heels he tried to rear and duck off again. Sorrells made him think he was going to gut him with his heavy blunt spurs. Roller quit rearing but he wouldn't go to the heels long enough to give Sorrells a throw. The heifer was bucking around on the end of Porter's rope.

"Give her slack, Dobie," Sorrells said. He took two coils of the reata in his loop hand and threw the loop underhanded over the twenty-five or thirty feet that separated him from the heifer. The loop yawned and whipped up under the flanks of the heifer as she walked away. She walked into the loop and Sorrells pulled his slack and caught her high above the hocks.

"*That's* the way, cowboy," Dobie Porter yelled. "Both hind legs and the end of her tail."

Sorrells wanted to smile but his mouth was too sore. He turned Roller carefully away from the heifer to keep him from rearing, took a dally, and walked him with the tight reata burning the horn until the heifer was down. He held her down while Porter branded, earmarked, and vaccinated her. Porter got back on Buck and rode up to Sorrells, coiling his rope.

"Goddamn, Bert," he said. "Old Roller got you, didn't he?"

"Yeah," Sorrells said. His lips were so swollen he could see them. They looked like a tomato. He felt his front teeth and they were loose.

"Did he get your grinners too?"

"I think they're going to stay in," Sorrells said.

"That sonofabitch'll kill a feller."

"He's had the heels jerked on him."

"That comes from a gunsel catching a pair of heels and just driving off and running the old horse against a slack rope. It's the same as if he'd caught a post and ridden off. It jerks hell out of a horse. It hurts his back."

"Yeah," Sorrells mumbled.

"I do thisaway with one spoiled like that. Ride off slow till all the slack is tight then start him once and pull steady. That way he ain't been jerked to a stop and hurt and started again."

"Yeah," Sorrells said.

"You done just right," Porter said. "That was a nice heel loop you threw. Like it was glued on."

Sorrells didn't say anything.

"They's some good reata men come out of your country in Arizona."

It hurt Sorrells to talk.

"I used a reata a lot when I was young. They's a lot of difference between a reata and one of these damn stiff nylons."

Sorrells got down off Roller and led him out of the corral. He rearranged the fire so the irons would heat faster. He took out his knife and sharpened it on a whetstone. Porter heeled the baby calves and Sorrells branded, earmarked, vaccinated, and castrated. He scraped out some good coals and put the mountain oysters on them to braise. When the branding was finished, he and Porter ate the oysters without salt.

Wilson came with the stock truck and the men began loading weaner calves, bulls, and old cows to take to headquarters. The calves and old cows would be sold. The bulls would be fed hay and rested until spring. When Wilson went in with the last load of cattle, Sorrells stayed at the corral with the horses. Porter and Cunningham went in to headquarters in the pickup.

Sorrells was out of cigarette papers. The first day out and he found himself alone, ashamed of his day's work, with a busted mouth, a sore hand and no cigarette papers. A dis-

tinctly bad day the first day out. He was keeping the tally
book on cattle that were being left on the range. He tore a
leaf out of the book and built a fat cigarette for company.

Wilson came for him in the late afternoon and they
loaded the horses. On the way to headquarters Wilson suddenly pounded on the steering wheel and said, "Sonofagun."

"What's the matter, Wilson?" Sorrells asked.

"I forgot to count that last load of cattle I took in and I
turned them in on top of the others we've gathered."

Sorrells laughed. "Hell, just figure what you had before
and count what you've got now and you'll have it."

"It isn't that simple. We'll have to gather them all and
count the whole bunch again."

Sorrells thought a few minutes. "Well, let's see, Wilson.
You took seventeen head, didn't you?"

"I don't know. I forgot to count."

"You took seventeen head."

"Did you count them?"

"No, but I know what cattle you took."

"Now, Bert."

"Sure, Wilson. You took two bulls, didn't you?"

"Yes."

"O.K., two bulls. You took seven old cows: two high-
horned cows that looked a lot alike; two muley cows, one was
red-necked; one motley-faced cow; one red-necked, tipped-
horned cow; and one wild, old, line-backed, crooked horned
cow. You took eight weaners: four steer and four heifers."

"Now, Bert," Wilson laughed. "You don't really remember those cattle, do you?"

"Of course, Wilson, of course. Stick with old Bert."

"Awww!" Wilson said.

"That's right, Wilson," Sorrells said. He got Wilson's
tally book out of the glove compartment and tallied the last
load.

At the headquarters compound Wilson maneuvered the
truck to a chute to unload the horses. Feathers and the
white-headed cat driver were standing on the platform by
the chute. They were wearing big hats and boots. Wilson
opened the door of the stock truck. The white-headed man
climbed up on the rack and began clapping his hands and

hollering at the horses. While the other horses walked out, Roller threw up his head and began lunging and sliding in the corners of the rear of the truck, terrified of the man on the rack.

"Roller, you silly bastard," the white-headed man hollered. His tongue was thick. He was full of beer. He was now going to show Sorrells and Wilson how to unload horses.

"Whitey, get down from there and he'll come on out," Wilson said.

"Roller!" Whitey yelled and clapped his hands. The other horses were standing down in the alley.

"Get down, Whitey," Wilson said.

"Look at that ringy bastard!" Whitey said and got down. Roller dodged and slid like a quail in a cage. Feathers went to the back of the truck and ran him out. Roller banged the side of the stock truck as he went into the chute. He stampeded with a terrible downhill momentum through the chute, into the alley, through the other horses, fell, and picked himself up. "Whooeee," yelled Whitey. "Go," yelled Feathers. Sorrells' Mexican saddle had slipped and was hanging on the horse's side, one stirrup whipping underneath him. Roller jumped a gate, charged down the long alley, ran into the gate at the end, and knocked himself down. He got up kicking the saddle. He left the saddle on the ground. He staggered a few steps and fell.

"Whooeee," Whitey yelled, slapping Feathers on the back. "That's the end of *that* crazy bastard."

Sorrells and Wilson walked down the chute and through the alley. The horse was getting up when Sorrells got to him. Sorrells caught the lead rope on the bosal. Wilson walked over to the saddle. Sorrells saw him pick up the horn. It had been sheared off cleanly where the base met the swell. The clean, hard grain of the red Mexican wood shone there. The stirrup leathers on one side were torn. The skirts were torn away from the tree. One stirrup was smashed.

Feathers and Whitey walked up.

"Hell, the leather's tore right off the seat," Feathers said.

"Naw," Whitey said, looking at Sorrells. "That's the way them cheap Meskin saddles come, ain't it?"

Sorrells took the horn from Wilson.

"You a Meskin?" Whitey asked Sorrells.

"I can glue that back on so it'll be plenty stout," Wilson said to Sorrells. "It might still be a saddle a man could use."

"You call *that* a saddle?" Whitey asked.

Sorrells smiled. "At least it *was* a saddle."

"That cheap thing?" Whitey said.

Wilson stepped back, looking at Whitey. Sorrells bent down and picked up his saddle. Feathers snorted through his downy mustache.

"How much did that saddle cost, hombre?" Whitey kept on.

"It was given to me," Sorrells said.

"And you was *using* that thing?"

Feathers laughed.

"That's the kind of *cowboys* Famous is importing to take our place," Whitey said, looking at Feathers. Feathers kept on laughing. "I don't know how you got that rig, fella, but *I* wouldn't have it even as a gift." Feathers clapped his hands and laughed. Roller sat back on the lead rope.

"Whoa, Roller," Sorrells said and led the horse away.

"Ho, Roller!" Whitey yelled. "You loco caballo, ho!" He clapped his hands and the horse almost ran over the top of Sorrells. Sorrells turned toward Whitey ready to fight. Roller sidled and swung away on the lead rope, dragging Sorrells down the alley.

"Now just watch it, Whitey," Wilson said. Whitey and Feathers laughed at him, climbed out of the alley. They got into a car and drove away.

Sorrells led Roller to a stall and grained him. He took off his chaps and spurs and walked to the bunkhouse. He undressed and got into his bed. His mouth was too swollen to eat supper.

In the night Sorrells was awakened by the loud voices of Feathers and Whitey coming in from their drunk. The door to the room Sorrells and Porter shared opened to the kitchen. They had left it open. When the drunks turned on the light in the kitchen it shone in Sorrells' face. He lay there listening to their drunken talk.

"Old Ruthie's got it for me," Feathers was saying. "She's

going to play up to me once too often when her husband is
gone to Keno."

"You think so?" Whitey asked.

"Well, Whitey. You've been around a lot. What do you
think about it?"

"You want to know?"

"Sure, that's why I'm asking you."

"Ruthie'll go after anybody when her old man's not
around."

"She brings my drinks to the pool table and is always
talking to me."

"She sells more beer that way."

"She took my side when that long-haired flower boy
came into the bar. Why is that, Whitey? Why is it a hippie
won't fight. I called him every name there was."

"They don't fight, I guess. That one didn't look stout
enough to wipe his own ass. Hey, Chief! Chief!" Whitey
hollered. "You want a beer?"

"No," Wilson answered.

"Don't get him started. He'll drink all our beer up and
then he'll go on the prod. Indians can't drink," Feathers said.
"They get mean."

"You afraid of a damn Indian?" Whitey asked.

"No, but I don't like drinking with one. That is just
asking for trouble.

"Shit. I've known tough Indians and got along with them
drunk or sober. I used to run around with a Yaqui Indian in
the service and they are the toughest Indians in the world."

"Yeah?"

"You bet."

"Did you ever fight a Indian?"

"I damned near killed that Yaqui one time in Japan. He
got mean drunk and tried to pin me to the bar with a
switchblade. I busted a full bottle of whiskey over his head
and then stomped him good."

"Boy, he must have been tough if that didn't kill him."

"He was tough but I was tougher. You got to be tougher'n
they are. There ain't any Indian or Meskin alive can whip a
tough white man."

"What about that new guy? You think he's a Meskin?"

"He's some kind of off breed, dark as he is. He's part Indian or Meskin or both." .

"You think you could whip him?"

"Shit!"

"He's purty big and he's mean-looking."

"They're all mean-looking. Hey, hombre! Hombre. You want a beer? Beer, hombre!"

Sorrells didn't answer. He wondered why Mexicans in Mexico hollered Spanish at him as though they thought he was deaf and idiots like Whitey hollered broken English at him. He lay there with his eyes opened only to slits, watching them.

The kitchen was a big room and had plenty of floor space. The bunkhouse had once been the Ethel, Nevada, meeting house and an old piano left over from those times had been rolled into the corner of the kitchen next to the door to Sorrells' room. Feathers and Whitey discussed something quietly for a moment and then Feathers began pounding on the piano. Whitey watched for Sorrells reaction.

"Beer, beer, beer," Feathers sang while he pounded with his fists on the piano. Sorrells got out of bed and stepped up behind him. He grabbed Feathers by the hair of the head, lifted him off the piano stool, and slammed his face down on the keys.

"You like to sing and play?" Sorrells asked him. "Play... play... play... play." Feathers slid below the keyboard. Sorrells pulled his head back and punched his face. Whitey grabbed his arm. Sorrells turned, took Whitey by the throat, and slammed him into the wall.

"Tough guy," Sorrells said and hit him. The tooth bone against the bone in his hand shocked all the way up his arm into his shoulder. He let Whitey slide down the wall. He positioned Whitey's face by the hair on his head. "Tough," he said and drew back to hit him again.

"Bert!" Wilson said from the door. Sorrells saw him out of the corner of his eye standing brown in his shorts in the doorway. He let Whitey fall back, his kneeling knees still under him.

"No, don't do that," Wilson said to Feathers. Sorrells turned around in time to see Feathers putting a butcher knife down. He stood there looking at Sorrells. "I don't want to fight," he said.

Sorrells went to his bunk and started dressing. Porter was sitting up in bed rubbing his bald head.

"You can turn on the light if you want to," he said. Sorrells pulled the ragged cord of the fly-specked light and began rolling his bed.

"You quittin', Bert?"

"No, I'm going outside to sleep," Sorrells said.

"Hell, they ain't going to bother you now."

"I'll sleep at Flatcar Springs."

"Do you want us to bring you anything?"

"Bring Roller. I'm going to use him until I wear him down to where I can find his heart, if he has any." Sorrells found food, coffee, and utensils in the kitchen. He put it all in a box and took it and his bed and grip out to Carlotta. He drove to the saddlehouse, got his gear, then drove out to Flatcar Springs.

He got out of Carlotta and walked to the pool where water seeped clearly under the moon. His mouth was very dry. His lips stretched nearly to cracking from dryness and swelling. He lay down and drank sweet, cold water. He sat up and looked at the moon's reflection in the pool.

He didn't mind the work, the injuries, the seldom wages, or the enemy horseflesh. It was the society he minded. He walked back to Carlotta and unrolled his bed on the ground. The cows whose calves the men had taken away that day walked around the camp all night bawling and searching for their calves. Coyotes, attracted by the bawling and hoping that perhaps they might find some calves in trouble, came and barked near the springs. Sorrells slept and rested well in that society.

Chapter 4

THE SON OF THE OUTFIT

The word leppie is from the Mexican lepe, *meaning a stunted calf, a calf that has been deprived of his early nourishment. Maybe his mother didn't make enough milk, though cows that don't seem to give more than a teacup full raise big, strong calves. Some cows give a lot of milk but their calves don't thrive. These cows might make too much milk for a little feller to be able to get his mouth over the swollen teat. Some cows might take to loco weed or sustain some other shock to their systems that dry up their mother juices. Certainly no calf's sire ever knew him.*

At any rate, until a cowpuncher takes him from his mother, a leppie is a dried-up, snot-nosed, pot-bellied little waif, and permanently beggarly.

Cunningham notified the front office in Los Angeles when the crew had gathered the first shipment of cattle. The crew would be branding and readying the cattle for shipment on Saturday of the first week Sorrells was at the Outfit. Word came from the front office that Bobby Lang would be at the ranch on that day to supervise the working of the cattle. Bobby was sometimes able to give his weekends to the ranch.

The crew was saddling horses when the son of the Outfit

31

flew high over Ethel in a silver plane, circled once, and landed on a strip down on the flats. Cunningham was waiting there to pick him up. From the corrals Sorrells saw Maudy Jane hurrying in and out of her back door with brooms and mops and rugs and rags, getting her house cleaner for the son of the Outfit.

Sorrells saddled Big Red for the first time that morning. Wilson caught Front Office for Bobby and left him standing saddled at the hitch rail while he and Porter and Sorrells rode out into the horse pasture to bring in the bulls and old cows. They were penning the cattle when Bobby rode out with Cunningham to help them.

The cattle crowded into the alley between the pens. Sorrells got off his horse to close the gate. Porter rode up and shook hands with Bobby. Wilson got off his horse and saw to his cinches. He stood beside Sorrells while they waited for the horsemen to ride through the gate. Cunningham stopped Bobby at the gate and introduced him to Wilson. Bobby had an open, smiling face that froze and did not speak when it met Wilson. Sorrells looked at Bobby's tight, highwater, white Levis that barely reached the top of his wellington boots. Bobby reached down from atop Front Office, squeezed Sorrells' sore hand, and called him Bert with a nice smile as though he had known him for years. He was bareheaded. Sorrells had seen him on television doing a soda pop commercial. He looked at the son of the Outfit in the high morning light of Ethel, Nevada and saw that his hair was bleached. Sorrells didn't hold that against him. Who knew what a man had to put up with in that movie and television business? Sorrells guessed bleached hair was part of the business, like getting manure under the fingernails was part of the cowpuncher business. Thank God for the man, bleached or no. He had a job for Sorrells on a thousand sections and no fences.

Sorrells got on Big Red and he and Wilson ran the weaner cattle into an alley. Sorrells began cutting the steer and bull calves off the heifers. Wilson, Porter, and Cunningham worked gates to separate pens. The bulls and steer calves were cut into separate pens, the heifers into another, and the dogie or leppie calves into another. Bobby Lang was handling the gate to the leppie pen.

Ordinarily Sorrells would have cut these little cattle on foot, but since this was his first day on Big Red, he wanted to see how the horse handled before he used him to cut any big or wild cattle in an alley. Big Red turned out to be lazy and afraid of cattle. He had the body and the action for cow work, he wasn't dumb, but he wouldn't do anything without a lot of encouragement.

Sorrells was wearing a heavy pair of Chihuahua spurs for Big Red's encouragement, and the horse soon found out what was expected of him. He did not like being ridden in front of the calves. Like Roller, he tended to rear up when work hurried him. Almost any work hurried him. Just looking at cattle hurried him. Sorrells gave him plenty of rein and a lot of steel and almost got the job done.

The last three cattle in the alley were heifers. One of them was a little, runty leppie. Sorrells let the two healthy heifers go by and stuck Big Red, who weighed about 1350 pounds, in front of the leppie as she trotted on weak legs to follow them. Something about the runt, alone in the end of the alley, bearing down on Big Red, gave him an excuse to act afraid and throw off on Sorrells. He ran backwards in the face of the leppie, and when Sorrells gave him the steel he fell over backwards. Sorrells did not have time to fall clear. The top of an iron post gouged his back from his belt to his shoulder but that same post kept Big Red from landing on top of him. The horse sat for an instant on his haunches after he slammed Sorrells against the post and the man stepped clear of him. Sorrells heard the son of the Outfit laugh and sing out, "Ride him cowboy!" He walked away to the end of the alley so the other men couldn't see his face and vomited. Cunningham came up to him, leading Big Red. He stood quietly behind Sorrells until he was through being sick.

"You O.K., Bert?" he asked.

"Yes," Sorrells said.

"Looks to me like you drawed all the spoiled bastards."

Sorrells was sure that was true.

"I watched for you to hit the back of your head on the top of that post."

Sorrells looked at Big Red. The big counterfeit son of a bitch.

"You didn't pull on him either. He went over on his own accord. He ought to be dog chowed before he kills somebody."

"It ain't him, it's who's been on him that ought to be dog chowed," Sorrells said.

He led the horse out of the alley to the shade of the barn. He squatted in the shade and rolled a cigarette and smoked while the other men finished working the cattle. Big Red, shot hipped, dozed. After a while Porter came to Sorrells with a cup of water and a handful of aspirins.

"Here, Bert. Swallow three of these," he said. "I've got some more if you want them. I need them all day myself."

Sorrells chewed four of them while he followed Porter to the squeeze chute. Porter fired up the butane burner to heat the branding irons while he arranged his vaccine and syringe. He and Sorrells sharpened their knives. Neither of them had ever worked on the squeeze here on the Outfit but if they could be given a dollar for every bovine they had run through a squeeze they could, between them, buy the Outfit and Bobby Lang's airplane to boot.

Sorrells worked on the front gate of the chute. He caught the cattle in the squeeze when they came rattling through. They saw the hole of daylight in the gate and tried to charge through it and Sorrells caught their heads. Then he closed the sides of the chute, squeezing them, holding them still. He scooped out the nubbin horns and earmarked the calves. Porter branded, vaccinated, and castrated.

Bobby was trying to help on the squeeze. He prodded the cattle into the chute and scurried around to supervise and give orders to Sorrells and Porter. He kept a commentary going on the proper running of a squeeze. If Sorrells was one second slow closing the squeeze or getting his knife out, Bobby almost ran over him to do what he thought had to be done. When an animal had been handled smoothly and dispatched with the proper urgency, according to the pace set by the son of the Outfit and the staff on the Boulevard of Dreams in Los Angeles, Bobby would congratulate Porter and Sorrells. The running of a bovine through the squeeze with no difficulty proved the value of the time and motion studies the staff in the front office made.

All Sorrells knew was that a man had to be strong and quick to handle the work on the front gate of the chute all day. He had to stand in one place. A man scurrying and skulking around distracted the handler of the gate. A skulker also endangered himself.

Sorrells watched out for Bobby so he wouldn't get hairlipped by a steel lever, his teeth knocked out by the dehorners, burned by a branding iron, cut by a sharp knife, or accidently vaccinated for blackleg. Any one of these misfortunes could hurt Bobby's earning power in Hollywood. Bobby escaped accident all day without noticing the narrowest of margins.

Dobie Porter tried to teach Bobby his method of knowing if the older heifers were pregnant. He was not using the clinical technique. He used the experience of his nearsighted eyes. Sorrells would not have bet against Porter's judgment. He turned out a heifer Porter had judged to be pregnant. Bobby ran a weaner heifer into the chute. He was talking about plans his front office was busy making at that moment concerning these cattle in this squeeze chute operation. Porter set the heifer to squirming and bawling with the branding iron. Choking smoke weighed down the hot air.

"Is this one pregnant?" Bobby asked.

"No," said Porter.

"Why?"

"Ain't been bred."

"How can you tell?" Bobby demanded to know.

"She's just a baby. She can't be over eight months old."

Bobby looked at the calf. "Oh," he said. Porter kept busy. Sorrells was not surprised that the planners in the front office had not told Bobby that sucking calves did not breed.

A bull calf was next. Sorrells caught his head and squeezed him. He lifted his near hind leg by a rope suspended from an overhead pulley on the back of the chute. Porter began castrating him. Bobby very conscientiously watched the operation as though interested in learning how to perform it himself.

"What are those growths on its belly?" he asked Porter.

"What growths?" Porter asked.

"Those," Bobby said, pointing. "I have read of a good iodine solution that will burn off growths like that in just a few days. I wish I had brought some."

"What growths? Where?" Porter asked. He turned his head away from the calf to look out of the corner of his eye without using the lens of his glasses. Sorrells had come to know he did this when his nearly blind eyes had exhausted all reasonable possibility of seeing and he didn't want a person to know he had given up seeing what the person wanted him to see.

Sorrells looked at the calf's belly too. He could see no growths at all.

"These. That one, that one, that one, and that one," Bobby said.

Sorrells saw what he meant and turned away, embarrassed.

Porter straightened up. "His titties," he said.

Bobby thought he had Porter now. He winked at Sorrells.

"But he's a bull, Dobie. Or he was up until a minute ago."

"Bulls got titties too. You do, don't ya?" Porter said.

The crew finished branding in the late afternoon. The men began loading the heifers on the stock truck so Wilson could take them out to pasture. Sorrells was in the chute behind the file of nervous, hot, and harried heifers, crowding them up the ramp of the loading chute. The son of the Outfit leaped into the chute behind him carrying an electric prodpole. He reached around Sorrells and hotshotted the heifer in front of him. The heifer kicked Sorrells in the groin. Sorrells groaned and relinquished his position to the son of the Outfit. Bobby attacked the heifer with new intensity as though he had not seen the violence he had caused. He kept the heifer at arm's length so *he* wouldn't get kicked. Sorrells walked down the chute as straight as he could so as not to show he had been hurt. He went and found a prodpole.

Wilson came back for another load. Sorrells walked up by the son of the Outfit and hotshotted a heifer. The heifer kicked Sorrells in the shins. Sorrells was too close to the son of the Outfit to groan.

Loading the last of the cattle he tried once more to get

back at the son of the Outfit with the hotshot. This time the
heifer kicked between them and fanned their ears with her
hind feet like a mule. Bobby stopped and looked at Sorrells.

"You're having a hard time today, aren't you, Bert?" he
said.

Sorrells looked at him. Yeah, all by myself I'm having a
hard time today, he thought. With my back, my shoulder, my
poor old balls, and my shins.

"You want to watch how you handle one of these hotshots
in close quarters like this. A man could get hurt," Bobby
said.

Sorrells turned and limped away.

Chapter 5

THE BUNKHOUSE

When ranchers began outfitting themselves, they built edifices to house cowboys called bunkhouses. When a cowboy was at headquarters, he had shelter and was expected to unroll his bed in a bunk and was not obliged to sleep on the ground for awhile. He had a warm place in which to rest. He had card games and hot water. He had hot meals and a place to write his letters. He had social demands on his person.

Sorrells headed straight for the bottle of whiskey he kept in his grip in the bunkhouse. He pulled it out and eased his sore places with a swallow. He sat on the edge of his bunk and watched over the spirit seeping in his innards. Wilson walked by the door of the room and Sorrells wordlessly handed him the bottle. Wilson smiled and took a swallow and handed it back. Sorrells put it in its place deep in the cool bottom of the grip. He went into the bathroom and washed and went to the supper table.

The crew ate its meals in the bunkhouse. The cook was a fleshy man with a pale face who never took off his black hat and wore it cocked over one ear. He had a loud voice and was always bragging in a thick, contrived accent.

Feathers and Whitey were at the table. They were now trying to be friendly with Sorrells, and each time one made a joke he would look to see if it had amused Sorrells. Sorrells had cooled off and was sleeping in the bunkhouse in the room with Porter again. The two real clowns of the crew, who were always in some greenhorn difficulty, were the two hay haulers, Alabama and Pruney. Alabama was a good-natured loud-mouth who, as Porter said, "didn't have enough sense to pour piss out of a boot." Pruney was an illiterate boy who went bareheaded in the sun and had walked into the ranch one day in a torn shirt, torn jeans, and worn-out shoes. He had been at the Outfit a month and he still had not improved his wardrobe. He slept in his clothes in a blanket Dobie Porter loaned him. Both he and Alabama had been paid and gone to town twice but had been to the whores and the crap tables before they made it to the clothing store.

The man in charge of all the water holes on the ranch was Jack Roberts, an ex-jockey. He was small, slim, proud, and clean in his habits. Cunningham told Sorrells that Roberts had been banned from racing. Jack suffered from ulcers, was losing his hair, and was an insomniac.

Tom the welder sat next to Sorrells at the table. He was the last one in to supper. He slid quietly onto the bench and said hello to Sorrells. The man's voice was resonant. Each time Sorrells heard it he was as surprised as he would have been if he heard deep flamenco from an old and scuffed guitar lying in a corner under a pile of oily rags. Tom had found a pair of bib overalls that would fit a fat, short man but he was tall and slim. He was stringy. Sorrells kept passing him food but he took very little of it. He smiled and told Sorrells he couldn't eat much because he wasn't very good at it.

The meal tasted good but was a soiled meal. If a diner chose to look, he could see the weeks-old grease that had accumulated and then been brushed or shaken off the sides of the oven into the food. He could smell the residue of boiled over pots and dripped grease from the places on the stove where the flame in the burners charred it to tar. Sorrells saw the cook pick up a jar of jam in the kitchen to bring it to the table. The lid fell off and landed with the jammy, sticky inside on the unswept floor. The cook picked the lid up with black fingers, fingers ingrained black below white, unwashed fore-arms; wiped dirt, hair, and lint off the inside of the lid; patted the lid back on the jar; and set it on the table in front of Jack Roberts.

"How about some good, fresh, grape jam, Bert?" Jack invited.

"You don't see me licking my lips," Sorrells said. Pruney picked the jar up and scooped half its contents onto his plate.

Sorrells made a cigarette. He didn't need any more of that kind of a meal. Tom tried but could not keep his eyes off the tobacco. Sorrells offered him the makings. Tom reached out to take them.

"You want a dollar cigar?" Dobie Porter asked. Tom pulled his hand back. Porter was mocking him for not having his own tobacco. Sorrells watched Tom. He had been a long time down to be cowed by an old boar like Porter.

"I mean it," Porter said. "I've got a dollar cigar a man give me and I don't smoke."

"No thanks," Tom said.

"I'll go and get it if you'll smoke it," Porter said, making no move to rise from his chair.

"I'll get it," Sorrells said. "Where is it?"

"In my drawer," Porter said. When he looked at Tom out of his thick glasses, Sorrells knew Tom was in for a badgering. Sorrells went and got the cigar. He handed it to Porter. Porter held it up by one end, showing it to Tom.

"You want it or don't you?" Porter asked Tom.

"No thanks, but thanks anyway," Tom smiled. He had a crooked, beaten, pounded smile.

"What's the matter? Dollar cigars is good. Didn't you ever have a dollar cigar?"

"Yes sir. They are good. I don't think I'll smoke this evening, though."

"You'd be surprised how much better expensive things is. Even a smoke is better if it costs more. You ought to try it."

Tom left the table and walked toward the kitchen. The flaccid cook was leaning in the door. He did not step aside for Tom.

"Excuse me," Tom said.

"For what?" the cook taunted.

"I want to get by."

"Whatsa mattah, yew don' lak seegahs?" He glanced at the side of the table where Feathers, Whitey, Alabama, and Pruney sat. He knew they would enjoy it if he made a fool of Tom.

Tom stood with his head down, looking to the right and to the left of the cook. He saw no way to get around him. He turned away.

"If'n yew don' lak them dollar seegahs ah gots one ahangin' here yew mat lak," the cook said and grinned at his audience.

Whitey, Feathers, Alabama, and Pruney grinned with pleasure for being included.

Tom straighten. "Watch your mouth," he said.

"Mah mouth? Mah mouth?" the cook roared. "Ah'll break your mouth if you talk back to me, bum. I'll teach you more respect than to talk to me like that." He had lost his accent and was putting up a barrier of sound between himself and Tom. Tom walked toward him and the roaring words became howling words. Tom turned and walked toward the outside door. The howling lowered to a roar again and followed him outside. The cook then turned, shaken, back into his kitchen.

"I've never seen a bum or an Indian or a Mexican could smoke a dollar cigar, have you Bert?" Porter asked, wanting Sorrells to join him in his after-dinner play.

"You make funny jokes, Dobie," Sorrells said. Wilson got up from the table, stretched, and walked outside.

"Bums like that. Indians. They ain't got the feelings a white man has. A dollar cigar makes them nervous. They can go on a drunk until long after it would kill a white man but they never have a dime for a new shirt or the makings of a cigareet or a bar of soap."

"Tom's a white man, ain't he?" Sorrells asked him.

"He *looks* like a white man but I bet he ain't a full blood. He's bound to have some red hide in him or he wouldn't be such a bum."

"I'm part Indian, Dobie. Probably more than Tom." Sorrells got up from the table.

"The hell you say!" Porter said, looking away. He was quiet a while. He ate the rest of the canned peaches in his plate. The other diners got up from the table and left him there. Sorrells stepped outside the bunkhouse. Feathers followed him.

"That old cook sure scared the bum, didn't he?" Feathers asked Sorrells. Sorrells couldn't answer him right away.

"I wish we could scare him clean off the place," Feathers persisted.

"You have trouble with people, don't you feller?" Sorrells said to him.

"Why?" Feathers asked, trying to smile and be a friend.

"You're always making mistakes about people. You made your mistake about me just a few days ago and now you are trying to get in trouble with old Tom."

Feathers stopped trying to smile.

"I don't see what trouble a bum like that could be unless it's stinking the bunkhouse up."

"Let me tell you something, little man. Watch out for that man. A man who tries to stay out of trouble as hard as he does has been in bad trouble before."

Feathers didn't understand a word of the advice. He looked away.

"If you don't believe me, just back that man into a corner," Sorrells said, smiling. "He won't play piano with you. He'll see what you ate for breakfast."

Wilson was looking through a small satchel in the back of his pickup in front of the bunkhouse. He closed the satchel when Sorrells walked up to him.

"We've got a thief in the bunkhouse," Wilson said.

"The hell," Sorrells said. "What did they steal?"

"Two twenty-dollar bills I left in a wallet by my bed."

"Who do you think did it?"

Wilson shrugged. "I don't know. Somebody who's got time in the bunkhouse we don't have."

"Well, me and you and Dobie are always together. If old Tom had done it, the cook would have known about it and yelled his head off. I don't think Jack would make himself out a thief for two twenties. Who does that leave?"

"I don't know," Wilson said.

"Well, I don't either, but I bet we find out." Sorrells walked away and went inside to his bunk. He was too sore to stand with Wilson any longer to prove his innocence. He undressed and looked at himself. His thighs were black and blue. His skin was peeled. His thighs were turning green. He got Porter to smear monkey blood on his back. He rolled into his bed and went to sleep.

Tom's bathroom-bedroom was on the other side of a wall of the room Sorrells and Porter shared. Tom slept on a shelf above the toilet. If the door had opened into the room, he would not have been able to store anything in the room. He didn't have anything to store but his carcass. In the night the deep voice like a base viol vibrated off the walls of the little room.

> *These chains, these chains,*
> *Holdin' me down,*
> *These chains.*
> *These chains, these chains,*
> *Keepin' me bound,*
> *These chains.*
>
> *When I was free to run and to go,*
> *I cut down a path of sadness and woe,*
> *I ran and I fell like a fool headlong,*
> *Off the hill of my life to the God-awful wrong,*
> *Of these chains.*
>
> *These chains, these chains,*
> *Oh, how they keep me down,*
> *These chains.*
> *These chains, these chains,*
> *Lord, just like your frown,*
> *These chains.*
>
> *If you'll take me back and make me all right,*
> *I'll stand up straight and trust to your might.*
> *I'll do a man's work and walk like a man,*
> *I'll find my own children and maybe they'll ban,*
> *These chains.*

Chapter 6

COWBOY

All the parade and fairground fellows can wear straw hats and fine boots and silver trophy buckles, talking big and taking the rides in front of all the people, but those shows do not make them cowboys. Deceiving the people who want to be deceived by a big hat and a pair of boots does not make them cowboys.

Having a young dedication of mind and body that few professions have in caring for the bovine so it is able to provide tasty protein for man, is being a cowboy. Doing it at a pace measured by the shod steps of the equine animal and disdaining any other conveyance is cowboy. Using natural tools of flesh and blood, leather and hemp and hair, in any country hot or cold, open or brushy, wild or tame, with verve; by himself with no audience, no ticket sale, and no background music, not even a just wage, is cowboy.

A cowboy would be a fool to do it for the money. He would be a fool to do it for the right to wear the big hat and pair of boots. He does it to care gently for the lives of the tough, smart bovines in country where the bovine, the mule deer, and the wild horse use the same trails and he does it so people can eat beefsteak which, he believes, is why the bovine is on the mother earth.

"You awake?" Sorrells heard Porter ask. Sorrells lay quiet. He knew what would happen if he answered. Porter would begin his monologue.

He was liable to start a conversation during any one of his four trips to the bathroom every night. Sorrells now knew the reason Porter had been left to this room by himself. Sorrells had heard the first versions of Porter's stories. He was dreading the time the old man would begin repeating them. He hoped he wouldn't start this night.

"Bums," Porter said. "Moanin' in the night. You awake, Bert?"

"Yes."

"You hear that bum amoanin'?"

"Yeah."

"Didn't it scare you?"

"No."

"Well, it did me. It's a helluva note when a cowpuncher has got to put with them kind of weird noises in the night. The nights is short enough as they is."

Sorrells didn't answer.

"Bert?"

"Yes."

Porter raised up in his bed and pulled on the light. He sat on the edge of his bed in his long underwear. His sock feet hung short of the floor. He rubbed his bald head. He coughed in a voice harsh with phlegm. He talked. Cunningham was right. Every thought that came into Porter's mind had to come out of his mouth.

"I done thisaway. I pulled that tarp right out from under that agent," Porter was saying. His own great tarp was under his blankets and billowed around his bed. He sat on the tarp and his many expensive blankets. Sorrells bet the man had a month's wages invested in that bed. Well, the poor old man. He'd never had a wife to spend his money on or to keep him warm. The blankets were full of hay dust and dry manure that he spilled out of the cuffs of his Levis when he got into bed at night. He had the habit of undressing in bed because of the many cold nights of his life he had to undress outdoors and sleep on the ground.

"Here's the idee. He owed me and I didn't have no other way to collect," Porter was saying.

For all his set ways, Porter was a cowboy. He could do any job that could be done horseback. He was always in the right place at the right time. He knew by instinct more than a cow knew and *that* was what made a cowboy. Old Porter never forgot an old cow. If he saw her calf once, he could ride on to that calf a month later and know which cow the calf belonged to.

Porter got down from his bunk and stumped on his tiny feet and his stiff, bowed legs into the bathroom. He made four trips every night. A man could set his clock by them.

The old man had dedicated his life to the cow. She was his sole interest. His horse was an appendage of him, a flesh and blood tool he used in his husbandry of the cow the same as his own body was. He had already given his eyesight, the grip and feeling of both hands, half his stomach, and the capability of walking upright on his own two legs in his pursuit of the happiness of the old cow. He believed he still had plenty to give.

He came back and climbed like a child onto his blankets and tarp. He brushed roughly at some trash he sensed through his heavy underwear. He was almost totally blind without his glasses. He had the chest, trunk, and arms of a heavyweight, the small feet and legs of a child.

"Them's the only kind a man finds on these outfits anymore, for, here's the idee, a good hand won't work for these wages."

Not even Porter knew how many good, stout horses he had worn out in his trade, but he had never been as hard on a horse as he was on himself. He was hard on the cowboys that rode with him too, not by ordering them to work but by setting the example of work. He had managed to ride Wilson and Sorrells into the ground every day. His was the drive that started them every morning at four thirty and directed the ride until it got back to headquarters. During the first week of work they had not come in before nine at night. They carried a cold lunch but they usually didn't make it back to the truck in time to eat it. Sorrells and Wilson could take the hours and the short feed. They could bear it. Porter didn't even notice it.

Porter had shut down his talk and was snoring. Sorrells kept his mouth and eyes shut and his breathing regular during the rest of the night each time Porter woke him going to the bathroom. Porter yawned in three octaves each time he got up. He pulled on the light when it was time for Sorrells to get up. He was sitting at his place at the head of the table drinking a cup of canned milk and hot water when Wilson and Sorrells went to the table with their coffee.

"Well, fellers. Easy day today," Porter said. "It's Sunday so we'll go out to Pipeline Basin and just rim around and get back at noon in time to maybe go in to Keno and have a chicken dinner."

Sorrells felt good about that. He was sore as hell.

"I'll ride my little colt. I'll get a lot of miles on him and won't have to rush him into any cow work. Here's the idee, I'll do thisaway. I'll get the flightiness out of him. I'll work the birds out of his head and get him tired without dinking him."

Porter's colt was only a four-year-old with the rough taken off him. He didn't have any meanness in him but Sorrells thought he was too alert, too quick and full of life for an old man. He offered to top the colt off for Porter.

"No," Porter said. "He'll be all right. You just hold him so I can get on him when we get out to Pipeline."

Wilson drove the truck to within a mile of Pipeline Basin. The basin was in a badlands country. Sorrells was riding Roller and Wilson was riding Front Office. The three men rode through a high saddle into the basin. The basin was probably three miles wide and five miles long. A deep wash ran down the middle of it. Canyons full of piñon and joshua ran to the wash. Smooth, deep ditches had been cut by water in the sandstone bottom of the wash.

The horsemen took a canyon that ran parallel to the wash and rode toward a high bluff on a mountain. They came to a trail where they found fresh cow tracks. The trail got steeper and brushier as they rode up. They came to an old pipeline. Porter had told them about it but he didn't brag about knowing it was there when they rode onto it. He had not been in this canyon in fourteen years.

Wilson saw the cattle after the men had already passed them. Some instinct of Wilson's always told him where to look and Sorrells had never seen the Indian's equal for seeing hidden or distant cattle. This time Wilson turned back and saw the cattle from the only angle from which they could be seen. Two cows with two long-eared calves, two branded heifers, and a maverick heifer were bunched with their heads together like deer behind some trees watching the horsemen.

The men rode on up the canyon until they found the spring where the cattle were watering. They satisfied themselves that the seven head they had seen were the only cattle watering there, so they went back down the canyon to get them. The cattle were gone when they got back and the men tracked them down a ridge between the pipeline canyon and the limestone wash. Wilson and Sorrells left Porter and rode fast along the top of the ridge while Porter stayed on the tracks.

"Here's the idee," Porter had said. You'll make better time without tracking and you'll probably see the cattle first. You're mounted to catch and hold them. I'll stay on their tracks with the colt and make sure they go the way we think they're going."

Wilson and Sorrells were standing their horses on a high bluff above the junction of the pipeline canyon and the limestone wash when they saw the cattle high on a mountain on the other side of the wash. Porter was closer to them but he was down in the wash and could not see them. He was trying to make his colt cross one of the ditches in the limestone. The colt wasn't cooperating. Each time he was urged by Porter's spurless heels to the edge of the ditch he paused, considered the short hop he would have to make to cross, decided he didn't know how to do it, and whirled and lunged away. Wilson and Sorrells laughed and waited to see if the colt was going to leave Porter in the ditch. The old man took down his rope and encouraged the colt with the hardtwist until he lunged over the ditch.

Sorrells and Wilson rode into the wash. The cattle saw Porter and ran down toward Sorrells and Wilson. They were looking back at Porter when they came around a bend in the wash and ran into Sorrells and Wilson. One maverick cow split from the bunch, climbed a ridge with her calf and fell into another canyon with Sorrells behind her. He turned her uphill to slow her down and roped her. The calf climbed out of the canyon and ran on. Sorrells tied the cow. He tracked the calf until he saw her running down the pipeline canyon. Roller carried him off the ridge, through the rocks in the bottom of the canyon, overtook the calf, rated her through the joshua, and gave Sorrells a throw. Sorrells and Roller were getting along very well. Sorrells caught the calf and tied her in the canyon. He rode back to the place he had left Wilson and Porter. He found Wilson holding the cow and calf and the two branded heifers.

"Where's Dobie?" Sorrells asked.

"Who knows?" Wilson said. "Didn't you see him? He took off in your direction after that maverick heifer."

"I didn't see him."

"He'll turn up," Wilson said.

Sorrells and Wilson drove the cattle to the cow Sorrells had tied and let her up. They drove the bunch to the calf and let her up. They held the cattle on a ridge above the pipeline canyon and waited for Porter. They called for him but he didn't answer. Sorrells held the cattle while Wilson rode to a high point and called. After awhile Wilson walked his horse back down.

"Here he comes," he said and pointed toward the draw that led to the high saddle on the edge of the basin. Sorrells and Wilson started the cattle that way. When they came to Porter, he stayed in the lead of the cattle and pointed them up the draw toward the saddle. Sorrells figured he must have lost the heifer. No one could blame him. He was riding a green colt. The heifer had weighed at least seven hundred pounds and had probably never seen a human before. Certainly she had never been touched by a human. She was at least a three-year-old and could run like a coyote. If Porter had caught her she might have tangled the colt in the rope and hurt someone.

They were near the saddle when Sorrells saw Porter rein the colt over to one side of the draw and stop. He and the colt were looking at something in the brush ahead. Sorrells saw the white face of a bovine flash across the draw in the brush and jerk and stop and disappear. When it reappeared he saw it was the maverick heifer. She dashed across the draw again and he saw that her horns were tied by the full length of Porter's rope to a joshua tree.

Porter had caught her and reined to the other side of a joshua tree to keep her from jerking his colt down. He had tied the end of his rope high on another joshua without dismounting.

Sorrells heeled the heifer. They branded her and tipped her horns and earmarked her. They let her up and she joined the bunch where she felt safe. They got the bunch to the corral by dark.

Chapter 7

LAME BULL

On an outfit a wet cow is a cow with a suckling calf by her side. A dry cow is a cow that doesn't have a calf this year. A barren cow does well in her production of beef but does not, has not, will not give birth to a calf.

A dogie is a motherless calf, a calf that has been unmothered by drought, disease, or distress and left to shift for himself. Most dogies, if they do not suffer the same misfortune that orphaned them, stay alive if they are lucky enough to get their mother's first milk. This vital potion she made for him while she was making him, to give him resistance to the diseases that assault him in the first waking days of his warm, vulnerable life. After a dogie had been off milk a few days, he loses his taste for it and goes on trying to make a living by grazing, as he is born with a set of teeth. Some dogies, however, learn to steal milk. They wait and when a mother is nursing her own calf, they slip in and steal a tit. The mother is bound to nurse her own calf and this obligation often keeps her from effectively fighting off a small, persistent, rogue of a dogie. Young cows in artificial surroundings have been known to drop a calf and never turn to look at him and walk right on without even knowing the smell of him, caring as little for their offspring as they would for their other droppings. These calves are orphaned so small that they lack the strength, the will, and the answers they need to stay alive. They are little fellows yearning for a father or a mother or a school. Cowboys hope to find them before

51

*something gets them, as yearning will keep them alive only a
little while.*

Out in the flats, in the Sep-
tember heat, in a hot wind, the crew of the Outfit was
working cattle at a set of corrals called Poisoned Squaw. The
dust was like talcum powder six inches deep in the corral and
the men were white with it. It mixed with the moisture of
their bodies and turned stiff and hard like adobe on their
clothes. The wind deposited it in the soft, moist parts of their
faces.

Dobie Porter's thick glasses were caked with dust that
ran on the lenses like water. Wilson's long black hair under
his hat was gray with dust. Cunningham's face was pale with
it, and Sorrells coughed and blew it, brown, into his
handkerchief.

Alabama and Pruney were helping them that day. They
worked afoot loading the weaner calves, bulls, and old cows
onto the truck, daubing the range cows with yellow paint
when they were tallied, flanking the baby calves for branding.
The horsemen cut the cattle into a crowding pen off the
loading chute so Alabama and Pruney could daub them or
load them. The two boys were dangerous to the cattle, to the
cowboys, and to themselves. They were hurried and inept.
Their feet, legs, minds, and hands were in their way.

Sorrells cut off a bunch of weaner cattle and followed
them into the crowding pen. Alabama and Pruney began
shouting and dancing to scare the calves up the chute. This
scared Baldy, the horse Sorrells was riding, into a dance.
Pruney lost his temper when a bull calf turned back from the
narrow opening of the chute and knocked him down. He ran
to one side of the corral and picked up a shovel. He cut off
the calf and charged him, swinging the shovel. The calf, alone
in one end of the corral, away from the other calves, was
afraid. He ran into the corner where Baldy danced. He
lunged into the iron pipes of the corral hunting a hole big

enough for escape. Pruney went at him and made a swipe at him with the shovel. The blade brushed hot wind into Sorrells' face. The calf ran between Baldy's legs and he reared. Pruney scooped up a shovelful of dust to throw at the calf and scattered it instead into Sorrells' face.

"Here, now!" Sorrells yelled at Pruney. Pruney stood still and looked at Sorrells.

"What you doin', boy," Alabama shouted and ran at the calf swinging a six-foot length of stiff, plastic hose. Sorrells rode out of the corral. The calf saw the open end of the chute and ran to join his brothers. Alabama followed him, pounding on his back with the hose. He raised the hose, the end sprang in an arc over his head and whipped Pruney on the forehead. Pruney spun away and wobbled back out of the chute. Alabama, in a frenzy shouting, pushed the calves up the chute into the truck. He ran back to the crowding pen. Pruney was rubbing his forehead.

"Boy, what you doin'?" Alabama demanded. He looked to see if Sorrells was listening. "Don't you know nothin' about working livestock?"

"You hit me with the hose," Pruney said.

"Yeah, and I'll keep ahittin' ya if you keep gettin' in the wrong place all the time. I'll swear, I never seen anybody so always in the way. Now stand back and watch me and I'll tell you what to do from now on." Alabama looked at Sorrells and shook his head. "Dumb prunepicker," he said.

The cowboys drove a bunch of cows toward the pen to be tallied. One roan muley bull was in the bunch. He was lame in a front foot. He turned back from the gate when the cows passed into the crowding pen. He was left alone in the large corral. Alabama and Pruney dipped cloth daubers on the ends of long sticks into buckets of yellow paint and painted the cows on the hips. Porter called out the ages of the cows and their status as producers of livestock for the Outfit while Sorrells wrote it down in a tally book.

"One three-year-old wet," Porter said as Alabama daubed her. "One four-year-old dry," he said as Pruney daubed one and got kicked in the shin. Pruney ran to daub another and she ran over Alabama. Alabama poked his dripping dauber at another and it bounced off a hip and splashed paint in

Pruney's face. "One five-year-old wet," Porter said. Pruney swung his dauber like a bat along the back of a cow and knocked Alabama's hat off. "One six-year-old wet," Porter said. Pruney followed the cow to paint her better and stepped on Alabama's hand as he reached for his hat. Alabama stood up and punched Pruney in the back of the head with the dauber. Pruney, surprised, turned and faced Alabama. "Watch what yo adoin', Prunepicker," Alabama bawled. "One California Prunepicker," Porter said. "Wet." Pruney looked at Alabama. He was afraid to move. "What you standin' there now for?" Alabama yelled, the veins popping in his neck.

"Well, I'm sorry," Pruney said.

"Sorry, hell. We've got to get this livestock out of here. Get to work."

When the boys were through daubing, Cunningham decided to break for lunch. Wilson built a fire in the high wind and boiled coffee water in a gallon can. He dropped a handful of coffee on the water, sprinkled it with cold water to settle the grounds, and set it aside to steep. When he thought the grounds had settled, he picked the can up.

"Coffee, Bert?" he asked.

"No you don't, Wilson," Bert said. "First cup gets all the grounds."

"No grinds this time, Bert," Wilson said.

"Wilson!" Sorrells said.

"Honest. Look, no grinds," Wilson smiled.

"Give me a cup now you got it in your hand," Alabama said. Wilson poured him half coffee, half grounds and smiled at Bert.

"Now give me a cup," Sorrells said. When Wilson had poured the coffee, Sorrells asked, "How come they call this place Poisoned Squaw, Wilson?"

"*I* wouldn't know," Wilson smiled "How would *I* know?"

"A miner who used to camp here poisoned his squaw in the shack," Porter said. "I knew him. His squaw was a drunk and he got tired of her."

"What did they do to him?" Sorrells asked.

"Nothing."

"Why not?"

"He was a white man. Besides that, he told her the whiskey was poisoned."

"And she still drank it?"

"Well, he had put arsenic in a jug of whiskey and hidden it. I guess he was watching it because when she started to drink it he told her it was poisoned."

"Why did she drink it then?"

"He was just a little too late. She was already drinking it when he told her."

"Didn't she stop?"

"I guess not."

"Why not?"

"I guess she liked her whiskey too much and probably wasn't listening too close while she was drinking. Anyway, he took her to Keno to the doctor."

"Why couldn't the doctor save her?"

"He was too busy. He still had a handful of change," Porter laughed. "He was crazy for the slots and he was playing when the miner brought her to town. She was in the back of the miner's pickup. She was a great big old squaw. Somebody ran to tell the Doc she was dying. The Doc told the miner to have her brought in to where he was playing if she was so sick. They laid her out by him while he was playing. He looked at her. He pulled the handle of a slot and said, 'Roll 'er over.' They did. He put a coin in the machine and pulled the handle. He looked at her again. He said, 'Roll 'er back over, she's dead!' " Porter laughed.

"Aw hell, Dobie," Wilson said. "That's not right."

"That's the story, anyway," Porter said. "Maybe it ain't exactly true. Maybe the slot was in the Doc's office. He had one in his office."

Porter's eye fell on Pruney. He would now call attention to Pruney distracting his audience away from the improbability of the tale of Poisoned Squaw. He became, of a sudden, very solicitous of Pruney.

"Where's your hat, young feller?" he asked Pruney. Pruney never wore a hat and everyone knew it. He put one hand on top of his head.

"I don't have one," Pruney said.

"Well, I'll be damned," Porter said. "Huh! Don't have a

hat. I only knew one cowboy in my life who never wore a hat. He was a Navajo over on the Arizona Strip. He was a good cowboy though. Even if he never wore a hat. How is it you don't wear a hat, cowboy?"

"I never owned a hat," the boy smiled. He was shy and none too bright. "I've never been a cowboy before."

"Well, you ought to have one, a cowboy like you. You need a pair of boots so you can keep the manure out of your oxfords. You didn't bring your saddle or your horse to the Outfit, did you?"

"I don't have a horse or a saddle either."

"Huh. That's *unusual*. Now, when I was a young buck your age, I couldn't of done without a horse and saddle. All my first wages went toward a horse and saddle. You say you was raised on a big California cow outfit?"

"No. My uncles have vineyards."

"Huh. I understood you to say you was from one of them big California ranchos."

"No."

"I bet you're in the market for a horse and saddle."

"Well, maybe."

"Well, sure. I'll tell you what. I'm getting old and I want to find a home for Buck. I figure I don't have many more years of this kind of work and I'll be moving to town where I've been offered a job selling neckties. On the other hand, old Buck has got many good years left in him. I'll just sell you old Buck there as he stands, saddle and all."

"Well, I don't know. How much did Buck cost?"

"He only cost me four thousand dollars but I wore fifteen hundred off him. I'll let you have him for twenty-five hundred and I'll throw in my good saddle."

"Twenty-five hundred *dollars*?"

"Well, yeah. I know he's cheap but I want to see you get started right."

Pruney wasn't sure Porter was hoorawing him. He looked far away, a token smile on his face. He was thinking and holding the smile during the serious thoughts. Sorrells knew $2,500 was more money than he thought existed anywhere in the world, least of all in one horse. With $2,500 Pruney was sure he could break the crap table in Keno, have the youngest whores, and all the beer and wine he could drink for a month.

"Podnuh, that Prunepicker don't know nothin' about a good hoss," Alabama said. "I know. Mah uncle has the best hosses in Alabama and he raised me up ridin' the range."

"Yeah?" Porter asked innocently.

"Shore. Look here," Alabama said and took out an old wallet. He let a fold of pictures unravel from it. The pictures were of Alabama and an older man. Both wore gun belts holstered low on their thighs and black cardboard hats on the backs of their heads so the pompadours on their foreheads would show. An old plowhorse stood at one side. He was saddled with a cheap, single rig saddle. The uncle was holding him by a set of reins three yards long and three inches wide. A limber, three-quarter-inch hemp rope with big knots tied in each end hung from the saddle.

"Where was that picture taken?" Porter asked.

"On my uncle's spread. That picture was taken during roundup just before the Outfit hired me."

"Oh, you hired on to cowboy?"

"Shore. I'm just haulin' hay till the Pruney learns the ropes. I'll be drawin' my string of hosses soon."

"You don't say?" Porter said. "I didn't know."

"I'll tell you somethin'. The Pruney don't know nothin' about hosses."

"I can ride a horse," Pruney said.

"Boy, what, just what, do you know about a hoss? Tell me."

"I'll show you," Pruney said and started to unwrap Buck's reins from the fence.

"What you doin'?" Porter asked him.

"I'm going to prove I can ride this horse," Pruney said. Porter took the reins out of his hand. "Can I?" Pruney asked.

"Well, sure you can if you're goin' to buy him. But not until then. Old Buck wouldn't like it if I was to *lend* him to you."

"I just want to show you I can ride."

"Boy, you don't just get on a man's hoss out here in the West," Alabama said. "Don't you know nothin'? You don't ride another man's hoss. That's the Code of the West."

"Oh," Pruney said.

"Maybe you'd better think for a while before you buy old Buck. You should know more about how he works," Porter said. He walked up to Buck. "Ho, Buck," he said. "Whoa, now, you, Buck." He mounted the horse.

"Let's load that lame bull before we do anything else this afternoon," Cunningham said. The men looked at the lame bull. He, alone in the corral, was also giving them *his* attention.

"Say, he'll *look* at a feller, won't he," Sorrells said.

"He's going on the fight," Wilson said. "I'm glad he doesn't have horns."

Sorrells led Baldy out of the corral. Wilson mounted his horse in the corral. He was riding a short, chunky horse that belonged to him. Wilson rode around the bull. The bull pivoted in Wilson's direction and shook his head. He was not going to let Wilson drive him anywhere. He chose a corner of the corral, put his wringing tail to the fence, and armed himself to fight. Wilson couldn't drive him out of the corner.

Sorrells jumped into the corral and took off his hat and waved it at the bull as he ran in a short half-circle in front of him. After all, the bull was lame and would be unable to catch him in a charge. The bull spun, whipped his tail back and forth, and pawed the ground. Sorrells wanted to attract him out of the fortress he was defending, to untrack him, get him moving. Maybe then he could be driven into the smaller pen. Sorrells ran closer to the bull and shook his hat under the bull's nose. The bull was tall, heavy. He was a large, live hulk above Sorrells. Suddenly he was not a mass, slow and lame, but charging quickly down on Sorrells. Sorrells did not run in a straight line. He changed directions as he sprinted across the corral. Each change of direction was prompted by the hot sniff of the bull's breath on his fanny. As he reached the fence the bull was close upon him.

"Bert!" Wilson shouted and Sorrells heard real fear in his voice. Wilson rode his horse into the bull's flank, breaking the bull's momentum, changing his mind about Sorrells. Sorrells climbed the fence. The bull wheeled and charged the horse. He was nearly as tall as the horse. He scooped his head under the horse's flank, lifted the horse's hind end, and drove on, unhorsing Wilson and slamming the horse into the fence. Wilson hit the dust on the side of his face and his hands and knees. He bounced once and crawled in a hurry, churning dust like an outboard motor, to the fence. The bull had cleared the men out of the corral. He backed into his corner, his eyes challenging them again.

Porter rode up and handed Sorrells a rope. "See if you can get a loop on the good front foot, the one that ain't lame," he said. Sorrells took the rope and climbed into the corral. He knew the ground the bull would defend. He knew what ground was safe to stand in to rope the bull. He knew the bull would charge him if he got close enough to rope the front foot. He moved carefully around the bull.

Alabama jumped into the arena. He would show everyone he had no fear of the bull. Sorrells stood back and watched. Alabama danced and waved his hat. The bull raised his head, opened his nostrils and eyes as wide as they would go, and waited. Alabama took a timid step closer to the bull. He had the stage now. He must have a reaction from the bull. The bull pawed the ground nervously in an invitation. Alabama got down and faced the bull on his hands and knees and pawed the dirt with one hand, flinging dust behind him.

"Now, be careful, Alabama," Cunningham said.

"Attaboy, Alabam," Porter encouraged him. Alabama grinned nervously and scuttled ahead on his hands and knees. Porter laughed. He was happy at the prospect of seeing a gunsel rolled and stomped by a bull. "Be careful, get up from there," Cunningham said. Then Alabama got too close and threw dirt into the lame bull's eyes. At that moment Pruney decided he wanted to be noticed too and arrived in the arena at a spot close behind Alabama. The bull, aroused by the dust in his face and with two fine targets in his range, charged. He did not lower his head but ran looking at his victims. Alabama, scared by the suddenly growing size of the bull, turned and tangled in Pruney's feet. Pruney kicked him convulsively and ran away. Alabama buried his head in the dust under his arms, his rear end a shining target for the bull. The bull drove into the exact middle of the target and bumped Alabama along before him until his momentum carried him over the boy. He raised his head and lunged after

Pruney. He caught up to him just as the boy was making his jump to the fence. He caught this target between the tattered hip pockets and ironed him, spread-eagled, into the fence. Every inch of the front of Pruney's body seemed to strike the fence like a handful of mud. Sorrells though the boy would fall to the bull's feet, but the bull stopped, the boy bounced back, kept his feet, grabbed the top of the fence, and jumped out of the corral. The bull turned to do more battle.

Porter rode to a spot across the fence from the bull and caught him around the neck. "Now rope his front foot, Bert," he said. He rode Buck away and held the bull's head against the fence until Sorrells caught the foot. Each time the bull tried to charge, Sorrells threw him off balance by running against the rope on the foot. The bull could see no way of protecting himself against this new circumstance and sought escape. What he thought was escape misled him through the crowding pen, up the chute, and into the truck where Wilson slammed the door on him. The bull immediately attacked the other cattle in the truck by butting at them through an iron partition that separated him from them. He lifted the partition out of the slots in the floor and tossed it upon the backs of the cattle and began slamming cattle against the sides of the truck. The crew climbed onto the rack and tied the bull's head into a forward corner with Porter's rope. They put the partition back in place and tied it down so the bull couldn't lift it again. Sorrells was leaning into the truck taking the rope off the bull's foot with a stick when Alabama released the rope on the bull's head. The bull saw the toe of Sorrells' boot move before his eyes inside the truck. He drove his big head into Sorrells' foot at the instep, squashing it into a corner of a brace of angle iron on the rack. The pain turned Sorrells' face white.

"Now, be careful," Alabama mocked Sorrells and laughed. Cunningham took Sorrells on his shoulder and helped him down off the truck.

"Are you hurt bad, Bert?" Cunningham asked.

"I think it's going to be all right," Sorrells said.

"I knew somebody was going to get mashed. I'm sorry it wasn't one of the gunsels," Cunningham said.

"Why man, I knew that bull couldn't hurt me if I laid down still and quiety," Alabama laughed.

"Oh?" Porter said. "I thought it was just an accident he didn't kill you."

"Hell no. I've handled lots of bulls worser'n that 'un. Say, you goin' to be able to ride horseback now, Bert?"

"Yes," Sorrells said. He was thinking, did he always have to be in the path when one of these morons played cowboy?

"I was gonna say, I could take over for you a few days while your foot got better. Would that be all right with you, Mr. Cunningham?"

"Oh, I think we can get along O.K.," Cunningham said. "We don't have any horses good enough for a man like you, anyway."

"I could get by on Bert's string until you get some new hosses."

"Why, I'm ashamed of you. I thought you believed in the Code of the West," Cunningham said.

"I do but I just thought since you don't have no more hosses . . ."

"And you believe you could make a hand on Bert Sorrells' string?"

"Well, a hoss is a hoss, ain't it?"

"Why, boy. You couldn't even untrack one of Sorrells' string."

"I could try. Anyone could try."

"Listen, boy. 'Trying' don't get it. 'Trying' is for the dudes on the dude ranches that pays for it and for boys posing for pictures. I don't need anybody 'trying' around these cattle anymore. Your 'trying' got a cowboy hurt just now." Cunningham turned away to help Sorrells to the shade of the corral.

"I'm sure sorry about that and I'd sure like you to consider giving me a riding job." Alabama persisted. "Me and the Pruney talked it over and we decided we don't want to stay with the Outfit much longer if we are just gonna be hay haulers and not ever get a riding job."

"Since you are in that kind of trouble you don't need to haul any more hay. Not one more load," Cunningham said.

"Well, finally we're gonna get to ride," Alabama said and grinned at Pruney.

"Yes, you'll ride," Cunningham said. "You'll ride the pickup to the bus stop tonight. You're both fired. Get in the pickup now and I'll take you to headquarters to get your gear."

When Sorrells and Wilson got into the bunkhouse that evening, Sorrells invited Wilson for a drink of whiskey. Wilson took a swallow and made a face.

"There's something wrong with your whiskey, Bert," he said.

"Wrong?" Sorrells took a mouthful. He spat it out. "Water," he said.

"Somebody watered your whiskey. They drank most of the good and watered it back."

Sorrells limped through the kitchen to the main room of the bunkhouse. Jack Roberts had come in and was sitting on his bunk, taking off his boots. Dust caked his hair and face.

"Jack, who has been around this bunkhouse today?" Sorrells asked.

"Nobody, I guess, I just got in myself, Bert. Why?"

"Some son of a bitch watered my whiskey."

"I don't know who it could have been."

"The goddam cook," Sorrells said.

"I don't think he's been here. When I was coming in I stopped at that place on the highway for a beer and the cook was in there roaring drunk."

"He's the one then. My whiskey gave him the urge to go to the bar. I'll kill him. I don't mind too much a man stealing from me if he needs something more than me, but I can't stand a son of a bitch watering my whiskey. I'm going to kill him when he gets back here."

Cunningham saw that the crew had to cook for itself that night. He saw the cook at the bar on the highway when he took Alabama and Pruney to catch the bus. The cook never came back.

Chapter 8

BUCKAROO

A Nevada cowboy is called buckaroo. He is like the wild horse. A buckaroo will leave bed, board, wife, possessions, his good sense, and any instinct of self-preservation to go after the wild horse or the wild cow. He prefers commoner livestock than professional livestock breeders would like to see running free. Because of this preference, the livestock breeders look down on the buckaroo. The breeders say, justly, that it costs as much to raise a cold-blooded animal as it does to raise a purebred. They are sure only purebred livestock is worth money, since it is what they sell.

The buckaroo believes mustang blood is necessary in stock that is to thrive in Nevada. A human must have some of it too, called buckaroo, if he is to make a living in Nevada. The buckaroo, like the vaquero, believes in the saying, "Mejor saber el terreno, que ser el mejor vaquero,"—better to know the country than know all there is to know about cowboying. The point being, it is possible to know terrain, never possible to know all about cowboying.

The cowboys of the Outfit got a Sunday afternoon off one day after they shipped cattle. Dobie Porter told Bert Sorrells he would buy him a chicken dinner if Sorrells would drive him to town in Carlotta.

Sorrells wanted to do the driving when he and Porter went places together. Porter, when driving, had a propensity for the shoulder of the road, either shoulder, when he wasn't straddling the white line. He seldom used the part of the road that was legally his to drive on.

The town they were going to was Keno, about seventy miles away. It consisted of a hotel-casino, a few bars, a motel, a barbershop, a drugstore, a Western store, a tiny twelve bed hospital, everything a cowpuncher needed. The crew seldom made it to town except on Sunday afternoon when everything but the restaurant, casino, and bar in the hotel were closed.

Bert Sorrells had the complete emptiness of belly and voraciousness of appetite a month on the ranch without going to town could cause. Porter's idea of an evening in town was to have chicken and ice cream in the restaurant, two forty-cent games of keno in the casino, a telephone call to some bigshot ex-boss or to his old sister in Arizona, a drink of rock and rye just before he got into the car to go back to the ranch, and to be home in time to sanely take his many pills, do his extensive and complicated toilet, and climb early into his bedroll.

Sorrells had two martinis under Porter's stern watch before the chicken dinners were served. Porter was suspicious of more than one drink of anything. The chicken was good but Sorrells didn't want the ice cream because when his dinner settled he intended to have whiskey. He watched Porter eat both his and Sorrells' ice cream and listened while Porter bragged to a complete stranger sitting next to him at the counter. Sorrells decided he didn't need to stay any longer in Porter's company when the old man took hold of his slick teeth, withdrew them clacking from his mouth, brushed the remnants of chicken off them, and wiped them with his shirttail. He never paused in the steady brag he was making to the stranger about the wild horses he had ridden in his lifetime.

Sorrells got up and walked into the casino. A voice on the loudspeaker was telling the numbers of a new keno game. The sound of the voice over the casino came at exact intervals as the keno balls rolled from their cage down a ramp and revealed their numbers to the talker. The inflection of the voice promised that each ball bore a special number for somebody. The keno players were sitting in two rows of desks on one side of the room watching the numbers light up on a board. They were natives and dedicated keno players. They were elderly, wind creased and desert dried, shabbily clothed and comfortable about it. They were home.

A trim young woman dealt blackjack to two workingmen. Every hair on her head was in place. It was long and hung to the middle of her back. Her hands dealt surely and they took the players' money quickly and efficiently. The players seemed fascinated by feeding money to the dealer and seemed unable to stop until they had no more. The girl never lost a hand and her doll face behind a set of hornrimmed glasses was unconcerned.

Sorrells stood up at the bar and watched a tall man with a cow milker's crease in his hat tell some dudes about his life as a mustanger. Sorrells saw that the dudes didn't believe a word of it.

Sorrells had a drink of whiskey and watched the people. Their sounds and movements mesmerized him. He watched a clean-shaven, neatly dressed man standing at the crap table. His well-coiffed young wife stood by him. His big stack of five dollar chips was growing. The man's black hair gleamed. His eye was bright. His brow was flushed. He was winning. His clean, white hands below golden cufflinks in the cool, white shirt flashed before him with the red dice. The woman by his side held to one arm of him as though in this way she could accompany him, but Sorrells had the idea from the look on her face that she had no idea in the world where the man was going.

Sorrells wanted to play, but he didn't feel lucky yet, so he drank whiskey. He would contribute his five dollars soon enough. He noticed Keno's sorriest condition, no good-looking girls. He walked over to see what the slot machiners looked like.

One dumpy little lady, her adequate buttocks locked together in peddle-pushers, her mottled feet in white, imitation Indian beaded moccasins, had to reach above her head to grasp the slot machine handle. She was playing three machines with great speed and dexterity, like a veteran of work on a conveyor belt in a factory. She kept going without missing a beat in the settling click of the fruits in the eyes of the machines. She pulled the handles smoothly, effortlessly scooping spare coins from their maws with her other hand and passing them unerringly to the slots without looking to see if they found their proper way. When the lady gave Sorrells a look, as if she were worried that he wanted to play her machines or might be worsening her luck, he moved on.

A man in a phone booth in a corner by the slots was saying, "I know I shouldn't have done it . . . I know we can't afford it but I did it and now I have to have some to get home on . . . I know, but it's done and none of that kind of talk will get it back or get me home now. . . . You'll have to wire it. . . . Keno. K–E–N–O. No, wire it tonight. I haven't got a dime. How'm I going to stay around here until you get off work tomorrow?"

Sorrells left the slot machines. He saw Porter standing short and bowlegged under his broad, brown, town hat and walked up behind him.

"Yeah, I'm cow boss," he was saying. "But it's a hell of a job. I've got to do it all, you know. I ain't got no help."

Sorrells put his hand on Porter's shoulder and he turned around. "Oh, hi, Bert," he said. He did not act surprised or worried that Sorrells might have heard what he said. "Meet Gilbert Lombard," he said. Sorrells shook hands with the man. He was a tall, heavy shouldered, heavy headed man who looked part Indian. His hair was gray. His hands were big. He wore a broad-brimmed, high crowned, well-shaped felt hat cocked on one side of his head. His eye was kindly appraising Sorrells. It had seen a lot of sun and many cowpunchers.

"So you're dealing blackjack here in the hotel now," Porter said to Lombard.

"Yes, it pays me and keeps me busy. I get my pension now, so I can't work at it all the time and I can't run no cows."

"Say, Gilbert, I was trying to think what was the name of that spring where we penned those wild horses that time in '48. Remember that spring?" Porter asked.

"You mean Hoover Spring?" Lombard asked, his eye

completely interested and intense with remembering his trade.

"That's it. Hoover Spring. I was trying to remember the other day when me and Sorrells rode through that country. I thought it might be Roosevelt or Hoover or Coolidge or something like that."

"Hoover Spring. That's all I ever heard it called."

"Now Gilbert, we done thisaway, we rode down the canyon that runs under the north side of Black Mountain watching for trails to that spring. What side of that canyon is it on?"

"Well, you ride on down, the best I can remember, until Black Mountain is about behind your right shoulder." Lombard gestured with his two hands over his right shoulder the same way a man riding a nervous horse would brush a fly by his ear without looking at it, keeping his head and eyes straight ahead so as not to scare the horse. "And then you turn left up one of them canyons that run into the main canyon. You'll find that spring up one of them canyons."

"I can find it now," Porter said. "Me and Sorrells were in a big hurry when we went through there. It's been a long time since you and me worked that canyon together, Gilbert."

"Twenty years," Lombard said.

Sorrells excused himself and went to the blackjack table. Sorrells was a sandbagger. He played to stay in the game, to entertain himself with the cards as long as his five dollars lasted. He enjoyed playing the sharply colored designs on the cards in his hand against the green felt. When he played he warmed to the occupation of gambling for the luck it took to stay in the game. He had to win to stay and this wasn't his night to win. He lost his five dollars in half an hour. He got up and went to hunt Porter.

He found Porter in the restaurant over another dish of ice cream talking to another stranger. Porter introduced the man as Newt Stacy. Stacy was small, wiry, and red-faced. He had a short, wide, pug nose. He was wearing a sweat-stained straw hat, a clean shirt, and clean, patched Levis. He was looking for a job and Porter had just recruited him. Porter wanted Stacy to get settled back at the ranch. Stacy was broke and wanted to get out of town. Sorrells gave up wanting to make an evening in Keno. On the way home he listened to Porter brag to Stacy. Porter had found a new listener for his stories.

Stacy and Porter had a few acquaintances in common. Stacy called them buckaroos. He said he had not known many men he could call good buckaroos. By his talk Sorrells figured Stacy judged himself to be a good buckaroo.

The crew moved cattle the next day, the first day Stacy saddled a horse for the Outfit. Stacy was assigned a little black mustang horse that had been born on the Outfit. He immediately began calling him Nigger. The horse just fit Stacy, and when he bucked a few jumps in the morning, Stacy rode him with style.

Stacy didn't make a perfect hand on the drive, but the cattle the crew was moving were wild, he was on a strange horse and with cowpunchers he did not know. He was a good roper. He caught well in the open. When they got the herd to the corral he showed he was a good heeler, but when he missed his first loop he went mad. His face got red and he started "gawdamming" through his gritted teeth. He missed again and blamed his horse. He cussed the cattle. He began throwing bad loops, old lady loops that collapsed ignominiously on the ground or tangled in Nigger's feet.

The crew dismounted and Wilson lined the stock truck up with the loading chute. Sorrells and Stacy went afoot into the crowding pen and began pushing the cattle up the chute. The cow brutes didn't want to step up onto the chute and the constant, patient drive the job required disturbed Stacy to fury. Sorrells was looking for Stacy to club a calf to death or drop in his own tracks in a fit of apoplexy, but the calves and Stacy survived the job. Stacy did seem to have a good sense of self-preservation.

While Wilson was driving the last truckload of cattle to headquarters, the crew had one more chore to do. They had to brand, earmark, vaccinate, and castrate one newborn calf. Stacy rushed to his horse so he would get to rope the calf. He heeled the calf handily and then sat his horse giving orders to Sorrells and Porter. Sorrells tied the calf down. Stacy told him he should tie him better. To Sorrells, who had been tying calves for over thirty years, three wraps and a hooey had been all anyone needed to tie a calf down. He ignored Stacy and castrated the calf. He vaccinated the calf while Porter earmarked him. He held him down while Porter branded him. He started to untie him.

"Wait. Don't untie him," Stacy ordered. Sorrells stopped untying. "You didn't vaccinate him."

"I did," Sorrells said and let the calf up.

"You just think you did."

"I guess you didn't see me," Sorrells said.

"Gawdammit, Bert, you didn't vaccinate that calf," Stacy said and roped the calf again.

"He's already vaccinated," Porter said and Sorrells let the calf go again. Stacy's face turned redder but he said nothing more.

Sorrells made a pot of coffee on the branding fire. Stacy tied his horse by the bridle reins in the corral and took a cup of coffee. As he sipped the coffee his face took on a more natural color. When he finished he walked toward his horse. The black leaned back until the reins were tight as he watched Stacy approach. The horse was alarmed. He was not well enough acquainted with Stacy to accept so familiar and confident an advance from him. Stacy strode on just as though he couldn't see the horse needed time to look him over.

"He's gonna break your reins," Porter said. The reins broke. The black horse fell back onto his haunches in the dust with only two short remnants of a fine pair of braided rawhide reins hanging from the bits.

"Gawdam you," Stacy shouted. The black ran away from him in the corral.

"That boy does have a time," Porter said.

The next morning Sorrells and Wilson had fed the horses and were walking back to the bunkhouse when they met Stacy coming out of the bunkhouse. Stacy didn't answer Sorrells' "Good morning." Stacy had stayed in bed during breakfast in the bunkhouse. He had either been asleep or feigning sleep. Sorrells couldn't see how he could have slept while the whole crew of the Outfit scraped and slopped ten feet from the foot of his bed.

Later, when Sorrells and Stacy had to work together,

Stacy answered all of Sorrells' most polite conversation with sour looks. Sorrells finally asked Stacy good naturedly what was wrong with him.

"Gawdammit, Bert, why didn't you wake me up? Everywhere I've been the rule is a man wakes his buddy in the morning. You make me think you'd like to see me fired."

The accusation took Sorrells by surprise. "You can think what you want to but I never thought about you being asleep. I thought you wanted to stay in bed," he said.

"Well, from now on you'd better think about it," Stacy said and turned and walked away.

The crew was working cattle in the corrals that day. Whenever Stacy came near Sorrells, he strutted and circled him like a fighting cock. Sorrells saw that Stacy was looking for a chance to Sunday him. At noon when Stacy separated himself from the crew and headed for the bunkhouse, Sorrells followed him. He caught up to him at the door.

"I guess it's time we talked," Sorrells said.

"Sure, Bert, what about?" Stacy had cooled off.

"I'd like to know where the hell you get the idea I'd like you to get fired."

"Why bring it up, Bert? Forget it. I have. I was just peeved because you didn't show me the courtesy of waking me up."

"Now let me tell you something," Sorrells said. "I didn't take you to raise, so you can get mad at your horses, at the cattle and at yourself all you want, but don't get mad at me, because then I get mad."

"I didn't mean for you to make a big thing out of it."

"Just remember this. I'm for you one hundred per cent, but you get mad at me and I ain't going to be for you anymore. I don't know whether that makes any difference to you, but I figure we'll like the work around here better if it does."

"Hell, Bert, I want to get along."

The next day the crew hauled the Outfit's portable corral with them behind the stock truck. This corral was a loading chute and panels that could be assembled into a corral in a short time. The loading chute had wheels on it and also served as a trailer to haul the panels. This corral was the only means the men had of penning cattle on most of the ranch and it was adequate. The Outfit had no fences. The fence Cunningham had thought cut the ranch in two was never found. Sorrells was happy about no fences on the Outfit. If he had his way, fences would not have been invented. Fences showed up behind people who thought they owned the country. Sorrells knew no one owned it and would never own it, even though someone a hundred years from now would have a fence up like a farmer to try and prove a portion of the country was his.

The crew set their corral up in a canyon below Mud Springs. Sorrells and Stacy rode north out of Mud Springs Canyon. Stacy was riding Nigger again. Sorrells was riding Baldy.

They topped out of Mud Springs Canyon and came to another spring. A large covey of quail flew up. Stacy was riding in front of Sorrells. He sat very straight in the saddle with his knees stiffly locked, his heels in, his toes pointed out in the stirrups. When the spring was at eye level with Stacy as he rode up the mountain, the quail saw him and flushed.

The two men stopped to roll cigarettes and let their horses blow. Stacy had to dismount to roll his cigarette. He wasn't very good at rolling cigarettes. His best cigarette was lumpy in the middle, flat at the mouth, and leaked tobacco out the bottom. Sorrells kidded Stacy about the whole world stopping to watch while he rolled a cigarette. Stacy took the kidding because he admitted he was no good at it. He admitted it because he knew Sorrells could clearly see he was no good at it.

Quail continued to start up against the dark green of the thick piñon on Silver Peak Mountain over the heads of Sorrells and Stacy.

"That's a fine bunch of quail," Sorrells said.

"Average," Stacy said. "I've seen real bunches on the Bar Z."

"They look good to me."

"They're thin."

"Are they fat on the Bar Z this time of the year?"

"Everything's fat on the Bar Z, especially the cattle, the horses, and the buckaroos."

"It's got to be a good ranch then. That's what everybody sets out to do, get everything fat, ain't it?"

"Actually no. The Bar Z herd was so fat a buckaroo didn't have nothing to do, so the buckaroos got fat. Their horses *couldn't* do nothing, so they got fat and learned to buck, and not a buckaroo could ride one. I was the only one on the outfit even interested in riding one, so I was the only one never got fat."

"Well, you had it all to yourself then, Stace," Sorrells said.

"I guess so. My one big ambition in life is to be a good buckaroo. I'm not a good one yet, because I've only been at it a year and a half. But I'm good enough for this job."

"What did you do before you became a buckaroo, Stace?"

"I was a dealer in the casinos. I'll tell you, I'm bragging I know, but I am a good dealer. I ain't a good buckaroo yet, but I can get a job as a dealer anytime I want one and make real good money."

"By God, I'd be in one of them cool casinos looking across the tables at them good-looking, big-chested, female gamblers and taking a break with a different one and a drink of whiskey every hour if I could deal," Sorrells said, joking.

"Naw, I don't feel the way you do about that," Stacy said seriously. "I can see more of a challenge in becoming a top hand. I'll be one someday. That's why I picked this ranch. There's nothing but potential for a guy like me here. Do you know this outfit has had four managers in three years? There's not a man on this ranch who could hold a job one week on a ranch with a bunch of top buckaroos."

They rode on from the spring until they came to a plateau that ran flat and smooth parallel to Mud Springs Canyon. They crossed the plateau and climbed again up the mountain while they watched the country below them for cattle. They were high when Stacy saw a cow and a calf and a two-year-old heifer going over a ridge into a canyon below them. Stacy rode on around the mountain to stay above the cattle and Sorrells picked up their tracks and stayed with them.

The tracks followed a trail that rimmed the canyon. The tracks were deep, because the cattle had been moving fast downhill. Wild horses had also moved along the trail recently. Sorrells didn't have time to see where the horses had come onto the trail, but he looked above him and saw a big basin high under Silver Peak that he knew would be a good running ground for wild horses. The trail crossed a bare saddle and fell off into a long, deep, broken draw, and Sorrells saw the cattle going along the bottom of it. They were canalized now. They weren't going to leave the draw until it spread out and widened into a big open country. They were trying to make miles. Sorrells stopped to see if he could signal Stacy. Stacy was down in the deepest end of the draw, riding among some old mine buildings, and Sorrells waved and hollered to him and drove Baldy in a sliding fall off the mountain after the cattle.

He went at a long lope down the canyon until he rounded a bend and came into their sight. The cattle saw they were being crowded and left the canyon for the plateau that paralleled Mud Springs Canyon. They were going just right because Wilson and Porter would be along the lower end of the plateau. Sorrells fell in behind them and kept them going.

Suddenly a three-year-old maverick bull coasted up from behind Sorrells with Wilson behind him. The bull ran through Sorrells' cattle. This gave all the cattle new impetus and they ran on. Wilson caught up and Sorrells circled the cattle and got ahead of them. He tried to hold them up but they scattered. The bull hooked at his horse and went by him.

Sorrells ran ahead of them again to contain them and keep them pointed in the open. He saw Porter holding up a small bunch of cattle. Sorrells pointed his wild ones into Porter's bunch. The heifer and the maverick, each going different directions, shot through the bunch. Sorrells caught the heifer and tied her down. Wilson caught the maverick and tied him down and Porter kept the bunch from scattering.

They had settled the bunch and their horses were getting their wind back when Stacy came over a rise, cussing, spurring, whipping, and jerking his Nigger. He charged, straight toward the bunch. The cow Sorrells had followed off the mountain hooked by Wilson and was gone. Her calf ran before Stacy. The black horse followed the calf with Stacy red-faced and cussing, whipping, and spurring off the plateau into Mud Springs Canyon out of sight. This new disturbance set the whole bunch off again. Porter and Sorrells ran ahead to hold them while Wilson roped the cow. A calf broke from the bunch and Porter roped him. He tied the calf and held the bunch. Sorrells heeled the cow and held her down while Wilson tied her. The storm cleared with four cattle tied down. Only four were standing. One calf had removed Stacy from the field.

The three men let up the cattle they had tied down and drove the bunch into Mud Springs Canyon. Stacy had tied his calf in the bottom of the canyon, but had disappeared again. They started the cattle up the canyon and after a while Stacy rode up behind the herd whistling and swinging his rope. His little black horse was lathered and prancing. Every once in a while Stacy would jerk the horse and spur him at the same time, and when the horse didn't know whether to stop or go, Stacy would jerk and spur him again. He would also "gawdamm" him. Porter rode along watching Stacy. Sorrells knew he wanted to say something but he was keeping quiet, a rare effort for Porter.

Later, Sorrells and Porter were riding in the drags when Porter proclaimed, "In Arizona, before I came to Nevada, we always used to say we knew there must be a lot of good buckaroos in Nevada because none was ever seen out of the state. None ever escaped Nevada. We was too kind in them days. I ain't seen a good buckaroo in the state since I been here."

Chapter 9

A JOB OF WORK

A cowpuncher probably gets as much sun as any living being. The sun warms the backs of his hands and his cheeks. It warms his breast through his shirt. A cowpuncher partners with the sun raising cattle. He's glad to see it come up in the morning and usually has enough work to do so that he is not always happy to see it go down in the evening.

Tom struck the arc and the blue-white explosion of light sprayed over the weld he was making. The arc spat, hummed, and cracked, and left a smoking bead on the iron before him. The grill for Mrs. Cunningham was almost finished, and Tom was taking a lot of care with the job to make it last. The work contented him and he didn't want it to be finished.

When he finished he would have to deliver the grill in person to Mrs. Cunningham. Then he would have to go to the bunkhouse. After he had his supper, he would have to go on back to his room. All his life he had found himself alone in a cell like that after a good day's work, after the supper with his mates, after a day of doing his best to make a hand and usually always making a good hand. Soon tonight he would find himself alone again with nothing to do. He was not good at sleeping.

He had married very young, before he had known how a wife would have kept him from a cell all by himself. He had been sixteen years old. His girl had been younger. He had been so wild he had taken his wife-child to their first privacy together, and instead of remaining and bedding, he had realized he was sorry he had allowed himself to become walled in with another child so soon in the very beginning of his long life. He had looked at his wife and seen a little girl who had no mother anymore, only Tom. He had run away.

He had gone back. He had sons with his wife. His wife was good company, slight company, but a pleasant Texas girl who talked Texas music to Tom. He did not know why, but he always found himself a night after leaving her in a cell by himself on some place like the Outfit, far away from the arms of his wife. He was always a night away from her before he realized how good it was for him to be with her.

Mary was her name. Bright Mary. He would go back to East Texas to see her this winter, maybe. Right now he had a good job to do. He was building a new lumber and steel rack for the Outfit's stock truck. A steel rack for one of the new pickups. A new carrier for his welder. New gates for the chutes. He had many hours of work to do. He knew if he went back to Texas to see Mary, He would be years making his return to the work he had found on this outfit. He could never be sure where he would be a night after he left Mary again. He knew he was content here with his job and loath to be gone again, even to see Bright Mary.

The sheriff in his county in East Texas had that eight-year-old warrant for him and he would gather Tom in if he went back. The sheriff would make it stick too, for Tom was guilty. He had committed assault against a cottonpicker with the picker's own blade, assault with all intent to kill. The picker had lived after seeing his own guts blaring out from under his knife in Tom's hand. The sentence for assault could put Tom in that cell for the rest of his life. They'd do it to him too. He was guilty of all they said he had done. He had not taken the knife from the picker to scare him with it or to throw it away and fight fair. He had returned it sheathed in the picker's guts. He wasn't proud of the knifing and he wasn't sorry. He had done it because it was the only thing to do with the knife after the picker had let him take it away.

Now, behind the window of the heavy welder's mask in the dark shed seventy miles from any people who might be interested in seeing him isolated from them in a cell, he struck the free white light snapping on the end of the rod, insuring his own immunity from capture as though he were standing behind the sun. No one could look at him through his light by day and no one ever followed him into his own private hole at night. His cell might be a misery for him, but he had it mostly only at night and he could leave it for another one anytime he pleased.

Tom had thought of sending for Mary at times when he felt especially secure. Their kids were grown. The boy already commenced to give her trouble. She would be glad to come to Tom. He never had sent for her because he knew he would not have been able to stay in one place as long as anyone in Texas, even Mary, knew where he was. He would not have been able to stand the picture of Mary hurrying from Texas without looking back and of himself reaching for her when she arrived and seeing the law over her shoulder.

The law had sent him to Prison Farm when he had sent for Mary the first time. He had not minded the farm. He had learned welding and mechanics at the farm, and reading and writing. He had just naturally taken to mechanics and welding and had learned his arithmetic and reading so he could be better at mechanics. The other two terms he had served in other schools in other states had increased his learning, but he did not ever want to go back.

Each time he had been in trouble it had been for assault. He owned a blind white temper like the smoking white light of the arc. His temper produced in him a purpose as pure and impersonal as the arc light, and he never knew until after each time he fought that his temper had done him any wrong. For many years he had been proud of his temper, feeling it strengthened the fiber of him, not realizing it caused the very trouble he used it to extinguish.

His temper had been like the bulls he rode in the Prison Farm rodeos. He had never been able to understand why a man who had a chance to ride a big and powerful bull did not take it. Tom had never passed up a chance to ride a bull, nor had he ever passed up a chance to mount and ride out his temper when it rose and presented itself to him. He just couldn't find it in himself not to ride out and spur it on and see what would happen. He felt he lived a little more each time he rode a bull or had a fight. Giving up all caution, giving up all the spectator's sense of well-being and throwing himself into an arena upon the back of a bull made Tom feel good. It made him trust himself.

For a long time he had not understood why he had landed in jail or in some other kind of cell after he had turned himself loose. Now he realized people put those bulls up there to scare a man off, and it shook hell out of them when a man got on him and rode him toward them. The people would rather a man looked at a bull and then went off somewhere dark to hide.

They were making Tom hide now. He had checked it to them. He might never have to ride another one unless he decided he just had to see Bright Mary again. He knew he still had it in him to someday get on his bull and ride him out to see her. Seeing her again would be worth it. Even if he didn't get to see her it would be worth it.

Chapter 10

THE EXPERIMENT

When a cowboy speaks of "the Company," he means the owners of an outfit. To the cowboy, the company is the entity in the outfit that understands and decides on all money matters, the machinery of which the cowboy absolutely refuses to understand. The company's money matters may never reasonably be wed with a cowboy's husbandry of the bovine. Most of the time the cowboy sees and performs his husbandry with no regard for money, and the company cannot understand why he does. The company does understand that this difference is why a cowboy does not have an outfit of his own.

"**B**y God, we need a cook!" Porter said. "A man can't ride all day and cook too. Here we are, in at nine thirty after working fifteen hours for a millionaire outfit and it a famous one and that can't provide a cook."

Sorrells was working too hard unsaddling his horse to answer. He did not have the energy. He led Roller to a stall and got a bale of hay to feed the horses. He turned on the water in the horse trough. He made a cigarette and smoked while the trough filled. He turned off the water, went to the saddle house, turned off the lights, and walked slowly toward the bunkhouse.

A light was on in the machine shop. Sorrells heard the welder crackling and saw the blue light reflecting off the walls. He stopped by the door. Tom was bending over a piece of his work.

"How is it, Thomas?" Sorrells asked.

"O.K., Bert. I've got her licked now," Tom said.

"What're you building?"

"A grill for the indoor broiler for Mr. Cunningham's lady."

"At nine thirty? Don't you ever quit?"

"I see you ain't quit till now, Bert."

"Yeah, but the bovines are my bosses and they don't carry watches."

"Well, I might as well work. I cain't sleep. Mr. Lang will be here tomorrow and Mrs. Cunningham asked me to have this ready if I could. She's a nice lady. I don't mind doing it."

"Yes, she is, I'll see you later, Tom."

"See you, Bert," Tom said and dropped the welder's mask down over his face.

Sorrells dragged his sore foot up the hill to the bunkhouse, relishing his tired steps because he was sure there was no more work to be done that night and only a few more steps to take. He sat down on one of the long benches at the bunkhouse table and took off his chaps and spurs. He carried them into his room and dropped them on the floor. He took out his pint of whiskey and drank a swallow. It warmed his empty belly and revived his lank spirit. He swallowed more of it and put it away. He was sitting on his bunk looking at the palms of his hands when Cunningham came in.

"How did you make out today, Bert?" he asked.

"We got seven head," Sorrells said.

"Is that all?" Cunningham was peeved.

"That's all."

"Hell, Bert, I would think four men could do better than that."

"We didn't get any more but we didn't let any get away."

"What was the matter? At this rate we'll be gathering until the first of the year.

"They've just been let get away so much they're wild as deer. These cattle are scattered all over the ranch. There's good water and feed everywhere in the high, rough country and they can hide."

"Maybe we aren't doing right. There might be some other way."

"The only way I can think of is the way we're doing it. We're moving the portable corral and working a different country every three or four days. It's a big country, Roy."

"Well, something is wrong."

"Yes, the weather's hot and the cattle are scattered in the high country where we can't find them and they run when they see us. That's what's wrong. They're used to getting away. We got two yearlings and a two-year-old today that had never been touched by human hand."

"Bobby Lang will be here in the morning and I promised him we'd have more cattle than we've got."

"I wish we could have them. Poor Bobby."

"Maybe we need more men."

"What would they ride?"

"Hell, I don't know. I'm just trying to figure this thing out so I can keep the job."

"Tell Bobby Lang to get ten more men and he can come along too. He wouldn't do it, would he? So don't worry about it. We'll gather the cattle."

"He's bringing some bulls he bought in Las Vegas."

"What kind of bulls?"

"I don't know, but they are probably Brahmas."

"He's on a Bremer kick now, is he?"

"It's his ranch."

"We've gathered about one Bremer calf for fifty native calves. Those big red Bremer bulls of his stand around together like monuments and look on while the little native bulls get the cows."

"Bobby's got a program. He's experimenting to see what breed of cattle will do best on this ranch."

"Hell, the buyers tell him that. They've been giving him eight dollars a hundredweight less money for his Bremer calves. He's lucky he doesn't have more Bremers."

"Well, he's trying."

"Yes, Roy? What was that you said the other day about trying? Tell him to ask the old cowpunchers who owned this ranch before him what kind of cattle do best on this ranch. Tell him to ask old Porter. That won't *cost* him anything."

Cunningham batted his hands as though to keep a fly away from his mouth as he turned away. "I've got to go to supper. Come on and eat supper with us. Maudy's got steak."

"Naw. Thanks. Porter is fixing us something. That's another problem you've got. Porter wants a cook."

"Find one. Just find a cook. I had to fire the last one to keep you from killing him. I'll get you the best cook in the country if you'll just find him for me."

"It's not my job to find cooks."

"No, *your* job is to gather these cattle as soon as you can." Cunningham left the bunkhouse.

Sorrells and Wilson were feeding the horses the next morning when the truck came with the new bulls. They unloaded the bulls and put them into a pen by themselves. They were not good bulls to sire calves for any outfit. They were degenerate, hide bound, narrow between the legs, long headed, and small boned. Some sharp trader had seen the son of the Outfit coming from a long way off down the Boulevard of Dreams. The bulls were common, the kind of cattle meat-packer buyers called standard and paid sixteen to eighteen cents a pound for. The Outfit was selling yearling natives for beef at twenty-six and twenty-eight cents a pound that were real sire material.

Cunningham and Bobby Lang walked down the alley to where Wilson and Sorrells were standing looking at the bulls. Bobby was beaming. Cunningham stood apart and looked at the bulls.

"What do you think of them, Bert Sorrells?" Bobby asked, shaking Sorrells' hand. He did not see Wilson standing there too.

"What did they cost?" Sorrells asked.

"Two hundred dollars a head. Don't you think they're pretty good little bulls?"

Sorrells laughed. Wilson turned, the Indian face closed, and walked away down the alley.

"You figure you got a good deal?" Sorrells asked.

"Yes. The men that sold them to me were asking two hundred and fifty dollars."

Dobie Porter had been taking the morrals off the horses. He walked up with the morrals hanging from the crook of his elbow.

"Hi, Dobie," the son of the Outfit beamed, shaking his hand. "What do you think of my bulls?"

Dobie had already seen them. He did not look at them again. He smiled from way off behind his glasses. "Well, sir," he said. "I don't know nothing about these kind of bulls as herd sires. I've seen lots of them on cheap feed in Imperial Valley going for sixteen cents a pound. Their daddys and mamas was common and they was *uncommonly* common."

The son of the Outfit turned off his beam. "These cattle are half Charolais," he said.

"They might have *smelled* a Charolais once but that don't make them Charolais. They look like common old Laredo Meskin gray Bremers to me, but I could be wrong, I've been wrong before."

"You're wrong this time. These cattle are from good Charbray stock."

"Charbray is half Bremer and half Charolais?"

"Well, no. I don't know just what the percentages of the blood are, but I know the breed comes from those two kinds of cattle. Anyway, these cattle come from that stock."

"Huh!" Porter snorted. "Could be, I guess."

"They are," Bobby said. He turned to Cunningham. "Roy, let's get the rest of the bulls up and sort them so I can see what I've got."

Cunningham called Sorrells aside. Sorrells was almost sure what Cunningham was going to ask him to do and the thought didn't amuse him. The men were going to spend the day shuffling Bobby's play prettys around the corral so he could watch.

"Bert, I want you to cut these native bulls deep. Keep only the very best. Bobby tells me he's going to replace the natives with red and black Angus, Charbray, Brahma, and Santa Gertrudis this year. If he wants to spend, let's let him spend all he wants to."

"He *is* trying, ain't he?" Sorrells said.

"As long as he's replacing bulls, let's get rid of all the bad and mediocre natives."

"If you ask me, the bad and mediocre already on this ranch are better than these longheads or registered cattle you'll have to wait on."

"No one is asking you and no one is asking me."

"I'll go and catch my 'sortin'' horse if I'm going to 'sort' the cattle," Sorrells said.

Sorrells saddled Big Red and he, Porter, and Wilson drove the bull herd in.

Newt Stacy liked to whistle and dance on his way to work. On this morning he had been busy with himself in the bunkhouse and he came to the corrals late. He was whistling and dancing up the alley, intent on his shuffling step and the volume of his whistle when he noticed, accidentally, the crew driving the one hundred and one head of bulls to the corral. He stopped, did not think, and made the mistake of turning the new bulls out of their corral so that they mixed with the one hundred and one bulls.

The men held the bulls in the alley while Sorrells cut out the old, shorter, narrow-hipped and thin bulls. He kept the young, long, rangy broad, and tall bulls. The best bulls on the Outfit were big, roan bulls. These bulls were all in fine shape and were throwing good, big boned, stout, choice calves. Sorrells kept every one of the roan bulls. He tried to cut out all the Brahmas but he didn't get away with it. Cunningham was watching him and each time he tried to cut a Brahma "by" Cunningham caught him down the alley and cut him "in." Cunningham didn't say anything to Sorrells. Sorrells kept on trying to "by" the Brahmas just to exasperate Cunningham. He tried to "by" every one of the new longheads but couldn't get a reaction from Cunningham. When he cut one of the longheads that was particularly bad, so bad that even Bobby Lang could see he compared unfavorably with the worst bulls the Outfit was keeping, Bobby shouted to "by" him too. Cunningham turned him into the "in" corral.

"Hold it," Bobby shouted and walked down the alley to Cunningham. Sorrells rode Big Red close to them so he could listen.

"I know I said I wanted to keep the Brahmas, but maybe

we ought to cull that one and sell him, Roy," Bobby said. "He's an evil-headed brute, isn't he?"

Cunningham stood by the gate and said nothing.

"He won't be hard to get back out of there, will he?" Bobby asked.

"You don't want to cut that one out," Cunningham said.

"Why not? He looks bad beside the rest of them."

"He is one you just bought, one of the bunch that arrived this morning," Cunningham said, and leaned on the gate.

"That one is?"

"Yes, sir."

Bobby looked at the bull for a long time. The bull was swaybacked and bobtailed, besides being longheaded and droopeared. The bobtail was only about a foot long and had a sparse, hairy tuft on the end. The bull looked back at the son of the Outfit from his place in the "in" corral.

"We have to keep him then, don't we?" Bobby said.

"Yes."

"I'll get him out of there in just a jiffy on my 'sortin'' horse if you want me to," Sorrells said. He grinned at Cunningham.

"No. He'll be all right. As rough as he looks, he's got good blood in him. He probably looks bad because he had a rough trip," Bobby said.

Sorrells turned Big Red around so the son of the Outfit couldn't see him laughing, grinned at Cunningham's cloudy face, and went back to cutting the bulls.

Cunningham got Sorrells to supper at Maudy's with Bobby Lang that evening. Tom the welder was finishing setting up the grill when they walked in. The grill was set in a small, waist-high fireplace in the kitchen. Maudy already had her coals glowing in the big fireplace and Tom silently carried them to the kitchen. He hurried with his head down when he left the house, as though he felt he would offend someone by looking at him.

Maudy's food was good, her table well set. Her house was well prepared for her husband's business with his boss. She kept quiet and served the food and provided her ear in audience. That was all Maudy did. She did not speak when dinner and sleeping in her home involved business.

Bobby Lang was in a magnanimous mood. He had brought with him the most expensive New York steak cuts he could find on the Boulevard of Dreams. He had the same definite ideas about cooking steaks as he had about herd sires, which is to say he knew a bull must bellow when he breeds much the same as he bellows when he bleeds, and he advised Maudy that she would do well if she applied his ideas. Although Maudy had been successful in the business of cooking steaks all her life and Sorrells knew she didn't agree with the son of the Outfit, she smiled and did as he advised her to do.

They sat down to supper and Bobby began telling Sorrells and Cunningham about all the improvements the Outfit would be getting. Bobby was going to till four thousand acres and plant crested wheat grass to see how it would do. He was going to build many dams to hold the rain water and he was going to fence waterlots on all the springs. He was going to buy a helicopter and Cunningham was going to learn to fly it. He was going to buy two new four-wheel-drive pickups. He was going to send Maudy and the bunkhouse new washing machines. He was dickering, even then, with a Japanese motorcycle company to see if he could, economically, make good use of motorcycles on the Outfit and thus do away with much, if not all, the horseback riding. He had men in the front office at that moment doing studies on a system of underground reservoirs for the Outfit. The new bulls, from then on, would be only the best that could be bought at livestock shows where there would be no question of their bloodlines.

"This is one of your ideas that will have a hard time succeeding, in my opinion," Cunningham said.

"Why won't it succeed? Any program we institute toward infusing new blood on this ranch *has* to succeed."

"You must not be thinking about the product you will be trying to sell so that you can pay for all your new bulls."

"Sure I am. We'll have the new bulls' calves."

"Buyers want uniformity. You will have six different kinds and colors of cattle. You won't get as much money for crossbred calves as you are getting for straight Hereford, native calves or the Hereford-roan calves."

"I was meaning to ask you about that. How come you kept those roan-looking bulls? They are a funny color. *They* aren't uniform."

"Any buyer knows the roan blood helps these natives and will give high prices for them. Your Brahmas pull the quality down."

"Maybe so but we will get more calves because Brahmas are better rustlers in this kind of country."

"We've only been getting about one Brahma calf for fifty natives."

"Roy, we're only learning now. Experimenting. Maybe the Brahmas we've bought up to now have been sterile or deficient."

"They might be but, most important, they aren't used to the country. They don't know what to eat when they get here. Their feet are soft. Their lungs are too small for rustling in the high country. They bunch together like queers, sometimes four or five in a bunch. They aren't interested in cows. When you buy, you should buy cattle that have been raised in country similar to this, thrifty cattle."

"From now on we're buying only the best kind of bulls, bulls we can get out of the stock shows, of proven stock, and semen tested."

"That will be even more a waste of your money. Those cattle have been raised in meadows and stalls. They can't walk a hundred yards before their feet start to fall apart and their tongues to hang out. They'll starve to death where a native would fatten. We'll have to wait on them hand and foot and you won't get any calves."

"You'll wait on them, then. What else do these riders have to do?" The son of the Outfit smiled at Sorrells, a concession. He called his cowboys "riders" and he, before Cunningham, had hired mechanics and paid them more money and had let them ride as a fringe benefit. Sorrells didn't smile back at him.

"I don't know how I'm going to keep good cowboys at two hundred fifty dollars a month," Cunningham said.

"When we get the programs working I'm going to start a

profit-sharing program for all the crew. The wages will stay the same, but the crew will divide about 15 per cent of the net profit of this ranch."

"Then you'll be making us partners in the Outfit?" Sorrells asked, laughing.

"Exactly."

"Partners in the net profit?"

"Right. You get it, Bert Sorrells."

"I think, with all the money you will be spending on improvements, it will be a long time before anyone sees any profits on this outfit. I think I would rather have a raise in salary and not be a partner. I don't want to own any of these bovines I'll be waiting on."

"When you've been here awhile we'll talk about a raise. We have been having so much transient help I haven't seen any such possibility before this. If you prove yourself to be a good rider, as I'm sure you are, we might think of a raise. I can't, right now, authorize any raises for our Indians or transients or old has-beens, if you know what I mean." The son of the Outfit smiled at Sorrells again.

Sorrells laughed, shook his head, leaned back in his chair, and relaxed. He wondered what the old "has been," Dobie Porter, and that Indian, Wilson, would say if Sorrells told them the enterprise of Famous had plans for Sorrells that didn't include them.

"You say you are experimenting," Cunningham said. "I don't see how this ranch can pay for these experiments if it can't produce."

"Don't worry about paying for it. Archie Lang and Son can pay for it. We make enough in one night to keep improvements going on this ranch for a long, long time."

"I see. That, of course, is a different story. I just want to make clear that the ranch can't pay for these improvements."

"It will in the long run. It will be a storehouse of the money we make in the entertainment business. My dad is a smart, tough businessman. He doesn't give anything away and he doesn't pay any money he doesn't want to pay. You see him as a comedian, a generous clown on TV, but let me give you an example of how hard he is in business.

"Just recently we were in New York for a meeting of all

the executives of Famous Enterprises. Just before the meeting my dad found out that one of the highest paid of his executives had accidentally let out a piece of confidential information involving a transaction Famous was about to make. This transaction involved two and a half *million* dollars." Bobby paused to let his audience grasp the significance of a multi*million*-dollar deal.

"This meeting had been called for the purpose of finalizing plans for the transaction. The executive's betrayal of confidence had aborted the whole purpose of the meeting. A rival corporation had beat Famous to the deal.

"My dad found out about this executive's indiscretion just as he was walking into the meeting. I asked him what he was going to do about the executive. He just laughed and said, 'There is only one thing to do to a person when you have him by the balls. You squeeze.'"

Cunningham laughed nervously and nodded. Maudy was committed to her dishes. Sorrells excused himself and went back to the bunkhouse.

Chapter 11

RODEO

The first rodeos were roundups held by Spaniards for the purpose of joining all the cows with all the herd sires to assure the best calf crop. Geography sometimes kept cows and bulls apart too long. These rodeos took several weeks and often involved several brands when fences did not exist.

When families of the owners of the brands began enjoying these meetings, rodeos evolved into gatherings of people. In the cattle country of the United States rodeos were no longer for cattle breeding. They were for celebrating birthdays and anniversaries, holidays and centennials. At rodeos the men showed the prowess they had developed in their husbandry of cattle in contests of roping and horsemanship. Women showed off their best sewing and cooking and their babies. In the evenings the men and women danced to fiddle music while the young and the lonely courted.

In early October the sheriff's posse of Las Vegas sponsored a rodeo. Sorrells, Wilson, and Jack Roberts, the ex-jockey, had been working two months without a weekend off. Wilson pulled for Las Vegas with his sorrel horse in the back of his pickup. Sorrells went ahead with Jack Roberts to pay their rodeo entrance fees. The car radio played the music of Tex Ritter and Patsy Cline going a hundred miles an hour on the road to Las Vegas. Sorrells was going to town and no one could stop him.

Sorrells liked Jack Roberts, he liked the cushioned bucket seats in Jack's car, the music, the speed, the clean clothes, the more because he knew if he had not spoken up he would be horseback in some canyon chasing a wild bovine. Someone else could do the chasing for the next two days, not Sorrells. For three nights someone could chase Sorrells while he did some running and playing. He was free of the Outfit and might never go back.

Vegas was the town Sorrells most liked to run and play in. When the town came in sight he squalled and yelled, "Hang it in 'er, Jacky, we're almost there," and the closer they drove to the center of town the happier he became. They went straight to rodeo headquarters. The first big hat he saw that he knew was Andy Elias, the producer of the rodeo. The man turned and saw Sorrells and said, "Bert Sorrells, I thought you were dead. I saw the letter you wrote to enter the rodeo. I couldn't believe it was you." He did not smile when he shook hands.

"Not dead yet," Sorrells said.

"I thought you'd of been killed by a good horse or bad whiskey by now."

"I'm not even sick."

"What are you here for, to give my young athletes competition?"

"I came to see if all that chocolate milk and orange pop they drink makes them good hands. If it does, I might quit the whiskey and go rodeoing."

"You'll get my young athletes to runnin' and playin' is what you'll do. What are you 'up' in?"

"In the team roping and the dogging. I need for you to mount me."

"You're mounted."

"I'll give you a third of what I win."

"O.K."

"You never would turn a feller down."

"I never turn down a sure thing." Elias walked Sorrells over to the desk.

"Take Bert Sorrells' money in the steer wrestling and the

team roping," he said to the blond in the tight pants behind the desk. A bunch of rodeo cowboys half Sorrells' age were standing around a Coke machine. They were as clean and sober as a high school basketball team. They turned and looked at him. They had heard of Bert Sorrells if they had been around rodeo very long. He had been rodeoing as a boy twenty-five years ago when the Rodeo Cowboys Association had still been called the Turtles by some. Sorrells had never seen the purses these boys saw and he had only quit going to rodeos ten years ago.

"Come on," Elias said. "I'll introduce you to some real champions who would have made you and me in our day look sick."

"I'm already sick just looking at them," Sorrells said. "I'll meet them in the arena. Right now I'm going to meet another old guy at the Horseman's Club. You better come along. He's an old friend of yours too."

"Who's that?"

"Old Crow."

"I'll see you there later."

"O.K.," Sorrells said and started away.

"Wait a minute," Elias said. "Talk to me a minute before you get started runnin' and playin'."

"Ain't got a minute," Sorrells said and went out. He and Jack Roberts drove to the Horseman's Club. They got their grips out of the trunk and carried them through the crowded lobby to the desk. They registered and started to the elevator. A bellboy who had been watching them turned away when Sorrells faced him. Sorrells and Roberts, just off the Outfit, must not have looked prosperous enough to him because he didn't offer to help them with their grips. Sorrells dropped both grips at his feet, handed him the key and headed toward the bar.

"Come on, Jack, we're wasting time," he said.

The bar of the Horseman's Club was eighty feet long and made of hardwood. Mussed and tired people sat there on that morning. These were people who had gambled and caroused all night and were about to give up. None of them were fresh and starting with appetite like Sorrells and Jack Roberts were.

"Wanda's my name and cowboys my game, so give my cowboys a drink," a voice shouted from behind Roberts and Sorrells. "Howdy, my little Jacky Baby." A plump woman, immaculate in new Western clothing, caught Roberts in her arms and hugged him. Jack broke free and introduced her to Sorrells. She was the madam of the Rabbit Hutch, the bordello in Keno. She stood up to the bar like a man; one tiny, red booted foot on the brass rail; her small, white hands covered with diamonds before her. She threw back her head and bragged.

"I'm a gilflirted mare with a wring in my tail, gold in my pocket, and meat in my belly," she shouted. She was also drunk. "Give us cowboys a drink. A drink, my man, a drink."

"How long have you been at it this time?" Roberts asked her.

"I'm on the town to screw it up brown," she answered, paying no attention to his question. "I'll race my horse down the paved streets and match my whores against any town bitch feats."

"Bad, bad," Sorrells laughed and shook his head. Wanda looked down her nose at Sorrells.

"I'm going to ride a bull," she announced.

"*You* entered in the rodeo, Wanda?" Roberts asked.

"Now, *that's* what I come to see you about. You are going to enter me."

"Now, Wanda," Jack said. "You're no bullrider."

"The hell I ain't."

"Have you ever rode a bull?"

"How in the hell do you figure I make a living if it ain't riding bulls?"

"I thought they rode you."

"Yes, and by God I'm going to do the riding today."
Wilson walked in.

"Wilson, my smiling, pudgy, Paiute brave, I'm riding a bull today."

"Aw, Wanda," Wilson laughed.

"Lend me your chaps and spurs and rope. Little Jack has gotta lope on out and enter me."

"I'll lend you the gear, but you're not riding any bull, Wanda."

"I'll ride a big bull in spite of you, and if you don't get me the gear I'll beat you black and blue."

"Let's go get it, then," Wilson said. He took her by the arm and led her out of the bar. When she came back she was wearing Wilson's red chaps, a pair of tied down bullrider's spurs, and was carrying Wilson's belled bullrope over one shoulder.

"Now," she said to Jack. "You go down and enter this woman for to back out now would be less than human."

She produced a bankroll and handed Roberts a $100 bill.

"Hell, Wanda, the entrance fee is only about $25," Jack said. "I'm not even sure I can get you entered."

"The bulls always need new meat. Ye tell Elias it's Wanda they'll eat."

"Well, give me a smaller bill. This is too much money."

"Use the rest of that dough in any way it takes to pay the drinks today," Wanda brayed. "Now get agoin' and come right back cause I'm a halfbreed buckskin with no respect, the king of England's a clapped up wreck."

"Gawd almighty," Sorrells said.

"Give Wilson a drink, give us all a drink fine, for the day is begun and the day is for wine."

Soft hands covered Sorrells' eyes from behind him. They smelled good and were warm. He turned. They were Bonnie Sorrells' hands.

"Hello, my own man," Bonnie said. She had always, in Sorrells' memory, had the finest bosoms, the straightest body, and the brightest face he had ever known, and here she was standing in front of him calling him her man.

"Can't you kiss me?" she asked. She was smiling brightly to stave off his looking her over too closely. He kissed her but didn't know for even an instant what it was like.

"I knew you'd be here. I called rodeo headquarters and Andy told me you were in town. I came right over."

"I'm glad to see you, Bonnie."

"I knew you would be. I'll have just one drink with you and then I have to go take care of some things."

"Wilson, this is Bonnie Sorrells," Sorrells said.

"Sorrells?" Wilson asked.

"Bert is my husband," Bonnie said.

"Ex," Sorrells said.

"You'll always be my husband," Bonnie said. Her smile must have been making her jaws ache.

"Bonnie, Bonnie, Bonnie," Wanda said. "I never see you any more. When are you coming to see me to help me keep my store?"

"That'll be the day," Bonnie said, not looking at her. "Come on, Bert, come with me. I've got to go now." They walked out of the bar. Sorrells was happy to be with her again. "I'm Hot Wanda from Keno and I'm dry for vino" was the poetry that followed them down the street.

"You got any money?" Bonnie asked.

"Sure."

"Good. You can buy me a new outfit for the rodeo."

"Now, listen. I can't afford no Hart Schaffner and Marx stuff."

"You idiot," Bonnie laughed. "That's men's clothes. I just want a pair of Levis and a pair of boots if I'm going to be around you."

"Wear a dress." He saw the long, tan legs. The trim little fanny. She moved so lightly the slightest accidental brush of the back of his hand bounced her away from him, but she would always drift back close to his side as they walked down the street.

"I'm always in a dress. I want to wear a pair of Levis again."

"I'd like to play right now with you without a dress and no Levis."

"Oh, Bert, you're just like all the rest of the men in this town. You only think about how you can get a girl to bed."

"What wrong with that? It seems to me we always got along good in that department."

"Well, just forget it," Bonnie said, and led him into a store.

She bought a pair of men's Levis that hid her figure when she put them on. She bought a frilly white shirt. She rolled the cuffs in her Levis. She bought a pair of boots. Sorrells picked out a hat for her. The hat was a fine red felt with a wide ribbon hatband that flowed off the back of the brim like a swallow's tail. He put the hat on Bonnie's head with the sharp, pointed brim just over her fine eyebrows. When she looked at him out of her grave eyes from under that hatbrim, he loved her again. He was going to be with her now for a celebration. He felt his breast fill up with sweet air as though he had been long near suffocating. Bonnie placed the hat carefully on the back of her head and cocked it over one ear like a dude. She didn't like herself the way Sorrells liked to see her. He knew some women, even though they were not raised on a ranch, had an instinct for looking good in a hat and Levis. Bonnie had been raised on a ranch and been around cowboys all her life and didn't know how to wear a hat.

"You look like hell," Sorrells said to her.

"Never mind. I'm going to have fun, so don't worry about how I look," she said.

"Let's get something to eat," Sorrells said. He took her into a restaurant and ordered her a steak. While they waited for the meal, Bonnie got restless. The table with Bert Sorrells didn't hold her attention. She kept her eyes busy looking at the people who came and went in the restaurant. She was shopping for a good time, any person or place for a good time.

When the meal came she posed and postured with her fork and her glass but didn't eat.

"What have you been doing? How do you make a living in this town, Bonnie?" Sorrells asked.

"I do fine," Bonnie said while she looked around. "There's always something to do in this town. I have a lot of fun."

"You make a living having fun? How do you do that?"

"You have fun cowboying, don't you?"

"Sometimes. It's mostly just hard work."

"Where *are* you working, by the way?"

"Over by Keno for the Famous Outfit."

Bonnie shrilled, laughing. "You work for Bobby Lang? Mmmmmmmm. I like that man. How about introducing me?"

"You talk like a woman on dope. I asked you where you were working."

"Well, I just work."

"Doing what?"

"I have a lot of friends. This is a friendly town. I can get a job any time at any hour I want to work."

"Doing what?"

"For one thing, shilling on the strip. I work down on the strip mostly."

"Now if *that* ain't something," Sorrells said, and bent his head to his steak.

"In case you haven't noticed, I still have my looks. Some people still think I look like Ingrid Bergman."

Sorrells ate steak for a while. He could see Bonnie's fingers poking her fork at her steak without ever getting a tine into the meat.

"I make good money. I bet I make a whole lot better money than you do. I have a lot better things now than I ever had when we were together."

Sorrells did not look at her face. He knew too well what it would be expressing—her idea of haughty disdain. She had a cheap ring on her little finger, and that finger crooked and hovered in an arc around the fork. He remembered a fine ruby ring she had worn on that finger when they had been married. He had hocked that ring one time when they needed money and the first thing she had done when they had the money was go to a picture show. That night had been "Cash Nite" at the show, and he had hoped they might win the money the theater gave away. They got to the show after the money had already been given away. In those days he was so full of hope for the things Bonnie wanted that he had been fooled into thinking he wanted them too. For a long time after Bonnie and Sorrells were first married they had never missed a "Cash Nite."

"Why in the hell don't you eat instead of looking around so damn much?" Sorrells asked her in the restaurant. Bonnie smiled brightly at him so anybody watching would think she charmed him.

"But, I'm not hungry," she said.

"You're skinny. You never could just sit down and clean up a meal and go on about your business. You've got to make a production of it without ever getting any food in your stomach."

"You know me, don't you? I never could fool you, husband. You are the only one who ever cared about me."

"I ain't your husband anymore."

"You are too."

"Hell, Bonnie, we've been legally divorced for a year."

Bonnie's inattention stopped. Her face fell off the frozen cliff it had been holding on to.

"I didn't know that," she said. "Why didn't you let me know?"

"Where in the hell were you for the last two years?"

"I told you I was going to come back some day."

"Bonnie, who in the hell did you think was going to wait for a scatterbrain like you?"

Bonnie began to weep. She always could turn on the tears faster than any human he'd ever known. She didn't have to mean them from her heart. She had a good supply of tears in her head that could splash down and moisten her cheeks at exactly the area that caught the light best to move Sorrells to do what she wanted him to do.

"Now, stop bawling like you just lost your happy home. You quit two years ago," Sorrells said.

"I didn't think you would ever hurt me like that," Bonnie whimpered.

"Of course you didn't. No one ever hurts anyone else in your wonderland world, Bonnie. What you do to people makes them 'better off,' as you put it."

The tears ran on. "It's that I'm just no good," she said.

"Sure, that's right. Bonnie. You're a martyr and you always go away from people so you can have fun for their own good."

"I just knew you'd be better off without me, but I always intended to come back to you. You are such a man I never would have been able to stay away from you for long."

"Sure, Bonnie. Eat your steak."

"I'm not hungry any more. How could anyone eat?"

"Let's get out of here, then," Sorrells said. They met Roberts, Wilson, and Wanda and drove to the rodeo grounds. They parked by a stand that sold hot dogs fried in corn batter and served on a stick. Bonnie jumped out of the car and bought herself one of the huge wieners. She took it from the vendor and turned toward the car while she licked the top of it joyfully with the tip of her tongue, laughing at Jack

Roberts. The vendor handed her a Coke and she flounced off toward the arena with Wanda. Roberts was watching her rear.

"Man, how in the hell did you ever let that woman get away?" Roberts asked.

"She didn't like beefsteak," Sorrells said.

He knew better than to follow Bonnie. She was headed straight for the bucking chutes below the announcer's stand where the bull riders and the bronc riders were congregated, testing their rigging and watching the first round of the bucking stock as it was being driven into the chutes. He watched her as she kicked and horsed with the young men. She was horsing like a young mare in heat and she knew this was acid to Sorrells' feelings. Sorrells had never let her act that way when she was with him, though she had tried often. Now she was showing him how much "fun" she could have. She periodically looked his way to see if he was watching and each time she raised her tail a little higher.

"Come on, Bert. Let's get ready," Wilson was saying. He had been standing close to Sorrells long enough to see what he was watching.

Sorrells found Andy Elias up in the announcer's stand.

"If you still want that horse I won't use him to pick up broncs," Elias said.

"I want him," Sorrells said. "Where is he?"

"You can have him after I ride him in the grand entry."

"Fine."

"Isn't that Bonnie down there, Bert?"

"That's old Bonnie."

"I thought so. You separated now?"

"Can't you tell by looking?"

"That's too bad. You kids used to have a lot of fun together."

"Yeah, we did when we were kids on the Fourth of July and New Years' and at the rodeos."

"What are you doing now, Bert?"

"I'm chasing the wild bovine for the Outfit up near Keno."

"Famous?"

Sorrells nodded. "Archie Lang and Son."

"That's a big outfit. You running it for them?"

"Just cowboying."

"Why not follow my string and rodeo for a while?"

"Hell, no. I'm just here to have a little fun and contribute my money to these boys of yours. I've got a good job."

"How much does cowboying pay nowadays?"

"Two hundred and fifty dollars and found."

"You can't make any money that way. These little old kids make three times that much rodeoing. A guy like you would be a champion the first year. That cowboying ain't no good no more."

"Rodeoing never was good for me. I was in town for the celebration too much."

"You've got to look at it as a business."

"I never got that way about it. It was too much fun. I always felt good about going to town to a rodeo, but I felt better when I got out of town after a rodeo."

"I'll give you a job with me that'll pay you twice what you're making, and can make a full season without it costing you to travel."

"No thanks. I've got plenty to do."

"Think about it." Elias turned away to other business. Sorrells looked down at Bonnie who was now romping and playing with a boy in a flowered shirt. She had a smudge of mud on one cheek. The soft dirt in the arena had been sprinkled by a water truck. Bonnie was screeching and throwing dainty little mud balls at the boy. She spread her legs, lifted one boot in a high stepping prance, pointed her toe *almost* like a ballerina, and tossed a mud ball. Sorrells climbed down from the speaker's platform and went over to her. All the slick dicks in front of the chute were watching Bonnie.

"Come on, Bonnie," Sorrells said. Bonnie turned to him, her eyes glazed with the excitement she was causing in herself. Her face was shiny with sweat. Sorrells knew she was working herself into a frenzy that would soon end with her throwing her body at one of these boys or she would break out into hysterical laughter or weeping.

"Wild man, Sorrells," she shrieked. She threw a mudball at him and ran. Her flower-shirted boy was sitting on the ground. She fell on his lap. "Save me from the wild man," she mewed to him.

"Hello, Bert. Glad to see you here," the boy said, offering his hand from behind Bonnie.

"Do I know you, kid?" Sorrells asked.

"No, but I know you. I've heard my dad tell stories about you and I've seen pictures of you."

My God, Sorrells thought. What the hell am I doing here chasing after this woman again. He turned and walked away.

Sorrells and Wilson were up early in the team tying. Wilson caught the steer around the horns quick out of the barrier, checked him, and turned his rear end toward Sorrells. Sorrells dove in on Elias's gray horse and heeled him. Sorrells dragged the steer down and stretched him out on the ground. Wilson tied the steer's hind legs before the dust had cleared. Their time was respectable and they got a good hand when the announcer told the people they worked on Lang's Famous Outfit.

Sorrells was up soon in the bulldogging and he had to hurry saddling Wilson's sorrel. He dropped his ropes and spurs in the cab of the pickup and got his racing bat. Riding toward the barrier, Wilson warned him the little horse might spin in the barrier when the steer was let out. Sorrells asked Wilson how often the horse did that and Wilson smiled and told him the horse only did it when a cowboy let him do it. Sorrells backed the horse into a corner of the barrier box, saw Wilson was ready to haze, and nodded for his steer. The sorrel put Sorrells on the steer so quick and Sorrells was so out of practice that he got down on the steer late. Too much of his weight fell on the steer's head at once. Sorrells just had time to catch the left horn and get his arm around the right when the steer buried his head in the arena, planting Sorrells' head with it. The steer vaulted on his horns and landed on his back in the classic "houlihan." Sorrells' neck crunched and snapped in his eardrums, but when the steer came back to his feet Sorrells was still on his head, still holding him by the horns. He banged the steer down on his side and the flagman dropped his flag.

"Not many men get up from a 'houly' like that," the

announcer shouted. "But this is Bert Sorrells, an illustrious man from illustrious country where cowmen know their business."

Wilson rode up grinning and shook Sorrells' hand. Sorrells swung up behind him and rode double out of the arena. He got down at the gate. Bonnie pranced to him and kissed him in front of all the people. Sorrells was glad to see her. He pulled her to him and kissed her again. He lost his balance and fell against her, almost pulling her down. Bonnie held him up and led him along a path where the most people could see them together. Sorrells didn't care. He was giddy. If this was what Bonnie wanted, he would give it to her. He was walking along with her proud of him. After all, he had been *lonesome* out on the Outfit, and a man had to get *civilized* once in a while. He grinned through a mask of blood and dirt while he shook hands with some people Bonnie introduced him to.

"Say, Bonnie," he said, hearing his own thick tongue make words. He stopped her. "Must of been purty good time, huh?"

"Seven seconds is good anywhere and after a fall like that it's superhuman. My man's a hero," Bonnie said.

"Well, say Bonnie. Let's go find a drink of whiskey and talk this over while we cool off. Let's think about how we're going to spend this rodeo's first day money. What do you say, Bonnie?"

"I want to see what you did to yourself first." She led Sorrells to Roberts' car. He sat down on the front seat with his feet on the ground. He was so weak he couldn't hold the door open and an alarm was ringing in his head. Roberts handed him a pint of whiskey. Wilson and Wanda were standing nearby.

"Yeah, you sonsabitches," Wanda bellowed. "We're ropers and fighters and wild horse riders and purty good windmill men and I'm the woman from Keno gonna ride a bull to Reno next."

Most of the skin on the side of Sorrells' face from his cheekbone to his forehead came off when Bonnie cleaned the dirt off. He got up and slapped the dirt off his hat and walked with the rest of them to the bull chutes. He sat in the shade in a corner of an empty corral behind the chutes with the bottle. Bonnie sat on the top rail of the fence above Sorrells where she could watch the rodeo. Jack Roberts watched over Wanda as she raved back and forth behind the chutes. Wilson was on the chute fixing his bull rope on the bull Wanda was to ride.

The bull riding was imminent. The announcer told the people that the first rider would be Wanda, of Rabbit Hutch, Nevada, the best and only lady bull rider in the state, on a white Brahma bull, Foolish Man. Wanda scrambled up the chute like she was ready to eat Foolish Man and drink his blood and claim his carcass. The bull fixed a dark, evil, eye on her, and she kept right on climbing until she was standing on the platform beside the speaker. The speaker said, "Here she is, folks, Wanda of Rabbit Hutch," and handed her the microphone.

"Turn the sonofabitch out, I'll get him later, to the Rabbit Hutch he's bound to cater," Wanda brayed. "For all old bulls my pot is brewed. They come to Wanda to get . . . ." This was as far as she got. The announcer snatched the microphone from her and covered it with his hand. She turned away from him and vomited over the rail of the platform. The chute was swung open and Foolish Man left without her. Wanda tried to climb down the ladder. Her legs didn't work for her, and she turned loose of the ladder and bumped into the corral on her rear end. Dust rose up around her. She lay down her head and went to sleep.

Sorrells was happy when they drove back to town. He and Wilson had won second day money in the team tying and Sorrells had won first in the first go-round of the bulldogging. Roberts stopped at Bonnie's apartment to let them out so he could take Wanda to her hotel. Wanda had passed out in the back seat, her blouse open in front, still wearing the spurs and chaps.

Sorrells walked up the stairs to Bonnie's apartment with her. He took the key from her to open the door. He was thinking, she might make a big show for the slick dicks but old Bert was the one took her home. Old Bert was the one dug up the treasure and slick dicks lay dead all around. He banged the door open, took off his hat, bowed to her, waved it behind him, and then sailed it into the room. Bonnie walked in and turned on him.

"Oh, no," she said when he started through the door.

'Well, no, but can't I even come in?"

"Oh, no. Not here. I'll come to the Horseman and you can take me to a dance tonight."

"Well, yes, but I want to come in a minute."

"Oh, no. I know you. You go on back and get cleaned up and I'll meet you in the bar at the Horseman in a little while," She closed the door in his face. He was thinking of pounding on the door and squalling but she opened the door and pushed his hat at his open mouth.

Sorrells stopped twice to drink at the whiskey springs on the way back to his hotel. Once in his room he shed his clothes and took a shower long enough to get out all the arena dirt imbedded in him and to clear his head. He put on clean Levis and a fresh shirt and joined Wilson and Roberts in the restaurant for a steak.

They were sitting at the bar drinking and listening to a girl on the stage sing with a good Western band after supper when Bonnie came in. She would not sit with them. She wanted to stand behind them where she could show off her white miniskirt, her long, stockinged legs, her little feet on high white heels, and the nice, full halves of her bosoms, while she wound and quivered in a dance to the music. Sorrells thought she must be good stock after all to be able to look so good after two years in this town on the kind of life she led. She still wore the hat Sorrells had given her. Sorrells could only be tolerant. He was used to it. It was the only way he knew how to be with her at this stage of an evening during a celebration. He knew by the shine in her eye and the flare in her nostrils she wasn't going to listen or decide on anything, but was keeping in motion until the time, later, when she would stop, look at someone, and fall on him like an axe in love. She was picking and choosing. She knew she wasn't his to worry about, anyway, and she was going to try to make him wish she was.

"I'll have to ask your ladyfriend to take a seat during the show," a security guard told Sorrells when Bonnie had been dancing too long.

"Hell, ask her. Don't ask me, officer," Sorrells said. "It won't do any good."

"Then I'll have to ask her to leave. She's disturbing other folks watching the show."

"Leave? Leave? Go where? I'm gone, man," Bonnie breathed to herself.

The guard put his hand on her elbow to steer her out. She jerked away and kept dancing. "Hit him, Bert," she said in rhythm to her dance. "Hit him hard for Bonnie."

"Hit him, hell," Sorrells said. He got off the barstool and took her arm. "Let's go where we can *all* do some dancing."

The four of them drove to a place out of town called the Red Barn. They found a table. Sorrells asked Bonnie to dance. She refused and took Jack Roberts to dance. When she came back she excused herself and walked away.

"That's a lot of woman," Roberts said.

"You have original thoughts," Sorrells said.

"What?"

Wilson laughed.

"*I* know she's a lot of woman," Sorrells said. "You're impressed. I'm impressed. You are too, aren't you, Wilson?"

"Aw, Bert," Wilson said.

"Shit," Sorrells said. "If you are so impressed with her, Jack, why in the hell don't you go after her? Bring her back. Buy her drinks. Dance with her. Take her home to our room and put her to bed. I'll go out and stay with Wilson at the rodeo grounds."

"Maybe I will," Roberts said.

"You couldn't start her. You'd miss her out of the chute and buck off so quick you'd rack your brain trying to remember you'd ever been with her."

"I didn't mean it, Bert. She's your woman. I wouldn't touch her. You ought to know that."

"She ain't my woman. I know *that* for sure."

"If I were you I'd go after her and make her my woman again. That's probably what she wants."

"You couldn't be farther from the truth. She does exactly as she pleases and exactly at this minute she's trying to torment me."

"Trying?" Wilson said. "She don't look like the trying type. Looks to me like she's got you *all* pissed off, Bert."

"Well, she ain't. I've been shed of her for a long time. I'm going to the bar. The service is too slow for me here."

The bar was in a room apart from the dance hall and was full of cowpunchers and boys who wished they were cowboys and dressed in a way they thought would make people think they were. Sorrells saw Bonnie's hat on top of a jukebox in the bar.

The slick dick who had been playing with Bonnie in the arena walked up to Sorrells and put his hand on his shoulder.

"Buy you a drink, Bert?" he said. He wasn't wearing his hat now. He was showing off his pretty hair.

"I've got a drink," Sorrells said and kept his back turned to Slick Dick. The boy tried to shake Sorrells' shoulder heartily, but he didn't have enough heart in him to do it right. He succeeded only in acting familiar and found out Sorrells didn't like it. He took his hand off Sorrells' shoulder.

"You sure showed them fellers a thing or two about bulldogging today," Slick Dick said.

Sorrells drank half his whiskey and shuddered. He was alive, anyhow. He didn't think a man shuddered after he was drunk or dead. He looked at the reflection of Bonnie Sorrells' hat in the bar mirror.

"You win first, didn't you, Bert?"

Sorrells thought, when she comes for that hat she'll be leaving and, by God, she's going with me. He drank the rest of the whiskey and order another.

"On me," Slick Dick said when the bartender brought the whiskey.

"Fifty cents," the bartender said to him. Sorrells pushed the change over the bar to him.

"I wanted to buy that, Bert," Slick Dick said. Sorrells turned and looked at him. "Get out of here," he said.

"O.K. I'll see you later, Bert." Slick Dick said lightly. He tried to put his hand on Sorrells' shoulder, failed and went down to a place at the bar by Bonnie's hat.

"Well, did you buy him a drink?" Sorrells heard one of the other slick dicks ask him.

"No, he didn't like me."

"Why not? He seems like a nice enough guy."

"He's got yellow eyes, and I don't fool with a guy that's got yellow eyes." Slick Dick laughed.

"Well, Bonnie asked you to watch him."

"Nobody watches that man. He does the watching."

Sorrells knew he was getting drunk if he looked so bad people thought he couldn't hear them when they talked about him.

A dark-haired girl sat down next to Sorrells.

"Hello, Bert Sorrells," she said. "Remember me?"

His eyes wouldn't focus on the girl long enough to recognize her. He could see she was pretty, she was sweet. He felt she was a warm girl and 100 per cent for Sorrells. Any girl who asked a man if he remembered her did it to be nice to him. He saw his brown face with the pink streak where he had skinned it under his drinking hat in the mirror and he clearly saw Bonnie's hat's reflection.

"Don't you remember me from Jackson Hole?" she asked.

"What was I doing in Jackson Hole?"

"You were in a matched team roping. You and I had a lot of fun together."

"When?"

"A year ago."

"I don't remember."

"Remember you won the roping?"

"Yes. I remember that. I didn't miss a loop at ten steers."

"You remember Margie?"

"Sure. Pretty girl. Prettiest girl in Jackson."

"I'm Margie, Bert."

Sorrells couldn't focus on her. "You're still beautiful, Margie." He bought her a drink.

Jack Roberts and Wilson stopped behind Sorrells and told him they were leaving. Sorrells told them he wasn't leaving Bonnie. "I brought her here and I'll take her home," he said. "You go on."

"Dance with me, Bert?" Margie asked when Wilson and Roberts had gone.

"Oh hell, no. I'm sore as a boil. You go on and dance if you want to."

"You remember how much fun we had?"

"You bet, Margie. Ten steers, ten loops. Them other guys are still trying to catch their steers. Who could ever forget Margie?"

A man came up behind the girl. "Ready to go?" he demanded. He wasn't asking her. He was telling her. He didn't look at Sorrells.

"Yes," said the girl. "I'll see you again some time, Bert."

"Hell, don't go," Sorrells said. The girl slid off the stool and walked away. She looked back once and waved from a place down by Bonnie's hat.

After they had gone out Sorrells realized the girl was going away from him and he went to the door. He looked out into the night and saw the girl getting into a car. The man wasn't even opening the door for her. He was already behind the wheel in a hurry.

"Come back, woman," Sorrells squalled. She didn't pay him any attention. She got in the car and shut the door. The man drove the car away.

Sorrells went back toward his place at the bar. When he passed by the jukebox he could have reached out and touched Bonnie's hat. He and Bonnie had been together buying that hat with a happy promise of whole days and nights together again. But, by God, he wasn't going to touch that hat. It wasn't his. He sat at his place at the bar and didn't know when he passed out with his head on his arms.

"You can't sleep here anymore, pard," the bartender was saying. Sorrells was almost sober when he woke up. The hat was still there. He was sick of that hat. He was sick of himself.

"You can have another drink or you can sleep it off back in my room, but you can't sleep here," the bartender said.

"Thanks. I'll walk it off," Sorrells said. He met Bonnie coming in the door with a whole number of slick dicks.

"You forgot your hat," Sorrells said.

"I most certainly did not. That's *my* hat," Bonnie said.

"Well, there it is."

"I know where it is. Now where do you think *you're* going?"

"To my bed."

"Well, good-bye, I'll see ya again sometime," she said, smiling up at her slick dick.

"I'll see you never," Sorrells said and walked out.

Bert Sorrells hated walking worse than any chore a man had to do. His feet were too small for walking. His saddle didn't fit on sidewalks. He walked two hours to get back to the hotel. He was sober when he got to the room. He was sober, angry, and not hurting anywhere special but over his whole carcass. Jack Roberts wasn't in the room. Someone had left a note under the door. It read, "You with the face. If you are brave enough to bulldog, you are brave enough to have a drink with us. Come anytime. Room 317 just around the corner. Signed, Polly, Sue, and Olga."

Sorrells dropped the note and went to bed. Now if *that* wouldn't be something, he thought. Get into a deal like that and the first thing you know you wake up some morning too late to feed the horses and in love with another man's wife. The best track for you, Sorrells, is to catch your stock double quick tomorrow, get out of town, and go back to work.

Chapter 12

DAY OFF

When a cowboy goes out on a "circle," he rides out to see a country with a certain job in mind. He might be out to drive cattle from an area. He might be going to doctor for worms, to find an old bull he has been missing, or to see if the country is making feed. He always comes back to the place from which he started. He might get out and find a job that takes him far away from the place he started and he might be sorry he went so far when he heads back on a tired horse in the dark, but he always has to come back and finish the circle.

Dobie Porter's old heart was singing the song it knew when Porter had a few hours of leisure time to himself. The song was happy because it told Porter he had time to enjoy a few restful pleasures with the few faculties he owned, one of which was a strong heart.

Porter didn't like to go off to rodeos any more except for one performance to see if he could run on to someone he knew and to watch the livestock perform. He knew very few folks at the rodeos nowadays. At rodeos Dobie Porter walked around looking at the people and the stock from under the stiff brim of his big brown town hat.

110

Now he sat on his bunk finishing up a set of hobbles for old Buck. He twisted the wet leather in his hands to make it twine roughly and dry in grooves. When time to go to work came again and all the other cowboys were rodeoed out and hung over, Porter would have a new set of hobbles hanging on his saddle.

Porter had too much age on him to feel like running off and wearing himself out having fun. He might be slower and stiffer than his pards in a work, but he was always readier for work and a step ahead of everybody else in keeping up his outfit, because he looked to his gear and to himself when he had a little time.

He hung the hobbles on a nail over his bed and stumped into the bathroom. He ran water into the tub, not much, just enough so he could get some all over himself but not enough so anybody could say he was depriving some old cow of a drink. He sat and pulled off his boots. He peeled off his Levis greasy from dust, cattle blood and sweat, and shiny from wear. He unbuttoned his long johns and emerged from them as though from a worn out cocoon. He stood in his loose drawers and socks while he decided if this was such a good idea after all. He stood there for nobody in the world to see, for everybody was gone and the door was locked. He caught a glimpse of his own paper-white skin under the baked neck in the mirror, looked quickly away, dropped his drawers and socks, and stepped into the water which, for lack of volume, was quickly cooling in the bottom of the big tub. He scrubbed with hands like sandpaper, bringing long forgotten feeling to various numb regions of his body and when he had scrubbed every inch with a lather of soap only rough rope-burned hands can make, from his bald head to his leather butt to feet so tender they could hardly stand it, he rinsed off, rubbing again, and was through. He let the water and the black iron-looking rocks and sediment pour out while he dried, dressed in clean drawers and long johns, brand new Levis, fresh clean socks, and pulled on his boots.

In his room he noticed that the bottoms of the new Levis were scuffing on the floor under the heels of his boots, and he paused to roll cuffs in them. His old legs had shortened and bowed so much he couldn't buy Levis short enough for him. Old Bert complained he couldn't get Levis long enough for him. Bert, he knew, would never roll cuffs outside his Levis if he should get them too long. Bert said Porter and dudes was the only ones could get away with that. Cowboys had rolled wide cuffs outside when Porter was young. Dudes thought the cowboys still did it. Nowadays cowboys streamlined their cuffs by rolling them inside their pantslegs so they wouldn't catch dust, hay, and manure. Times changed, but Dobie Porter still rolled his cuffs outside because it was easier to do when a working man was in a hurry and didn't mind getting a little trash in his pants but did mind dilly-day-dallying over being streamlined. Porter didn't believe he ran the risk of being called a dude.

He put on a new work shirt. He had bought it the day he suspended his social security pension after he had taken this job. Each time he drew a check from the Outfit he was adding to his pension. He wished he had been paying social security all his life, but he hadn't paid any attention to social security until the time a horse fell on him and laid him up when he was fifty years old. The people at the hospital had not believed him when he told them he didn't own a social security number. He didn't have a wife or any kids either, so he had decided maybe he ought to start paying social security.

He put on his hat, smelling the rank, salt sweat of the inside of it as though it for the first time now that he had bathed, and slipped it down over his clean brow. He was going to have to take out that lining pretty soon. That was sweat, dirt, and fibrous mud in there, not a lining anymore. He would wait until next season. That lining kept much sun off his head in the summer and held much warmth on his head in the winter. Next summer he would take the lining out and carve holes out of the sides of the crown and have a cooler hat.

He went into the kitchen and found a loaf of bread. He sliced himself two big slabs of it and kept the butcher knife in his hand as he walked around the kitchen slicing roast beef, onion, and cheese, and slapping the slices onto a slab of bread. When he had all the innards he wanted, he pressed the other slab of bread down on them, dropped the sandwich into a sack, and carried it with him out of the bunkhouse.

He jerked open the stiff door of his truck and climbed to the seat. He pumped the gas pedal with the toe of his boot. He could barely reach the floorboard. He stepped on the starter and fired it up. Every part of the truck was clean inside and out except for a little horse manure in the back. A little green gold was all manure was to Porter. He twisted the truck around, shifted to low, and drove all the way down to the saddle house in low. He backed up to a loading bank and shut off his motor when the truck bumped the bank. Leaving the truck in gear, he pulled on the brake and climbed out. He got his bridle off the horn of his saddle on the rack outside the saddle house and walked around to the stall where old Buck raised his head to look at him. The horse was still chewing his morning hay.

"Hoh, Buck!" said Porter. "I got need of you, Buck. No hard work today, though Buck. We'll just make a little circle and see what we can see."

Porter bridled his horse and led him out of the stall, thinking work was work to Buck, even if it was just "making a little circle" to Porter. Well, Porter didn't want to do it alone. If Bert had not gone off to the rodeo, he would have just as soon Bert were there to go with him. But fellers Bert's age still would rather go to rodeos than stay home and listen to old lame cocks like Porter. He knew he was tiresome even to just look at, he realized it, but he knew Bert was interested in listening to him.

He laid his clean Navajo blankets on Buck's back and rested his saddle on them. He leaned down and saw his cinches hanging flat and curving beneath Buck's belly. He wrapped his latigo on his front cinch and pulled it snug. He pulled his flank cinch and buckled it and Buck never moved or swelled up. Right. Everything had to be just right for an old lame cock so he didn't have to walk around his horse to see his cinches weren't twisted. Buck was relaxed and not afraid Porter was going to cut him in two cinching him up. Porter picked up his spurs and led Buck around the truck and showed him the back end. Buck never paused but walked on in and stood still while Porter lifted the end gate into its holes and slots. Porter limped down off the bank, his big chest heaving, his thick arms barely swinging, his eye not deigning to look down to see where his next stiff step might fall.

He drove away from headquarters, not stopping to look to the right or to the left as he crossed the highway and headed up a mining road to McGregor Mountain. He knew he did not drive well. He could not see over the top of his steering wheel and could not coordinate his nearsighted going to his machine's goings on, so he often caught his machine and reined it back just as it touched an edge of the road and showed him the bottom of a canyon. No matter how abruptly he might wheel his machine, Old Buck never made a bobble or a slide in back. Porter had confidence in his driving as long as Old Buck never lost his balance. He would never have listened to any advice about his driving as long as Old Buck was riding well.

He thought, now let us see, it's been fourteen years since I've been here, Buck, but I bet I show you the exact same country I expect to find. There is just some countries a man never forgets. I've seen pine countries and brush countries I couldn't call after so long, but this Nevada high and sage and piñon range with rock and canyon wall, I can. He stepped on the gas and the dust lifted up behind him so anyone looking could watch his progress from fifty miles away.

He stopped the truck where he could look over the tops of piñon trees on the slope beneath him to a long draw that separated McGregor from another mountain equally high called Dupont. The paved highway ran down another draw, intersecting the wide draw, and at the intersection he could see the tops of a grove of cottonwoods and sun shining on the water of a spring there.

"We'll make a circle to Dove Springs, Buck," Porter said and unloaded the horse. He led the buckskin around and stood him off the downhill side of the road, took his stirrup with his foot, and stepped upon him. Buck moved off with the sound of Porter's spurs on each side of him and Porter sighed a deep new breath, almost young again for a moment.

He thought, if he had gone to the rodeo he would have gotten older and older every hour during the two days there, until by the time he came back to the Outfit he would have been sour on the good times everybody else was having and tired in every corner of his bones. He had felt that first great anticipatory rush of promised fun every cowboy felt when he first heard "rodeo," but he knew it would start getting old for him the first hour he spent afoot in that town. Nowadays he had to be horseback to feel a man at all. He liked women as well as any man, but just looking was no good and he liked to be looked at too. Nowadays nobody looked at him unless he was horseback.

There had been a time when he rode broncs to rodeos that could eat the horses cowboys were contesting in the arena. Porter, in those days, had squalled and spurred his broncs right up into the big middle of bunches of town boys who were always running together in packs on their way to the rodeos. He'd done it just to show ladies on the other side of the street what a real cowboy on a real bronc could do. The ladies had looked at him and liked what they saw too, when he was a young buck, wild and tough. But in those days Porter had needed to dam up all the whiskey in town for a while before he could get the nerve to talk to a lady.

Not having a family of his own, he expected he had never in his life been introduced properly to a proper single girl his own age. The cowboys was on this side and the girls raised in the country was on that side and the only ones could dance with them or talk to them was the fellers raised in that country. Cowboys was known to be wild and not respectable. A cowboy seldom got to know a native girl. A whole lot of cowboys Porter knew had married dude girls who had come out from back East ahunting cowboys. But if there weren't any dude girls around when the dancing started after the rodeo the cowboys took their whiskey off to the whorehouse. Porter had worked on many a ranch where the daughter had never once looked his way or had anything to say to him. He guessed that was all for the good. He would not have liked to own a ranch where six or a dozen young proud cocks was always crowing and showing off for his good looking daughter. Hell, they didn't even have to be good lookin'. Fifty years ago in the cow country *any* young female thing was precious to a cowpuncher, even if she was harelipped, gotch eyed, big eared and clubfooted, and there was more of them kind than any other. The ones the cowpunchers did get close to was them that looked unsound or was so hot tempered and wild they sounded unsound to the white mice from town who was supposed to court them. Them unsound looking and bad sounding ones had all turned out to be the best and most desirable to the cowpunchers because they had all made a hellava hand in the cookshack and some had been better cowboys than most of the cowpunchers working for their daddys.

Well, they had all admired Dobie Porter's prowess with rope and horse, but he'd never had a wife. One thing about it, his face might not be handsome at all, but nobody had ever accused him of being a white mouse and he had never gone abegging after any girl or woman. A lot of them fine girls married them native town boys who had carried them off to have a whole raft of little kids and left them alone in some shiny city, too. Porter wouldn't have done that to any *body*. He bet them gals wouldn't have minded some whiskey drinkin' horseback son of a bitch coming along and taking them back to some ranch somewhere after half a life in one of them cities beside one of them town fellers.

This old cowboy might be letting all the coffee and almost all the whiskey wash by him nowadays, but nobody could ever accuse him of having half a life, and nobody was ever going to have to put up with him, baby him, pamper him, or listen to him whine in his old age. Married life just might have done that to him.

Buck gained the head of the wide, long draw, and the air was so still in the sagebrush there that dust rose and hung around and followed him along. Porter leaned over and looked for tracks on the trail beneath him and saw the big track of a bovine he sensed was a steer. Some look or smell of the dust around the track made him think of a big old steer. Porter suspected the Outfit had plenty of old steers running that had been bought with the Outfit but never counted. Dobie Porter would be tickled to death to see one.

Porter let Buck singlefoot as though to a Sunday dance around a bend in the piñon at the edge of the draw toward Dove Springs. He was only out joyriding today, but he couldn't help feeling a thrill in the pump of his heart as the springs came in sight and he saw the color of cowhide in a solid bunch under the cottonwoods around the springs. Buck looked too and perked up to almost a real pace.

The cattle under the trees began separating as the horseman got closer. Porter was disappointed when he saw no big steer. He rode Buck into the breezy shade at the spring, dismounted, and untied his lunch sack. He was going to have himself, by God, a picnic. No cowpuncher he'd known had ever carried a lunch, nor had Porter ever carried one when working, but this was his own day off and he was going to eat good. He was glad, however, no one was around to see him untie the brown bag from his saddle strings. Someone might get the wrong idea and figure he was taking time off to eat and putting his belly greed ahead of his day's work. He knelt by the spring and top-heavily, stiffly bent to drink of the clear water. He stood up and let Buck drink.

The spring ran into a dirt tank, a reservoir. The cattle around the tank were undisturbed by the horseman. Calves dozed in the sun, their necks flat on the ground their clean noses outstretched and sometimes cringing from a buzzing fly. Cattle reclined on the bank of the tank, eyes half closed, chewing their cuds. One old bull who had filled up on water and had started away in the heat of the day had not gone far when he had discovered a pocket in his belly was still dry. He had turned and was ambling back in slow, dislocated joints of his heavy steps toward the spring to drink again and lie in the shade until the sun offered him a more opportune time for leaving. He stopped to grunt and grouch and paw the ground, causing dust to fly and spread over his back to protect it from flies.

Porter led Buck to a big cottonwood and sat down with his back to the trunk. He dropped Buck's reins and let him drag them and watched the horse nibble at green leaves and twigs a wind had downed. He knew Buck didn't need hobbles. Porter had seen that leather in his warbag and now it was a set of hobbles. He bet Bert could use them. Porter would hang the hobbles on his saddle and the first time Bert needed them he would give them to him, though he would say he was only loaning them to him.

He admitted he liked Bert. Bert didn't think he was too good to learn from an old man. Bert was double tough, but he was considerate of Porter and Porter had not known a feller he liked so much since he had been working on the Arizona Strip twenty years ago.

Porter had been like Bert Sorrells. He had done as he damned pleased and would work at any job as long as it was all downhill at ninety miles an hour, no brakes and no track to follow. Hell, Bert must be getting along close to forty but was still a young buck by cowpuncher standards because he had not been stove up much yet. At forty, though, it was time for Bert to pull up a little and stay sound into his old age.

The Lord knew, Porter couldn't tell anyone to pull up. That would be like telling a race driver to take a chauffeuring job for a ninety-year-old lady. Porter had not noticed when he pulled up. He had one day found himself on slower horses and shorter, quieter horses, and when he asked himself why, he found he could not get on a tall horse as easily anymore and he had hell getting on one if the son of a gun didn't stand still. He had lost his old brag that there wasn't a son of a gun he couldn't get on. He might not *stay* on but there wasn't a son of a bitch could put any fear into Dobie Porter *before* he got on him.

He lost all his grinners getting on that paint horse up on the Strip. The paint had the whole crew looking the other way when the boss called out to ask who wanted him for his string. Porter knew the horse, a going son of a bitch for a circle horse, but no good in the corral and hard as hell to get on. The horse just flat had come to find out that if them stinky, bowlegged sonsabitches couldn't get on him, he wouldn't have to go nowhere that day. The crew was making big circles, fifty to seventy miles, and only changing horses at noon. It made a man ashamed to ride a good horse on circles like that in that country, a good horse who looked at a cow and was good in a herd. So Porter had glommed onto old Paint, the piebald paint.

The piebald paint would stomp in a circle, turkey trotting, when Porter tried to take his rein in one hand the horn in the other to mount him. The horse would swing his hind end away until he was facing a feller and then he would try to come right on over the top of a man. Plenty of cowboys had semi-busted toenails on account of that trick. If a feller was stout enough to hold him and get that stirrup, old Piebald would threaten to go over backward as the man swung on. Any man will loosen up and look to fall free when a horse starts over but the piebald wouldn't fall but once every ten tries. He usually jarred back to his front feet and bucked a few jumps while a man was all loosened up. He would jump two or three jumps with his head up watching his rider. He wasn't a dedicated bucker though. He wasn't that honest. After a hard start he would break out running and if a feller didn't gather him up fast the horse would brush him off in a tree or on a fence or a gate post. He had a good mouth though and was easy to pull up once a man caught up to him. Once he was pulled up and lined out, the horse would go like a maniac all day. He mobiled like the ground was a track and he was an electric train with no heart to beat and no fuel to burn. He was a perfect circle horse. He never looked at a cow and never had a thought except "move on," so no cowpuncher could have any sympathy for him. Porter never had one ounce of pity for him after the first time he got on him and he threw his head up to go over backwards and hit Porter in the mouth with the top of his head. He had cleaned out three of Porter's grinners. Porter's jaws had been clenched and the crowns of most of his molars had gone too. One by one they had started aching and had to come out. That dirty piebald son of a bitch! He had given Porter two years of nothing but pain. Porter had always taken the outside circle on him and the horse had been the same after it was all over as he had been the day he started, maybe wanting more country was all.

The horse had been a smooth-riding old thing though. Porter wondered what had ever become of him. The piebald paint. A feller never saw horses like that anymore. All that toughness was being bred out of horses nowadays. Nobody ever accused the piebald paint of being a white mouse. Just a cold-blooded, cold-hearted, leather-brained, glass-eyed, rock-

mashin', man-killin', widow-makin' son of a bitch that made
the circles that brought in the beefsteak that won a world
war. Not one goddam thing noble about him either. No little
girl ever made a pet of him, that's right. But neither did any
ever make one out of General Patton. Porter had never given
the horse a name. He had not called him anything but
sonofabitch and the like nor ever looked at him long enough
to see if the flies were bothering him.

The piebald paint was gone now, like all the other
pissheads Dobie Porter had ridden. He wasn't sorry he had
ridden his last pisshead but he was glad he had never been
afraid to get on one from the first to the last. He had taken
them all on, all his hurt, broken, and badly-healed places
notwithstanding.

Porter finished his sandwich and was folding the sack to
put it in his pocket when he saw Buck raise his head to some
new presence. Porter followed Buck's gaze across the wide
draw and saw the big white head of a bovine rising out of a
deep arroyo. The head was very large. It came on out and the
body started out and deep low music began rising from
Porter's heart as his eyes began to make him realize the size
of the creature coming out of the ground before him. The
bovine came slowly, not from any sense of caution but from a
sense of lordly independence only old powerful eunuchs must
have had. Porter saw that the creature was the biggest steer
he had ever seen outside a feedlot. The steer had not seen
Porter, or if he had, he was not bothered by the man. He
prevailed upon the draw. He dwarfed the other cattle by the
spring as he approached it sleepily, his spring and summer fat
rolling under his hide. He was a native steer with one loose
gotch horn and one large white spot on his side. The spot was
round and sprayed on the outside, like the smoke sprays out
from an explosion. It made Porter think of the spot a man
sees when he closed his eyes after glancing at the sun. The
steer around the blaze of white was calm and strong, confident of his strength, and acted as impartial to his use of it as
the sun. He came into the shade by the spring and drank, his
muzzle bobbing on the smooth water.

As he drank and began to fill, he noticed more around
him. His eye fell on Porter under the tree. His ears stiffened

forward and his head rose to examine the man. Drops of clear water returned quietly to the pool from his muzzle. Buck lowered his head to a green leaf and the sunspot steer moved his head to notice him. He was not alarmed. He was still relaxed from drinking, but he was surprised to find this new dimension under his sun. Porter did not move. Sunspot resumed his drinking. When he was full he turned and walked away. In a few minutes he was gone from the draw.

Porter sighed deeply and quietly and raised himself to mount Buck and ride back to his truck.

Chapter 13

MONTEZUMA MOUNTAIN

Sometimes a cowboy will decide to just "rim around"; he goes "rimming." He rides the high ridges and rims high on the mountains and rides the rims of the mesas where he can watch lower country for cattle, or tracks, or anything he might see for his work or his enjoyment. He usually suspects before he starts rimming that the ride won't have much import on the work he is doing, but rimming is necessary because it gives him time to decide his strategy on cattle, puts miles on a horse that may need them, or shows him country he hasn't seen since last year or may never have seen before. He and the country represent themselves to each other.

The mountain was on the border of the ranch and no one seemed to care to whom it belonged. The three cowboys wanted to work it for the chance of catching maverick cattle no one could claim. They did not want to keep any such cattle for themselves. They were on company time. They would carry any mavericks home to headquarters. But they wanted to do anything they could to prove to the company whenever they could that they were worth more than the $250 a month they were paid.

The cowboys unloaded their horses from the stock truck three miles from Montezuma Mountain. They had been finding maverick cattle in high country. Porter had said no cattle could be running on Montezuma Mountain because there was no water there. But today they had taken a road east to see new country, and ten or twelve miles from known water and three miles below Montezuma Mountain they saw wild horse tracks and fresh sign. They parked their truck in a hollow at the bottom of a big canyon that cut all the way to the top of the mountain. They unloaded their horses and started up the canyon.

The feed was good all the way up. Tracks covered the floor of the canyon where the horses had been grazing. As the canyon narrowed, the tracks were confined to a trail. Horse trails lead to water. The men knew if they found the water they might find the wild bovine, too.

Bert Sorrells and his companions followed a narrow, rocky wash full of piñon brush that topped out of the canyon on a high pass. They stopped their horses and let them breathe on the pass.

The summit of the pass was a mustang highpoint, a place where the wild horses stopped to rest and watch the country. Mounds of stallion manure were growing there, mounds like monuments that marked the supremacy of certain stallions over this country. Trails split from this summit in many directions. The men rode up a trail that wound on the side of another deep canyon. This trail was steep and rocky. They stopped and let their horses catch their breaths again.

"Bert, Bert, look!" Wilson said. "There they are!" Wilson was standing in his stirrups and pointing to a talus strewn crest on the mountain. Bert Sorrells looked and saw nothing. "A gray. Two grays. A dark blue and another. One, two, three, four head," Wilson said. To see the wild horses was a pleasure to Wilson.

Sorrells saw a dark shape move on the skyline. Another shape moved and the sun reflected off a light coat. The horses were so far away he could not have been sure they were horses if the Indian had not pointed them out to him at the moment they happened to be moving.

"Are you sure they're shitters?" Stacy asked.

"They ain't sheep," Sorrells said.

Wilson looked at Stacy. "Horses," he said. "Mushtangs."

"Those are the first wild horses I ever saw in my life,"
Sorrells said.

"Aw, come on," Stacy said. "You're foolin'."

"I've never seen a wild horse before."

"I don't believe it," Stacy said. "I thought you said you'd
cowboyed all your life."

"I have."

"Where?"

"Arizona mostly. Mexico."

"Bound to be wild horses in Mexico."

"I never saw any."

"None in Arizona?"

"*I* never saw any."

"I don't believe you."

Sorrells shut up and rode on. Wilson followed him.

"We have wild horses all over Nevada," Stacy said from
behind them. "It's hard to believe there are none in Arizona." Sorrells started to say that he hadn't said there weren't
any, just that he never had seen them, but he wanted much
more to be quiet and ride on and get a better look at the
horses.

The trail wound toward another saddle. The higher the
horsemen climbed, the harder the wind blew, and the colder
the day got. The sun was darkened by clouds, and Bert
Sorrells thought he probably should have brought his slicker,
but neither he nor his partners would have thought of turning
back to the truck for slickers when they had such good
prospects of getting closer to the wild horses, finding a water,
or capturing the wild bovine. They had not yet seen the track
of a cow.

On the high saddle they had a good look at the wild
bunch. The horses were watching the men and grazing slowly
around the crest. They would soon be out of sight. Sorrells
couldn't keep his eyes off them.

"They haven't been chased. If they had, they would be
gone by now," Wilson said. Sorrells watched them. Their tails
were long. Their manes were long. Their coats were bright
and they were fat. Their colors ranged from near white to
dark blue.

"They look like good horses from here," Sorrells said.

"They could be," Wilson smiled. "Most of the horses in this country have good looks. But they might be locoed. Lots of the loco weed in the flats. You can never tell about them until you catch one."

"They probably are runty little broomies," Stacy said.

"Maybe," Wilson said, smiling. "They might not be, though."

"They look good from here," Sorrells said.

"They always do," Wilson said. Just then three jet fighters whistled over the saddle very low and then climbed, blasting in single file almost straight up.

"Good-bye fellers, a few minutes and you'll be back in the club where you belong, telling your partners how close to the wasteland you flew," Sorrells laughed.

"Showoff sonsabitches," Stacy said. Sorrells looked to the wild bunch. Two of the band were already out of sight. The band was not in a hurry even though the jets had passed close to it against the mountain. It was accustomed to jet planes.

Trails led off the mountain. Sorrells rode down one of them, backtracking the horses. His partners stayed high, doubling back toward the direction of the truck. The trail off the mountain had been dug deeply by the horses. The green of the thick piñons was dark with the dampness of the day. Sorrells saw cow tracks and one shod horse track going toward country off the Outfit. He stopped Roller on a high point. He saw a windmill miles away down on the flats on a neighbor's range. The mill probably belonged to Duane Jones, the man Cunningham had fired. Duane partnered with a man called Maynard. Sorrells didn't think it likely that the horses were watering that far away at improvements. Cattle running on the mountain wouldn't be watering there either. Sorrells couldn't see cattle on the flats. He rode back and caught up to his partners at another saddle, another highpoint of the mustangs.

"I saw cow tracks, and one shod track headed off the mountain," Sorrells said softly to Wilson. "What would you think about that?" Stacy was off to one side whistling.

Wilson nodded. "I would say there shouldn't be any cow tracks. If anyone should ask me, which they probably won't, I would say there are no cattle running on this mountain."

"That's what Porter said, only those tracks came from the Outfit's side of the mountain, so the cattle that made them didn't stray from Duane Jones's mill. Somebody might have driven them toward that mill from the Outfit."

Wilson was looking off the mountain. Far below the horsemen, on the top of another mountain, at the end of a wide road that scarred the mountain, squatted a government radar station. Stacy rode over close to Sorrells and Wilson.

Wilson nodded toward the station. "Look," he said. "They haven't got windows. I bet they've never seen the wild horses on this mountain."

"By the tracks it looks to me like a lot more than four head of wild horses are running up here," Sorrells said. "There must be a lot of water near this mountain."

"Maybe," Wilson said. "For the mushtangs."

"I doubt it," Stacy said. "I bet there are only four or five head at the most."

Sorrells rode on and Wilson and Stacy followed him, circling back toward the steep canyon they had originally taken when they left their truck. When they came in sight of the canyon again, they were much higher than they had been when they left it. Directly across the canyon from them and only about a quarter of a mile away, a blue horse trotted up the side of the canyon.

"There's another one," Wilson said. "He's probably a young stud been whipped off the bunch." They stopped their horses and watched the wild horse. The gentle saddle horses under them watched indifferently. The climb had been hard. They were black with sweat now that they were on a sheltered part of the mountain. When the wild stud reached the summit he ducked his head under a piñon, turned behind it, and was gone. Wilson laughed. "He needs a friend," he said. "He won't find one on this mountain. He needs to get gone."

The horsemen went down into the deep canyon. They rode along its narrow floor. The walls of the canyon rose from their stirrups like the walls of a corridor. Many wild horses had used the trail and had got along well in this canyon. Sorrells wondered how long the mustangs had run here. Not as long as Wilson's people had. The trail was deep in sandstone. The men rode around a sharp corner into an open, sandy wash.

"Look, again!" Wilson said.

A gray mare with a black colt was topping out of the canyon. A black stud stood above her, looking back at the horsemen. The wild horses were less than fifty yards away.

"Now, what do you think of that!" Sorrells said, exultant.

"Lots of horses here," Wilson said.

"More than I thought," Stacy said.

"We should have found the water. We've come full circle now," Sorrells said.

"We have found the water," Wilson said.

"Where?" Stacy asked. "I didn't a see a spring."

"We circled it. It's here," Wilson said. "We know it now."

"Where?" Stacy demanded. "Where are the cattle then? How come we haven't seen the cattle if there is water here?"

"No cattle running here," Wilson said.

"Well, I guess not," Stacy said. "Wild horses won't run with cattle most of the time. All we've done is waste the day."

"Why is that, Stace?" Sorrells asked.

"We've been riding together as though riding the same horse all day, and we haven't see a cow."

"It's a pleasure to do it for a change," Sorrells said.

"We found the feed and the water," Wilson said. "The Outfit has a lot of good country over here."

"We know we won't have to ride over here anymore," Sorrells said. "Up to now we've been finding mavericks where nobody rode before."

"Nevertheless, a guy could get fired. We didn't catch one cow today."

"We saw the Montezuma Mountain for the Outfit, didn't we?" Sorrells said.

"We found water where Porter said there wasn't any," Wilson said smiling.

Chapter 14

RUN, MAVERICK, RUN

A querencia is an individual animal's own abode. It is a flesh and blood creature's mating, birthing, feeding, playing, sleeping ground. It is the place where he finds subsistence best for himself. The brave bull will often make a querencia of a certain area in the bullring and the matador feels he will do a better job of killing him if he can draw him out of his querencia. An Indian is united with his querencia no matter how far away from it he finds himself and no matter who thinks he owns it. The Indian yearns to be in his own home ground in this life and the next. A cowboy's querencia is anywhere he finds the seldom and meager society of other cowboys, open country and good horses for traveling it, feed and water for cattle, and a job to do with cattle.

The five cowboys made their horses climb the high mountain at sunup. When they reached the first crest, Porter and Wilson Burns surprised a buck mule deer, a doe, and two fawns. The buck and the doe ran away to a saddle below the men. The fawns circled high and almost ran head on into Bert Sorrells as he came riding around the mountain. The fawns almost fell when they turned away in fright. They ran to the saddle after the buck and the doe.

The cowboys grouped at the top of this first crest under Silver Peak Mountain and looked down at a draw below them. Dobie Porter gave each cowboy his assignment, and they spread out and rode off the crest.

Sorrells was riding Big Red. He was not a good horse to make the big circle on, but he was surefooted and powerful in rough country.

Sorrells rode to the saddle where the deer had gone. He wanted to ride on Silver Peak Mountain, cutting for sign and staying above any cattle running in the deep canyons. Piñon was thick on the side of the mountain. Sorrells was not able to see very far. If he rode onto any cattle in this brush, he was bound to surprise them and make them run.

He came to a fresh cow track. He followed the track into a canyon where it joined a trail and more tracks. The canyon narrowed. Its walls were so steep that a man on a horse would have a hard time riding up the sides. A cow could escape that way. The trail led into a thicket of willow where a spring seeped. Cattle were watering in holes made by their own tracks. The trail passed through the thicket. Sorrells knew that no one on the ranch knew about this spring.

Big Red poked his head into the thicket, Sorrells ducked his hat into it, and the brush closed behind them. The man could only follow the tracks by watching under his horse. He saw a new, heavier, larger track.

Sorrells saw the roan hips then. They stood motionless, close to one side of the trail. The willow thicket obscured the animal from flank to muzzle. The hips belonged to a bull. He didn't have enough room in the thicket or had not had the time to hide his whole carcass. He had frozen as the man approached him, hoping the man would not notice him.

Sorrells stopped his horse and looked at the roan hips. He could not tell if the animal was branded. The bull was young and was the owner of the larger track. The cowboy looked around him, moving only his eyes now, turning his head as little as possible and searching the brush. He didn't want any cattle in the thicket to move higher in the canyon. He wanted to get above them to move them out to the draw where his partners could help him stop them and hold them if they ran. He was sure when they moved they would run.

Standing up the canyon from him he saw part of the white face and the brown-ringed eye of a cow brute looking directly at him from the thicket. She was standing so still her face reminded Sorrells of faces he had tried to locate in gnarled trees of picture puzzles in books he had studied as a child. He backed his horse down the trail out of sight of the ring-eyed bovine. He rode on the steep side of the canyon to get around the cattle. He stopped his horse and listened. He heard the cattle moving and he saw the ring-eye join a horned cow and a big, fat, roan bull calf. The calf was unbranded and slick eared. The cow was branded. The ring-eye was a maverick three-year-old heifer. They stopped to look at Sorrells and he spurred Big Red through the thicket and gained the canyon floor above them. Cattle and horseman stopped again. The calf hid his head in the brush where he stood by his mother's side.

Sorrells knew he would never get the cattle to leave the thicket unless he gave them a scare. They were in their own place, their *querencia*, their haunt. He charged them and screamed. The cattle threw up their heads, threw up their tails, and ran away. Sorrells tried to run with them. The thicket beat at his face, and thicket was all he could see. Broken willow brush stacked around his saddle horn in his lap.

The cow had been run before and she wanted to have a good lead when she got to the open draw. She had to stay in the floor of the canyon so her calf could keep up with her. Sorrells saw the heifer climbing out of the canyon. He hoped the roan bull had been flushed down the canyon with the cow and the calf. The heifer gained the rim of the canyon and was gone. Sorrells had to go to the place she had topped out and find her tracks. The tracks were deep and easy to follow and at regular intervals the heifer had released the bright green, hot, runny, aroused bowel waste that is the mark of a disturbed bovine. Sorrells could follow the tracks easily at a run. He began to pick up the dust the heifer left behind. She was running like a coyote. She ducked close under the piñon and kept rimming uphill.

Sorrells was very close to the heifer when he saw her again. She had been running cunningly, gradually changing her direction and watching the steep footing, and she did not see the horse and man until they coasted to the uphill side of her. When she did see them, she turned and fled straight downhill toward the draw. She ran looking back at Sorrells, and because she was so uncautiously, fearfully fleeing, with all downhill momentum, she outran herself, lost the mountain beneath her, and houlihaned down the hill like a cartwheel. Sorrells took down his rope and built a loop. When the heifer regained her footing at the bottom, he caught up to her, roped her around the horns, fairgrounded her, and tied her down.

He remounted and picked up the tracks of the cow and calf where they came out of the canyon. He let Big Red out in a dead run and built another loop. Sorrells saw none of his partners in the draw. They probably all had similar business. Down the draw he caught sight of the cow. She was not looking back. She was going on steadily and saving her wind. Big Red was fast. Sorrells passed the cow and swung his loop to catch the calf. The calf dodged and bawled through the piñon and just as Sorrells had a throw, the loop caught the pliant top of a short piñon. Sorrells could not take the time to stop and free his rope. The calf would gain too much on him. Sorrells shouted, cussing, and drove his spurs into Big Red. The whole top of the tree came off and Big Red didn't break stride. Sorrells caught the calf and tied him down. The mother cow came on, braked, reached high with her front feet as she passed, and stampeded by Sorrells.

Sorrells stopped awhile so that he and Big Red could catch their wind. He did not see or hear any of his partners. He looked down at the roan calf. The cow had known he was too big to worry about and had looked to her own freedom. She had probably long wished to be rid of him, the big, overgrown, life-sucking baby.

"I bet that roan in that willer thicket is your daddy," Sorrells said to the calf. The calf lay flat, his head outstretched along the ground, his eyes rolled back, his muzzle covered with dirt it had plowed in the draw. "I bet I catch him." Sorrells mounted and rode back up the canyon.

He found the bull's tracks again and saw that he had stopped when the cattle and the horseman had run past. Sorrells tracked him up the canyon. He saw the bull near the end of the canyon.

The roan was a fine a bull as Bert Sorrells had ever seen. No mark of man was on him. He was big, long, and rangy. Sorrells guessed he was a four-year-old. His horns were shiny and perfectly symmetrical.

Sorrells rolled out a loop while he let Big Red blow. The Bull moved unhurriedly up the canyon. Sorrells was satisfied the bull could not escape by climbing the canyon walls. Not even a goat could get out that way. He hoped the canyon would end in a box with no trail out. The bull stopped in a thicket once, hoping Sorrells would ride by him again. When he saw the man was almost on him, he moved on.

At the end of the canyon the bull began climbing a good trail out. He was in the open now and wasn't going to stop until he was out of the canyon with a downhill run to cover. Sorrells charged him, swinging his loop so Big Red would know he was for catching the bull, not chasing him. The roan had watered and was heavy in the belly, but even so, he almost beat Big Red out of the canyon. Just as he topped the grade, he lunged at the last abrupt step and Sorrells caught him when his horns tossed high. Sorrells turned Big Red back down the hill and drove off. The roan came over backwards and slid down the hill. He caught on a tree. Sorrells rode back up to be above him when he got up. The fine bull was lying on his side, his head jammed into the base of the tree. One horn had dug a long furrow in the ground and was hooked under a root. The neck was bowed. The eyes rolled foolishly.

"Now, look at you!" Sorrells scolded the bull. "Why didn't you run when you saw me coming this time? You're so used to getting away you weren't in any hurry, were you? Now you got yourself captured and what the hell am I going to do with you?"

As the man cooled off, he began to be sorry he had caught the bull. By the time the bull was out of the canyon he would be mad and on the fight. He would be driven all afternoon and would try to get away and some cowboy would have to rope him and strangle him. Strangulation would set in if he didn't sull up and die anyway. If the men did get him to the corral at headquarters, the bull would be in jail for a week or two before he could be shipped. He was so wild he wouldn't eat in jail, and every time he saw someone so much as walk out of the bunkhouse he would run into the fence and knock himself down. The company was not keeping four-year-old mavericks. This bull took up the room all those high toned, high priced, front office cattle would need. This bull wouldn't bring what he was worth for baloney because he would lose all his flesh between this canyon and the place the butchers were waiting to lower the hammer on him. "What good are you? Answer me that," Sorrells accused the bull. "Not only are you unmerchantable but you don't have sense enough to run like a self-respecting mustang should."

Looking at the bull, Sorrells knew that if it was up to him, he would much rather have the roan bull than one of those ring-nosed play pretties the front office wanted to replace him with, and this bull had not cost the front office one dime. "Get up, goddammit!" Sorrells said.

He turned Big Red uphill and pulled the bull away from the tree. He gave the bull slack and let him roll. He got up and Sorrells let him run off the hill to the floor of the canyon. Sorrells stopped him there. He circled the bull once, wrapping the rope around the hindquarters just above the hocks. As he passed in front of the bull again he dropped the wrap below the knees and rode off behind the bull pulling the rope under the front feet so it wrapped around the hind legs above the hocks. The bull went down again and his head was pulled back to the rope that was caught and wound on his hind legs. Sorrells dismounted and built a fire and heated his running iron.

"Now, by God, bull," Sorrells said. "The company didn't buy you so you ain't on its books. You don't belong to me, so I can't put my brand on you. But I'm going to fix you so you'll have enough respect for a man to get the hell out when you see one." He branded RUN on the bull's left side where the company brand should go. He did not earmark the bull. He tied his hind legs together with his piggin' string. He put his rope on the hind legs and dragged the bull to stretch him out. He rode Big Red close to the bull and yelled and whipped him with a double of the rope. The bull would not get up. Sorrells dragged the hind legs up under the bull's belly and spun him on his side. The bull lay supine. Sorrells sighed and got off Big Red. He took his rope off the hind feet. He loosened the piggin' string on the bull's hind feet. He could not ride away and leave the bull on the ground. He wanted to see him standing upright before he left him. The loosened piggin' string on the hind legs would hamper the bull enough so Sorrells could get back to Big Red when the bull got up. Tied loosely, the piggin' string would fall off after the bull stood up. The bull lay there peacefully. Sorrells kicked him in the hams and started toward his horse. The bull raised his head, looked at the man, and laid it back down again. To Sorrells this was strange bull behavior. This bull had not even bellered since the beginning of the storm that had descended on him. "Maybe you're hurt. Are you hurt, bull?" Sorrells asked. He stepped up to the bull's head and stomped him on the nose. The bull came instantly to his feet. Sorrells ran. The bull came on, running smoothly after Sorrells with both hind feet held together by the loose piggin' string as though he had been running in that manner all his life. He came on faster and much smoother when the piggin' string fell off. Sorrells downed his head and really ran. He ran away from Big Red so the bull wouldn't be attracted to the larger target. Sorrells didn't want to have to walk home. The bull was snuffing at Sorrells' buttocks. Sorrells threw his hat behind him in the bull's face and swung around a piñon. The bull hooked and dodged at the hat and then at the tree and kept on going to his trail out of the canyon.

Sorrells picked up the piggin' string and hat and caught Big Red's reins. After a while he mounted. He was going down the canyon when he began to laugh. He thought about the next cowpuncher who saw that roan mountain's great, unmarked ears. The cowpuncher, like Sorrells, would feel exactly like a man who had won a lottery. After the run old Roany gave him, the cowpuncher would discover the RUN brand and no place to put the company brand. Catching the bull was going to be difficult but turning him loose was going to be more interesting for the next cowpuncher. He would probably get hooked right in the ass if he wasn't awful rapid. Sorrells felt it was a shame the next man who tied onto Roany couldn't be a front office feller, but that would be too much to hope for. No, it would be somebody more than half a cowpuncher who would probably wonder why some cowpuncher had gone to so much trouble to give him a lot of trouble. Then he would have to turn Roany loose, too.

"By God," Sorrells said out loud when he stopped laughing. "This outfit has got one good bull even if he don't carry the company brand."

Chapter 15

I, PORTER

A cowboy wants to see tallow on his charges. He believes that no matter what color, breed, age, or class a cow is, if she doesn't have tallow, she is ugly. The old cowboy saying is, "Fat is the prettiest color." Some cattle make pones of fat, round bulges of fat, on their sides and hips between hide and flesh. Other cattle make it evenly, in fine thick layers and intruding like veins of marble through the flesh. The companies prefer some breeds of cattle because of the way they manufacture tallow. A cowboy enjoys seeing tallow on any bovine under his care. Seeing it on a steak, rolling under a hide, or adorning a saddle to preserve it is a cowboy's pleasure.

"**H**ow's 'I' Porter doing these days?" the barber in Keno asked Bert Sorrells one day when Sorrells rose to take his turn in the barber's chair.

"'I' Porter?" Sorrells asked.

"You're one of the riders out at the Outfit, ain't you?" the barber asked.

"Yes."

"Don't you know 'I' Porter? Ain't he out there running the Outfit?"

136

"You mean D. B. Porter? Yes. He's at the ranch. He didn't come to town today."

"We all call him 'I' Porter because he brags about himself so much. Nobody in this town knows his full name, but everybody knows who you're talking about when you mention 'I' Porter."

Sorrells looked at the barber, at his pale face and white, skinny hands. The barber had to make talk about somebody. He had probably never done anything else in his life but cut hair, gossip, and complain how his feet hurt him. He'd never imagine the country and the accomplishments Dobie Porter had seen if he cut another ten thousand heads of hair before his barber's heart failed him. One thing was sure, this barber was not half the man the seventy-year-old Porter was, even though he charged more than a fourth of that old cowboy's daily wage for every haircut he performed. Sorrells did not say any of this because he wanted to have an evening in Keno without getting himself scalped before he started.

"There isn't anyone around here like Dobie Porter," Sorrells said.

"Are you trying to tell me, buddy? I've known that crusty old man many years. I've heard his lies repeated so many times I know them all by heart," the barber said. Other customers and the other barber listened and smiled and made similar remarks about Porter, and Sorrells' barber began winking at them as though conspiring with them as he got wittier and smarter on the subject.

When the barber was nearly finished with his hair, Sorrells figured he was safe and said, "Well, Porter might brag a lot, but his stories are good and there's always some truth in them. He's been a cowpuncher nearly sixty years, and you can't do anything that long without being good enough at it to brag about it."

"Anybody who would buckaroo sixty years is probably so dumb he can't do anything else," the barber said, winking at the customers and whipping the cloth off Sorrells' lap and brushing his neck and shoulders with great verve, something *he'd* learned with real experience. Sorrells got up and put on his hat.

"How much do I owe you?" he asked.

"Two dollars and twenty-five cents, sir," the barber said. Sorrells took the money out of his pocket and paid.

"Thank you, sir," the barber said, grinning. "And give my best to old 'I' Porter."

"Oh, he'll be in to get a haircut one of these days, bald as he is. He does that often, doesn't he?"

"He sure does."

"You make money off Porter, that's no mistake," Sorrells said, smiling. "But then, you earn it, I guess, with all the lies you've got to listen to. Porter is too dumb to know he's imposing on you."

"No imposition, I'm sure. Next," the barber said and tried to ignore Sorrells.

"Two twenty-five in dollars ain't enough to pay a man like you to listen to a man like Porter. You time is too valuable."

"Next, next," the barber said.

Sorrells started for the door.

"Say hello to Porter for me," the barber said, not looking at Sorrells.

"I will. He'll be glad to hear from an old friend like you," Sorrells said and went to the hotel for whiskey.

He got back to the ranch in time for a few hours sleep that night. He carried with him a large paper sack full of chocolate bars for Porter. When he opened the bunkhouse door, the odor of a dead hog hit him in the face and gagged him. The odor was boiled cat mixed with dead hog. The odor was screw worm juice of cow mixed with boiled cat and dead hog bloated in the sun. This did not mix well with the Chinese food, beer, and whiskey Sorrells had taken on in Keno, and he ran to the bathroom and puked up the Egg Foo Yuke or whatever the hell it had been. When he had recovered, he went into the bunkhouse kitchen. He saw that the burner of the gas stove was on. He turned on the light in the kitchen. A gallon can of something was cooking, and from this was coming forth the odor. He lifted the tin plate that covered the can and new dimensions, richer dimensions, assaulted him deep in the sensibilities. The atmosphere in the room turned green and greasy. Porter was cooking his tallow.

A month ago the crew had butchered a big steer, and Sorrells remembered Porter had saved the tallow. The time to cook it had been the day of the butchering or at the most, two days later. Sorrells thought Porter had thrown out the tallow when he had not cooked it right away. Sorrells thought of throwing the tallow out the window but realized this was no longer the remedy. The sickness would have run its course or a worse sickness, the sickness of Porter's displeasure, would take over. Sorrells looked into the big room of the bunkhouse. Every bunk was empty and the bedrolls were gone. He went into the room he shared with Porter and laid the sack of candy on a bench at the foot of Porter's bed.

"You back?" Porter asked.

"Yeah," Sorrells said. "Your candy is on the bench."

"Hee, hee, hum, hummm," Porter sang with a yawn. "Everybody back from town?"

"Hell, I don't know. There's not a soul in the bunkhouse. It looks like you've run them all out."

"I ain't done nothing to them. What did I do?"

"Your goddam tallow would gag a buzzard. You aren't going to use that stuff, are you?"

"Why not? It's good taller."

"What are you going to do with it?"

"Going to grease my saddle."

"My God, you'll stink up your saddle and your clothes and all the country you ride through."

"Hee, hee, hum, hyum, hummm," Porter yawned. "Why?"

"It stinks that bad. *Man*, it stinks."

"I cain't smell it."

"You can't? It's got the whole bunkhouse stunk out. It made me puke up my two-dollar Chinese dinner."

"You're probably smelling that old steer skull the dogs dragged up outside the kitchen window."

"No, it ain't no skull. That particular skull has been out there two whole months. There ain't no meat on it anyway. It's your tallow. Now our bunkhouse will probably smell like a gutwagon for a year."

"Well, if it's the tallow, it'll cook out and quit smelling by morning," Porter said. "Hee, hee, hum, hum, hummm."

Sorrells shut up and in few seconds Porter was snoring.

Sorrells got into his bedroll, stuck his nose down against his flannel sheet, covered his head with his pillow and went to sleep.

Later, a wheezing, choking, gobbling sound awakened Sorrells. He uncovered his head and held his breath, trying to identify the sound. It was coming from near the foot of Porter's bed. Some poor thing was getting the very juices squeezed out of it. Then Sorrells heard a paper sack rustle and heard a candy wrapper being stripped impatiently from a chocolate bar and saw the squat figure of Porter in his long johns standing at the foot of his bed like a spectre. The sound was three pounds of nutty chocolate bar being gummed to death. Porter could not possibly have that much chocolate in his mouth and have room for his teeth at the same time. The nuts were the bad part. They were slick with chocolate, and Porter's salivating jaws were wallering them around, tumbling them, and he was trying to breathe through his mouth at the same time. He devoured and gasped and shifted the heavy bulk of wadded chocolate bar around until he found an air hole. He then sucked air gratefully, choked, chomped frantically, and swallowed whole what sounded like at least a pound of chocolate bar, gulped another huge drought of air and quickly replenished the vacancy with a new pound of chocolate. He then walked around his bed while he rolled his head to get a better prize with his gums on the nuts. He got back in bed. Sorrells thought he was going to strangle for the next five minutes it took him to get the chocolate down while lying on his back. He finally subsided. He had been gobbling, Sorrells though, exactly like an old ogre on a human head.

"Ho, ho, hee, hee, hummm," Porter said and before *one minute* was up he was snoring again. It made Sorrells so mad and uncomfortable thinking of those pounds of chocolate disintegrating in that old man's sour stomach while he snored on in peace that Sorrells couldn't go back to sleep.

Porter was always the first one up in the bunkhouse in the morning. When he got up he turned the light on, coughed and hacked his way into the bathroom and back, dressed in ten seconds time, put his teeth in his head, and coughed and hacked his way to the big room of the bunkhouse. He turned the lights on in there and overturned a chair or two to wake the men up. He never looked at a clock, and more than once he did all this at three A.M. instead of four thirty which was the usual hour of the crew's rising.

Sorrells was the last man to the breakfast table on the morning after the tallow and the chocolate. All the doors were open, and a cold wind blowing through the room was not enough to chase away the odor of the tallow. Porter was sitting at his place at the head of the table with his cup of hot water and canned milk. He always drank hot water and canned milk in the morning because he couldn't drink coffee on what was left of his bad stomach. Stacy was dishing up eggs and spuds and flapjack belly pads and toast and jam and coffee with both hands and grunting unconsciously as though he had a three-hundred-pound load on his back. The rest of the crew was sipping coffee and not saying a thing.

Porter was holding forth. He was sitting straight in his chair with both arms on the table telling a story. When Sorrells sat down, Porter finished it and attacked Sorrells with his nearsighted regard.

"Have a good time in town last night?" he asked.

"Who, me? Yes," Sorrells said and drank a big glass of cold, powdered milk solution without stopping. He immediately poured himself another glassful and drank it.

"Thirsty?" Porter asked Sorrells as he poured still another glassful. Sorrells drank it instead of answering.

"Didn't you get enough liquid in town?" asked Porter. "Didn't you get anything to drink since you left the ranch?"

Sorrells sighed.

"Like that old milk, don't ya?" Porter asked.

"I'd like anything wet and cold this morning after a night like last night," Sorrells said.

"I never did like milk," Porter said. "A man has to milk a cow to drink milk and I always figured the cow made milk for her calf. Maybe that's why my folks leppied all us kids back in Texas. The only time a kid got milk was when he was a babe in arms.

"One time when I was working for Morrow over on the Arizona Strip, his wife come to the roundup where I was running the branding crew. She had a little baby and she had forgotten his milk. He was settin' up a squall, so I done thisaway, I caught a range cow out of the holdup and the fellers got about a quarter of a tea cup from her, and Missus Morrow, Imo was her name, sopped it with a corner of her handkerchief and gave it to her baby thataway. It took about five of them old cows to fill that baby up. Here's the idee, the year was so dry them old cows wasn't giving a teacup full of milk." This story finished to his satisfaction he got up and said, "Now Stacy, don't founder," He then jammed on his hat and stumped out banging the door behind him.

When Sorrells and the rest of the crew got to the saddle house, Porter had already smeared the tallow on his saddle. The tallow lay in thick streaks on his slick latigos. It darkened the seat, skirts, and swells of the saddle and stunk only a little less in the open air than it had in the bunkhouse.

Porter went to the corral and caught old Buck. When Buck smelled the saddle he snorted, showed the whites of his eyes, and ran backwards, dragging Porter by the bridle reins.

"Buck!" Porter scolded. "What's the matter with you?"

"Buck, stop that!" Sorrells said. "Porter has a surprise for you, Buck. Don't you know nothing? Damn you, Buck!"

"Come up, Buck!" Porter said and tried to lead the horse up to the hitch rail. But Buck wouldn't let Porter saddle him. Porter had to turn him out and catch another horse that would stand for the stench. When Porter had gone the full circle of his string of horses and the saddle had been aired a full week, Buck finally condescended to be saddled with the tallowed saddle. He threatened to buck Porter off three times that day. Porter still would not admit the tallow had caused anyone any discomfort. When Buck tried to pitch on the way in to the corral that evening, Sorrells said, "It's the taller, Dobie. I don't blame old Buck. I can still smell it and if I can old Buck sure can."

"I cain't smell it," Porter said. "Say, how about old Buck? He still wants to buck. I had to work him over three times today. But you know I wouldn't own one who wouldn't wake a feller up and pitch a little now and then."

Chapter 16

NEIGHBORS

*When a cowboy says a man is a good neighbor, he means that
the man's concern for the bovine does not extend only to his
own boundaries. A good neighbor intends to be of service in
helping any bovine perform his certain duties.*

*A neighbor might not have exactly the same idea as
another company of what service to the other company's
bovine should be. If a good neighbor finds another company's
steer out of bounds, he might decide that steer lacks growth
and might rope him and bust him down to stretch his hide.
He enjoys this type of service. He might break the steer's leg
in the process. If such an accident happens, a good neighbor
may butcher the steer and eat the meat, divining that the
other company had sent the steer over to repay a favor.*

*A good neighbor might gather steers belonging to an-
other company at shipping time, sell them with his own
steers, and give the money to the company. Or he might keep
the money and think of a better way to be a good neighbor if
he is sure, deep in his cowman's heart, that the neighboring
company doesn't need money.*

The new cook was a delight.
He had cooked on the Pullman twenty years. He could fix
anything a cowboy liked to eat. He was a professional. He

shaved in the morning. He wore clean, striped cooks's trousers and an apron. He washed his hands. While he was preparing a meal, his kitchen was a holocaust, but when the crew was fed and gone, he straightened it out and swept the floors. He poured coffee for any man who came into his kitchen and no man had to ask for it. He asked cowboys what they would like to eat. He made pies and cakes and dumplings. He fixed lunches a man might call a picnic and take along for a lady friend. By paying the new cook good wages, the Outfit was taking care of its hired help, and the crew appreciated it. The cook was happy to have suppers hot on the table anytime the cowboys came in from the day's ride. Mealtime, which was part of his wages, pleasured Sorrells like a paycheck.

Tom the welder, who complained that his liver was so bad it periodically stuck fast to his ribs, began to come to meals on time. He no longer preferred to work in his shop at suppertime. The cook was courteous to Tom. Tom often stayed to smoke and talk with him when the rest of the crew had gone to work. They talked of special trains they knew and special places in America they both had enjoyed, Tom as a hobo and the cook as an elite member of the railroad fraternity.

Porter venerated the new cook. His worn life was the only good life he had left, and he handed it over into the care of the new cook. The bachelor, celibate Porter was a stranger to comforts of bed and board, but his poor eyes showed a gleam when he was near the cook or when he thought about mealtime. In the truck on the way back to headquarters in the tired evenings, Porter enjoyed speculating on what the cook would have for supper and remembering what he had been fed before. Mealtimes, for Porter, were much the same as formal religious services might have been for him. With the religion of a full stomach came new hope for him. He began to remember old ambitions. He spoke to Sorrells about ventures he had in mind, intimating he would try them again if Sorrells would help him.

Wilson became more confident that his presence and his work counted with the rest of the crew. He offered Porter suggestions about the way the crew should handle the day's work. He told Sorrells about mistakes he thought Porter had made in handling the roundup. He knew the country very well, and when he disagreed with someone he no longer smiled and agreed or "maybe'd" or kept silent. He demonstrated that he knew enough to run the Outfit. He and Sorrells had respected each other before the new cook. Now they became friends.

Stacy stopped grunting in desperation at mealtime. He became a special favorite of the cook because of his large capacity for eating. In the discussions about the cooking, only Stacy refused to praise it, saying he had known better cooking almost everywhere he had been. After ten days Stacy levelled off and only ate three helpings of the seven or eight courses the cook put out each meal. He began to taste the food instead of swallowing it whole. He offered suggestions to the cook. The cook listened earnestly to the advice, but happily for the crew, continued to cook as he pleased. Stacy's manners improved. He would pick up the platter, stick his fork into the last chop, wave the platter so everyone's attention was brought to the chop, wipe the platter with the chop and slide it onto his plate. Before the cook, Stacy had been like a cement mixer gone wild at mealtime.

As soon as Feathers, who was a very young man, began to fill out on the good feed, he quit the Outfit and went to work as a heavy equipment operator at a mine. Whitey, who was older, stayed on but set up his camp at the spring he was improving. He did not like supervision, society, or cooks fooling with his grub. Jack Roberts worked with Whitey. He ran equipment and pickups with supplies to the springs they were improving, but was in the bunkhouse every night. The bunkhouse was left to the cook, Porter, Wilson, Stacy, Roberts, Tom and Sorrells as the cold weather set in.

After a week of grazing at the new cook's table, Sorrells found more energy for doing his work. The work had become a joy to perform. The crew worked smoothly together harvesting the wild bovine. Each man knew what to expect from the next.

Wilson would unload Sorrells, Stacy, and Porter and take the truck to the place the portable corral was set up. He would pen cattle he saw near the corral and then ride toward a spot where he thought his partners would converge with cattle, or he would go to a place he suspected a partner might have trouble with cattle. More than once Wilson coasted up to help Sorrells when Sorrells thought the snuffy cattle he had flushed were going to get away.

Each day, when the crew started a drive, Stacy would leave for the area assigned to him and disappear for the day. Sorrells never worried about him causing a storm in the cattle by running through a herd anymore. He would reappear, long overdue but not missed, after the rest of the crew had joined and penned the cattle. He usually came in from a direction a pole apart from the country he was expected to work. When he was helping work cattle, he was usually chasing one head off out of sight or fighting his horse, so he never disturbed the work anymore.

Sorrells had never worried about Porter. Porter was the brains that moved the crew during the first months. No one bothered to look around and wonder where Porter was. He was at the right place at the right time like Wilson always was and anyone who thought he had to highpoint Porter was wasting time. The only trouble Porter had was his age. He could not chase the wild bovine off the steep mountain with abandon. He needed help when he was after more than one renegade, but Sorrells and Wilson were happy he couldn't handle too much of that kind of work. The big renegade was whiskey and milk, nights at the party, meat in the pot, and married life to Wilson and Sorrells. Then one day Porter worried Sorrells for a little while.

Wilson unloaded Sorrells, Stacy, and Porter at the foot of McGrath Mountain and drove the truck around to the flat where the portable corral was set up. The corral was on the side of the ranch that bordered the range of Duane Jones and his partner, a man named Maynard.

The men split up and worked the canyons toward the corral. Sorrells picked up some cattle and followed them into the flat. When they were in the open, he saw he had over fifty head, more cattle than Porter had believed were running in the McGrath country. He saw the cattle were moving well toward the corral and climbed back up the mountain to make sure he hadn't missed any. He stopped on a highpoint to look around. Smoke was rising four or five miles away in country Porter was working. Where Sorrells came from, smoke meant "Come to the fire." A man whose horse was down or a man injured or in a storm with livestock lit signal fires for help. Sorrells didn't think Porter would signal for help because of any trouble he might have handling livestock. He would let them go rather than admit he needed help with a bunch of cattle. But he might be afoot or injured. Sorrells rode toward the fire.

The distance Sorrells had to ride to reach the fire was cut with many deep washes. Big Red didn't care if he ever got across that kind of country. Sorrells was over an hour arriving at the fire. Sorrells was tired and cranky when he saw that Dobie Porter was not down under his horse with a broken leg at the place he had set two Joshua trees afire. He was not in sight, but Buck's tracks showed plainly that he had been there.

Sorrells rode all the way back to intercept the cattle he had left on the flat. He found Porter, Wilson, and Stacy pushing them along. Porter was on the opposite side of the herd and Sorrells didn't get a chance to talk to him until the cowboys were penning the cattle.

"Who in the hell has been lighting fires?" Sorrells asked.

"What?" Porter asked, smiling like a guilty child when he saw that Sorrells was angry. He was like a child who got his way when he smiled. The weather had turned cold and windy and Porter had put away his felt hat so it would not be blowing off his head. He was wearing a leather, billed cap with ear flaps. The bill was off center and neither of his ears was completely covered by the flaps. Clear drops of moisture clung to Porter's nose. His face was wind dried and unshaven.

"Who lit the fire?" Sorrells asked.

"I guess I did," Porter said.

"You made me ride nearly three hours out of my way," Sorrells said. "I thought you were down with your head under old Buck."

"I didn't think anyone would come to it."

"I was taught anyone who lights a fire wants someone to come to it."

"Well, I'm shore sorry about it. I got off and built that fire to warm up. I was getting stiff from cold."

The day was sunny. In spite of the cold wind Sorrells stayed warm enough without a fire, but Sorrells wasn't seventy years old. Porter might have needed the fire.

That afternoon Sorrells was riding high watching the flats

for cattle when he saw Porter about two miles away with a
bunch of cattle by a mining road. Another rider was helping
Porter. He watched them, trying to figure out who the other
rider was. It could be Stacy. Stacy was riding a dark horse
that day. Porter had lighted himself another fire. He was
pushing the cattle down the road away from it.

Sorrells saw a cow and a calf between himself and
Porter's bunch. Porter must not have seen the pair. Sorrells
rode to push the pair to the road.

The cow was in a draw. Sorrells saw Buck's track near
her. Well, he thought, she must have come into the draw
after Porter rode by. The cow and calf trotted ahead of
Sorrells. He didn't catch up to them for a good look until he
was near Porter. The rider who had been with Porter was
nowhere in sight now.

Sorrells thought he saw the Outfit's brand on the cow's
side, but it wasn't clear. She was better than the average
Maynard-Jones cow. The Maynard-Jones cattle were small
boned and off-colored. The calf was unbranded but had been
earmarked with the Outfit's earmark. The earmark was a
swallow fork cut in the right ear.

Sorrells suspected the calf had been "sleepered." Sleepering
is an old trick of the cow thief. A cow thief will catch an
unbranded calf and earmark him with the owner's mark. An
outfit always brands and earmarks calves at the same time.
When a cowman sees cattle from afar or from the off side of a
brand, he can tell if they are branded by looking at the
earmark. The owner sees that the sleepered calf is earmarked
and mothered by one of his cows and automatically thinks he
is branded. The thief waits until the sleepered calf is old
enough to wean, rides in and takes him, crops off the owner's
earmark and puts his own brand on the calf.

Sorrells drove the cow and calf into Porter's bunch and
rode up beside the old man, trying to remember the stories
he had heard about Porter before he met him on the Outfit.

"Where'd you find her?" Porter asked.

"Just behind you over those hills," Sorrells said.

"Does she belong to the Outfit?"

"The brand isn't clear but I'm almost sure she does.
She's the type we're running. She ain't anything like the

cattle Maynard and Jones are running. She's got the Outfit's earmark for females and the calf has our earmark."

"I saw her over there. I think she's a cow belongs to Maynard and Jones. They earmark their cows the same as the Outfit does and they earmark their bull calves with a swallow fork on both ears. They brand their cows on the same side with a bar in the same place the Outfit puts the bar."

"Seems to me that is mighty convenient for a neighbor of an outfit this size," Sorrells said. "No neighbor could get away with it where I come from."

Porter laughed and pushed at the air with one hand by his ear as though to brush away a bad thought. "You and me wouldn't stand for it, but you and me don't count," he said. He rode ahead of the cow and cut her out of the bunch.

"I'd keep her," Sorrells said. "Let's rope her and shave that brand and see for sure who she belongs to."

"Aw, we'll be working here a few days more and we'll catch her some other time. It's late. Her calf's too young to wean anyway."

"He's sleepered," Sorrells said to let Porter know he was no fool.

"I don't think so. Somebody just made a mistake. Say, wouldn't a feller do good if he *did* decide to do a little mavericking and sleepering on this outfit? A man with a pair of horses and a good truck could just hide out here and catch him a stake."

"A man with a good night loop," Sorrells said.

"The last time I ran cattle on this place I lost my stake. I got a lease deal with the Parkers who owned it then. Me and two big-shot Los Angeles packers went in together. They put up the cattle. They were supposed to put up all the operating cost and I was supposed to do all the work. We done thisaway, we turned fifteen hundred steers out on this ranch.

"Them packers was supposed to put up a pickup for me to use. They never did. They was supposed to get me charge accounts for feed and chuck in town. They never did. I had a little money so I used it to get along. They wouldn't pay me back so I done thisaway, I sold a big steer whenever I needed money. When they got ready to ship the steers they said they didn't need me no more. Here's the idee, they figured I would just slink off with my tail between my legs and they wouldn't have to pay me my cut in the steers or the money I had been out caring for them. I taken them to court and the judge give me my money back, but I couldn't prove I had anything coming in the steers. I finally figured out that the only money I saw in the deal had been from the steers I'd sold so I could stay alive and care for the rest of the cattle. I only contributed my time and money to them fellers when I could just as well have taken my cut by selling a hundred steers instead of just five or six. Here's the idee, they was a long, long time gathering them steers after I left here, and they never did hire cowboys enough to get them all. They never would have been able to prove I took any of them cattle.

"I've always been in sympathy with the cow thief. There was a young feller got caught stealing from old Jim Morrow, my boss up on the Strip. Morrow was called as a witness at the hearing. The prosecutor thought Morrow would identify the cow brute the young feller had stole and that would be that.

"This lawyer feller asks Morrow if the bull found in the suspect's corral belonged to him.

"Old Morrow says, 'Maybe he did and maybe he didn't. I figure, if he was going to bring him back, he belonged to me. If he wasn't, he might figure he was his bull.'

"The lawyer feller was put out. He'd figured Morrow would be for hangin' the young feller and he asked Morrow how come he wasn't.

"Morrow says the young feller might have needed the bovine and that was why he took him.

"The lawyer says whether he needed him or not was beside the point. The young feller had blotted out Morrow's brand on the bull so he must be guilty of *stealing* the bull. Then he asked Morrow if he didn't want to see justice done.

"Morrow said, well, now, no. If he wanted to see justice done as the lawyer feller seen it, he'd be in trouble with all his neighbors.

"The prosecutin' feller needed an explanation of this too.

"Morrow says a lot of people in that part of the country would go to jail if that kind of justice was done. He himself had got his start in the cow business with more than just one bull he got in the night from the young feller's daddy."

Sorrells bet Porter would not have remembered that story if he wasn't seventy years old and still working for $250 a month. Porter didn't have any cattle of his own and maybe he thought it was time he did. Now was a good time. The Outfit didn't depend on the income from its cattle for bed and board. The front office seemed to want the Outfit to lose money. The more the Outfit cost, the more deductions Archie Lang and Son could claim. If the front office kept from paying taxes because of the Outfit, Sorrells couldn't see any wrong in Porter's night looping cattle the Outfit would never miss. A cowpuncher ought to make something out of the old cow he took care of. Somebody ought to make the care of a cow profitable. It didn't seem right to Sorrells that the corporations buying up the ranches were creating an economy in their other businesses that prohibited a cowpuncher from owning a ranch. The way the corporations had inflated the cost of ranches, a cowpuncher couldn't buy an outfit on the credit anymore and work himself out of debt. A calf crop might pay his interest, but it would not get him out of debt in one lifetime. A man had to be a corporation and pay cash for land and cattle in order to get a reasonable return on his money. Sorrells wished Porter luck if Porter was stealing cattle, but Sorrells didn't want any part of it. He had lost as good an outfit a man could lose through trusting in hard, honest work, and he knew he wasn't smart enough to carry a night loop.

On that day, for once, Stacy came to the roundup with cattle from the direction Porter had sent him to work. He had not been riding with Porter at all that day. The men had finished for the day and were loading their horses when they saw a truck coming down the mining road from the direction Porter had been seen by Sorrells with another rider. The truck was a bobtail. It rolled up and stopped by the corral. The dark horses in the back had been ridden hard, harder than the Outfit's horses had been ridden. A heavy man with a flat-topped felt hat and a bandana around his neck got out of the truck. Duane Jones was in the cab. He did not get out or greet the crew of the Outfit. The neckerchiefed man walked over to the corral and studied the cattle.

"Afternoon," Porter greeted.

"How are ya," the neckerchiefed man answered gruffly without turning toward Porter.

"You our neighbor?" asked Porter.

"Yeah."

"Mr. Maynard or Mr. Jones?"

Wilson snorted and laughed. Porter was overplaying feigned ignorance or he was badly senile. Porter, Sorrells, and Wilson all knew Duane Jones, the man Cunningham had fired the first day Sorrells had gone to work.

"Maynard," the neckerchiefed man said.

"Oh. Well, is Duane Jones your partner?" Porter asked. He craned his neck and examined the man in the cab of the truck. "Is that you, Duane?" he asked, leaning on one foot and waving. Sorrells was standing behind him watching him perform. Porter's old spurs stuck out from under the sagging cuffs of his Levis. He was standing at Buck's head holding his reins. He didn't look capable of stealing cattle.

"My eyes ain't so good no more," Porter said. Duane gave him the merest sign of a greeting.

"Have you been seeing any of our cattle?" Maynard asked.

"Not many, Mr. Maynard," Porter said.

"Well, I've been having reports that you men have been moving our cattle with yours in your drives." Sorrells knew this wasn't true because this was the first day any of the crew of the Outfit had worked cattle near the Maynard-Jones range.

"No. Whenever we see any of yours we just drop them back," Porter said.

"I retrieved several head of our cattle from the Outfit last week."

"Those were probably your tracks I saw today on this side," Porter said. Sorrells never had seen him so humbly friendly.

"They were and I'm getting tired of having to ride over here every few days."

"We haven't moved any of your cattle," Sorrells said. He didn't like to watch Porter acting dumb. Maynard didn't need to think Sorrells was a fool, either.

"Well, see that you don't," Maynard said, looking Sorrells

in the eye. "I like to be a good neighbor and all that, but if I keep finding my cattle over here, I'll have to see the inspector about making the Outfit round up all the cattle over here for inspection."

"We are doing exactly that, rounding up the cattle. Invite your inspector over if you want to. Come and help us. Are there any of the Outfit's cattle over in your country?" Sorrells asked.

"No. I'm hauling water to a place where we border with the Outfit and I keep your cattle pushed back this way. I can barely haul enough to keep my cattle alive, let alone cattle belonging to Famous."

The Outfit's range up to the Maynard-Jones border was good, but Maynard's range was bad. Sorrells wondered why Maynard had any cattle there at all. Most of Maynard's flats were covered by an alkaline lake. The water he was hauling was probably to attract cattle belonging to the Outfit.

Maynard got into his truck. "Good-bye, Mr. Maynard. We'll keep a lookout for your cattle," Porter said. Maynard drove away. Duane Jones was looking straight ahead.

"Huh. That's the first time I've ever seen that Mr. Maynard. Did you know him, Wilson?"

"All my life," Wilson said and yawned.

"I never knew him," Porter said.

"Awww, Dobie," Wilson laughed. "He was here when you were here with the Parkers. He's been here for a long time."

"I cain't remember him. Say, he's kindly a grouchy feller, ain't he? I was going to ask him where he had been riding today, but he acted damned unfriendly."

"Didn't you see him, Dobie?" Sorrells asked. "The truck came from the direction of the country you were working."

"I didn't see him. I seen his tracks though," Dobie Porter said. "Say, that was sure a good truck he was driving. I wonder what a new truck like that cost. Do you know, Bert?"

"No, Dobie," Sorrells said. "I wouldn't have any idea."

The first snow, a heavy wet snow, fell that night and the next day was clear and warm.

Chapter 17
SUNSPOT

he had awakened in the night in his bunk over the
in his room, had leaned against the door to climb down,
had spinning fallen out of his room
cement walk.

*A hondo is the small, even loop, knotted on the end of a
lariat. Americans took the word "hondo" from the Mexican,
honda, which means the same thing. Lazo is also a Spanish
word. The lasso is the loop formed by passing the end of the
rope through the hondo.*

*A cowpuncher must take the time to make himself a good
hondo in a new rope. The rope must pass easily through the
hondo and the overhand knot which joins the hondo must be
thrown evenly so the hondo does not lie twisted.*

*A good hondo must be reinforced with leather, called
wear leather, to protect the hondo loop. A cowboy has to soak
his leather overnight, so it will stretch and be easy to handle.
He has to punch holes in the leather small enough so they do
not weaken the leather. The holes should be so small it hurts
his fingers to pass the thick thongs through them. He has to
pull and tighten the thongs to sew the leather around the
rope. He has to tighten them so tight the water in the leather
will ooze out. He has to let the hondo leather dry before he
uses the rope.*

*If he meets all these prerequisites, he will have a good
hondo and might not have to meet them again until he gets a
new rope. Only he can perform this chore for himself. No one
is going to do it for him, and he doesn't like to do it enough to
do it for anyone else. Making hondos is just too deep an
exasperating chore, requiring the very ends of the fingers, the
ends of patience, the end of the day, and the end of the rope
in the operation.*

Tom's eye was swelling shut. The heel of one hand was gashed by a deep, long-grained wound. He limped on one leg when he showed these hurts to the crew in the bunkhouse at breakfast one morning. He told Sorrells he had awakened in the night in his bunk over the toilet in his room, had leaned against the door to climb down, the door had sprung open, and he had fallen out of his room to the cement walk.

"I don't see how that could possibly have happened," said Stacy, who rarely spoke to Tom. Tom turned to him and patiently began explaining the accident again. Stacy grinned up at him. The gut inside of Stacy's upper lip was bared over his teeth. The cook handed Tom a slice of fresh beefsteak for his eye and Stacy's grin widened. The bright, white light from the fluorescent lamps in the bunkhouse in the early morning on the moist beefsteak in Tom's dry and shaking hand and on Stacy's grin, were too real to Sorrells' waking consciousness. He closed his eyes and wished he was still in his bedroll.

"Huh! I heard something happening out there in the night, but I thought it was coyotes dragging a beef belly," Porter said, and hid his face behind his cup of sugared canned milk and hot water.

"Why do you stay in that little toilet?" Jack Roberts asked Tom. "There's plenty of room here in the bunkhouse now."

"I'm used to it," Tom said.

"It's sure getting cold," Porter said. "The first snow came two weeks ago. It must be cold out there in that toilet. All that water and crock. It's cold in our room, ain't it, Bert?"

"I fixed up an old electric heater for myself," Tom said.

"I thought you'd of flown south by now," Porter said. "Even the crows leaves this country in the winter. It's warm in Southern California. That's where *I'd* be."

"I'll stay awhile longer," Tom said. "Mr. Cunningham asked me to stay and I'm making some hackamore bits for Bert."

"How does a feller get you to do custom work?" Porter asked. "I could use a little welding done on my truck."

"You could bring it over to the shop on a Sunday," Tom said.

"Hell, I wouldn't want you to have to work on Sunday. I know how mechanics hates to work on Sundays," Porter said.

"Might as well work. Cain't sleep," Tom said.

"Well, say, I'm much obliged. I've got some good dope mixed up that will be good for your hand if you don't mind it stinging a little," Porter said. He got up from the table and stumped back to his room. Sorrells knew that Porter's favorite cut and scratch medicine was a batter of turpentine and mentholatum. He had some outstanding remedies. Once he had put Vicks in Stacy's eye to cure an irritation.

Cunningham walked in and sat down. The cook gave him a cup of coffee. He talked cheerily to Tom for awhile. He liked Tom. Then, when Porter came in with the salve, Cunningham turned to Sorrells.

"How many did you guys bring in yesterday?" he asked.

"Five head," Sorrells said.

"Well, it's time we did something else about this. We've been at it ten weeks and haven't shipped many more cattle than they shipped last year in a month. I'm going to have to put on some more men or something."

"What the hell!" Sorrells said. "We've done a lot in ten weeks. We haven't shipped more calves but we've tallied the cattle, culled the cattle, and gathered over a hundred mavericks that they damn sure didn't gather last year."

"We've got to get *all* the cattle gathered, and *all* the steer calves shipped, and I want to get it over with. Why are you guys so damned slow?"

"The cattle are scattered," Sorrells said.

"What do you mean 'scattered'? They must have been scattered last year too, and the year before that."

"The weather's been cold."

"You told me before that they were scattered because the weather was hot."

"That's right. They are moving now from the high, broken country to the low, broken country."

"I don't care what they are doing. I want them gathered. Jack can ride with you from now until you finish."

"Good. I'll go for that," Sorrells said. "What the hell is he going to ride?"

"He can ride old Careful and the pigeon-footed grey and I'll loan him my blue horse," Cunningham said.

"Whoa, boy," Roberts said. "I ain't no cowboy. The only kind I know how to ride is the kind that run away in front of a crowd of people. I don't even have a saddle."

"You'll use mine," Cunningham said.

"You know why they call Careful, Careful?" Sorrells asked Roberts.

"No, and I don't give a damn," Roberts said.

"When he runs, he runs in forty directions at one time, so it takes you forty minutes to get him running."

"Why don't you ride your own horse and saddle?" Roberts asked Cunningham.

"Hell, I'm starting a hundred thousand dollars worth of heavy equipment building dams tomorrow. I'm expecting a crew of well drillers and a ten-man fencing crew this week."

Finding nothing more to talk about over coffee the cowpunchers of the Outfit left the bunkhouse, saddled their horses, loaded them on the stocktruck, and went to work. Wilson parked the stocktruck near the top of Dupont Mountain. Sorrells and Jack Roberts had ridden in the open platform over the cab of the truck. They were stiff when they climbed down. Dupont was the highest mountain on the Outfit and the morning was cold. Four men could ride in the cab, but when Sorrells had climbed to the platform in front of the rack, Roberts had joined him to keep him company.

The men eased themselves into their cold saddles, their faces down in their coat collars, their hats jammed on their heads against the cold. In single file, the horses blew heavy fog from their nostrils in the climb to the top of Dupont.

Each man had his own armor against the cold. Wilson would have looked like a Chinese Communist in a cap with fur flaps over his ears and forehead and a quilted jacket, were it not for his red bullrider's chaps.

Roberts looked trim and natty. He was freezing because he was wearing a thin waist jacket. He had recently been to

town and had bought a brown felt hat that did not conform
well to his head. He had also been to a barber who had used
his clippers all around Roberts' head and neck. Near the
mountain top a high, thin wind fanned the blood out of his
ears and bare neck.

Stacy wore the same thin, unlined brush jacket and the
straw hat he used in summer. The wind was turning the
highpoints of his face white and when Sorrells asked him why
he didn't dress warmer, he said the weather was not cold
enough yet for him. He rode along, straight and stiff in the
saddle, jerking involuntarily each time the wind chilled a
fraction too many of his corpuscles.

Only the top of Dobie Porter's black leather cap could be
seen over the high collar of the long, heavy sheepskin he
wore. Dobie tucked the overcoat under his seat, providing
him with three inches of padding over his saddle.

Sorrells wore long underwear, chaps, flannel shirt, blanket-
lined canvas jacket, a kerchief on his head that covered his
ears under his old hat, and leather gloves with cotton liners.
He was too warm for riding. He was manufacturing torturing
droplets of sweat under his arms that caught the cold in some
baffling manner and pricked his ribs with it. His feet, however, were so brittle with cold he was sure they would break off
without bleeding if he bumped them against the brush.

They stood their horses at the top of Dupont, nearly
eight thousand feet high. Below them they could see the
long, deep, wide Dupont Canyon stretching to the flats
bordering California. They could see badland country bordering
Highway Draw. They could see the many ruins of old mines
and shafts and roads leading to them.

Porter sent Stacy and Roberts into Dupont Canyon.
They would follow a road down its floor to the flats. They
would encounter springs and salt licks in the canyon. Any
cattle they found there would be easy to contain in a drive to
the flats. Sorrells and Porter would search the high country
between Dupont Canyon and Highway Draw. When Wilson
knew how Porter was going to work the country, he went
back to the truck to load his horse. He would take the truck
to the flats below Dupont. He would bunch cattle he found

there and hold them to stop any cattle that ran out of Dupont.

Below the peak of Dupont Mountain, Sorrells and Porter rode over three long, open grassy mesas. They were like steps. The descent from each step was over steep, malapais lava slopes. The horsemen saw tracks of a large bovine on the steps. The bottom edge of the third step was a bluff over many canyons separated by high, sharp ridges. The ridges were like spokes in a fan between Dupont Canyon and Highway Draw. The canyons and ridges were covered by a soft, tan loam. The horsemen could see many spots where talc had been mined. From above the last step, they also saw some of the owners of the large tracks. They saw two cows, two large calves, and one big steer.

"There's old Sunspot, I bet," Porter said. "I knew we'd find some big steers in this country."

"He's sure big," Sorrells said.

"I bet he is the steer I saw while you fellers was at the rodeo. If he is the same steer he'll have a white spot on his other side. He'll have one loose gotch horn that hangs over one eye. I saw him at Dove Springs one day I was rimmin' around. He'll weigh close to fifteen hundred pounds, that old feller will."

"How old you think he is?"

"I don't know, Bert. I'd bet money he's at least ten. He could be a steer my Los Angeles partners couldn't gather. That would make him fifteen years old. We ran some weaners that time."

"He'd have your brand then."

"If he does, it won't be clear. I branded those calves light that year because this country was bad for screw worms."

"We'll shave him when we catch him. We'll see if he could be fifteen years old."

"He'd be worth catching if only to mouth him, wouldn't he, Bert?"

"You bet," Sorrells said. Both men dismounted, reset their saddles and tightened their cinches. Sorrells unbuttoned his jacket. He put the glove of his roping hand in his chaps pocket. They remounted, ready to run the wild bovine off the steep mountain. They rode off the mesa. They separated to approach the cattle from different sides.

Sorrells was thinking the big renegade would probably split and try to rim out after he led a rider into the canyons. He would come back here eventually if he got away. When the cows were pressed, they would go downhill so they could keep track of their calves. If one of the men got a chance, he should rope the old steer and let the other man stay with the cows. Sorrells would know what should have happened with Sunspot when all five head of the cattle got away and no plan worked anyway. Sorrells and Porter had started out right. They had not wasted time making plans.

Sorrells was riding Baldy. The horse sensed a run and was hard to hold. Sorrells rode over the malapais without fighting Baldy to keep him quiet. Fighting him would make him more delinquent. Sorrells stopped him when he knew he would move the cattle if he rode closer. A cow and calf were about seventy-five yards from him. The cow was a four-year-old maverick. She was red-necked. The calf was an eight-month-old bull. The cow was wild eyed. She was sensing adventure. She sniffed the air and moved toward the other cattle. Her calf moved close by her side, trusting to her.

Sorrells moved from behind a piñon and the pair saw him. The cow trotted with her calf to the sunny slope of a hill near the other cattle. Porter was standing Little Red in the open on the other side of the mesa. Porter was able to ride closer to snuffy cattle with them looking at him and not afraid of him than any man Sorrells had ever known. Sorrells dismounted from the unquiet Baldy and stood behind a piñon to watch Porter.

He could see parts of the red and white hides of a cow and calf bunched together with the big steer in a thick growth of young juniper trees. They were not moving and probably hoped Porter did not see them. Porter walked Little Red toward them calmly. The horse seemed to move only in unrelated parts, presenting no menace to the cattle. The cattle started moving out of the junipers toward Sorrells. The big steer was first. Yes, he was gotch horned. The white hair on his head and on the stockings of his front feet was clean, the red of his hide on his shoulders caught the light in disturbed places like the red on velvet. He came on and he came on and he came on until all of him was out of the junipers. No other cattle came after him. Sorrells realized the steer was all of what Sorrells had believed were three cattle in the junipers.

The steer stood a full twelve hands tall. The big horn that hooked over one eye had been broken loose at the base and wobbled when he moved. On one of his sides a pure spot of white the size of a hat scared the red hair away. He was not fat. His frame was full of efficiently maintained brawn that made his movement fluid, graceful, and sparing of his force. Sorrells had seen Mexican oxen the size of Sunspot. Oxen possessed a used and shambled strength. Sunspot owned his force. It had kept him free. No insidious marbling of fat crept through him to make him a choice product for man's consumption.

Sunspot was no maverick, unused, untouched, uneducated about man. He was an outlaw who had once walked in the herd, ridden in the cattle car, been hormoned, castrated, branded, tagged, prodded, marked, filed, and had his tail bobbed. Now, he had escaped man. He was on the dodge. He was not a member of the beef industry. He was the Wandering Jew who had found his Promised Land and he was damned well able to defend himself now. He was the wild bovine whose very tracks Sorrells felt privileged to find.

Sunspot moved unhurriedly away from Porter. He picked up the cows and calves and they streamed behind him like small sloops in the wake of a great ship. They rounded the sunny hill with Porter on their tracks. Sorrells mounted Baldy and rode to keep them from going into a canyon that would lead them away from Dupont Canyon. If he could keep them pointed toward Dupont, he and Porter would have the best chance of getting them to the flats.

The cattle were quickly out of sight. Sorrells gave Baldy his head toward the bluffs under the mesa. He looked up once and saw Porter winding on the hill above him behind a cow and calf. He saw the red-necked cow going off a ridge on his downhill side. He spurred Baldy off the hill to turn her toward Porter. He lost her for a while. He rode back up the ridge and found her tracks. She had cut behind him and

stopped. She had run to the floor of the canyon about the
time he had found her tracks. Sorrells followed her tracks
until he was sure she had run down the canyon. He let Baldy
run. He caught up to the cow. She was going at an easy run
down the canyon. She slowed only when her calf crashed into
brush or bank. Sorrells slowed and let her go on out of sight.
If she saw him chasing her she might leave her calf and rim
out of the canyon. He followed her tracks, keeping well
behind her but in pace with her. He was going in the wrong
direction to help Porter with Sunspot.

The canyon began to widen and Sorrells rode to catch
the calf. The pair was running on a sandy, level, talc mine
road now. The road was downhill and level enough to allow
the cow and calf to run their fastest without danger of falling.
It was steep enough to make their flight headlong, the line of
flight Sorrells liked best. The calf was jumping and stretching
so truly along the road that Sorrells could see his front hooves
and his hind hooves in a straight line with the taut, white
belly streaming above the white road. Sorrells leaned over
Baldy's ears and looked down at the calf's wide back bunching
as he jumped. The calf's tail was waving high. His thick head
strained forward on the short neck. His tongue swelled when
his voice bawled. Sorrells threw a loop that would have
decapitated the calf had the loop been keen edged. He felt the
true angle and heft of the loop as it left his hand. He pitched
his slack high, as a man throws away his hat in celebration.
He sat down on Baldy as the horse slid on his haunches and
buried his tail to stop. The bull calf hit the end of his rope.
Sorrells watched him nose up as though to fly on and soar
out. The nylon rope stretched. It quit stretching. The calf
nosed back in an arc toward Sorrells, the legs stiffened in the
air, the tail whipped up. The calf returned to the earth.

"That'll stretch your hide so you'll grow," Sorrells said
when he had the calf tied.

He caught up to the red-necked cow at the open end of
the canyon with the highway in sight. She had slowed enough
so that she took time to wave her head from side to side to
look at Baldy bearing down on her. She did not look back for
long. For her, this horseman was all four of the Apocalypse in
one, and she was not waiting for her doom.

The flat between the end of the canyon and the highway was covered with high, coarse sagebrush. The brush concealed washes that ran parallel to the road. Into the sage the frantic cow dove, with Baldy rating her to give Sorrells a throw. She quit running in a straight line. She ducked and dived in the brush like a rabbit. Baldy stayed dodge for dodge with her. Sorrells did not try to catch her in the brush. He rode to keep her in sight, to stay on Baldy, keep his boots in stirrups the brush pounded, keep his loop from snagging, and to keep from losing a kneecap. He had to watch the ground ahead of the cow for deep arroyos and the remnants of old, rusty, barbwire fences he knew might snag his horse. The cow checked, scrambled with her hind legs spread and sliding, showed her sparse teats quivering behind her, and jumped a narrow wash. Baldy strode across it after her. Sorrells lost a stirrup against a trunk of sagebrush. He was five jumps catching up to Baldy again. He dropped his loop when he had to reach for his saddlehorn and pull himself back into his seat. He thought, oh hell, if that loop catches on something low on the ground Baldy is in for a jerk that will strangle him with his own tail. Sorrells' rope was tied hard and fast to the saddlehorn.

Sorrells caught the lost stirrup. He stood up and leaned forward to help Baldy take the jerk. The loop caught, the rope stretched. The hondo at the end of the rope popped and dusted Sorrells just above his right hip pocket where he carried the least cushion on the flat bone. He had no curve or contour there to deflect the hondo. He cussed his misfortune. He was too busy to rub it.

The next wash was too wide for the cow to jump. She nose-dived off the bank into the sand. Baldy was so hot he had no whoa in him, and Sorrells had to apply all his two hundred pounds to pull him up at the brink. The cow's front legs buckled under her when they tried to catch her in the sand. She plowed over them, her nose, jaws, throat, and brisket making a long furrow in the sand. She floundered in that position, her front legs swept back along her sides, her hind legs stretched out flatly behind her. Her free flight was over. She moaned. She had run too long. She had been in a start too long and her freebooting legs were cramping.

Sorrells tied the cow's hind legs together while she bawled her disdain of him. He hauled on her ears and tail until her legs were under her. Her muscles still twitched to carry her away. He imagined the cow must be shocked suddenly, unbelievably, to find herself so accessible to the touch of man.

He had tied the hind legs together above the hocks so the cow could stand up and move about when her cramps subsided. This tie would hold her for a few hours until she learned to walk with her hind legs tied together. He hoped to be back for her before she learned. If he tied her so that she stayed down, her cramps might stiffen through her will and she might never get up.

He loosened his cinches and reset his saddle, cleaning the sagebrush from under his blankets. He mounted Baldy. He marked the spot in the wash where the cow lay by picking out a tree by the highway. He rode toward the flat where the rest of the crew should converge.

Along the rising country below Dupont Mountain where the canyons opened and widened and levelled to the flats, Sorrells walked Baldy. The country was grassy and not rocky. This country was warmer than the mesa where he had started the cow. The kerchief was soaked with sweat on Sorrells' forehead. He unbuttoned his jacket and shirt. The November breeze cooled him unpleasantly. Wide grassy draws under the ridges off Dupont were covered with cow feed. Sorrells saw tracks that could belong to steers as big as Sunspot. He found a trail these cattle used. He followed the trail. Big deer used this trail, too. The trail crossed a rise and fat chukkars rose and stiffened in a long, low glide in front of him. He stopped Baldy and looked at a good spring of water where deer, chukkars, and cattle were watering. He turned Baldy toward the flats.

Before he got to the flats, Sorrells rode to a highpoint to locate his partners. He saw them miles away. One man was running his horse away from the other three horsemen. That must be Jack Roberts on the gray horse, Pigeon. Three other horsemen were close around a large bovine, maybe old Sunspot. Sunspot was roiling and probably exploding. The gray horse made a big circle and then his rider pointed him back toward the maelstrom. He ran by it again.

Sorrells joined his partners about an hour later. They had bunched the cattle and were driving them toward the highway. Porter was riding slowly along the flank of the herd. When Sorrells rode up to him, Porter grinned behind the porcelain facade of his false teeth. Sorrells saw big Sunspot walking jerkily in the center of the herd. He had been sidelined. A front foot had been tied on four feet of rope to a hind foot. The tie allowed him to walk but prevented him from running.

"You got him, Dobie," Sorrells said. "Nice going, you old thing."

"Let me tell you, no one has ever been as happy to see a red Indian ride up as I was awhile ago."

"Did you get in a storm?"

"I was in a horserace with old Sunspot off the mountain. Little Red was about to give out when I got the steer, the cow, and the calf down to the flats. I started hollering for help and Stacy and Jack come up. First thing they did was separate the cow and calf and run them off. Sunspot made a run at me so I tied on to him with my rope while Little Red still had breath. I figured at least one of my partners would think about me and come back soon. Hell no, when I looked up to see where they were they had run the cow and calf clean out of sight. Sunspot about had Little Red jerked down before Stacy come back. But Stacy was no help. He was afightin' his horse, as usual. He had to catch himself around the neck a few times before he could throw a loop at the steer. Sunspot made a run at Stacy. By then he had Little Red broke to lead and I couldn't hold him. I rode around a joshua. Sunspot pulled Little Red up against it and that's how I held him. Then Stacy ran back toward me with Sunspot following him and Sunspot took a wrap around Little Red against the joshua. About that time Jack came by and pulled Pigeon up astraddle of my rope between the joshua and the steer and instead of getting the hell out he tried to SAVE me and threw a loop at the steer. He caught a front foot just as Pigeon sold out. Pigeon hit the end of the rope, Jack's saddle slipped, Jack turned loose his dallies, and Pigeon ran off with Jack hanging and flopping on one side. Stacy took off to head Pigeon and save Jack and left me and Little Red snubbed to the joshua. Wilson rode up then and heeled old Sunspot and dragged him down."

"Why didn't you just turn loose your dallies and let him go when you got in the storm? You weren't tied hard and fast, were you?"

Porter grinned. "Well, we wasn't in *that* much trouble to let him *get away*. We could have held him a little bit longer. I knew I wasn't horseback enough to run the steer again and I don't think Stacy and Jack were going to catch him *for* me if they couldn't catch him *with* me."

When the herd reached the highway, Wilson turned back to go after the truck. Porter and Jack Roberts rode back to see if they could locate the cow and calf Roberts and Stacy had let go. Sorrells and Stacy started the forty head up the highway. The corral was set up at Dove Springs, by the highway. Wilson was going to take the truck up the talc mine road and load the calf Sorrells had tied there. He would then take the truck to the corral, unload his horse, and ride back down the highway to meet Sorrells and Stacy.

The first half of the highway route for the cattle to Dove Springs was through a canyon with straight, high walls of black rock. Two men could handle the cattle easily in there as long as they were kept bunched together. Sorrells rode in the lead. Stacy came along behind, whistling and practicing his heel loop at cattle in the drags. Sorrells let the cattle move along. They only had an hour of daylight left and he wanted to get through the canyon before it got dark. He did not want to meet any cars that might be going too fast in that canyon in the dark.

He knew he was going to have trouble ten minutes after he and Stacy started the cattle. Stacy was not pushing the drags hard enough to keep them caught up to the leaders. Sorrells held up the leaders and waited for Stacy. Stacy didn't hurry. He rode along whistling, his head down, his attention on his rope and the particular pair of heels he was bent on catching. Three head of his drags stopped on the road and watched him while he rode by them practicing roping another. After he threw his loop he noticed the three head.

They were not sure whether he was driving them with the rest of the herd or trying to cut them off the herd. Stacy cussed them and rode at them like a banshee, cutting them off and running them away from the herd. They made a big circle and ran back into the flank of the herd. Stacy downed his head again and went to playing with his rope.

The drags finally caught up with the leaders. Sorrells broke one of his own strictest rules and asked Stacy to keep the drags in step with the leaders so they could drive the cattle in a close bunch through a narrow gap at the end of the canyon. Sorrells didn't like to give or take orders. Neither did Stacy. Stacy paid no attention to him. He continued his whistling and roping. Sorrells also noticed that Sunspot's sideline rope had worn out. He was free. Only his herd instinct was keeping him in bounds with the rest of the cattle.

The gap where the road led out of the canyon was at the top of a steep rise. The road had been built on a fill that rose off the canyon floor. The cattle would be confined to the asphalt in the climb to the gap. Cattle hate to climb on pavement. Sorrells knew he would have to ride behind the cattle with Stacy in order to get the herd in a bunch through the gap in a hurry. If the cattle were allowed to stop on the rise the men would be stalled there with a herd of milling cattle on a blind side of a hill for oncoming traffic.

Sorrells held the cattle below the hill until Stacy caught up again. They started the cattle up the hill. Sorrells rode on one side of the herd under the embankment pointing the cattle up the road. When the leaders threatened to leave the asphalt off the other side, Sorrells rode across the road behind the herd to the other side and headed them back up the road. Stacy whistled indolently and waved his rope at the heels. Sorrells got back on the asphalt and squalled at the drags. He was beginning to realize he was not horseback enough to ride both sides and the drags too. He hoped no cars met the herd within the next few minutes.

Sunspot had gone ahead of the leaders. He saw the setting sun through the gap at the top of the hill and headed for it like he was going home. The sound of their own trotting hooves on the asphalt excited the cattle. They took a fix on the sight and sound of big Sunspot and followed him.

Sunspot was in the gap in the center of the road when the driver of a blue Oldsmobile sighted him from a hundred yards on the other side. Steer and car braked at the same instant. Sunspot slipped off one side of the road. The Oldsmobile skidded toward the other. The same foot that had been mashing feed into the Oldsmobile was now stomping the brakes to halt it. The car skidded past Sunspot and cut him off from the herd. The only containing force in front of Sunspot now was the sun in his eyes.

The mind in the driver of the Oldsmobile functioned briefly when it remembered hard braking caused skidding. The driver lifted the foot off the brakes to let the wheels roll and control the car's flight. Then the leaders of the herd appeared as a wall of hide and hair and horn before the driver. The heavy foot took over again and the driver, gaping at the cattle, remembered the words, "WATCH FOR CATTLE" on a sign he had just seen back up the road. From the Oldsmobile next was wrenched a sound of stress, the sound the car seldom had made, the sound which always heralds doom coming soon to machines of its kind: the rubbing scream of a car's earthbound tires when reminded it can't fly, has not been flying after all. Then the Oldsmobile went off the embankment in front of the cattle onto a pile of boulders.

Sorrells watched the cattle scatter off the highway and stream back down the canyon. Stacy spurred his horse to the Oldsmobile. This was the fastest Sorrells had ever seen him move. The Oldsmobile was stalled with its underbelly on boulders, its tires spinning in the air. Two men got out of the car and climbed off the rocks to the ground.

"Anybody hurt?" demanded Stacy.

The two men mumbled an answer while they looked at the spinning wheels and examined their machine for damage. They looked around at their new location, the new place in which they were suddenly finding themselves. They seemed concerned their machine could not fly them away from there. It had come to rest for a while upon a pile of stone in a desolate place.

"What do you mean scaring my cows like that?" Stacy bawled at them. "I ought to get down off this horse and work you both over."

The two men stared at Stacy's red face.

"Gawddammit, you scared those poor cows so bad they'll never give another drop of milk," Stacy shouted down from his horse at them. Sorrells rode after the cattle. He was laughing so hard at Stacy he could not see for the tears in his eyes and he had to hold onto the saddlehorn with both hands to keep from falling off Baldy. Baldy always meant business running after cattle, and Sorrells' fit of laughter put him out of rhythm with the horse.

Sorrells was still laughing when he and Stacy started the cattle up the hill again. He asked Stacy why he had bawled out the tourists.

"Gawddammit, the cattle and the buckaroos have the right of way in this country," Stacy said hotly. "You watch me. When I get back up the hill, I'm going to get their names and addresses. I'll teach them not to barrel through the cattle country. You've got to scare them sonsabitches so they'll go away and not bother you. Get their numbers. Make them show their driving licenses. That's why I told them these cows would dry up. They think a cow is only for the damned mother's milk them kind crave whenever anything goes wrong for them. You got to tell them off in language they understand."

"I guess you know that Porter's spotted steer got away," Sorrells said. "What are you going to tell him, Stacy? He was depending on you to get his big steer to the corral."

"Hell, I can't be responsible for *everything* that happens around here," Stacy said. "We'll just have to catch his steer some other time." He took down his rope and started whistling. He stopped it. He looked at Sorrells. "I don't believe that steer is as old as Porter is claiming he is," he said. He squinted one eye at Sorrells, though the sun was already down. "Besides that, I don't believe he ran him and that cow and calf as far as he said he did."

"He ran them a good, long ways. I was with him when he started them and I know they didn't come straight off the mountain to the flats. They must have done plenty of running."

"Naw," Stacy said and started swinging his loop. "That couldn't be." He began whistling again. He stopped again. "That steer couldn't be as old and wild as he said he was. You see how easy he was to drive?"

"He drove real well. Right uphill on the highway into the sun," Sorrells said.

"Well, you see? Most of these other cattle were harder to drive than he was, weren't they?"

"Yeah," Sorrells said. "But which one got away?"

Wilson met them at the bottom of the hill. Stacy rode ahead to warn any cars that might come through the gap. He stopped to scold the motorists again on his way.

Chapter 18

REMNANT

After the bulk of cattle have been shipped off an outfit, the cattle that have been missed are called the remnant. The work of gathering the remnant is the hardest work a cowboy does, but it is the most fun because it usually is done all downhill so fast a cowboy's eyes water. The renegade remnant's rule is RUN and they lead fuller lives than the ordinary bovine.

Sorrells listened to Porter's clacking, squishing jaws at the breakfast table and didn't mind. Nothing bothered Sorrells these days. He even liked the good stiffness that showed him his own frame was standing strong under hard work. The days were sunny and brisk. The nights and mornings were cold.

"I'd hoped the cold weather would drive the rimlant out of the high country but it looks to me like they're staying in there now that the days have warmed up," Porter said. "The feed is still good and they like it where they can stand up and highpoint a feller."

Wilson smiled. "They'll stay high until a deep snow and real cold runs them out. It's so warm now with moisture in the ground it almost looks like the feed is greening up again."

Sorrells swallowed the last of his coffee. "Work!" he

growled and smiled. "Work, work, work, Wilson. Time for work, fellers." He got up from the table with his dishes. "Time to saddle Big Red and catch runnygades," he said. "Tie down Sunspot today. Strangulate the sun. Raise big dust. Be proud."

Wilson laughed at him.

"Wild man," Roberts said, laughing.

Stacy was grinning at the arrangement of salt, pepper, worcestershire, ketchup, and syrup on the leftovers from breakfast on his plate.

"If the rimlant ain't as big as Sunspot, they'll be females smart as he is, steers almost as big, and calves miniatures of him from now on, fellers," Porter said.

"Work," Sorrells said, stomping on the flimsy boards under the torn linoleum as he charged the door of the bunkhouse with Wilson. "Work!" he shouted on his way to the corrals. "Work!" as he got his bosal out of the saddlehouse and walked out to survey the milling remuda. "Whoaaa, Reeolah!" he shouted at Roller.

Each morning Roller kept away from Sorrells as the man went after him to remove his morral after breakfast. This was a game the man and the horse played. The horse was not afraid, but he snorted at Sorrells and trotted away and allowed his teary eyes to start. Sorrells acted mean and angry. "Whoa, Reeolah, Reeolah, whoa," Sorrells growled with menace. Wilson's look cheered quietly for man and horse when Sorrells finally walked up to the Roller, removed the morral, and patted the horse on the neck.

Sorrells caught Big Red for himself and Buck for Porter. Wilson caught Rabbit, Careful, and Nigger. Stacy drove the rest of the remuda out of the corral to the horse pasture. Roller sidled and blew through the rollers in his nose at Sorrells as he went through the gate. "Reeolah!" Sorrells scolded him. "You, damn, Reeolah horse!"

On that day Wilson drove the crew to the top of Dupont Canyon. The men unloaded and started down the canyon together. During the normal roundup the men had driven the cattle as carefully as they could to their corral. Part of the plan of these drives was dictated by the country and another part was dictated by Porter's rule that driving cattle gentled them and would make them easier to handle the next time they were rounded up.

No desire to gentle the remnant governed the crew. The remnant was to be sold. All maverick or wild cows, big steers, and mustang or snuffy heifers were to be shipped and traded off for money. The crew, by general agreement, was not husbanding the renegades. The most profitable way of getting them off the ranch from now on would be fun for cowpunchers and hard on the bovine.

Each man carried as many lengths of piggin' string as he figured he could handle. From now on the crew of the Outfit was going to rope the renegades, lead them to the mining roads, tie them down, and come back for them with the truck when the run was over.

The crew split when it spotted the first bunch of cattle in Dupont Canyon. The cattle were catching the morning sun on a ridge on the side of the canyon. Wilson started them off the ridge. A heifer rimmed out toward the top of Dupont. He followed her. She had the high ground on him and was across a small, deep gorge from him.

Stacy turned the cattle onto the road on the floor of Dupont. They ran toward Sorrells. They did not stop. Porter and Roberts each picked out a calf and charged to rope him. Sorrells ran down the canyon ahead of the rest of the cattle to hold them up. The cattle split and went by him. He caught two calves and tied them down by the road. He remounted and ran after the others. He rounded a curve and surprised a big, buck mule deer with the morning sun shining on antlers like streaks of lightning. The buck was standing near a steer as big as Sunspot.

The sides of the canyon offered no exit for the cattle. Sorrells got in front of the cattle he had been chasing. The big steer joined them. He was not the least bit excited. The cows hid their faces in the piñon from Sorrells. He saw no more of the buck. He waited and let Big Red blow. He was sure his partners would be along soon. The canyon got very quiet.

Sorrells heard the peep of a whistle up the road and knew Stacy was coming. As the man approached, the peeps joined with the other tuneless sounds of Stacy. The cattle moved quietly into the brush. Stacy whistled to the bend. He couldn't see the cattle. Sorrells raised a hand for him to stop. Stacy stopped and looked around, seeing nothing.

"What's the matter?" he shouted. Sorrells pointed to the brush where the cattle were. He wondered what Stacy thought Sorrells was stopped and quiet for, if not for cattle.

"You got cattle?" Stacy shouted and came around the bend. The big steer came out of the piñon at a high, lumbering trot. He was wanting room. His sides rolled heavily, "Jeez," said Stacy, when he saw the steer. This sound pushed the big steer toward the quiet Sorrells. Sorrells let him by, rode behind him to cut him off from the cows, and tied onto him at a run.

Big Red weighed thirteen hundred pounds. The steer was not any lighter. Sorrells tried to pull up on the smooth, hard road. The steer was fresh. He started towing Big Red. He towed Big Red off the road, into a wash, up a bank, and onto loamy ground covered with sagebrush. Sorrells spurred his horse so he could get some slack and the horse could get his feet under him. He set the horse down again in the soft ground. He pitched the slack at the big steer and Big Red planted a sliding V with his hind legs. The steer ducked behind a tree. The nylon stretched and Sorrells had time to wonder what was going to give first of breakable horn, horse, rope, or saddletree. The end of the rope popped at the base of the steer's horns as though a puff of gunpowder had gone off there. The end cracked and whistled and whipped around the tree and a spray of fine fragments of the factory-built nylon stopped and hovered in the sunshine. The steer raced on. Sorrells coiled his rope on the run and saw that his hondo knot had broken out.

Wilson and Rabbit rattled by on the road after the steer. Sorrells reined Big Red onto the road behind Wilson while he was tying another hondo on the run. Wilson reined Rabbit off the road, fell in behind the steer, and threw his loop. The steer lost his balance and slowed when Wilson's rope jerked the horn and snapped off. Sorrells relayed Wilson, caught the steer around both horns, pitched him his slack and jerked him to a stop. Wilson heeled him down and Sorrells crossed a front leg and hind leg on the same side and tied them together. He rolled the steer over so the tied legs would be under him and he couldn't get up. The big legs were like corner posts on a fence. The steer was fat and clean. They left him there when two cows and heifers ran by them on the road.

The heifers were mavericks and one of the cows was a maverick. Wilson was ready first. He aimed Rabbit at a heifer and she headed into the sagebrush and piñon beside the road. Rabbit was rating her well and Wilson was standing to throw when the heifer went into a wash no one had seen. Rabbit stood on his head and somersaulted into the wash spilling Wilson ahead of him. Wilson was back on his feet holding Rabbit the instant he stopped sliding. Sorrells' laugh turned into an exultant squall as he rode by Wilson. Wilson and Rabbit both turned faces half white with dust on him. Sorrells caught and tied the heifer. Wilson relayed him and caught the other heifer. Sorrells mounted to go after the maverick cow. He noticed Wilson was sitting his horse waiting for Sorrells to heel the heifer. Sorrells heeled her and looked at Wilson. Wilson sat Rabbit without paying any particular attention to his daytime duties.

"Anybody home?" Sorrells asked Wilson, smiling.

"I guess so," Wilson answered good-naturedly. His teeth looked yellow behind the white dust. Small blood spots were turning the dust black on the side of his face.

"You, as the feller says, kissed your mother earth," Sorrells said. "I was glad to see you scoot clear. Old Rabbit went down awful sudden. I didn't see that wash either. All three of you just went clear out of sight. I almost ran over you."

Wilson got off his horse. He wobbled on his feet as he tied the heifer. He loosened his cinches and reset his saddle. He was bareheaded. His shoulder length hair stuck out all over his head. Sorrells watched him a moment.

"I'll tell you, Wilson. You better find your hat in this sagebrush before you go any farther away. If you'll go back and get your truck, I'll go after that other maverick cow. You can come on down to me and we'll load her and come back up loading the rest of the cattle as we come. Maybe you can find

out what happened to our partners." Sorrells didn't wait for
an answer. He turned Big Red and loped away.

Wilson looked up at the dry sky. It would probably stay
dry and run those high, thin clouds fast now for a while, he
thought. What did he care what happened to their partners?
He and Bert did it all anyway. He would go get the truck and
drive it down to where Bert would have the last cow tied. He
didn't care what kind of a storm them white men were in. He
was going after Bert. That damn Bert! He'd tie on to anything
big and pitch him his slack. He just pitched them his slack
and set 'er down as though to see if everything was going to
fall apart before his eyes. He didn't give a shit about anything. It made Wilson feel good when he could ride onto Bert
and help when Bert was in the middle of one of those
hurricanes he was always diving into.

Wilson looked at the sky again when he had found his
hat and was riding up the canyon. His hat didn't fit down on
his head like it ought to. Maybe he'd flattened that side of his
head or ground it down when Rabbit turned over. No, that
side felt bigger standing out there. A promontory was the
word for it, the proper word. Word the white man used in
the art class in prison for the overhang on the cliff face over
the valley Wilson had been painting. Up there in my dry sky
over the land on which I was born goes the flying hot wire,
my word for airplane. What the hell has that white hot metal
got to do with a bird? Big Bird, my ass. Wilson laughed in his
heart, no sign of it on his face. Big Silver Eagle. He smiled.
Don't they know an eagle smells like a lion or a dog that's
been rolling in the rotting hide of a carcass? They don't know
what being a real eagle is. They never knew a real Indian
who smelled good to them, so why do they think a real eagle
is so fine?

They will stay here until I am old like my father. I like
the play of this cowboying here now because it has been fun
since Bert came. I would like to paint a picture of him tied to
that big steer. Maybe I should tell him about how I learned to
paint in prison. He would know if it was right to paint
pictures. He would tell me to do it. He is like my father. He

likes what is good and leaves what is bad alone. What Bert has of the white man must be good because I like him.

The high, fast clouds in the dry sky reminded Wilson the time had passed for his appointment. Sheriff Bowman would be hunting him up and asking him to explain why he'd missed reporting on his parole. Porter and Stacy would find out he'd been in prison. Porter probably already knew it. Seeing the sheriff would remind Porter and get him to talking, talking, talking. How that white man talks, never says anything right out, but he accuses. Other Indians see me and stare away, away, away like I still took scalps. That would be all right, taking scalps. I know some Indian scalps I'd take first. They know who they are, too. Bowman would never take me this time. I'd be *gone*.

I could tell Bert if I wanted to. He'd just laugh because he don't give a shit. He has fun because he don't *care*. He just pitches them his slack.

Sheriff Bowman's Holstein-colored car was leaving headquarters when the stock truck got back there that evening. Cunningham stood by while the crew unsaddled. He laughed with the men when Sorrells told about Wilson's kissing mother earth. Cunningham was pleased with the remnant the crew had gathered. When all the feeding was done and the men had started toward the bunkhouse, Cunningham asked Sorrells to accompany him to his house.

The two men used Cunningham's bootjack to pull off their boots inside the kitchen door so not to track manure on Maudy's kitchen floor.

"Are you going to stay on the Outfit, Bert?" Cunningham asked when they sat down at the kitchen table with hot coffee.

"Sure," Sorrells said, watching Cunningham. "As long as my duties stay as they are."

"We're going to work this ranch differently next year, and I want to know if I can count on your help."

"Well, I don't know about next year. I do know I'll stay if you mean for tomorrow's work."

"I want to know if you'll stay on as cow boss."

"What the hell is a cow boss?"

"You know what a cow boss is, Bert."

"No, I don't know what a cow boss is."

"In Nevada the cow boss runs the cowboys and all the cow work. He's foreman of the cow work."

"Would that mean he'd be an executive?" Sorrells laughed.

"Don't be funny. Next year I want to run two crews and see if we can't gather all the cattle in thirty days. I'm too damn busy with the other work we're doing to worry about the cow work."

"Does that mean I'll have to be human? Will I have some real responsibility?"

"Well, yes. You'll be responsible for the weighing condition of the cattle, the calf crop, the replacement cattle, everything."

"Don't count on me, Roy."

"Why not? You're the best hand I know, and you know how to work a crew."

"If I had to give up being a don't-give-a-damn cowboy, smiling and always happy, I'd have to become a servant and give good service to become a boss. If I got that domestic I would probably get smart and need more money just like any boss does. Dobie will take the job. He knows the ranch better. His eyes ain't too good and he will only see what Bobby wants him to. He wants to stay with the Outfit."

"I don't want Dobie for the job. He gripes too much. He's always seeing the wrong side of everything. He's too negative, too old, and just goddam drives me crazy."

"Wilson is really the man for the job. He's better than me or Dobie, either one. Besides that he was born here and he belongs here."

"Wilson's got a prison record. He's on parole to Sheriff Bowman."

"What did he do?"

"Bowman was here today to see how he was doing. Wilson was eight days overdue reporting to him."

"Hee, hee, hee." Sorrells laughed. "What did Wilson do to them?"

Cunningham smiled. "He took a rifle, a case of beer, and a fifth of whiskey to that cliff above Silver Hill and kept the whole town indoors for twelve hours."

"How'd they stop him?" Sorrells laughed.

"Bowman waited until he was sure Wilson had drunk all the booze he had bought in Silver Hill that day and then got the drop on him after dark."

"That shouldn't be any reason for locking a feller up. I bet he could have shot somebody if he wanted to."

"He's lucky to be free. Bowman stood up for him and he behaved in prison or he would have been an old man before he got out."

"I admire that not one person in Keno has ever let on to me that Wilson did anything like that. Not once has anyone run him down to me."

"Bowman says he's bad when he gets painted up with whiskey. Everybody in the country wants Wilson to stay out of trouble because of how bad he is when he wants trouble. People are afraid of him. He hates all humans when he's drunk, especially white men."

"If Bowman is on his side, he'll be all right. Wilson is a man. He ought to be cow boss of this outfit."

"You recommend him, Bert?"

"Hell, yes."

Sorrells got up and left after that. Maudy didn't ask him for supper. Sorrells didn't know why she wasn't so good to him anymore since he was hired help. He didn't mind. The cook would have a fine supper ready for him.

Walking by the corrals in the dark Sorrells surprised the big renegade he and Wilson had caught that day. Wilson had shut him up on the scale. The scale had a cage over it and the steer couldn't jump out. He looked through the steel pipe away from Sorrells. The man looked away from the steer, too. The steer would be butchered for the crew.

Chapter 19

HIGH LONESOME

*A man who has been working hard and driving himself with
no thought of self-preservation will sometimes feel like freeing
himself of the leases and holds anyone else has on him and
driving himself to distraction. This is known among cowboys
as going on a high lonesome.*

Wilson Burns drove to Keno
the evening after Sheriff Bowman had been to the Outfit
checking on him. He stopped at the courthouse and the
deputy told him Sheriff Bowman had gone to Reno. He
stopped at the laundromat and put a load of clothes in
the washer. While he was waiting for the machine to wash his
clothes, he took out his tally book and began sketching his
memory of Bert Sorrells being towed by the big steer. The
laundromat was on one of the few side streets in Keno.
The street was not lighted. A cold wind off the mine-gutted
hills around the town was funneled through the street. It
blew a fine debris of trash and broken leaves through the
open door and brushed it around Wilson's boots.

Wilson was alone in the room with suds-smeared machines. The room was unheated and the door would not stay
closed. Wilson tried to close it once, but it rattled awhile and
the next hard gust of wind blew it open. Wilson sketched by

the light of one small bulb in the ceiling. He had no place to sit, so he rested the tally book on the warm top of the working washer while he sketched. He forgot about being cold and beholden to the Sheriff as the outline of a big steer took form on his page. He looked at the smooth point of his pencil and reached into his pocket for his knife to sharpen it. His friend, Ernest, another Paiute, came in from the street.

"Hey, Brudder," Ernest said. Ernest had his hands in the tight pockets of a pair of bell bottoms two sizes too small for him. Four inches of his dry, thin wrists showed between the pants pockets and a light shirt that had no pockets. The shirt was open four buttons from the collar and Ernest had no undershirt. His chest showed thin and pinched between his shivering arms. His hair hung straight from the natural part at the top of his head and was cut in a straight bang over his eyes. He wore a runover, misshapen pair of sharp-toed Italian pumps.

"Hey, Ernest," Wilson smiled, putting away the tally book.

"I seen your pickup outside, Brudder," Ernest said. "What you been doing, man? You still working?"

"Yeah, Ernest."

"I'm going work soon for the Forest," Ernest announced, shivering and leaning an arm against the warm washer.

"What doin', Brudder?" Wilson leaned on the other side of the window of the machine.

"Sharpen tools. I'm goin' to make all the tools sharp for the next fire season. All the fire tools dull now."

"Good job for you."

"You goin' stay at that Outfit?"

Wilson laughed. 'Might quit," he replied good-naturedly, lapsing into the laconic grunting Ernest used. "Too much work." Both Indians laughed softly.

Ernest composed his face. "Too much pay for you, Wilson," he said and bent down against the quiet laughter in his belly muscles.

"I must pay too much . . . income tax," Wilson said to keep Ernest laughing. They laughed gently for a time, not looking at one another.

When they had subsided, Ernest thought of something

more to laugh at. "I might take your job, Wilson," he said, and set them to laughing comfortably again. "They might make me boss soon if I go to work at Ethel. Maybe I better tell Forest I might not work for them."

The two men stood quietly content, each looking at his own feet and musing with satisfaction over their encounter in this forlorn place.

"*Indians* too dumb, Ernest," Wilson smiled. "Maybe after I quit I study to be medicine man. Bring back Ghost Dance. Scare hell out of white man again." He affected a mighty, faraway, noble savage look over Ernest's head. This made Ernest laugh very hard. The laughter tortured him. He knew Wilson was good at scaring white men. While Ernest laughed, Wilson took his clothes out of the washer and put them in the drier. When he put a quarter in the drier, the sight of the coin in his hand sobered Ernest. Ernest spread both arms over the washer and hugged its warmth. Wilson went outside to his trunk, got his saddle blankets, and put them in the washer. He poured detergent over them and set the machine to going with another quarter.

"You washing your blankets now?" Ernest asked. Wilson looked at Ernest and saw that his friend had been hoping Wilson was almost through with his chore, but the blankets were going to delay him unendurably.

"Yes, I might need them to cover my ass after I quit the Outfit," Wilson said, laughing.

Ernest acted tickled by this joke but he did not laugh long. He was cold and wanted to be moving. "Brudder, I watch your laundry if you got important business right now," he said. He took his arms off the washer and put his hands back into his pockets. A wind banged the door and blew trash by him. He looked through the door miserably.

"No, I don't have no other business," Wilson said.

"I thought we'd get some muscatel. Have a party."

"No. Don't like that wine. What's the matter you, Ernest? That wine make you crazy."

"Gets me warm. I want to borrow a dollar, Wilson. I pay you back first payday from the Forest."

Wilson took a dollar from his billfold and gave it to Ernest. "O.K., Ernest," he said.

"You want some?"

"O.K. Bring me a pint of Old Crow whiskey. I been liking that Old Crow now." Wilson handed Ernest a five-dollar bill.

"I use your truck, Brudder. I'm cold," Ernest said, and started out the door. He turned. "You got the keys?"

"They're in it," Wilson said. Ernest hurried to the truck, started it, ground the gears, and lurched away from the cold, quiet street. Wilson got out his tally book and worked on his picture.

Ernest had not returned when Wilson's laundry and blankets were dry and carefully folded. Wilson did not want to sketch more in the weak light. He wrapped the clean-smelling garments in his blankets and walked to the main street. He did not see his truck by any of the bars or the drugstore that sold liquor. He walked to the small house outside of town where his father and mother lived. Their truck was not there. His black dog, Scout, did not meet him. Wilson figured they must be out at the half section ranch he and his father owned in the mountains.

Wilson went into the house, built a fire in the stove, and worked late rebuilding Sorrells' Mexican saddle. A strong glue was drying the pieces of the horn together when he remembered the whiskey. He washed his face and hands, combed his hair, put on a clean shirt from his laundry, and walked back to town. He went to the All Hang Out, a bar on the unlighted end of the main street. The All Hang Out was lighted inside by the neon beer and whiskey advertisements behind the bar. All who hung out there were not there. Wilson looked at a glowing clock for a whiskey ad and it was two o'clock in the morning. The bartender was filling the beer chest. He looked up, recognized Wilson, and looked him over closely to see if he was drunk. His expression did not change. He greeted Wilson and did not smile.

"What's yours, Wilson? I'm closing up," he said and placed his hands flat on the bar before him. He did not look at Wilson again.

"A glass of beer and a shot," Wilson said. The bartender brought the order, stepped down the bar two paces from Wilson, and placed his hands on the bar again. He gazed across the room. Wilson got his billfold and took out a ten-dollar bill.

"A quart of Old Crow," he said, looking down at the bill. He had not once looked at the bartender. The bartender kept the across the room focus to his gaze, picked the bottle from a shelf, put it in a sack, twisted the sack around the neck of the bottle, and set it on the bar in front of Wilson. Wilson paid, drank his shot and beer, counted his change with care, took his bottle by the neck in a careful grip, stepped down from the stool, put his change in his pocket, and left the bar. The bartender, safely alone again, sighed with relief. He decided he was too tired now to finish loading the beer chest and went to the door. He watched Wilson walk heavily, like a bear, down the street. He closed and locked the door quickly when he felt Wilson might turn back and look him in the eye.

In his father's rooms Wilson opened his trunk and took out the fine desk lamp and sketch pad and pencils he kept there. He unwrapped the heavy clean flannel cloth from about the lamp. He placed the kitchen table near the wall socket, plugged in the lamp, and switched it on. He opened the pad and placed it under the lamp. He opened the whiskey bottle and set it by the pad. He sharpened his pencils, got a glass, and sat down at the table. He took out his tally book and began drawing Bert Sorrells' steer again on the sketch pad.

Later, drinking whiskey, he became dissatisfied with the steer. He felt a need to draw his country the way he would like to see it. He wanted to see buffalo. He drew one big bull standing defiantly looking at Wilson from atop a knoll. He drew a herd of buffalo in a draw behind the knoll. In the sky he drew the man Wovoka, the Paiute prophet, known as Jack Wilson to the whites and for whom Wilson Burns was named. Wovoka brought the Ghost Dance to tribes of the plains and the Southwest. Many tribes had believed the Ghost Dance would bring back the buffalo, bring back all dead warriors to make the white man disappear. Wilson drew the basin track of the Ghost dancers with the dancers moving serenely around the buffalo herd. Below the hooves of the bull, he drew the figure of Bobby Lang, tiny, hurrying toward his fragile silver airplane, both hands laden with heavy valises.

The sun was up and the whiskey was gone when the drawing was finished. Wilson turned off his lamp and went to his father's robes to sleep.

He awoke in late afternoon and washed himself. He went back to his drawing and straightened the uneasy lines he had made in Wovoka's face under the influence of the whiskey. He decided to paint the picture. He knew a man in Keno who had the canvas he would need. He hurried out of the house. The man might be at the hotel playing keno.

In the street he remembered Ernest had not returned his pickup. He would need the truck to go to the man's house after the canvas. He walked past the hotel searching for the truck. He walked to the edge of town and saw his truck a half mile away at Wanda's Rabbit Hutch. He walked to Wanda's. He hoped the keys were in the truck so he would not have to go into the whorehouse. They were not in the truck.

Ernest was sitting up straight at the end of the bar with Louis Grady, Wilson's ex-wife's new stud. Louis had been living with the woman since Wilson had left her. Wilson had not divorced her. He had gone away from her.

Louis Grady was a worthless Indian in Wilson's opinion. He sat by Ernest whirling Wilson's keys on top of the bar with his forefinger. He wore an Indian hat of imitation felt with a high, creaseless crown, straight brim, a dyed feather stuck in the band. Two imitation braids of hair hung down his neck from the hat.

"Hey, Brudder," Ernest said. He tried a friendly grin. He was not too drunk to show he was afraid to see Wilson.

"I come for my keys, friend," Wilson said.

"Hey, no, man," Ernest said. "I was just goin' take your truck to you. You didn't need to come out here. You walk?"

Grady twirled the keys on their chain in front of his face. "These the keys you want?" he asked.

"Yes," Wilson said.

"Man, you want to leave us here without no wheels?" Grady was mocking Wilson.

"Come on, Brudder, have a drink on me," Ernest said.

"I ain't got time," Wilson said.

"Wilson gots no time for us Indians," Grady said. "Wilson goin' go out and make money today too. You keep on making that money Wilson. Your family *need* it. Your *wife* need it. Your *kid* need it."

"You need a sock in the mouth, Louis," Wilson said.

"Maybe not, Brudder. Not by you, anyway, unless you miss that penitentiary place so you want to go back. Don't go to that place again, Wilson. You family need you too much."

"You ought to try supporting yourself for a change, Louis," Wilson said.

"Don't need to. I'n 'merican Innian, man. Not many of us real Innians left. You oughtta try bein' Innian, Wilson, 'stead of all around handy man for rich Hollywood whites."

Wilson started around Ernest toward Grady. Ernest put his arm around Wilson's waist. Grady slid the keys down the bar past Ernest. "There your keys, man," he said. He pointed to the door with his chin. "Go on."

"Have a drink, Brudder. I buy it," Ernest said.

"Wilson!" someone said from the door. Wilson turned and saw Sheriff Bowman standing there. The sheriff crooked his finger and Wilson started walking reluctantly toward him.

"Go to White Daddy, fat papoose," Grady said.

"Wilson!" Sheriff Bowman said, deterring him again. Wilson walked up to the sheriff. "What the darn heck are you doing in here?" Bowman asked him. "I thought you knew better than to hang around a place like this, the trouble you're in."

"I was just leaving," Wilson said.

"By darn, you're right, you're leaving. Go and get in my car."

"I've got my own wheels."

"Don't argue with me. I see your darn truck. You didn't even bother to hide it. You're not driving it anymore today. Get in my car." Wilson walked past him and went out the door.

Ernest held the truck keys up for Bowman to see.

"Take that truck to old man Burns' house, Ernest, and don't wait around here another minute or I'll get you for drunk driving," Bowman said. Ernest nodded sagely, as though he too had been taught a lesson. He walked to the window and watched Bowman drive away with Wilson. He turned and pitched the keys to Grady. "Two more beers," he said gaily to the girl behind the bar. He held up two fingers so the girl would understand Indian talk.

"Fo' da *road*," said Grady. "Wilson's buying." He smiled at Ernest and laid a five-dollar bill on the bar. Ernest doubled with laughter.

Sheriff Bowman drove out on the highway away from Keno. He got on the radio and talked briefly to the dispatcher. He drove on slowly.

"When was the last time you saw your wife and son, Wilson?" he finally asked.

"What wife? What son?" Wilson smiled.

"Willie, that's who. Willie's your wife, remember? The mother of your son?"

"Why ask me? Ask any other Indian around here. Ask Louis Grady. He pimps for her. Ask half the white men in this town. Ask your own deputy."

"Bull! She's the best little Indian gal in this country. She's a real princess. She came to see me the other day. She brought the boy. He's a fine boy."

"Where did you see her?"

"At my office."

"Ask your deputy why she was there. I didn't send her."

"My deputy my eye! She said she didn't have any money this month. I don't mind you not reporting to me when you're working on the Outfit but Willie needs her check on time."

"I sent the check the day I got it and I reported to your deputy yesterday."

"My deputy said you were there. You got smart with him. Why the heck do you have to make trouble with him?"

"With your deputy? I didn't know I had any trouble with him. Ask him why he's got trouble. I don't know why."

Bowman turned the car around and headed back to Keno. He rubbed his eyes tiredly. Wilson looked down at the toes of his boots. He was thinking he was wasting a lot of time in his life. Now he was riding around in a cop car for nothing. He was never going to be able to finish anything, not his Ghost Dance painting, not his marriage, not any friendship with any man he knew.

"Well, I'm telling you something right now, Wilson

Burns," Bowman said, accelerating the car. "You've had it with me. If you step out of line one more time or neglect that little family of yours again, you are going back to School for the full term. I won't stand one more complaint about you. There are too many good people in this country who want to see you back in the pen and they might just be right."

Neither man spoke again until Bowman stopped in front of the house Wilson had shared with Willie.

"You get out and go in there and try to do right for a change," Bowman said. He reached across Wilson's lap and opened the door. Wilson got out and shut it.

"Wilson?" Bowman said kindly.

"Yes?"

"Let's have some good reports about Wilson and Willie from now on."

"Wilson and Willie who?" Wilson said as Bowman drove away.

He went to the door. He didn't have his key but the door was ajar. He went in. A dirty diaper dried stiff lay in a corner inside the door. Mussed clothes were lying beside empty bottles and beer cans in the front room.

"Willie," he called. He walked through the house to the kitchen. Willie was sitting at the kitchen table in her slip, her long hair in her eyes, her fat feet dirty on rubber thongs. Her bare thighs, crossed under the table, looked leathery.

"What do you want?" she said, moving hair aside and peering at him.

"I wish Bowman could see his Indian princess now," Wilson laughed.

"This is my private home. Who asked you to come in?"

"It don't seem hard for anybody to get in."

"*Shat*, can't I have any privacy? Haven't you learned any manners at all? What the hell do you want?"

"I'm reporting, Willie. I got orders to report to you."

"Well, it's about *shat* time you came around to see about us. Another day and me and that kid will be in the street begging."

"What for? Beer? Wine?"

"*Shat*. You smart guy. Give me some money and get out if you so smart."

"No. No more money."

"*Shat*. What you good for then, you bastard fart. What you want here, anyway?"

The child cried. Wilson found him on a pallet on the floor of the bedroom. The room was cold and the child was naked and uncovered. Wilson picked him up and he was icy small in his hands. His voice was thin. Wilson rubbed him until he squalled warmly and then wrapped him in a flannel sheet. A new Polaroid camera lay teetering on the edge of the dresser, the cover hanging over the edge, a roll of film exposed beside it. Wilson closed the cover so the camera wouldn't fall. He carried the child back to the kitchen. Willie was pouring beer from a half quart can into a glass, her little finger crooked elegantly and out of line with every other line of her slumping body. She poured the beer slowly and then lifted the can to make a nice head in the glass, set the can down, lifted the glass and inspected it, turning it indolently before her eyes. She pursed her lips and sipped through the foam.

"Why don't you offer us a drink? That's good manners ain't it? I don't know, though. You're the manners expert."

"*Sssssshhhhh . . . at!*" the woman said, without spirit.

Wilson looked in the icebox, found a can of evaporated milk, found a bottle, rinsed it with hot water, filled it with milk and water and set it in a pan of water on the stove. He found a nipple and lid and dropped them into the pan beside the bottle. He sat across the table from the woman. The child squalled past his little gums toward Wilson's face. The smallest calf born in Dupont Canyon was doing better than this little man.

"What did you do with the last check I sent you?" Wilson asked, bouncing the child gently.

"You call that money? *Shat!*" The woman pushed at the hair in her face disgustedly. "You don't know what money is. You don't know nothin'! What *do* you know? How much you think I can buy with a hundred and eighteen dollars?"

"You don't pay any rent. You've been taking in boarders, too."

"What do *you* know about anything?"

"I know you buy Polaroid cameras. Some outfit's been

dunning me every week for five weeks for that Polaroid you got in there. What do you do with a Polaroid?"

"I got uses for it. It don't work no more, neither. If you sent me some money I could get it fixed."

"Get the deputy to fix it."

The woman, alarmed, brushed her hair aside in earnest this time so she could look at Wilson. "You accusin' me of somethin'?"

"Why would I do that? *I* don't know nothin', do I? Why would I accuse you about the sheriff's deputy?"

"That man been nice to me. You let him alone. He ain't no cowboy. He's a gentleman."

Wilson got up from the table. The woman flinched when he moved a hand to the child's face as he walked by her. He went to the stove to get the bottle. The water in the pan was boiling. He put the nipple on the bottle and tested the milk. It was too hot. He ran cold water on the bottle to cool it as the woman replenished the beer in her glass. Wilson took the bottle and sat down again. He set the bottle on the table, still too hot.

"What'er you going to do with this child?" Wilson asked.

"What do you think? I'n his mother, ain't I?"

"You going to raise him to walk proud?"

"*Shat!*"

"Which one of your boarders going to be his daddy?"

"*Shat!*"

Wilson tested the milk again. Still too hot. "I'll be his daddy. He's got my name." He looked down to lick the milk off his wrist.

"You? *Hoo, hoo, hoo,*" the woman scoffed. "How *you* raise him? Like some old cow. What he suck? Some old shatty cow."

"My mother cares for him. It ain't his fault I don't know who he is."

"You not his daddy. Don't you know nothin'? He don't want you."

"I'm more his daddy than you his mother, and my mother wants him."

"Some buck Innian's his daddy, but not you," the woman laughed. Wilson tested the bottle again and gave it to the child, shutting off his squalls.

Chapter 20

JUST ONE

Cowboys will tie onto anything as long as it is robust. They will tie onto Satan to see if they can hold him long enough to fairground him and bust him down and break an egg in him. They will rope Doctor Timothy Leary, given the chance, and tie a cowhide to his tail to see if he will go out and have a runaway. Let any man, beast, or idea present a daring target to a cowboy, and he will spread his loop with strangulation and fun on his mind, as long as he is not already beholden to the man, the beast, or the idea.

Maudy's kitchen was warm and Sorrells welcomed his bones to it. He welcomed the sound of the stock truck going away in the early cold without him. He welcomed a cup of coffee and a cigarette at Maudy's table while he gave Cunningham the latest tally on the cattle. Sorrells studied his totals and leaned back in his chair.

"We've gathered over eight hundred cattle Famous Enterprises didn't even know they owned," Sorrells said.

"The front office isn't counting the mavericks and renegade steers on any tally but the bank book," Cunningham said.

"I hope you're getting credit for this roundup and they aren't on your ass for taking too long."

"How many more calves do you think you'll get?"

"We get a few every day."

"How many more big steers and mavericks?"

"How should I know? They kept hid a long time before I ever got here. I'll tell you when we have them tied down by a road somewhere."

"What can I tell the front office?"

"Don't tell 'em nothin'."

"I've got to tell them what they can expect in return for the wages the crew gets paid."

"Tell them they can expect a bad winter, a 10 per cent death loss, a poor calf crop, no profit this year, and broke cowpunchers."

"Bobby Lang told me this outfit never has had more than a 1 per cent death loss."

"Bobby Lang is full of crap. *Good* ranches expect at least six. Cattle on irrigated pasture get six. Is he running a fever?"

"That's what I told him. He says he knows better."

"All feverish farts knows better. Excuse me, Maudy. Which reminds me. Speaking of Bobby Lang. You didn't count the leppies we gathered in your last tally. How many of those did we gather? What does he plan to do with his leppies?"

"Sixty-one head of leppies," Cunningham said. "He said he didn't know what to do with them because this ranch never had any leppies before."

"What happened was they didn't know a leppie when they saw one, they didn't take them off their mamas and they died. That's why they didn't have no leppies."

"There you are," Cunningham said thoughtfully. "When they think they know better than the man on the job it always costs them."

"Well, I'm going to cost them a new rope today. Have you got any of that good nylon left?"

"Damn, Bert. It hasn't been two weeks since I gave you a new rope, Bobby says I've spent more on rope in three months than the Outfit ever spent in the three years Lang has owned it."

"Well, I need a new rope. My rope is about to break in two places and is so fuzzy it doesn't have any life. It's turning into a feather."

"How do you manage to break a nylon?"

"Loading renegades in the truck, that's how. Rub, rub, rub, that's how. Catching that strangle loop and not missing, that's how. Bringing in a hundred and fifty mavericks and big steers, not to mention the branded cattle the Outfit didn't know it owned, is how."

"This is at least the fifth new rope I've given you."

"I'm having so damn much fun I hope it costs you five more before we're through," Sorrells said. He went back to the office and cut forty feet of rope off a coil. He walked into the kitchen hefting the new rope and rolling the waxy hardtwist in his fingers. He didn't have time to soak a wear leather and lace it to the hondo. He was going to use his new rope that day. He tied his hondo knot, looped it on Maudy's broom, stood on the broom with his feet planted on both sides of the knot, squatted, wrapped the rope on his hips, and straightened his legs.

"Don't you break my broom, Bert Sorrells," Maudy said, alarmed.

"It won't break, Maudy," Sorrells said.

"*Crack,*" went the broom.

"Darn you, Bert Sorrells, you'd disfigure an anvil," Maudy said, dusting his dirty black hat with her dish towel.

"Maudy, you sure are pretty and no bigger'n a minute," Sorrells said.

"Oh! Out, out, out! Go back to your corral and break a fence post. I *knew* when you picked up that broom you were going to ruin something in my house."

Sorrells and Cunningham loaded Roller in the back of the new four-wheel-drive pickup and left headquarters. The crew was working near Dupont Canyon again that day. Cunningham took Sorrells to the top of Dupont Mountain and unloaded his horse. When Sorrells had wrapped the end of his new rope in a bight around the swells and horn of his saddle he said goodbye to Cunningham and started down the steps he knew Sunspot haunted.

Sunspot was alone sunning himself on the side of the hill on the edge of the third mesa on his mountain. He had been alone since the day several weeks ago when he had escaped the men in the draw after the hardshell had rushed close to him and frightened him, separating him from the cattle and the horsemen. He did not wish to leave his bed and grazing ground to seek the company of other cattle now. The rushing hardshells did not come to this side of the mountain. Sunspot knew the hardshells were used sometimes to contain the bovine and change his haunt. As long as he could stay away from them he knew he was safe. He had been contained by them before during times of great suffering to him.

Experience told Sunspot that yearning after his own kind could lure him to being shut inside the hardshell upon its pitching deck and then to corrals where horsemen poked him or cut him, burned him, or hugged him in metal. In the time of his life he had watched many of his fellows taken away in the hardshells.

Early this day he had smelled and heard the horsemen on the other side of the deep canyon. He had traced their foreign movements as they awakened the whole of the mountain on this side. The movements had hardly given enough sound to reach him but had been unmistakably the alarming sounds of searching horsemen. He had left his bedground and gone high to the sun on this hill earlier than usual. He could not hear the horsemen now, but an ozone of shouts, broken rock, and running animals still pervaded the whole side of the mountain, and he knew they had not yet gone away. The ozone made the sun not so bright or warm for him this morning.

He stood entirely still, nerves and muscles relaxed against his locked frame. His senses waited on all the sights, smells, and sounds on this side of the mountain. The only part of him not fully awake yet was the white spot on his side. The spot always numbed quickly on cold nights and warmed slowly in the morning. He stood with the spot broadly to the sun. When it warmed he would move to the colder, more broken, more hidden feeding places. He never moved of his own accord off his morning bed and warming ground until his spot had warmed.

Sunspot heard a hardshell when it grunted and whined at the top of the mountain. He heard the voices that always made him taste again the thick smoke of his own burning hide. He smelled his own blood as he had the time it had wrapped itself heavily around his bawling tongue. He could remember the pain of the pulling of the cords in him, the hot cords that had been sweet in him. He could remember it. He heard the equine hooves coming slowly off the malapais steps above him. Now the horseman must be on the second step in the grass, on the sod. Now he has stopped at the rim. He is searching my place with the eyes. He has not seen me. He is looking. He is looking at me now. Now he goes through the malapais again.

One of Sunspot's old legs started and jerked and one of its smallest functioning parts cracked like a tiny, dry stick. The sound of it reminded Sunspot to be careful as he moved away toward the steep shady side of the hill on the edge of the mesa. He stood in the shadow of some piñon while he listened to the horseman circle him. When he decided the horseman had come for him, he walked around the side of the hill until he was sure he was out of sight and then carefully slid down a ridge that separated two canyons. He had not once looked at the horseman to acknowledge his coming. Looking might make the horseman chase Sunspot. He dropped off the ridge, hit the bottom of the canyon running, and turned back up the canyon toward his bedground. He stopped in cold shadow at the end of the canyon where all the sides were steep. He listened and found the horseman on his tracks directly above him. He stood still and breathed carefully. When he heard the horseman coming down into the canyon, he climbed out.

Sunspot stopped to breathe and listen when he got back to his own tracks where he had started his descent into the canyon. This horseman was different than any that had come for him before. The others had usually come running at first sight and this first tight, circling maneuver of Sunspot's usually set them running on away. Many many times he had stood in plain view on the side of a hill like he was now and watched horsemen race away without knowing they were being watched by him from behind. He got rid of them that way without having to run.

This horseman was quiet and here he came up the

canyon. Sunspot had to look at him. He couldn't stand not looking anymore. He turned his big head downhill and looked on the top of the horseman. The horse saw him. The pair of eyes atop of the horse looked up and saw him. Sunspot jerked his eyes away quickly, too late to miss the dreaded meeting. The point of the loose, gotch horn over his eyes quivered and tapped him on his sore place. He moved on quickly, glided to the bluff off the mesa, dropped gradually along its sides into a canyon, loped on good footing along the bottom, climbed a narrow ridge out when the canyon became shallow, dropped into a deeper canyon, followed it down until he began to take long breaths, and then galloped across canyons and ridges to the first canyon he had entered. He stopped under a tree. He would rest and cool himself and wait here until he was sure the horseman had gone and then he would take this deepest, surest avenue back to his bedground. He was thirsty. He had not watered in two days. He could have waited another day and gone to water after dark, but now he would have to water tonight because he had been running. He had not reckoned on being disturbed again at this time of the year in his place.

Sunspot heard the horseman coming again. He took a few steps toward his bedground. He looked up in surprise to see the stiff front legs, the straining chest, the pulsing red nostrils of the horse come over the ridge above the canyon ahead of him, blocking him from his bedground. He stopped and watched the whole horse and man buck and scatter sand ahead of the front feet off the ridge into the canyon. He turned and ran straight down the canyon away from the horseman, away from the bedground, away, away, to change his winter range now, now today.

He reached and leaped until he had his great momentum coasting, his large feet supporting him surely, his enormous lungs devouring the air, the hurtling jar of his own bulk jogging his vision and deafening him, until he could not conceive any horseman could be in close pursuit of him. All downhill he ran headlong, and when he came to a wide, even path, his big feet pounded on reaching for more. Sunspot felt he could run on until snow fell again before he stopped this time.

Sunspot ran awhile longer before he decided not to run until it snowed. He looked up when he realized he should take stock of where he was and saw the horseman following close. He sprinted again and was surprised he did not gain his strong momentum. Sprinting was now an effort, with the horseman close behind looming taller and bigger and faster above him than he would have suspected. Being so aware of the horseman all of a sudden made him not so aware of the way he was going, and he ran through a filament, heavier than cobweb, more pliable than brush. He had noticed no brush in the wide, clean path he was taking. Whatever it was he had run through whipped around his neck, caught on his brisket, held strongly a moment, stretched, and popped free. Whatever it was checked Sunspot enough so that his balance fell behind his sprinting, and he skidded, plunged, drove into a claybank, fell, and rolled. He got up immediately. He did not know exactly in which direction to continue his flight. He stood a moment to catch his breath while he decided.

"Popped my hondo knot out. Damn, Maudy's cheap broom broke before I got it tight enough," was the form of the sounds that came from the horseman to Sunspot. Sunspot did not understand why the sound of the man, so much closer now than Sunspot would have chosen him to be, did not menace or frighten him. Sunspot stood a moment longer and took back all the breath he could.

"Ready?" was the horseman's sound this time, as the horse stepped toward Sunspot. "O.K.?" was the next, as Sunspot's eyes met the dreaded gaze, "Go, then," was the last, as Sunspot heaved around and ran again.

This time the filament was strong enough to hold him to the horseman. Sunspot was caught. He bucked and lunged until he choked himself to his knees and his tongue hung out to reach for breath. Sunspot did not bawl. He did not charge the horseman. He ran to overpower the shining filament that resembled and seemed no stronger than a slobber. Each time he ran against it he felt it stretch to breaking, but it always stretched on until he could go no more against it. Its strength did not daunt Sunspot. It stretched easily. He was sure, each time he tested it, that he would break it. It held each time only a little longer than he tested it. He could not

seem to get the correct run at it so that he could break away
and gather his momentum to him again.

Finally, after being jerked back against his own charging
length many times, he stood to catch the breath that had
become so hard to reach through the thin, tight collar that
held him. The horseman walked around his side and the
collar loosened. The sweet air rolled over Sunspot's tongue.
The horseman moved behind him and Sunspot felt the strong
filament hold above his hocks. The horseman came back
around in front of Sunspot, did not pause, but started behind
him again. Sunspot moved away to start again his downhill
flight. The filament was like a web around him. It was drawn
under his knees in front, pulling his front feet from under
him and making him kneel. It looped on his hind legs above
the hocks. It stretched and pulled against him as Sunspot
strained, too late, to stand. It pulled Sunspot's head back
toward his hind legs and he went down on his side. He lay
and gasped uncomfortably on his doubled bellies, his gorge
caught and held in his throat by the filament, as the man
detached himself from the horse and did something to Sunspot's hind legs. The man remounted and moved the horse
close to Sunspot and the filament relaxed and loosed his
head. When Sunspot tried to get up, he found he could not
move his hind legs. He fell over on his side, for a moment
stricken with hopelessness, his trussed legs trailing far behind
him, his eyes turned inside out. The man pushed his hind
legs under him, bent his front legs for him, and pushed him
over so that he was lying on them. Sunspot opened his eyes,
did not like what he saw, closed them, and rolled over on his
side again. The horseman went away. After awhile, when his
full bellies called for relief, Sunspot found a way to roll
himself back upon his legs. He stood, but when he tried to
walk, his hind legs refused him and he lay down again, this
time in a ditch upon his side. He was unable to rise again.
His legs were out of the ditch above him. He kicked helplessly.
He lay there in that bunched position, his heavy bellies
bearing down on him, so long that he knew he would soon be
dead with the warm sun on his side. He felt like lowing but
he did not. His white spot had warmed.

The sun had turned and was falling close to the horizon

when Sunspot heard the nearing sound of a hardshell. When it got so close that he could feel its weight shifting the ground, he began to low. He could not keep the utterance from his throat. When he was hauled from the ditch by his feet he stopped lowing. When he stood again, the relief of it made him dizzy. He saw other cattle through a narrow way, turned away from him, contained. He lowed again but they did not turn to him. He was pulled and choked, jerked and driven toward the other cattle. He trembled with weakness. He lay down. He was dragged and splinters of wood made him smell his own blood. He bawled and his tongue was trapped outside in dust when a filament tightened behind his jaws, popped his eyes, and cut off his breath. He gave one convulsive whip with his great head and spread his length upon the ground.

How would he escape? He had always managed escape. He would run on away inside himself and leave his inutile, captive carcass behind. He shuddered, an ecstatic shudder, a small movement he did not know he made, a move foreign to great fifteen-year-old steers, a movement identical to the first sign of life given by a calf in his mother's womb. The first, the last sure sign of life.

"He's dead. We've killed him," Bert Sorrells said, and what he hoped would happen, happened. His partners all looked away. Sorrells hurried and took all the ropes off Sunspot. "God damn it," he said. He shut the tailgate of the stock truck. The darkness was covering Sunspot now, but the white spot on his side was plain to see.

"You go on with the cattle, Stace. You guys can go with him, if you want to," Sorrells said to them. "I'll lead the horses down to the highway and meet you there when you come back for me."

When the truck was gone, Sorrells tied all the horses to a joshua and turned to Sunspot's carcass. He went to the sagebrush in which he had hidden the battery hotshot. If they had used the hotshot they surely would have killed Sunspot. A Sunspot cannot be prodded along by any man.

"Are you dead anyway, old Sunspot?" Sorrells asked. He was afraid to put his ear to the old steer's muzzle, afraid he was dead. His plan had been not to kill Sunspot. That is why he had hidden the hotshot from his partners.

"Wake up, Sunspot," Sorrells said and gave him a touch of the four batteries behind the twin prongs of the hotshot. Sunspot sent back the little shudder from the place where he had taken it inside himself. "Come back, Sunspot," Sorrells said. Sunspot bawled out half a breath and kicked and raised his head. "You damn Sunspot," Sorrells yelled in happiness, ready to bawl. "You broke my thumb." He gave the old steer the hotshot again in vengeance. Sunspot stood up. "Go and sin no more," Sorrells said and shocked him again. "Go, go, go," he said poking Sunspot's hams as he swayed up the road toward his bedground. "You're the one that got away."

Chapter 21

TURNING LOOSE
THE DALLIES

The cowboy term "dally" comes from the Mexican dale vuelta. *A cowboy's dallies are the wraps he takes on his saddlehorn with the end of his rope after he has snagged his loop on a fleeing bovine. A dallying cowboy is a busy man. He has no leisure time in which to contemplate his dallying. If his dallies go wrong for him a cowboy can lose a finger or even a hand between the dally and the saddlehorn. Because of this danger, a cowboy cannot be considered to be dallying in the ordinary sense of the word, as in dilly-dallying.*

The true dally hand uses a long rope and a smooth horn. The Mexican vaquero is a true dally hand because he works in country where stock is light and saddletrees are not as strong as tree stumps. His ropes are handmade rawhide or short-fibered maguey *and are easily broken by a sudden jerk. Horses are small. Cattle are raised a long way from market and must be handled carefully. A vaquero lets his rope run and burn on his saddlehorn so he will not jerk down his steer, bust his horse, break his saddletree, or snap his rope. Dallying is for small horses, cattle a man has to wait on, and men who have to be careful with their livestock to make a living.*

My thumb is busted, Bert Sorrells thought when Porter pulled the light cord in their room in the early morning. He sat up in his blankets and looked at it. It was dirty red and shiny, like a bloated goldfish, and would not wiggle. He put on his hat and swung his legs off the bed. He rolled a cigarette. He could roll a cigarette. He was going to have to watch that thumb or it was going to become a goddam travail. When he had dragged old Sunspot out of the ditch on Roller, the dallies on the slick horn of his saddle had slipped, and he had turned them loose to keep them from catching a finger, and the Turk's head on the end of the rope had come unwound like a buzzsaw and rapped Sorrells on the back of the thumb. The new rope he had cut had a neat Turk's head tied in the end since it was the first rope cut from a new spool. Sorrells blamed himself for not having sense enough to untie the knot and replace it with a soft braid. He prodded the thumb gingerly through his clothes. He did not enjoy the buttoning of the steel buttons on his Levis, tight over the extra thickness of his long johns. He began trying to forget he had a broken thumb.

"How's your thumb?" Porter asked him when he came back into the room, Porter *knew* Sorrells would be trying to forget it.

"Fat," Sorrells said.

"Huh," Porter said. He smiled with all his charm. "Sounded like a piece of meat under a cleaver on a butcher's block when that Turk's head found it, didn't it."

Sorrells didn't say nothing.

"I always did say them Turk's heads never fail to chop a feller sooner or later."

Sorrells kept quiet. His thumb was throbbing after buttoning his Levis.

"You know, I hated it when we killed the old runnygade," Porter said. "I guess we should of left him alone. Don't you think so, Bert? Here's the idee, them old things ain't merchantable no more and they're too tough to butcher by the time you worry 'em around and get 'em hot and mad. Get 'em in here and they won't eat or drink." He brushed both hands by one ear, turning his head the opposite way in total rejection of the idea of catching Sunspot and old steers like him unless, of course, Dobie Porter was the one doing the catching. "Then you get somebody like Stacy takes six thirty-

thirty bullets to stun him down when you go to butcher him. Hits him six times in the corral and only gives him a nosebleed. I'll tell you, Bert, it's just no use, now, to be trying to bring in them old steers. What we ought to do is bell 'em with a good leather strap around their necks and turn 'em aloose. That way they'll always lead us to cattle in them bad countries like that."

"We need straps and bells," Sorrells said. "That's what we need."

"I just happen to have one good strap and one good bell in my bag," Porter said. He pulled a canvas bag out from under his bed and dumped a conglomeration of gear out on the floor. He had old whiskey bottles purpled by the sun, ore samples, slashed off boot tops, broken whetstones, headstalls cracked with age, bent bridle bits, rowelless spurs. He handed Sorrells a piece of ore with an assay report attached to it by a rubber band. "Now, there is a good piece of mercury ore," he said. He unwrapped the rubber band and handed the report to Sorrells. "Look there," he said. Sorrells stared at the paper dumbly. "You and me ought to take some time off next spring and go and work that claim. Mercury's getting scarce. In ten more years the world won't have no more mercury. That claim you're holding in your hand might just have all the mercury in the world."

Porter held up a wide leather strap and a bell with the clapper muffled by burlap. "Here you are," he said.

"You got any more of them?" Sorrells asked him.

"What we need any more for?"

"Suppose we catch more than one big steer, say in Last Chance, or on Black Mountain, or over on Montezuma, or Gold Mountain, or McGrath, or Shannon, or Horse Corral. If we bell one, we ought to bell them all, oughtn't we?" Sorrells demanded of the old man, and, out of patience early in the day, felt his eyes focus quickly in anger.

"We'll get more bells," Porter said, looking down and away.

"Hell, it's like pulling teeth to get new rope on this outfit. How you going to get them to buy you bells and collars?"

Porter began stuffing his gear back into his warbag. "I

just thought it was a good idee," he said, not looking up. Sorrells watched him a moment, was ashamed for being cranky, and got down and helped him gather his accumulations. "Let's take that bell and strap it on the next old outlaw we see. We'll not say anything about it to anybody and see what happens," Sorrells said. "You've got a good idea, Dobie."

"That's what I mean," Porter said, straightening up and letting Sorrells finish the chore with his sore thumb. "We don't have to broadcast what we're doing. We'll just do it." He went in to breakfast.

Sorrells pushed Porter's warbag into the dust under his bed and went to the breakfast table. He said good morning and sat down and poured himself a cup of coffee. He was thinking, if Porter's idea of belling the old steers was outdated, it made Porter extinct. It made Porter useless around a ranch. If Sorrells liked an idea he was sure the front office would laugh at, then Sorrells was becoming extinct. Sorrells refused to believe Porter would ever be unable to help a ranch produce livestock. He had seen old fellows help run a ranch who were like old, belled outlaws, hardly able to get around, griping, hard to get along with, impossible to advise, too old to believe, too broken, dirty, and profane to have any apparent physical or moral value, absolutely ignorant of any formal or mechanical knowledge and proud of it, but who made the company money until the day they left the outfit to die.

All of them left their outfits to die, probably because they knew their broken, dirty, and profane carcasses were not appreciated, partly because they wanted not to leave any mess around camp for somebody else to clean up, and partly because they, like old wolves, had shame and pride and didn't want their outfits to watch them die. They would rather pay a professional who makes a living watching folks die, as was proper.

"Want more coffee, Bert?" Porter asked him, grinning at him and holding up the pot.

"Sure," Sorrells said. Porter poured coffee for Sorrells and then poured for the other cups he could reach from his place at the head of the table. Porter always kept the coffee cups full. He didn't drink coffee, "Because of my old belly," he always said, but he liked to pour his poison into everyone else.

"I thought so," Porter said. "A feller always needs plenty of coffee on a cold morning before a big circle."

"I never could get along with any son of a bitch who could only drink one cup of coffee in the morning or one drink of whiskey on a Saturday night," Sorrells said to Porter.

"Say, you ought to soak that broke thumb in something before you go out in the cold," Porter said, grinning. "It's all swoll up. You'll be *cranky* before you get in tonight. You want more coffee, Stace? No? You want more, Wilson? No? You fellers all better have plenty of coffee in you. You'll wish you'd filled up when your horses start getting tired along about ten o'clock."

Sorrells was thinking today was Saturday and he was ready to go to town. He could get a room at the hotel in Keno and take a hot bath and watch the football and drink hot whiskey and sleep and rest his broken thumb. He could air out for today and tomorrow instead of grinding two half-hearted days' work out of himself. He would, by God, do nothing but rest and do his laundry for two days in town. He placed his half-full cup of coffee on the table. He had not yet started to eat.

"I'm going to town," he said, getting up from the table.

"What time you coming back? I thought we might work the Last Chance today," Porter said, knowing Sorrells would not want to miss working the Last Chance.

"Maybe I might see you all Monday morning."

"Roy said he was going to ride with us today. What do you want me to tell him?"

"Tell him I ain't coming," Sorrells said. He went to his room and packed his grip with everything he needed. He got his drinking hat and his drinking boots and headed back through the bunkhouse.

"Aren't you going to have some breakfast?" Charley the cook asked him, smiling. The whole crew was grinning at him. Not one of the men said anything to him. "Hell no," Sorrells growled, hurrying toward the door. He was fearing someone would think of a reason to hold him on the Outfit.

He wanted a high lonesome. The door opened before he got to it and Cunningham cut him off.

"Where are you going? You quitting?" Cunningham asked him, looking at the grip, hat, and boots.

"Not quitting. Going to *town*. Going to civilization for a while," Sorrells said, starting around him.

Cunningham stepped out of his way. "Well, O.K.," he said. "But I was going to take you and Jack with me today."

"Give my regards to all the wild bovines in Last Chance, but tell 'em I ain't coming," Sorrells said. He began to regret he might miss Last Chance. He stopped at the door. "I'll see you all Monday," he said.

"Don't you want to go to Reno with me and Jack?" Cunningham asked.

"Reno?" Porter asked. "I thought we was working Last Chance today."

"No. I got a letter from the front office yesterday that said for me to go pick up some Red Angus bulls at Reno," Cunningham said, sitting down and looking over his shoulder at Sorrells. "I was going to take Bert and Jack. Why don't the rest of you take today and tomorrow off? We'll all start fresh on Monday."

Sorrells thought about two whole days riding the stock truck, no whiskey, no football, and waiting on a bunch of bulls. "Oh, no, not me. I'm going to Keno," he said and went out the door. Cunningham caught him trying to start Carlotta.

"You'd better come on and help me, Bert," Cunningham said, opening the car door. "I'll put us up in a nice motel and turn you loose in Reno tonight. Reno's a better town than Keno any night. I want to look at some saddle horses while we're there, too." Sorrells tried to start Carlotta one more time and gave up. He got out, put his grip on the platform over the cab of the stock truck, helped gas the truck, put on his good hat and boots, and got in the cab between Cunningham and Roberts.

Sorrells awoke from a nap while they were passing the hotel in Keno. "Right here. *Stop* this sonofabitch," he said. Cunningham smiled the little smile it hurt him to hold and stopped the truck in the middle of the street. Sorrells got out, took down his grip, and the truck was rolling before he stepped off the running board. He walked across the street to the hotel. The live business of the casino was balm to him as he went to the bar and ordered his whiskey. He was drinking it when Wilson walked up quietly and joined him.

"What you doing in town so early, Bert?" Wilson asked.

"I'm going on a *high lonesome*. Cunningham's on his way to Reno to get a bunch of Angus bulls. I bailed out here." Sorrells laughed. "I know that sonofabitch; he'll promise a feller a party and at party time he'll start yawning in your face. He could bring an eagle to ground by yawning at him."

"Is he going to bring back any horses?" Wilson asked.

"Horses? Who needs horses? Didn't you know the Outfit's going to get rid of horses and mount us on motorcycles?"

"Bert, I'm afoot. How do they expect us to finish the work on the horses we've got?"

"Say, Wilson, let's have a good time and let our horses rest today. What do you say about that?"

Wilson nodded his head but Sorrells knew he was stubborn about his horses. He was not smiling. Sorrells knew if he didn't divert Wilson, the Indian's only topic of conversation for the rest of the day was going to be horses. Wilson was not wearing his hat. His long hair was combed. He was not himself.

A man seated down the bar from Sorrells and Wilson had been watching them and listening and making little drunken, mocking faces and signs about them to a noncommittal bartender. He turned on his stool to stare at them.

"Hey, Chief! Chief!" he finally said.

Wilson turned to him. "Who, me?" he asked.

"I don't care. You or the other one is all the same to me. You want a drink? You guys have a drink with me. I wanna know where I can catch some wild horses around here. I like horses, you know? I wanna catch me a wild mustang horse."

"*I* don't know anything about wild horses. How would *I* know?" Wilson said. He was grunting when he talked.

"You guys are from around here, ain't ya?"

"Who me? Not me. I'm from California. Hollywood," Wilson said.

"Oh, well. You wouldn't know nothing about mustangs,

would you. How about your brother over there? I bet he knows where I can catch me a mustang."

"Not me," Sorrells said, holding up his empty glass and rattling the ice. "I'll have a crow and water, though."

"Now, wait a minute. Don't you guys put me on," the man said. He picked up a hat from the stool beside him and walked over and stood between Sorrells and Wilson with his arms over their shoulders. Sorrells saw he had his spurs on and remembered seeing him once before in this bar bragging to the tourists about what a great mustanger he was. The man put on his hat. It had a cow milker's crease and the brim was turned up in the back.

"We wouldn't put you on. You look like a real mustanger," Sorrells said. "You got on your spoors and your hat."

"Do you guys work around here?" Spurs asked.

"My brother told you, didn't he? We're from Hollywood. We're out of work at present. You know anybody hiring?"

"Not offhand. I've been looking for work myself," Spurs said.

"Only trouble is, I ain't got no spoors," Sorrells said. "You got to have spoors for work around here?"

"If you want a riding job you do. What kind of work do you do?"

"We're actors, only we forgot our spoors today," Sorrells said. "We didn't think the barstools pitched in here so we didn't bring our spoors."

"Say, you're a smart feller, ain't you? What makes you think you're smart? I offer to buy you a drink and you get smart with me." The man pulled Sorrells' and Wilson's shoulders together as though testing to see if he could handle them, maybe bring their heads together.

"I'm smart cause I'm skeerdy," Sorrells said. "I don't even wear my spoors in town cause I'm skeered I'll get them caught on somebody."

"Smart guy. I'm warning ya. I can handle any Hollywood Indians any day they think they can come in here and act smart. Now that I look at you, I don't think you are even a real Indian. He is, maybe, but you ain't."

"I don't wear moccasins, if that's what you mean," Sorrells said and stomped his boot heel down on the man's instep.

"Oh!" exclaimed Spurs, and Wilson took his head in a hammer lock and led him out the door. Sorrells picked up his change and walked over to the crap table. The pit boss walked up to him.

"You have trouble with Calico Dave?" the pit boss asked Sorrells.

"Is *that* who that was?" Sorrells said. "I thought that was Buck Fartino."

"Calico Dave is what he calls himself. What happened?"

"He hurt his foot. He started crying and my partner helped him out the door."

"Let's not have any more trouble," the pit boss said and handed Sorrells a red token, good for one free drink at the bar.

Sorrells watched the players. He felt lucky. When he got the dice he put a dollar on the line. He made three passes and ran it up to eight. He bet he would roll eleven and rolled it twice. He bet on boxcars and rolled a pair of them. He bet on eleven again and it turned up fifteen to one again. He bet his dollar once more on the line and lost it. He walked away from the crap table to the cashier and cashed in his chips. He went to claim his free drink at the bar with over eighty dollars in winnings in his Levis and Wilson wasn't even back from taking Calico Dave home. Sorrells was camping at the bar on the same stool when Wilson came back.

"The sonofagun only had three dollars on him," Wilson griped.

Sorrells laughed. "You didn't roll him did you, Wilson? Poor old counterfeit thing."

"No. He made me the loan of all he had. He only *had* three dollars. He apologized for not being able to loan me more. I meant to tell you, Bert. Your new saddle came in on the bus. It's in there at the hotel desk."

Sorrells had ordered a new saddle from Tom Ford, a cowboy from Vega, Texas, who was good at making saddles a cowpuncher could get some use from. Tom Ford was an old friend and partner of Sorrells. Every time Sorrells thought of Tom Ford during the work at the Outfit, it did Sorrells good.

Sorrells claimed his saddle from the baggage room. It was in a good burlap sack. He unsacked it and set it up on a slot machine so he and Wilson could look at it. "Lookee there at my beautiful new rig, Wilson," Sorrells said. The saddle was a three-quarter double rig on a low association tree. Sorrells looked at it for as long as he could stand to look and then he squalled and mounted it. He caught the stirrups and blew wild air through his head and spurred the slot machine from shoulder to flank. Wilson held the cantle down from behind and Sorrells squalled and spurred again. A big dealer from the casino came in and good-naturedly invited Sorrells and Wilson into the bar for a drink. When they had finished the drink, they tried to order another and were told they were eighty-sixed, meaning they could do no more business at the bar. Sorrells shouldered his saddle, thanked everyone, and he and Wilson walked out.

"Say, Wilson. You know where we'll be welcome?" Sorrells asked.

"Yeah," Wilson said. "At Wanda's."

"The Hutch," Sorrells said with glee. "Old Wanda wants to see our new saddle." They went to Wanda's in Wilson's pickup. Sorrells kicked the door open, saddled the bar with his new saddle and sailed his hat at Wanda who was standing behind the bar.

"Lock the doors. Hide the whores. Don't dare frown. We're under seige. We've lost the peace. The Outfit's come to town," Wanda bellowed.

In the morning, Sorrells went to work singing the dirtiest song he knew at the top of his voice. A red Angus bull was standing on top of a ten-foot manure pile in the horse pasture. The manure pile dominated the section of sagebrush horse pasture and the fat, young bull was acquainting himself with the sights, smells, and sounds of the Outfit. He had been tired and cold arriving on the Outfit and had spent an uncomfortable night on a pounded rocky bed in the corral surrounded by cold concrete and metal posts through which the cold wind had blown. He was yearning for his ration of warm mash.

Chapter 22

LITTLE BARNEY

"Caballo de pobre, pobre caballo"—*Poor man's horse, poor horse, is the Mexican saying. It is true a poor man's horse might not get much to eat, but the horse earns what he gets or the poor man would not keep him. On the other hand, a man can own thousands of dollars in horseflesh and hundreds of thousands in horsepower and still be afoot. Among horsemen this is sometimes known as being "horse poor."*

The cold light was fresh on Sorrells' face as he and Porter mounted their horses to rim new slopes of Silver Peak. The last drink of whiskey Sorrells had swallowed at Wanda's was beginning to profess its loneliness in his stomach, and he was glad to face his work and let his whiskeys howl. They would subside with a good day's work.

"We'll just rim around today," Porter said, and when the two horsemen crossed wild horse tracks he said, "Maybe we'll get a run at some horses today."

The country was grassy, smooth, and open. The two men stayed high, where they could see it well. They rode into the higher of two basins, which were separated by two hills with a low saddle between the hills. Sorrells looked through the saddle and saw a sorrel horse grazing on the far edge of the lower basin. He stopped Porter and told him about the horse. Porter rode to higher ground and saw a band of horses grazing under one of the hills. He rode slowly back to Sorrells and stopped.

"You take Big Red and wait on this side of the saddle," he said. "I'll go around the hill and make a run at them. Maybe they'll come to you." He rode away.

Sorrells rode to the saddle. He took off his hat and stopped Big Red by a tree. He stood in his stirrups until he could see over the edge of the saddle. He counted ten head of horses. They were about a half mile below him. The sorrel stood apart from the band. He was a stud, their sire. Sorrells took down his rope and wrapped a bight on the swells and horn of his saddle. His hondo leather had dried tight and hard while he was in Keno. He was riding his new saddle. The ground was soft and even here, for as far as a horse could run. He would never in his life be better prepared to catch a wild horse.

Porter came around the hill in sight beyond the band. He was riding slowly, his thick torso so short his capped head barely cleared his horse's ears. The band began to notice him. Each horse raised his head and turned toward Porter to watch him. He came on and they bunched closer together. He charged them and whooped and waved his rope. They ran toward the stud, away from Sorrells. They were going fast, with a long start Big Red would never overtake, but then, bad luck for them, the stud charged them viciously from his side. Ears back, head darting, teeth snapping, he herded the band toward Silver Peak and the brushy steep cover he knew would protect it. The way to Silver Peak was through the saddle where Sorrells waited. Sorrells watched them come directly at him. They were looking back at Porter. Porter was closing with them. Sorrells waited. When they came through the saddle he spurred Big Red in time with them and rode in among them. He was among them before the trailing half of the band topped the saddle. Most of the band did not know he had joined them. The horses that saw him seemed incapable of shying away from him. They were trapped by their instinct to stay together. Sorrells kept Big Red in the band, revelling in the run, loath to do his business for a while. He chose the horse he wanted, a blond bay yearling stud colt with no white on him, running on a flank in the front. The man pointed Big Red through the surf of horses, rated the colt on the edge, threw a strong and yawning loop, jerked his slack, and peeled the bucking, kicking colt out of step and off the edge of the band. He forgot about the band a moment while he watched his colt. The band was soon gone over a ridge of cedars.

The colt whipped on the end of the rope and, in a quick, wiry flip, was down. He was up at once and when he went to the end of the rope again, Sorrells spurred Big Red to him to keep from busting him again.

The little fellow began whinnying and looking for his mammy, but Sorrells didn't mind. Now was time he quit her anyway for business of his own. His business would have to be a man's work or someday, Sorrells was sure, some company man was going to decide these horses were costing the Outfit money and was going to come out here, rest himself on the hood of his pickup, and gather these horses with a rifle.

Porter rode close to the colt. The colt nickered and trotted up to Porter's horse. He saw that Porter's horse wasn't anyone he knew so he trotted toward Sorrells' horse. He knew the rope had an end to it now and he didn't run hard against it again. The little fellow had sense. His dark eye was afraid but did not show any white ring of meanness. Porter rode away and the colt followed him with Sorrells giving slack.

Sorrells drove the colt on the rope without leading and choking him. They tied him with piggin' strings to a joshua by a mining road and went on about their day's work. They had not cost the company an hour of its time.

Riding away from the joshua, Sorrells could not keep from looking back every once in a while. Finally the colt was all alone on the flat and so far away Sorrells could no longer distinguish him from the joshua. The colt had not whinnied since he had made sure his elders and partners had gone away from him. He had not tried to hurt the men when they had tied him to the joshua, though he had been very afraid of them.

"You've caught yourself a fine little horse," Porter said when he caught Sorrells looking back.

"I guess he'll be all right until we get back," Sorrells said. "He's tied so he can't hurt himself."

"He ain't going to hurt himself. As long as he's alone, he'll be all right. It's when we were around was when he was most afraid. Who wouldn't be afraid the first time he seen our class of humans? On top of that, we didn't give him time to think. He's got a surplus of sense. What you going to call him, Bert?"

"The first name I thought of was Barney."

"Barney he is. I like Barney," Porter said. "I used to have a little horse just like him I called Barney. A coincidence, you thinking of calling him Barney."

I wish I had a son to give him to, Sorrells thought.

In the evening they joined with Wilson and took the truck and loaded the little horse behind the partition that would separate him from the cattle. Wilson said he liked the colt. They went back to the portable corral and loaded the cattle. They were dismantling the corral when Cunningham drove up in the company pickup. He asked them how many cattle they had gathered that day. They answered and he frowned and looked at his watch, as usual.

"Say, Bert gathered a yearling maverick he is mighty proud of," Dobie Porter told Cunningham.

"What yearling maverick would that be?" Cunningham asked.

"Have a look for yourself. He's in front of the partition," Porter said.

Cunningham climbed the rack and looked in. He dropped back to the ground. He looked very big. He was not happy.

"Whose idea is it to run broomtails on this outfit now?" he asked.

"Mine, I guess. I caught him," Sorrells said.

"What the hell do you want with a damned scrub like that?"

"Hell, I thought he was a nice little horse. Get back up there and take a good look at him," Sorrells said.

"I don't need another look. I bet you a month's pay I can take a hundred dollars and go anyplace in the State of Nevada and buy ten head better than he is. I'll do better than that. I'll *give* you a hundred-dollar horse if you want a horse just for your very own."

"We'd *all* appreciate a hundred-dollar horse," Sorrells said. It was his turn to hold a little smile it hurt him to hold.

"What're you going to do with him?" Cunningham asked.

"I'm going to take him to headquarters and gentle him this winter and break him next summer."

"Who is going to feed him?"

"Hell, I'll feed him if you figure it will break the Outfit to put out a little hay for him."

"It ain't going to break anybody to feed him. Not even you. He'll never be big enough to pull a sick whore off a pisspot, let alone pack your big carcass next summer."

"Jack will ride him for me until he's big enough."

"Let me tell you something, Sorrells. I'm the one decides what Jack Roberts does. He is going to have more important work to do than ride hairy little scrubs like that."

"I'll figure something out," Sorrells said. He had to look down.

"*You'll* figure something out. *Damn*, Bert, how about figuring out how I'm going to keep a crew working and paying it wages when the front office finds out you are running broomies half the time."

"Now let me tell *you* something, Boss. We don't have an hour's work in that little feller, and I'll work on him on my own time and pay out my own money to feed him. You are going to see a good horse on this outfit next year. I'll make a bet with *you*, Mr. Boss. I'll bet you six months' wages on that proposition, and if I win, you get the horse and I get fifteen hundred dollars, the price of that Front Office horse Wilson rides. If I lose, I work six months just for my room and board."

"I ain't going to stand here and argue with you all day. I've got *work* to do. Do as you please with the horse, I don't give a damn anymore what you do." Cunningham took himself to his company pickup.

At headquarters, Sorrells walked Little Barney off the truck and put him in a small pen by himself. The pen was by the main alley next to the leppie and dogie pen, where the

colt would be a witness to every bit of work that went on in
the pens. His neighbors during the long days would be the
gentle leppies. Sorrells haltered him and put a block of hay
next to the fence that separated him from the leppies. If he
wanted to eat, Barney would have to compete with the
leppies and dogies that crowded to the fence and ran their
tongues through the bars to get at Barney's hay. Sorrells
didn't want the colt to develop any great love for the bovine.

Sorrells had been noticing that Maudy had female company. He was running water in the trough and rolling a
cigarette when Maudy and friend started strolling toward
him. He lit the cigarette and took a look at Maudy's friend.
Oh, oh, he thought, I bet it's that damn Bonnie. The two
women came on. It *was* Bonnie and she'd seen him. She
smiled at Sorrells as he watched her. Well, we'll see, he
thought. Maybe she just felt like coming out and seeing a
feller.

"Look who came to see us all the way from Los Angeles,"
Maudy called to him.

"Hello, Bonnie," Sorrells said. She looked well. She had
put on weight and wasn't wild looking. Her eyes were clear.
She had on a nice, plain dress.

"Hi," Bonnie said. When she smiled up close, Sorrells
saw she had lost a tooth out of the side of her mouth.

"Is that the little horse you caught today?" Maudy asked.

"You bet. That's Barney," Sorrells said. He remembered
he and Bonnie would have called a son Barney.

"He sure is a pretty bay, isn't he?" Bonnie said. Barney
raised his muzzle to smell her from across the pen. Horses
always had liked the way Bonnie smelled. "Come here, little
man," she said and held out her fine hand to him. Barney was
not afraid of her at all. He widened his eyes to see all of her
he could. Sorrells never could help admiring Bonnie when
she was around a young horse.

"I thought you headquartered in Vegas," Sorrells said.

"I quit that town for good," Bonnie said, looking Sorrells
in the eye. "I came back to get the rest of my things this
weekend and decided to come and see how you were doing."

"The hell," Sorrells said. He turned off the water and

stepped out the gate. Bonnie put her arm in his and fell in step with him.

"We've got supper ready at Maudy's," Bonnie said. "I made you some biscuits."

"Oh, you did," was all Sorrells could think to say. All he could think to do was walk along to Maudy's with his head down while Maudy and Bonnie talked at him. In the house he sat down in Cunningham's easy chair where he could watch Bonnie and Maudy. Cunningham stayed in his office in the back of the house to show he still was not altogether satisfied with Sorrells even though he had invited him to supper. When Cunningham finally condescended to join them, he said with a big smile, "Well, did you finally capture him and lead him in, Bonnie?"

"There he is, the Wild Man," Bonnie said, looking at Sorrells too long and with too much a proprietary air.

"He's sure been quiet," Maudy Jane said, and Sorrells found himself holding the damned smile it hurt him to hold while he thought, yeah, you phonies, all three of you, it's just too damn bad you are the three I love most in the world.

They sat down to supper, and Cunningham asked, "Are you going to stay with us for a while, Bonnie?"

"I don't know," Bonnie said, looking at Sorrells. "I've been offered a modeling job by the Arizona Western Shops I used to model for. They have an office in Los Angeles now."

"Bonnie, you don't want to live in Los Angeles," Maudy said. "Stay here with us. Halter old Bert. He's *always* loose with the saddle on anymore."

"Are you going to make the Outfit your permanent job, Bert?" Bonnie asked.

Sorrells' scalp tightened. "At least until day after tomorrow," he said.

"We're going to build a rodeo arena here next spring so we can have some fun," Cunningham said. "We'll have a matched bull riding once in a while. Remember that bull riding we had on New Year's Eve that time at the feedlot?"

"I'll never forget it," Bonnie laughed. "Everyone was drunk and you and Bert matched a bull riding at midnight."

"I let Bert have the best bull," Cunningham said, acting innocent.

"Yeah," Sorrells said. "You let me have the bull that had never been rode." .

"What were the rules?" Maudy asked. "I never did know."

"The one who rode his bull the farthest won the match," Cunningham said.

"Yeah, and you gave me the bull that had bucked off every cowboy in the country and you took the one that didn't buck at all. You said your bull was a chute fighter and you didn't want me to get hurt. You didn't say your bull didn't buck. My bull stood in the chute like a gentleman and when they opened the gate he slung me like a slingshot and when I came down he kicked me with both hind feet before I hit the ground."

"I remember what Bonnie did," Maudy said. "Those people who were at the party were really high class dudes. They were scared to death when they saw Bert was just lying there like he was dead..."

"Roy just ran over and drew a line with his bootheel across my carcass and said, 'That's as far as you got,'" Sorrells said.

"Bonnie ran into the arena," Maudy said. "She had a few words with Bert and when she came back we asked her what had happened. She never changed expression. She said, 'Oh, nothing, the bull kicked Bert in the balls.'"

Bonnie looked at Sorrells. She wasn't affecting pride of ownership anymore. She was happy to be remembering the Great Matched Bull Riding.

"I got a hundred dollars of Bert's money for winning that contest and all it cost me was a little bark off my knees," Cunningham bragged.

"Yeah, but I had to keep shoving down on your head to hold you on your bull while he fought the chute," Sorrells said. "I didn't mind paying you the hundred after the working-over that bull gave you."

"Well, I rode my bull and you paid a hundred to watch," Cunningham said.

"I could afford a hundred in those days. I ain't that big of a shot anymore."

"Hell, by this time next year you'll be able to contribute

several hundreds toward bull riding," Cunningham said.
"We'll all be making more money by then. That's why I want
you to stay, so I can get your wages back in bull ridings and
matched ropings."

"You think the Outfit will be able to afford the crew a few
hundred-dollar horses?" Sorrells asked innocently.

Cunningham laughed. "I apologize for bawling you out
about your little horse today. I just couldn't figure how I was
going to explain him to the son of the Outfit."

"I wouldn't explain nothin' to him," Sorrells said.

"Bert, you've got to learn to be patient with Bobby
Lang. He's learning the cow business. He's a good businessman. People like the Langs don't get where they are by
making mistakes. He'll come around. You watch him. Have a
little patience. He listens to my advice more each time I give
it. I'll tell you, I like him. He's agreeable as hell to me. He
just needs to be shown the right way to run a ranch, that's
all."

"I sure like him," Maudy said. "He is a perfect gentleman and he's the handsomest man I've ever seen. He's just
plain charming."

"Mmmmmmmmmmmm," Bonnie savored. It wasn't her
supper that was tasting so good to her, because she was
picking at her food as usual. "I want to meet that man. When
does he come to the ranch?"

Sorrells finished his supper and smiled to himself. He
rolled a cigarette. Hope be damned and love be damned, he
thought.

Maudy got up from the table to bring Sorrells coffee.
Bonnie held her ground. She had a beachhead on the subject
of Bobby Lang. "I'll have coffee too, Maudy," she called. "Are
his offices in Los Angeles, Roy?"

"Yes, right smack dab on the Boulevard of Dreams,"
Cunningham said proudly.

"The most elite street in Los Angeles," Bonnie dreamed.
"I wish Arizona Western was down there. The boulevard is
closer to where I want to live this time."

"The building Famous Enterprises is in has its own
bank, an executive club, insurance offices, travel offices. That
building is a small city in itself," Cunningham said.

"Bobby travels all over the world between visits to the Outfit," Maudy said, placing Sorrells' lonesome cup of coffee before him. "But he's about due for a visit here. You ought to stay a few more days, Bonnie. You might get to meet him."

"I sure want to meet him," Bonnie said. "He emceed that Miss Liberty model contest in New York last month, you know. He and I would have a lot to talk about."

"You know, it's a wonder he ever has time to visit us. He makes more clear money in one night on one of those emceeing jobs than he makes in a year on the Outfit," Cunningham said. "The Outfit has yet to make him a profit. But, you know, he won't always be able to do that kind of show business work. Someday he'll have to slow down and then is when the Outfit is going to be a business he can fall back on."

"Well, he won't always have his boyish good looks," Maudy argued. "But he'll get more of a sort of executive business to tend to as he grows older. He'll always be a busy, busy man. I just wish he had more time for his family. I wish he'd bring his whole family out here and stay a month or so. I'd like to get to know them all."

"How large is his family?" Bonnie asked.

"They have two children," Maudy said.

"I bet he gets lonesome away from them," Bonnie said. "He must be away a whole lot."

Sorrells got up from the table. "It's eight o'clock and time I was hittin' for the bunkhouse," he said.

"Aren't you going to stay here with us tonight?" Cunningham asked. "You and Bonnie can have the whole back bedroom to yourselves and nobody'll bother you." He winked at Sorrells.

"Naw. I'd have to clean up and I have to get up awful early. No use waking Bonnie up, too." Sorrells put on his hat and gained the door.

"Aw, come on, Bert. You two haven't seen each other in years. This is no time to sleep in any old bunkhouse," Cunningham said.

"Now, just let them alone. Let Bert and Bonnie figure things out for themselves," Maudy said. She was muffling her

words when Sorrells went out the door. He had gone fifty
yards in the dark before Bonnie called to him.

"You can stay here with me if you want," she said in the
little girl voice she had not forgotten how to use. She always
offered him something in that voice so he would know she did
not want to give it to him. He made her walk out to where he
stood, and she didn't want to do that, either.

"Come on, Bonnie," he said. "You don't want to sleep
with me. Save it for when it will do you the most good."

"Well, maybe it is best we don't have sex just now.
Maybe you and I need to get reacquainted first. You know, we
should find out if we really want each other again before we
rush off to bed."

"That's right, Bonnie. You decide between me and whoring
around. I'll decide whether I want you or my bed and
saddle."

"We both have to decide whether or not we want to
make something of ourselves. I mean, you know, like you
won't probably always be a hired hand, but I've reached the
time in my life when I have to be sure the man I decide to
live with is going to have ambition to get somewhere in the
world. Whether you believe it or not, I never was a whore.
You can be so dumb. It doesn't make me mad because I know,
no matter what you think of me, I'm going to be somebody
someday, and no man is going to keep me from having what I
want."

"Who knocked your tooth out? Were you being somebody when a man got mad at you and knocked your tooth
out?"

"He was a man I believed in. A man a lot like you. Yes, a
man did hit me. He put me in the hospital. I didn't have a
soul to turn to, and when I got out I decided never again
would I have anything to do with some damn fool with high
hopes and big talk and nothing but muscles to back them up.
Wait a minute. Don't turn away from me."

"Bonnie, you're wasting your great thoughts on me. You
and I both know you'd rather be in the house finding out
more about Bobby Lang. So go on back. But listen. Find out
all you can tonight, because you ain't going to be here
tomorrow night. You do your pursuing elsewhere. You ain't

going to get after Bobby Lang while I'm on the Outfit. I won't stand to be rimfired by you. You leave me and the Cunninghams out of your golden schemes."

"What? You think I'm after Bobby Lang, you idiot?"

"You ain't here to give me any loving kisses."

"Bobby Lang. That's not a bad idea, Bert, old boy."

"Just you lift your hot little tail on out of here tomorrow or I'll take a double of a rope to it."

"You think you can intimidate *me*? You know what I could have done to you if you harm one little hair on my head?"

"You probably know all the nighttime habits of all kind of thugs. But let me tell you something, you ain't mine to give a damn about anymore, and if you fool with me, I won't give you any more consideration than I would any other predator on this outfit. You be gone by the time I get in tomorrow evening."

"Well, just remember *you* said it. Not me. I came to see how you were and now I've seen you and I don't see very much. I know I'm not looking at a *man*. Good-*bye*."

Sorrells walked on. He stopped at the corrals and looked back in time to see Bonnie go through the kitchen door. The trouble was, he *had* run her off, hadn't he? He had a chance to be with her a few days and instead of taking it, he had threatened her. "Just what *would* you do to her, Big Man?" he muttered out loud. "Knock her teeth out? Big Man. One week with her could be better than a lifetime alone on any damned outfit like this." Little Barney turned to the sound of his voice.

Chapter 23

RIMFIRE

Rimfiring is a hazard in the work of a cowpuncher. Once a horseman has roped a bovine, he must be careful that he doesn't rimfire another horseman near him. He must control the bovine he is tied to. If a roper lets his catch wrap another horseman in the rope, he rimfires that other horseman. No matter how gentle a horse is, he will explode when rimfired. A man who has been rimfired is liable to regard the person who rimfired him in much the same way he would regard a mule, always sort of half an ass and not to be trusted.

"**H**op, bop, deeree, zonk," Stacy sang to himself as he did his little dancing step on the dark, dirt road. The road was so dark he never knew exactly where it was until one of his oxfords struck it. He was walking from the highway to Ethel after four days in town with the person he called his girl, who was his ex-wife. "Hop, deeree, hop, deeree, boppity rock, zonk," he sang and pumped his fists. His girl had let him off at the turnoff. She wasn't used to driving on dirt roads in windy snowstorms. She was afraid, and besides, she might not get back to work in Oakland before her vacation was over.

The wind was blowing a dry snow that whipped around Stacy's socks under the cuffs of his trousers. I might pull these cuffs out and turn them down, he thought. Looking down, he could see the lighter ground of the road with the grainy sheet of snow and dust blowing over it. He knew the dust wasn't being settled by the snow, because he could feel it sting his ankles through his socks. I should have worn my boots, he thought. I see other guys in town in hats and boots and not one a buckaroo. Hop. She likes me better in sport coat and sport shirt and oxfords. Zonk. Right now she's warm and cozy driving down the highway. The wind don't touch her. She's past Beatty by now and out of the snow. She went south instead of north. She didn't like the stormy passes. A good thing. She could roll the car. Eighteen more payments for me to make and she gets to keep it. How have I done eighteen payments up to now? I'll never know. It's easy after you get out of town. Easy, man. Rock. Bop. *Zonko*.

I'll be getting better money by next spring when she comes back to see me. Easter Rock, zappyo, Jjjjeeeosie, it's cold. Can't take the name of the Lord out here in vain. I've only come two miles about. Eighteen to go. Eighteen miles like eighteen payments. Easy, man, zeezeezee. Should make it to the bunkhouse by two or three and just melt into them blankets, man, and get them most important two or three hours sleep I ain't been getting recently, the *first* two or three hours learned in seventh grade health period. *Get* eight to ten hours sleep and rest with ddddoors and wwwwindows open. Don't need fresh air today, though, damn. *Drink* nine times a ddday at the bbbubbler fountain. Should have worn my sweater under my sport. I pppledge allegiance . . . to the flag . . . to the flag . . . g . . . guh.

In the morning we'll all wake up together in the bunkhouse. Wait until they find out old Stace *walked* in. *Nobody* ever done that before. Old Stace could walk a mustang down. Walk him down and pen him afoot. The others, my partners, all asleep now. They have two hours sleep on me. I'm two hours behind them already and look where I am and how far I have to go. It beats me to figure out how come I'm here, right now, where I am all the time. Always behind. Bert's stuck up, Porter's an old man, Wilson's an Indian, Cunningham's a boss. I don't even know Jack Roberts. But what I'd like to know, God, is what makes them so special they're in their blankets and I'm this far behind them again? Charley the cook is a helluva cook, and I wish I had some of that black coffee of his. In awhile I'll get some. Pretty soon. Hop, bop, soon. Nigger is going to be a good horse if he keeps getting the work. I'm the buckaroo to give it to him.

Oh, fellers, this flat is a bad place for a man to be on a night like this. An ordinary man, run of the mill, would freeze to death his tocus. Hop, bop, deeree, zonk. Not old Stace. Stace has his girl and the reason he does is because he's willing to sacrifice. Whups, look out, sacrifice all you want, but don't lose the road. Find the road, find, find, find the road. Ohhhh, boy, here it is. Good boy. Good old road. Nice road. Now keep your sacrifice on the road, boy, on the road, or they'll find you out here with your toes shrivelled up. If they look. Would they? Stuck Up would look. With my luck he'd be the one to find me, too. He'd say old Stace really done it up good this time. Now there's plenty of good road to see. Straight on now. Giant step, step, step, step. Trot. Stretch your lazy legs.

"Ohh, God, ohh, God, my feet," Stacy groaned when he walked into the bunkhouse. The others will not have heard a car, he thought, and might not know I'm here yet. He looked at the luminous clock on the shelf over the gas stove. Forty-five minutes is all the rest I'll get. To hell with that! Forty-five minutes can be a lot. "Gawdam!" he muttered, "I won't get a full hour of sleep and I've got to wait until Easter before I see her again. At least I made it before the cook got up."

"I didn't hear a car drive up," Wilson was saying when Sorrells walked in to the breakfast table.

"His girl friend must have brought him in," Porter said. "I didn't hear a car, though, and I've been awake since about three."

Sorrells looked at Stacy's bunk in the corner. The man was crumpled there in his blankets. The toes of the wet oxfords under the bed were curled in a puddle of melted snow. The wet socks helped form the puddle.

"How's the weather?" Sorrells asked.

Wilson shaded his eyes at the window. "Blowing snow," he said. "You suppose Stacy walked in?"

"Better wake him up," Porter said.

"Hell, let him sleep," Sorrells said. "It's storming."

"Won't he be put out at us for not waking him up?" Porter asked, putting on his innocent old child's face.

"Coffee," Charley the cook said, setting his big pot on the table. Porter overturned a chair and looked to see if the noise stirred Stacy. Jack Roberts came in carrying his towel. "Morning," he said. "Morning," all answered.

"Wake Stacy up," Porter said to Roberts and crouched, watching from over the top of his cup of canned milk and hot water.

"Stace . . . Stace," Roberts said, trying to find a shoulder or a hip bone under the blankets to shake.

"Hell, Jack. Look how wet his shoes and socks are. Let him sleep," Sorrells said.

Roberts uncovered Stacy's head. Stacy moved. He turned his face to the room. He almost didn't have a face that morning. His face was a swollen flush with no eyes.

"Time all buckaroos was up," Porter said. "Coffee's ready."

Stacy moved his carcass as though it had turned into angles of numb edges. "My feet," he said.

"Your feet? What's the matter with your feet?" Porter asked. He knew he could get away with hoorawing Stacy if he acted solicitous.

"Froze," Stacy said.

"Huh!" Porter said. "Been walking?"

"Walked in from the highway," Stacy said. His smile did not show his gut lip. He did not look around for approval of his feat.

"Huh!" Porter snorted. "Walked in from the highway." He looked at Sorrells as if to say, "I told you he was an idiot." Sorrells poured himself a cup of coffee.

"My God, Stace. Didn't you have a ride?" Roberts asked.

"No," Stacy said, trying to move toward the clothes hanging on the wall over his bed. Sorrells couldn't watch him. He couldn't talk to him. He never could. Too much misery there all the time. Old Hard Way Stacy. But much of a man. Can't watch him. Would have to feel sorry for him and that wouldn't be right.

Tom the welder came in the bunkhouse. "Morning," he said. Sorrells poured him a cup of coffee. "It's clearing up," Tom offered. He sat down. He watched the men for a while. He got up and left his coffee. He came back from his room with a pint of whiskey. He stood over Stacy and held the bottle in front of Stacy's face. Stacy acknowledged Tom was there by taking the bottle and drinking more of it than any decent man should this far away from the supply. He smacked his lips and grinned up at Tom showing his gut lip. The grin was not a grateful one, it only showed that the whiskey was good and was a windfall. Stacy would be all right, Sorrells thought. He had not asked for any help. He was not the kind who felt sorry for himself on any morning. Stacy got up and dressed for work and hobbled to the bathroom. His constitution was so ruined this morning he wasn't whistling, but Sorrells was sure he'd be whistling again after his attack on the breakfast chuck.

Tom offered his bottle around the room and everyone let him keep the rest of it. Stacy headed him off again in the kitchen and took it all but half a swallow.

At noon that day Sorrells and Porter were holding cattle at Dove Springs, waiting for Wilson, Roberts, and Stacy to come in with their cattle. The yellow leaves of the cottonwoods lay around the dirt tank. They were still falling from the trees and catching the light of the clear day in their first and last flight. They floated lightly on the tank water as though walking on their curled edges. Their predecessors formed a mat on the bottom of the tank that made the water seem dark.

The storm had blown over. At noon the sky was clear, the sun was warm. A remnant of snow under the thick sagebrush on Highway Draw was melting fast. Sorrells and Porter were both sweating. The cattle they had brought to the spring had been hard to contain in the high sagebrush, and each bovine had a different idea about which part of the ranch he preferred to leave the springs for. Sorrells' horse, Roller, was hot. His steps had become nervous and shaky.

Sorrells turned a bunch off the side of a hill and stopped

Roller there. From his vantage point he saw Stacy on Brandy, one of the high-priced horses the front office had sent from California, cross the highway and ride into the sagebrush. Stacy was driving a young bull. He had the bull roped. He was yow-yowing for help, because he thought Sorrells and Porter ought to leave what they were doing and help him. Sorrells and Porter could not leave the herd.

The animal Stacy was driving stopped in the brush and, by the way Stacy was acting, Sorrells knew the animal had turned on him. Stacy's bovine was on the fight. Stacy drove his horse belligerently into the brush, flipping and jerking the slack in his rope. Sorrells could tell Brandy's proximity to the bull by the altitude of his head. When he was real close to the bull, Stacy pulled so hard on him all the horse could possibly see was the sky. Stacy's red and swollen face looked very big from Sorrells' vantage point. Stacy got the bull moving toward the springs again.

As he came on through the brush, Sorrells began to understand the words Stacy was cussing. "Gawdam," of course, was his favorite. This word exploded often from his bursting head. Sorrells then heard, "Gawdam it, Bert, come on over here. Move your big ass and help me." Sorrells reined Roller to head off some cattle walking away on the other side of the herd. Stacy's voice became more subdued as he neared the spring and by the time he was within fifty yards of it, he was as quiet as the leaves floating in the tank. His face began losing its color and bloat as Sorrells rode around the cattle, taking his rope down. It was set and white, every muscle in it clenched, when Sorrells rode by to turn back cattle on Stacy's side.

"I see you captured a maverick," Sorrells said. "A bull. What is he, a two-year-old?"

Stacy kept his eyes on his prize and did not answer. He whipped his slack at the bull and pulled on Brandy's reins. Brandy rolled his eye and opened his mouth to ease the strain on his jaw. His eye strained to look down and see the bull. Sorrells saw a red and leaking puncture low on the horse's ham.

"You must have had a time with your bull. I see you got your horse hooked," Sorrells said.

"Huh?" Stacy asked, surprised. He leaned over Brandy's flank to get a look at the wound and caught Brandy in the opposite flank with his spur. Brandy lunged and wrapped Stacy in the slack of the rope tied to the bull. Stacy hauled on Brandy's numb jaw and unwrapped his dallies, hooking with his spurs at the same time to keep from being unhorsed. Brandy didn't know whether to stop or to go, so he hopped and pawed the air with his front feet. Sorrells spurred Roller to get out of the way of Stacy's rope. When Stacy gave Brandy slack, the horse sold out to run away. When Stacy hauled on his reins, the horse offered to rear over backwards. Stacy took his dallies again just as he rimfired Roller.

"Turn loose your dallies! Drop your dallies!" Sorrells yelled at Stacy. "Whoa, boy, whoa!" he coaxed Roller to talk him out of the fit he was about to have. Stacy's rope burned like a fuse on Roller's hams and the horse caught Brandy's fear and fired. He floundered in the brush and went down to his knees before he picked up momentum. The rope burned across Sorrells' ribs and he gaffed Roller to make him pitch out of the brush. Roller whirled and bucked toward the bull. The bull lowered his head against the rope and hooked at Roller, tightening the rope on Roller's thighs. Roller bucked clear and froze, his muscles cramping, as Stacy and Brandy made another run at him. Sorrells whipped Roller over and under with his rope and the horse jumped clear before Stacy could set him afire again. Stacy stopped Brandy when the bull, dragged into the sagebrush, lost his footing and fell.

Sorrells looked at Stacy. The man was showing his gut-lipped grin. Porter was pushing the herd against the hill so he could hold it by himself. Sorrells could tell by the set of his back he didn't want to watch any more of Stacy's and Sorrells' goings on.

"Now, if *that* wasn't something," Sorrells said. He walked Roller away to the cottonwoods, dismounted and reset his saddle and blankets. He rode back and caught the bull's heels as the bull was getting up. Roller whirled and bucked to the end of the rope as though he had forgotten how well he and Sorrells had been getting along. The bull was jerked and stretched to breaking on the ground. Stacy got down off Brandy and ran over to Porter to get a saw the old man carried on his saddle. Stacy was hurriedly stumbling, intent on revenge, when he came back.

"Now, you dirty bastard," Stacy said and dropped his knees on the bull's neck. "We'll see if you gore another horse." He sawed off half the bull's horns and the bull's hot, excited blood spurted on Stacy. The business done, he took his rope off the bull. He knelt on the bull's flank and passed the bull's tail between the bull's legs and held him down with it. He grabbed Sorrells' hondo on the bull's heels.

"Slack!" he ordered. "Slack!" he commanded again when Sorrells didn't move. Sorrells started to tell him he would hold the bull down while Stacy got on his horse. The bull would step out of the loop when he got up. Sorrells would have liked to be decent and not let the bull catch Stacy on the ground.

"Slack!" Stacy ground through his teeth and jerked on Sorrells' rope as though to overpower Roller and pull him forward.

"Suit yourself," Sorrells said and nudged Roller to give the slack.

Stacy opened Sorrells' loop and as he did, the bull came alive and kicked and rolled, pulling Stacy over by his hold on the tail. Stacy rolled over the bull's hip. For a moment Stacy was supine. He saw the bull was getting up over him. Stacy kicked and rolled too. He and the bull gained their feet at the same time. Sorrells saw that his loop had closed again on one of the bull's hind feet. The bull looked Stacy in the eye and charged. Stacy had buttocks like two saltine crackers rubbing together and the bull hooked at them close enough to shower salt off them. The race was even. Both Stacy and the bull had already covered twenty miserable miles that day and neither could gain on the other. Sorrells felt like letting the bull run Stacy a little farther to see which had the most bottom, but Stacy ran toward his horse. Before Stacy got to his horse Sorrells braced Roller and stopped the bull by the rope on the hind foot.

Stacy mounted Brandy and rode away to help Porter with the herd. He had *his* rope free. Sorrells dragged the cramping bull down again and took his rope off. Now *he* was on the ground and the bull was free to catch *him*. This time the bull sulled and didn't get up when Sorrells freed his rope.

When all the cowboys were together again, they drove the herd by the bull so he would get up and walk away. He refused to get up. Porter and Wilson put their ropes on him and held him to brand, earmark, and vaccinate him. The crew drove the herd away and left him alone.

"Gawdam," Sorrells heard Stacy tell Jack Roberts from the other side of the herd. "I wanted to take him in to headquarters and show him off. Now who is going to know I caught a maverick bull?"

The crew returned early to headquarters that day and changed horses. They had to move the weaner heifers from a pasture to the corrals. The best of the heifers would be hauled to warmer country and fed hay through the winter. The culls would be sold. The heifers were loathe to leave their pasture. They were hard to drive because they had never been moved before without their mothers. The trail to the corrals was through the old buildings and rusty junk of Ethel.

The crew bunched the heifers in a corner by a gate and held them while Porter rode through them. He opened the gate and rode outside to be in the lead of the cattle when they streamed out of the gate. The heifers began milling in the corner and trying to break by the cowboys. The job of holding them was not a hard one if the cowboys, as a team, gave the cattle room. If one man pressed too close, the cattle would break by him and weaken the whole line of cowboys.

Stacy always worked too close to cattle. He was riding Nigger, and Nigger had been intimidated so much that he watched Stacy instead of the cattle. Inevitably, a heifer got by Stacy when he tried to prance Nigger over the top of her instead of standing back and facing her off. When the heifer got by, Stacy "gawdamned" and plow-reined Nigger after her. The rest of the herd started through the hole Stacy left.

"Let her go," Sorrells shouted and rode in to turn the herd back into the corner.

"Gawdam!" Stacy was chewing through his teeth, in full pursuit of the heifer.

"Let her go. She can't get away in the pasture," Sorrells

yelled and laughed. The herd would be easier to hold with
Stacy gone. The four men backed off and gave the herd room.
They watched Stacy. He had his rope down. He was trying to
make Nigger follow the heifer so he could catch her. Nigger
wasn't taking any chances. He wasn't going to take his eyes off
Stacy long enough for the man to do something to him by
surprise. Whenever the heifer ducked away from in front of
Nigger, Stacy needed an acre of ground to turn the horse
back and get him to tracking her again. Stacy made another
wild charge at her, swinging his loop higher and higher above
his head as he closed on her. She ducked off again just out of
range of his loop. Finally, when the heifer was run down so
her tongue was hanging out, Stacy dabbed a loop on her. He
had to relax his death grip on Nigger's jaw to make his cast,
and while the loop was on its way to the heifer Nigger's eyes
turned green. He took a fix on the hay barn and saddle house
a half mile away and sprang to see how soon he could make it
back there. Sorrells marveled at how quick Stacy could stack
his dallies with his horse stampeding one way and the calf
ducking off another. Stacy got the dallies on in time to jerk
the heifer three feet in the air and stretch her neck as much
as it took for her to swap her direction for Nigger's. Stacy
stopped Nigger just before he hit the pasture fence, but
Sorrells didn't think he could have done it if he had not been
using the heifer for anchor.

Stacy dismounted, took a new hold on Nigger's bits, and
made him back up, educating the horse on how properly to
hold a strangling calf. He then took his piggin' string and tied
the calf. Seeing Stacy thirty-five feet away was too much
pleasure for Nigger and he relaxed, causing about half a coil
of slack to appear in the rope holding the calf. This breach of
discipline turned Stacy into an angry, angry man. He ran at
Nigger to jerk on his bits again. Nigger misunderstood.

He was not the type of horse who could read the mind of
a man like Stacy. He thought Stacy was going to kick him in
the belly as the man had done before on similar occasions.
Nigger left there, on the run. This time the heifer looked
more like a pennant trailing behind him. Just at that moment
Roy Cunningham, the boss, drove by the pasture in the
company pickup.

Cunningham was in the pasture helping Stacy head Nigger into a corner when the heifer herd started out the gate. The crew drove the herd to the corrals without Stacy. The men were unsaddling and Stacy still had not come on. Cunningham drove up in the pickup. He got out and joined the crew at the saddle house.

"Did Stacy ever get his horse unhitched, Roy?" Porter asked.

"Unhinged," Cunningham said. "That man is crazy, you know that?"

"He does have a time," Porter said. Sorrells, Wilson, and Roberts busied themselves with their own affairs.

"I think if he had a gun he would have killed old Nigger. Is he always that way?"

"He thinks all brutes ought to know better," Porter said.

"If he thinks that way, he ought not to be horseback," Cunningham said.

The crew was walking by Tom's shop when Stacy rode up to the saddle house and dismounted in front of Cunningham. Sorrells turned his face away from Nigger because he couldn't stand the sight of the way the man had used him. Tom walked out of his shop to greet the crew. "Did Stacy make it through the day all right?" he asked. He was a man who had a pint of whiskey invested in Stacy that day.

"The hard way," Sorrells said and went on.

The crew was sitting at the bunkhouse table when Stacy came in.

"Well, fellers," he said, grinning. "My horses are getting a rest. Somebody's got to haul hay to the heifers and bulls from now on and I'm it." He hobbled on his sore feet into the little skip dance he liked to do as he started through the kitchen door. "Hopdebop," he chanted low for his audience. He turned back to the men and showed the palms of his hands. "Zonk," he said.

Chapter 24

HOULIHAN

*If a steer stands on his head and overturns and cartwheels,
or a horse somersaults with a peculiar, neck-buckling sudden-
ness, these vaults and falls are known as houlihans; hoolies
for short,*

*A hoolie is also a short, overhand, backhanded toss a
roper gives his loop in a herd. He does not swing his loop
before he tosses his hoolie so not to broadcast to the herd that
he is about to catch one poor unfortunate. Whether houlihan
or hoolie is used in describing a fall or a loop, it always
describes an arc, always comes as a surprise, and is always a
misfortune to man, or beast.*

Wilson Burns carried the
Mexican saddle into the bunkhouse one morning after he had
spent the night at his father's house. Sorrells was pleased
with the way Wilson had repaired it. The horn was welded on
by wide, clean, scraped strips of rawhide. The skirts and
stirrup leathers were sewn in place. The saddle was tallowed
and ready for use. Sorrells laid it on a bunk and spread the
stirrups out to admire Wilson's work better. The saddle
reflected light. It had been burnished.

"Hell, Wilson. It's like new. I've already got a new

saddle," Sorrells said. "I didn't know you had been working on it."

"Not much work," Wilson smiled.

"Listen, I know how much work had to go into that saddle to fix it after Roller got through with it."

Wilson stood up. "All I had to do," he explained, "Was soak those strips and..."

"Listen, Wilson," Sorrells said. "I want you to have the saddle."

Wilson was quiet a moment, looking at the saddle. "I'd like to have it. I like the saddle. It has a good seat and good balance."

"It's your saddle, Wilson. It just fits you. You keep it."

"Thanks," Wilson said.

Sorrells went into his room and took his time readying himself for work. When he was sure all the crew had gone to the corrals, he took his soft, tallowed reata from his rope can. He went back to the Mexican saddle and laid the reata on it. Tom and Charley the cook were sitting at the table drinking coffee.

"It's been a long time since I seen a reata," Tom said. "I've seen some men that could damn sure put them to good use back in Texas."

"Hell, sit down and have a cup of coffee. You don't need to go hurrying off, Bert," Charley said.

Sorrells' cup was still on the table. Charley poured it full. Sorrells ignored his sore thumb and rolled himself a cigarette. "I'm wore out," he said and handed the makings of his cigarettes to Tom.

"Did you give that rope to Wilson too?" Charley asked. He walked over to touch the reata.

"Yeah," Sorrells said.

"It's a damn nice present," Charley said. "What'll you take for it?"

"Aw. Wilson ought to have it," Sorrells said. "I wouldn't sell it."

"Wilson'll appreciate it," Tom said. "You ain't doing wrong, Bert."

"That's what I figure," Sorrells said.

"Didn't you want it anymore?" Charley asked.

"No use giving him something I don't want," Sorrells said.

"It's a real nice present," Charley said. He sat down at the table and looked at Sorrells. Sorrells sipped his coffee under Charley's new scrutiny. "I'm wore completely out," he said to distract Charley. "What's today?"

"Today is the eighth of December," Charley said, still not taking his eyes off Sorrells.

"Are you almost through gathering the cattle, Bert?" Tom asked.

"Hell, I don't know," Sorrells said. "Sometimes we get to thinking we're almost through and then we run into more cattle."

"You guys better keep at it while you can. I've never seen the winter hold off as good as it has this year," Tom said. They heard a motor. Tom leaned back to hold the blind away from the window so he could see outside. "It's Mister Cunningham headed for the corrals," he said.

"I'd better get to work," Sorrells said and got stiffly off the bench. His sore foot hurt him and his thumb was no good at all. He was full of breakfast, but his Levis sagged on his hips. His shirttail was getting longer every day. He was just downright losing flesh. He walked to the saddle house.

Cunningham and Bobby Lang were standing by the saddle house. The crew had not caught horses yet at seven o'clock in the morning. We're *all* of us wore out, Sorrells thought, and the boss is catching us going to work late. Cunningham saw Sorrells and looked at his watch. Bobby Lang smiled when he saw Sorrells. He was a pleasant fellow and had a hearty handshake. Sorrells went into the saddle house without saying anything to Bobby Lang.

"Where are you going today, Bert?" Cunningham asked in the loud voice he always used when he wanted to get an answer, any answer, from Bert Sorrells. "Bobby wants to go with you."

"North side of Black Mountain," Sorrells said. "Horse Corral Canyon."

"You want to catch Streak for Bobby?"

"Streak? Who's Streak?" Sorrells said. He turned back into the saddle house and got Bobby's bridle from its special

place. He went outside and handed it to the son of the Outfit.
"Here you are," he said. "Show me which one is Streak." He
walked away toward the corrals. He had never in his life
asked a man to catch his horse for him unless one roper was
roping horses out of a remuda. If the son of the Outfit wanted
to ride, he would have to catch his own damned horse. Streak
was Front Office. Wilson had seen Bobby coming and had left
Front Office in the corral. Bobby Lang was going to know
what it was like to ride a tired horse today. He would be
considering buying motorcycles again by sundown.

The crew saddled their horses and loaded them in the
stock truck. Jack Roberts rode with Cunningham and Bobby
in the pickup. Cunningham didn't saddle a horse that day.
After he unloaded Bobby and Roberts he left for Keno to see
about buying more hay to feed the heifers and bulls.

Wilson unloaded the crew near the top of Black Mountain and then drove away toward the flats where the crew had
set up the portable corral. Porter, Sorrells, and Roberts
tightened their cinches and mounted. They were anxious to
ride into the brush out of the direct blast of a wind that was
like wind off a great mesa of dry ice. The movement of riding
would warm them, but they had to wait while the son of the
Outfit fussed with his gear before he mounted. Roberts and
Porter turned their backs to Bobby and the wind, but Sorrells
felt obliged to watch him. Sorrells didn't want Bobby's gear to
come loose during the work.

Bobby didn't wear a hat. His long, bleached hair waved
in the wind. His sideburns ruffled. Sorrells figured Bobby
wanted his cowboys to see his hair do that or he would have
worn a hat. People's hair did that in the movies about men
out West. Bobby's hands were long and white and nervous
about doing anything that might hurt them. They would
surrender if they had to take hold of anything. They floated
superficially over the task of readying Bobby's gear for work,
and when they became overwhelmed over tightening Bobby's
cinch, Sorrells got off and finished the chore. He held Front
Office while Bobby mounted. "Whoa, Streak," Bobby grunted
when he got on.

The crew rode into the piñon across the base of Black
Mountain, over country that was like a giant apron full of rock

and brush. Horse Corral Canyon cut down through the middle of the apron. Mustangers had used the canyon to channel wild horses to their traps.

Sorrells and Jack Roberts were about to separate from Porter and Bobby, when Bobby asked cheerfully, for conversation and companionship, "What's on the agenda, Dobie?"

"What on the *agenda*? What d'ye mean, 'what's on the agenda'? Work. That's what's on the agenda. Huh! The *agenda*," Porter said and rode into the canyon.

Bobby rode close behind Porter. Porter was an implacable unit with Buck, starting off on the day's work. He was ignoring the son of the Outfit now, but after they settled down to the work, he would talk Bobby to downright weariness and perhaps even physical exhaustion. Bobby was quietly, obediently enjoying his ride, content to follow and observe, like a child. He was paying no attention to Porter's grouchiness, or to the direction of the work. He was enjoying "horseback riding." Before he rode out of sight, he raised a hand to smile and wave to Sorrells and Roberts. What the hell, Sorrells thought. Why shouldn't Bobby enjoy a day on the Outfit? He hardly ever got a chance to be outside. How would Sorrells feel if he ever needed Bobby's help on the Boulevard of Dreams? If Bobby didn't like the Outfit, he wouldn't have a job for Sorrells.

Sorrells was riding Big Red. The renegade cattle had broken an egg in Big Red. The horse couldn't regain his strength with only two days' rest. Baldy was the only strong horse in Sorrells' string. Today had been Baldy's day to work, but Sorrells had ridden Big Red, gambling this would be an easy day with the son of the Outfit along. Big Red had never been a willing horse, but the small amount of will he did have had deteriorated, so that he no longer concentrated on his work. He required constant prodding if he was even to travel across country in a purposeful straight line. Roberts was riding the clumsy, limber Careful. That horse was a disaster to ride. He couldn't carry weight, his feet and his eyes and his brain were completely unrelated, and to rein him was a game of chance on whether he would avoid, trample, or collide with an obstacle.

Sorrells stopped on a highpoint to watch the country for

a while. He was about to tell Roberts that they should separate when he saw a bunch of cattle flush out of Horse Corral far below where Porter and Bobby should be. The cattle were running, streaming like deer behind one big, barren cow and rimming toward Sorrells and Roberts. Sorrells waited until he saw Porter come out of the canyon alone on their tracks. Porter kept his head down watching the tracks. Buck was moving slowly. Porter was not going to catch the cattle by tracking them.

"Let's get after them," Sorrells said and spurred Big Red off the mountain. The two men had no time for caution. They had to ride with rein and spur, their only concern being to keep their horses between their legs while they fell off Black Mountain to head the cattle. They crossed two ridges and Sorrells caught sight of the cattle again as they gained a level, grassy mesa.

Sorrells pitched Big Red all the slack in his reins to cross before the cattle got off the mesa. He heard leather slap and wood crack and Jack Roberts' voice slammed from him. Sorrells looked back in time to see Careful rolling with feet kicking the air and Jack mixed up in his saddle beneath him. Careful got his front feet bracing in front of himself, his hind legs still tangled and stepping on Jack before he stood up and pushed free of the man. He stood over Jack a moment, dazed. Sorrells caught him and led him clear while Jack moaned and pulled himself along the cold ground on his stomach.

Sorrells tied the horse to a piñon. He went to sit by Roberts while the man clawed the ground and cried and chewed the sleeve of his jacket. Sorrells could only wait quietly. He put his hand on Roberts' shoulder, but knew at once it caused the hurts to be more acute and he took his hand away. His hand had only been more unsupportable weight. After a while, Jack subsided. He sighed and raised his head.

"I'm sorry I made so much noise," he said.

"Hell, that's O.K., Jack. Holler if you want to. I would."

Roberts tried to sit up. "Oh," he said, and then he did sit up. "That god damned counterfeit son of a dirty bitch," he said.

"Where do you hurt, pard?" Sorrells asked. Blood was on Roberts' face and dirt and blood were in his mouth and nose. He began to clean his mouth and lips with his mangled tongue. Sorrells took the kerchief off his head, wet it with spit, and dabbed at the dirt on Roberts' face.

"He got my grinners," Roberts said, letting a piece of tooth fall to the palm of his hand. Rock was imbedded in the hand.

"He sure did, pard," Sorrells said. "He caught all of you under him, didn't he?"

"He got this wrist and this shoulder. I thought it was happening on the track. It was just like I was on the track again and it happened all over again just like the first time."

"Can you get up?"

"I think so."

Sorrells stood behind Roberts to help him. The man was very small and, from behind him, away from the face, he was mute and broken.

"Not that way," Roberts said. "I can't raise my leg."

Sorrells knelt beside him and picked him up to hold him all together. He carried him and sat him under a piñon with his back against the trunk. Sorrells used his stock knife and cut branches and stacked them against the piñon behind Roberts for a windbreak. He unsaddled Careful and propped the saddle between the tree and Roberts' back and used the saddle blankets to couch and cloak him. He laid a small a fire and broke a supply of dead branches for it.

"You got any aspirin?" Sorrells asked and gave him his supply of eight or ten. "You need anything else?"

"No," Roberts said.

Sorrells got on Big Red and stood him a moment. "You got your cigarettes? You want my tobacco and papers?" he asked.

"I've got my cigarettes."

"It's not far to the Horse Corral road. I'll go and get the truck and bring it back up the road as quick as I can," Sorrells said.

"See ya later, then," Roberts said and tried to grin. Sorrells turned Big Red away and headed in the direction of the portable corral. Wilson sometimes drove the truck to meet the cattle drive if he found no cattle near the corral. Sorrells might find the truck before he had to ride all the way to the corral. Sorrells had too far to go, too much country to cross, to hurry. He kept Big Red alive with his spurs and headed for a mountain he could use to look down on the flats.

The mountain was big, rocky, and barren. Sorrells rode up a dry, narrow wash that looked like an avenue to the top. The wash closed behind him. The climb was steep and he could not see far ahead. The wash became a canyon with high, rock walls, and he felt he was in an unending room and making no progress. Each corner he turned in the canyon showed him the same room. Roberts could be in shock by now. Sorrells dug at Big Red with his spurs, the first time he had ever spurred him cruelly. He felt trapped in the canyon but he had to go on to see the top of it, now. To turn back would mean backtracking and riding miles out of his way to get around the mountain.

The floor of the canyon was no longer sandy. The floor was bedrock. Boulders in the canyon were like head-high brown walls in a maze. Big Red was creeping, his hooves sliding, his heart pounding against Sorrells' legs. Sorrells gritted his teeth so their edges ground and he spurred Big Red harder, urgency crowding him. Big Red grunted and tried, but could not give more, and Sorrells stopped him. He saw no difference in Big Red stopped from Big Red climbing in that maze. The horse's head did not rise with Sorrells' pressure on the reins. It hung close to the ground in a sharp and bony angle from his withers. Red examined the rock where he would have to place his next step.

Sorrells wondered if he had been pushing Big Red up that maze long enough to kill him. He hoped Jack would not give up and die before he got back. He hoped he was not taking a losing gamble in this canyon. He was afraid, at that moment, his gamble in this high, lonesome place was going to prove no purpose. He couldn't see how he would progress toward helping Jack by going around the next corner.

Sorrells took off his gloves and rolled a cigarette. He knew if he had to walk out and lead his horse because he had ridden him down, he would not help his partner any sooner. He made himself subside. He thought, a tired horse, running for a dying man, on a track where nothing lives, gave your chicken heart intimations of death.

He stepped off Big Red and reset his saddle and blankets and pulled up his cinches. He leaned against his horse and smoked his cigarette. When it was gone, he mounted and coaxed Big Red to take the next step up the canyon. Around the corner was a slope of scree to a high saddle. Big Red wound slowly up the scree to the top. The stock truck, blue, was parked on a road about an hour's ride away. Sorrells looked up and saw an eagle floating on his stoop and watching Sorrells.

Chapter 25

NIGHT LOOP

A thief works best in the night, but a cow thief cannot drive cattle or chase them to rope them with facility in the night. If he is not too greedy and is content to glean only a few head in a night, he might, if he is a skilled cow thief, use a night loop. He rides close to another man's stock and slowly, effortlessly, drops a hoolie over the head of the stock, or rides beside the stock as though to go on by, and drops a loop across his chest. A bovine on his bedground, chewing his cud, or one just standing up in surprise, swallowing his cud, is usually too surprised, when caught in the dark, to bawl.

Sorrells did not wait long in Keno after he had delivered Jack Roberts to the hospital. He drove back to the Outfit that night, as soon as he found out Roberts was going to go on living for a while. He stopped at Cunningham's house.

"How's Jack?" Cunningham asked when Sorrells walked into Maudy's kitchen.

"Old Careful broke his collarbone, sprained his wrist, cleaned out his front teeth, and they were x-raying his pelvis when I left," Sorrells said. "Aside from being all skunt up, he still thinks he's handsome as hell."

"That bad?" Cunningham asked, as though Roberts were

being unduly, unreasonably grave in his hurts, an affront to
the Outfit, especially while the son of the Outfit was visiting.

"Hell, Roy, old Careful flipped on Jack instead of taking
his next step. I thought the horse had killed him."

The son of the Outfit was smiling as though he believed
accidents like Jack's couldn't happen. Bobby Lang still did
not believe his play-pretties could be deadly.   ®

"I signed for the Outfit," Sorrells said to Bobby. "The
nurse wanted to know who would be responsible for the bill."

"We've got insurance," Cunningham said.

The son of the Outfit arose from the table and poured
himself a cup of coffee at Maudy's stove. He moved stiffly. He
looked harried. He was probably thinking he had to get some
sleep.

"Have you eaten, Bert?" Maudy asked. Sorrells shook
his head. "Sit down and I'll give you your supper. I'm fixing
Bobby a steak. He just got in, too."

Sorrells looked at the clock. The time was eleven thirty.

"Well, what do you think, Bert? Will Jack be all right?"
Cunningham asked.

"Hell, yes," Sorrells said. "The little fart is tough as a
horseshoe. He was joking with the nurses. He said that fall
didn't break his maiden."

Bobby sat down at the table. "Oh, *boy*, I'm sore," he
groaned.

"Did you just get in?" Sorrells asked, grinning at the son
of the Outfit. Bobby didn't answer. He stretched on the chair
and flexed his arms like a wrestler pulls the ropes in the ring
to show his muscles. He opened his mouth to yawn, but he
didn't mean to yawn, he meant to make Sorrells think he was
unconcerned with the question.

"That damned Porter," Cunningham said. "He led Bobby all over the State of Nevada today. When I got back here,
Maudy told me what had happened to Jack. I took the truck
back out to the corral about five o'clock and not a soul was in
sight. I drove up the road, looking for the crew, and found
Wilson with seven head tied down. We loaded his cattle and
went back to the corral. It must have been seven o'clock
when I saw them come out of the canyon with the cattle and
they were still three miles from the corral."

Bobby tried to yawn and stretch again, but gave it up. He leaned on the table. "After we separated from you and Jack, Porter said he was going to follow some tracks out of the canyon," he said. "He left me holding three cows and was gone at least two hours. He came back with a bunch of cattle and we held them in that same spot for at least another hour."

"Those must have been the cattle Jack and I were after when Careful fell. We saw Porter on their tracks," Sorrells said.

"*I'll* never ride with Porter again," Bobby proclaimed. "When we finally started the cattle, they wanted to trot and he wouldn't let them. He kept holding them up. He didn't care if they *ever* got out of the canyon."

"Gentling them," Sorrells grinned.

"What?" asked the son of the Outfit.

"He likes to drive those shitty cattle slow, so they'll be easier to handle the next time he wants to move them."

"I don't believe he was poking along for that reason. I believe he wanted to keep me in that canyon."

"Well, he probably figured he would never get to the corral with the cattle *or* his boss if he didn't go slow. That canyon must be twenty miles long, and trotty cattle get hot might fast. A trotting horse can wear a feller out, especially a horse like Streak."

"I don't *mean* that," Bobby said.

"Bobby's been hearing stories about Dobie," Cunningham grinned. "A man in Vegas told Bobby that Porter is suspected of using his night loop in this country."

"Aw, hell," Sorrells said.

"What better way would he have of finding cattle he wanted to steal?" Bobby asked. "If he had someone to help him, all he would need to do was steer the crew away from the area his helper worked."

"I know he doesn't need to work for two hundred and fifty a month if he has the skills of a good cow thief. He don't need to spy in the bunkhouse."

"How much longer will this work continue, Roy?" Bobby asked.

"We should be near finished," Cunningham said. "Bert knows a lot more about the work than I do. I've been too busy with the fencing and the heavy equipment. What do you think, Bert?"

"How many cattle did you get today?" Sorrells asked Bobby.

"Eleven calves, two mavericks, and a big steer," Bobby said. He had learned to observe and remember cattle by riding one long day with Porter.

"There you are," Sorrells said. "I didn't think that many cattle were running in Horse Corral. This ranch is so big, we might never get them all."

"Can't you and Wilson finish the work before the weather closes in?" Cunningham asked.

"Hell, Roy, let Porter stay. Me and Wilson can't work Last Chance alone."

"Bobby doesn't want him on the Outfit. All he can do from now on is cause trouble," Cunningham said.

"I don't know of any trouble he's caused except trouble for renegade cattle on this outfit," Sorrells said. "No one thought he was any trouble when we started this roundup and he was the only one who knew the country."

"Wilson knew the country. Wilson can run this ranch as well as Dobie can," Cunningham said.

"Wilson will not be the cowman Dobie is until Wilson is seventy years old," Sorrells said. "We're not talking about Wilson. We're talking about Porter's job."

"You're almost through with the roundup?" Bobby asked.

"I guess so. We might not have all the cattle, but we'll have bad weather soon," Sorrells said. "That's why we need to keep Porter, so we can gather all the cattle before the weather closes us out."

"Keep him as long as you need him, but we better let him go when this roundup is done," Bobby said.

"Hell, he would be the last one to beg for a job or stay around where he wasn't wanted. So would I," Sorrells said.

"We want you to stay around, Bert," the son of the Outfit said. "Roy has been telling me his ideas about working the crew next summer and they are good ideas. You figure in all our plans for next year."

"That's comforting," Sorrells said.

"Don't worry about Porter, Bert," Cunningham said.

"He can take care of himself. I'm tired of him because his attitude is so bad. He never has anything good to say about the Outfit or the way it's run. He even spreads stories about us in town. I don't care how good a man is, or how much he needs a job, if he doesn't have any loyalty, I don't want him around."

"What stories has he spread about us?" Sorrells asked.

"The other day he went to the assessor's to get the license for his old truck and he told everyone in the office that he had to do all the work and he only had Indians, has-been jockeys, and mechanics for help. He said I didn't have any business on a ranch. I belonged someplace where I could bigshot it around hotel lobbies with a bunch of cattle buyers. He said you were too wild and impatient and he had to watch you all the time or you would turn this ranch into a rodeo arena."

"Why, that old son of a gun," Sorrells said, surprised. "After I fetched and carried for him four solid months."

"See what I mean?" Cunningham said.

"No I don't, Roy. You have your reasons for letting him go, I guess. Just because he talks about us is not reason enough for me. That old-man talk never bothers anyone. He's no different from a hundred old cowboys I've known. He's just cantankerous because you ain't running the ranch to suit him. No one does anything to suit him."

"I don't *have* to put up with him. I don't *have* to work with him. I'm letting him go."

"Keep him as long as you need him," Bobby Lang said.

"Porter will always be needed on an outfit like this," Sorrells said, looking at Bobby Lang. "He's a cowman."

"He must be," Bobby Lang said, laughing. "Everyone keeps telling me he is. Look, I don't want Dobie Porter too close to my business. I don't think he has my best interests at heart. I rode all day with Dobie Porter listening to him praise himself. I know from reliable people that he has been responsible for cattle theft. He is trying to woo me. He is wooing me for the same reason that prostitute in Keno tried to woo me, to get a hand in my pocket."

"What prostitute?" Sorrells asked.

"One of Wanda's ladies is Bobby's pen pal," Cunningham said, grinning. "She wrote to him offering her services."

"Yes," Bobby laughed. "One of Wanda's girls sent me a letter marked 'personal,' telling me she admired me. She said she realized I must often be lonely on my trips to Nevada, and that she would be very happy to meet me anytime to 'share delights' with me. She said she was beautiful, discreet, well-dressed and 'knowledgeable in the pleasures of Eros.' She said she wasn't any common prostitute, I wouldn't be ashamed to be seen with her in any party in Nevada. She was from a good family and had only 'fallen by the wayside' when she 'became destitute after her husband abandoned her.' I framed the letter and hung it on the wall in my office. I get offers from women in my business, but that one is written in language that makes it a classic."

"Listen," Sorrells said. "Porter is an old man, who has accomplished a whole lot in his life. No one would know what he has done with his life if he didn't tell people how good he is. He has no family to admire him. He has to tell *someone* his reasons for living. He probably thought you were listening to him."

"I was listening, all right," Bobby Lang laughed. "I only wish I could frame what he said beside Wanda's girl's letter."

Sorrells excused himself. He drove Carlotta to the bunkhouse. The lights were on in the main room. Sorrells took the bottle of whiskey he had bought in Keno and went in, screwing off the lid as he walked. Porter, Wilson, Tom, and Charley the cook were all dressed and drinking coffee at the table. Stacy was in bed, but he sat up when Sorrells started pouring whiskey.

"Don't you guys work hard enough to go to bed early?" Sorrells asked.

"We wanted to know how Jack was doing," Tom said, Charley brought Sorrells coffee, as the bottle got back to him. Sorrells handed Charley the bottle.

"His grinners are busted and his collarbone is broke, but the rest of him is probably only a little bashed in," Sorrells said.

"He's all right, then?" Stacy asked.

"Yeah," Sorrells said. "Come on over and have a drink, Stace." Stacy came over in his shorts and boots and turned up the bottle. The whiskey rolled and bubbled inside the bottle. "Oh, God, that's good," Stacy said. He drank more.

"You like that stuff, don't ye?" Porter said to Stacy. "Take another one. Take a stiff one this time."

"It's looking at me, ain't it?" Stacy said and sat the bottle on the table and watched it.

"Stacy's carcass is sore. He ain't found the right handle on them hay bales," Porter said. "Is that good whiskey?" He had not accepted a drink when the bottle had gone by him the first time. "Pour me just a little here in this hot water, will ye, Bert?" he said.

Sorrells poured. "Whoa, whoa, whoa," said Porter. "You'll get me drunk."

Tom was holding one of the Chihuahua spurs Sorrells had use on Big Red that day. He rolled the rowel with his finger, listening to the ring of the metal.

"How did Jack get hurt?" Porter asked.

"We were running to turn those cattle you were tracking and old Careful turned a fart knocker. How did you and Bobby get along?"

"I didn't have no trouble. *You* know. We just held the runnygades until they settled down. One old barren cow kept turning off, but once she quieted down, she lined out down the canyon."

"Did Bobby get tired?"

"No, he held up right well for a front office feller. Why, did he say he got tired?"

"He wasn't too bad off."

"I kindly like him. He might be all right," Porter said. "Well, fellers, I'm going to bed down. Three o'clock ain't far off," he grinned. "Stace, you can have my place at the table. It's closer to that whiskey." He got up from the table and walked away to his room. He walked like a man on broken stilts. He liked to prod the crew about three o'clock calls. He knew Stacy didn't like them.

Tom was humming and ringing the spur. Charley had begun his vigil over Sorrells again.

"I fed little Barney for you, Bert," Wilson said and drank from the bottle.

"How is my little horse?" Sorrells asked.

"I think he's going to be a good mushtang," Wilson said. "If you want to, we can keep him at my dad's place. That is, if you want to take him off this place."

"Why, is somebody griping about him?"

"No, but just in case. I think Bobby was asking Roy about him."

"They didn't say anything to me about him. I'm going to keep him here at headquarters as long as I am here. He's what we're going to have instead of Careful."

"I think you are right about that, Bert," Tom said. "A horse that has had a cowboy on him from the start ain't likely to fall and kill a man. If you break him and teach him the ways of the cow, he's liable to made a good little horse. A good little horse," he sang and strummed the spur rowel:

> *"Ride your little horse, spin him round,*
> *Teach him to work but keep him proud.*
> *Don't be mean to him, don't get mad,*
> *And the little old feller will never turn bad."*

Stacy drank from the bottle and went to bed.

"More, Tom," Sorrells laughed. "Tom and Wanda would make a pair, wouldn't they, Wilson?"

Tom held up the spur. "I've always liked a Chihuahua spur," he said. "They're hefty and give a man balance. They look mean, but they're not as mean as a light spur, because a man don't need to use them as much as he does a light spur. They've got music, and a horse gets to moving when the music starts. A horse knows a man's got spurs on. He don't need gaffing after the first time."

"Have you ever used Chihuahuas, Tom?"

"I had a pair of iron Chihuahuas once. They weren't silvermounted like these," Tom said.

"You can have the spurs if you like them," Sorrells said. "Have you cowboyed much, Tom?"

"Bert, I cowboyed and rode broncs on the first job I ever had back in Texas when I was a boy, but I never could stay in one place long enough to keep my outfit together. I never could learn the ways of a cow. That's why I'm a mechanic. I understand mechanicking. A mechanic can always find work and he don't need to own his own tools to go to work. I learned mechanicking in a school where I had to teach my hands a trade or go crazy."

"You been to School, Tom?" Sorrells asked.

"I've been to the Big School, where the bulls walked on their hind legs." Wilson laughed.

"I'd rather cowboy than do any other work a man does," Tom said. "Maybe Mr. Cunningham will let me help in the cow work sometime."

"Take those spurs to start your outfit," Sorrells said.

"I sure appreciate it, if you *want* to give them to me," Tom said. "Thank you."

"I'll be damned!" Charley cussed. He took out his wallet and handed Sorrells a ten-dollar bill.

"What's that for?" Sorrells asked.

"Me and Charley had a little bet about these spurs," Tom grinned. "Charley thought you'd be married to them." He got up from the table and went back to his room. When he returned, he was carrying a pair of hackamore bits he had been making for Sorrells. They were very well made and hanging on a new headstall Sorrells had left hanging in the saddle house.

"Here's your bear trap, Bert," Tom said. "I finished it today."

"Hell, Tom, thank you," Sorrells said. "Here, take Charley's ten dollars for your time. You won the bet, not me."

"No. You owe Famous about a dollar for the material," Tom said.

Chapter 26

THE GATE

An old bull, whipped by a society of younger, stronger bulls, may choose to remain longer in his summer querencia than is safe for him. He might stay after all the other cattle have gone, even though frost is covering him each morning, all the feed is gone, and his watering place is drying up.

Water holes are often fenced for the purpose of controlling the cattle watering there. These fenced areas are called waterlots. If an outfit wants to gather an area it shuts the gates to the waterlots and the cattle are held there by their desire to drink until the cowboys come to gather them.

Unless waterlots are inspected often for cattle, their gates should be left open. If they are not left open, an old bull whose range has become limited by his age, might wait too long to go to water, and arriving at his favorite water hole, find the gate closed. He will usually force his way through the fence because he is driven by his thirst, but once full of water, he does not always, for some unknown reason, realize that he can force his way out. He may starve to death inside the waterlot.

Tom walked back to his room carrying a cup of whiskey. The wind was holding the door of the small bathroom open and the water in the toilet bowl was freezing. Tom closed the door and switched on the electric heater he had rehabilitated in his shop. He sat on the lid of the toilet, his head bent under the shelf of his bed, and sipped his whiskey while his adequate, though out of balance, heater banged warmth into the room. He could see the top of his head in the mirror. He knew he needed a haircut. He had been on the place four months without going to town. He thought he ought to go to town for a haircut and a crap game and some new clothes. Then he would decide whether to buy the blankets and come back here or not buy them and go south. Bert had talked about Mexico at times. If Bert was to go to Mexico this winter maybe he could go too. He might go for a while to see if he liked it and then go on over to Texas and see Bright Mary.

The room was warming up. He stood up and started undressing. He banged an elbow against his bunk, recoiled, and banged his other elbow against the door. He did not notice pain. He felt like going to town tonight. He wouldn't want to bother anyone to take him, with them having to work tomorrow. He could take Bert's car, though, Bert had offered to lend it to him. He could fix the muffler on it to pay Bert back. You could hear that old car coming a mile off. He could ask Bert tomorrow if he caught the crew at breakfast. He could have a day or two in Keno and if he didn't want to stay on the Outfit after that he could bring the car back and get Bert to take him to the highway. Maybe he could meet Bert someplace down south this winter.

He stepped on the lid of the toilet and climbed onto his bunk. The rags he slept in were oily. He could go to town and rent himself a good bed and some sheets in the hotel and bathe and put on new clothes. When he came back to the Outfit he could bring nice blankets, a set of sheets, and pillowslips and a pillow of his own. He ought to try having a good bed again and sleeping clean. He kicked and poked his feet until all of him was covered. Carefully, he reached under his bunk and found his cup on top the toilet. He raised it and sipped on it, careful his movement wouldn't uncover him.

All cleaned up in town nobody would bother him, and if they asked him if he had work he could say out at the Outfit. Nobody usually bothered a man in Nevada. In fact, usually nobody even saw a man in the casinos, everybody being so busy gambling. The only place they noticed a man was at a place like Wanda's and that wouldn't be bad.

Tom swallowed the last of his whiskey and followed its warmth down into his bed and slept. He slept knowing he never slept too well with his old liver sticking and unsticking against his ribs, and after the peace the whiskey had given him began to wear off, he rolled over on top of his liver so he could bear down on it and hold it still until it started to swell. As it swelled, his consciousness rose, and when he decided to move he realized the room was too warm. He raised his head as he rolled off his side and his head went dizzy and did not stop in the arc it made toward the edge of the bed. The room was black and he did not know where his dizzy momentum was carrying him. He pushed at his bed with one arm, a strong arm. He stuck out his other arm when he started to fall and it struck the door. He fell on his temple on the frozen sidewalk outside his place.

"Tom, coffee. Coffee, Tom," Sorrells yelled in the morning. He pounded on the wall between their rooms. He went to breakfast without waiting for an answer.

"Are we going to wait on the son of the Outfit again today?" Porter asked Sorrells at the breakfast table.

"I don't think so. Bobby'll probably think of a thousand more important jobs to do than jobs that pay two hundred and fifty a month," Sorrells said cheerfully.

"I saw Roy's pickup going out just before I called you guys," Charley the cook said.

"Probably taking Bobby to his little silver plane," Sorrells said, filling his plate with beefsteak and eggs.

Wilson was standing by his bed. "Here comes Roy," he said, as the headlights of the pickup shone on the window. Cunningham came into the bunkhouse, looking at his watch.

"Did Bobby already zoom away in his little silver snorter?" Sorrells asked him.

"Damn right," Cunningham said. "Me and him have already done half a day's work."

"Was his little butt pink this morning?" Sorrells asked.

"No, why?"

"I just thought he would have wanted to go horsebackriding with us again. We're really going to see the country today," Sorrells said.

"Is Tom up yet?" Cunningham asked.

"I pounded on his wall. He's awake," Sorrells said.

"I need to take him out to the well rig with me this morning," Cunningham said and walked through the room.

"Where are we going today, Dobie?" Sorrells asked, hoping the old man would have a good reason to avoid Last Chance Canyon. Dobie would be through after Last Chance.

"Last Chance. Don't you think so, Wilson?" Porter said.

"The cattle seem to be moving that way, finally," Wilson said.

Cunningham came back into the room. "Old *Tom* is dead," he said.

Sorrells went with the rest of the men back to see what he could do for Tom, but Tom was not what he saw lying on the sidewalk. The barest features of Tom were lying there, but no recognizable form of Tom was there. That was his nose and his cheekbone, but the two features together on the end of the pale form a few feet long did not make it Tom. The pale, bare skin over the shoulders, dingy like the undershirt, covered by a sort of speckled grime worn into skin and cloth alike, did not identify Tom. Tom was a man who wore dirty bib overalls too big for him. He had an old black shirt with grease all over it. He had a healthy flush in his dirty face. It was not small and pale and turned away forever like this corpse.

"I couldn't think of anything to do except to cover up his feet," Cunningham said. "I couldn't cover up his head and leave his feet and that old rag wouldn't cover him all up."

"Is that all that's left of us?" Sorrells, who had seen many corpses, asked.

"That's all, I guess, when we're dead," Stacy said softly.

Wilson spread a blanket over Tom. Porter walked to the open door of the bathroom, placed both hands on the door jam and peered inside, cocking his head.

"Does anybody know who we can notify?" Cunningham asked.

No one answered.

"Didn't he ever say where he was from?" Cunningham asked.

"Texas," Charley said. "That's where he was from, I think."

"I thought he was from Oklahoma," Porter said.

"Aw, Dobie, everybody's an Okie to you," Stacy said angrily.

"Well, I did. I thought he was from Oklahoma," Porter smiled. His feelings were hurt. "What's wrong with that?"

"I didn't even know his name," Sorrells said.

"Tom something," Charley said.

"I've got it written down at the house," Cunningham said. "Once he told me he'd been in the army. Maybe the veterans will help us find his people."

"If he was a veteran, the veterans will even bury him," Wilson said.

"Well, let's don't leave him here, poor old thing," Cunningham said. He walked to the front of the bunkhouse and drove the pickup back. The crew loaded Tom in the bed of the truck and Cunningham covered his feet again when he saw them sticking out from under the blanket.

The veterans in their makeshift uniforms buried Tom in Keno. He had been a soldier like them and they were proud to do it. The crew of the Outfit stood by and gave a hand to carry him. Maudy Jane laid flowers on his grave. No one ever found his people.

Chapter 27

LAST CHANCE

A running iron is a short branding iron with a hook on the end in the form of a J. It can be carried on a saddle and used to run any brand a cowboy wants to brand. Branding irons used to stamp a brand on an animal are too cumbersome to carry horseback. The running iron can be used any place a cowboy can build a fire to heat it, and the accomplished wielder of a running iron can draw a brand that looks better than a stamped brand. For this reason, and for the reason that a running iron can be used to change a brand and make it look like a different brand, the cattlemen's associations look upon a man who carries a running iron in much the same way a bank teller would look upon any man he does not know who walks into the bank carrying a gun.

The old cow had been in the waterlot at Last Chance for many days. She had worn a trail around the fence on the inside. She was so thin the outline of her skeleton was clear. She was not much more than hide and bones. She was narrow as a knife when she turned to look at Sorrells and Porter riding up. She was crazy with hunger and she ran from the men into a corner of the fence, though she did not strike the corner with much force. She fell back, squatting on her hind legs. She tried hard to stand as she kept her eyes on the men.

"Why in *hell* that Whitey leaves the gates closed on the waterlots he build, *I'll* never know," Porter said, stopping his horse by the gate while Sorrells got off to open it. Sorrells untied the wires off the gate post, dragged the gate away, and threw it on top a piñon. He led Roller into the waterlot.

"Now let's just ease around her so she won't go on the fight," Porter said, following Sorrells. The cow stood up again, trembling and tossing her horns at the men. She decided against an immediate fight and moved toward the gate. She tried to keep her legs coordinated beneath her for a fight, but they could not keep up with her. She looked around for a way to escape the men. She headed through the gate. She was so weak and dizzy, she barely got through it without hitting both sides.

"Looka there, tch, tch, like a gutted snowbird!" Porter said. He dismounted from Buck and walked along to the spot where the clear water was rolling out of Last Chance Mountain. Buck followed close to his shoulder on a slack rein. Porter eased himself to his hands and knees and dipped his head to the spring. His old, dry lips touched the pool and he got back to his feet.

"Now, that's a drink," he said. "Here, Bert. Get ya a drink of that. Right here is the best place." Sorrells knelt and drank. He stood up and loosened his cinches.

"Let's sit a minute and rest ourselves while we decide what to do," Porter said. "Roll yourself a cigareet."

Sorrells offered his pouch and papers to Porter and was surprised when the old man took them. Porter didn't smoke. He rolled a perfect cigarette, wet it with an abundance of spit, and handed it to Sorrells.

"Here, smoke a goodern," Porter said. "You Southern fellers and Mexicans always roll humpy ones."

Sorrells struck a match to it with Porter watching. For an instant, Porter was like an old dog watching a bone.

"Here, take your makings," Porter said, "I cain't smoke no more cigareets nor drink coffee. My old belly."

Sorrells sat flat on the ground and stretched his legs.

"Now, you see?" Porter said. "This waterlot is just wasted here, because there's running water all through this canyon most of the time except right now. Close the gate here in the spring when you need to trap cattle and they'll just turn back down the canyon and drink. The cattle are all watering way down low now. I just wanted to start high today for just such a reason as that old cow we saved."

"This waterlot is another way to spend money," Sorrells said.

"Famous is just flat going to spend itself out of the cow business," Porter said. Look at that four sections they're fencing over above Dove Springs to plant crested wheat grass. Crested wheat will kill a lactating cow certain times of the year, and look at all the country they're changing from the way God made it.

"They're agoin' to conserve themselves right out of the cow business. When they have this whole ranch fenced and planted, the old cow won't have a chance to get away from the poisons to go and find a healthy bite to eat. Then, with all the expense and the death loss the companies will be having in the experimenting, the price of beef will get so high a poor man won't be able to afford it. Then the government will move in and force a subsidy on the cowman and start tellin' him what to do. The cowman will be working for the government the same as any other bib-overalled son of a gun.

"The government is giving people like Famous all the rope they need to hang themselves. You mark my words, Bert, the rich dudes' greedy ways is trying to change the cow country from the way the Good Lord made it and I don't think it's good. Get you another drink, Bert."

"I'm all tanked up, Dobie."

Here, let me roll you another cigareet."

"Aw, I'll roll it," Sorrells said, not wanting to burn any more of old Porter's spit.

"You know, Bert, I never ride up to a spring like this, but what I take a little drink of it and thank the Lord for it. You and me is lucky, Bert. We get to work out here in the open country just the way the Lord made us. We're lucky we don't know how to make better paying jobs. There's some people whose bosses owns the water they drink and the air they breathe.

"You take old Roller there. What chance would he have if you hadn't come along? All three of the horses in your string could go out and make good horses for any cowman now. But they wouldn't be able to do the work the Lord made them for if a cowpuncher hadn't come along.

"That's what I've enjoyed in this life. To make a good horse out of any goober-lipped pisshead and to help an old cow make a living for herself and raise a big calf. A cowpuncher helps God that way. He helps an old cow to help herself. But now, when a man starts waiting on one and buying her all kinds of doodads, he starts to lose his feeling for the cow brute. A man can't make a cow shit a quick dollar. She needs time and a lot of country, needs to be allowed to do it her own way, and when people forgets that, then *anybody* can own a cow, and you and me and old Roller and Buck is out of business."

"Where will you go after we finish gathering, Dobie?" Sorrells asked. "I don't know about you, but I ain't gonna winter on this iceberg."

"I'd kindly like to make a trip to the American Cattleman's Convention in Hawaii after New Year's," Porter said. "I've never been off the continental United States, and I've been reading up on that convention from material a friend of mine sends me. I think I'll just go."

"Won't that cost a lot of money, Dobie?"

"I've got a little cash money, Bert. Enough to take you along, too, if you want to go."

"Well, no. I've already seen Hawaii when I was in the Marines, Dobie." Sorrells stood up and tightened Roller's cinches. "Hawaii is awful green, Dobie. Just the smell of it would fatten cattle. Then there's all that water."

"Well, I'm agoin' to try and see her just once, too." Porter said, as they mounted and rode out the gate of the waterlot.

The two men rode across a short mesa into Last Chance Canyon. Porter dismounted when the trail began to descend into the canyon. He limped and slid, the soft, beaten clay in the trail making him take longer steps than he wanted to. Sorrells, behind him, thought of the picture Dobie would make under the palm fronds in the luxury hotels in Hawaii; standing on his tiny, booted feet with the rolled cuffs of his

Levis dragging the sidewalk; cocking his head on that neck that was so short. His broad, brown town hat would appear to be set on a shelf, when he was seen from behind. He would do much peering through those thick glasses at all the "half-nekkid" girls. Hawaiians were going to see at least one real, Western cowpuncher if Porter went to that convention.

A joshua tree leaned out from the side of the canyon over the trail and Sorrells had to duck to ride under it. Roller was nervously careful of his steps as were Buck and Porter. At the bottom of the canyon, the men came upon a cow and calf where the trail forked and straddled a long, high ridge in the canyon. The cow hurried down the canyon ahead of the men, her calf close beside her. Porter and Sorrells split to cover both trails. Sorrells followed the cow and calf.

Roller seemed stronger that day. Tom's death and funeral had given him extra days off. Sorrells rode down the dry canyon, following the cow's tracks. He seldom saw the pair as it scrambled through the canyon ahead of him. Sorrells rode onto a bend in the canyon where a deadfall blocked the trail. A new trail climbed straight up the wall of the canyon over the promontory that caused the bend. Sorrells reined Roller to follow the tracks up the new trail.

The top of the promontory was as abrupt as a board standing on edge. The last yard to the top was sheer. Sorrells could not dismount. He had no place to stand beside his horse. He was at least a hundred feet above the floor of the canyon. He did not check Roller while he decided he could not dismount. Roller needed his momentum to make that last yard. Roller's front feet slipped and he lost the traction in his hind feet at the same time. He began sliding backwards. He reached forward again with his front feet. His hind legs stopped sliding. Roller began a backward somersault. Sorrells reined him and pointed him downhill and Roller's front feet landed one hundred and eighty degrees opposed to the spot he had intended to plant them. Sorrells lost sight of Roller's head and got a very good look at the bottom of the canyon, as Roller began the fall to the bottom. Sorrells was glad no one was around to hear the unrobust squeak he squeezed out from behind his wide eyes during that ride. The horse kept his feet under him, but he was going much faster when he reached the bottom than he had been when he started.

Sorrells dismounted and rested, waiting until he no longer felt the climb was impossible. He mounted again, deciding that if Roller couldn't carry him over the trail the bovines had walked, then Roller wasn't the horse Sorrells thought he was and Sorrells wasn't any horseman. He did not spur Roller or coax him. Roller already knew more about the trail than Sorrells did. Sorrells made himself look down, as Roller tried the ascent again. Sorrells wanted to know at any moment which way to point Roller if they fell again. As they passed the tracks of Roller's descent, Sorrells wondered how the horse had kept his feet. At the last step, Roller paused, and with his nose inches from the step, made a standing, uphill leap. His front feet pawed the step and cleared it.

Sorrells saw the cow and calf from the highpoint. He hurried Roller down into the canyon after them. Sorrells had to keep on the track. He followed it over an hour before he saw that the pair had run into more cattle at a small running spring of alum water. Sorrells stopped to taste the water. It was flat and chalky. Roller drank, too. Sorrells rode up the side of the canyon and saw the cattle strung out and trotting toward the flats where Wilson waited. An hour later, Sorrells met Wilson holding the cattle. Sorrells looked them over. His Last Chance cow and calf were not in the herd.

"Did you see a three-year-old muley cow with a big, spotted calf, Wilson?" Sorrells asked.

"No, Bert. Maybe she didn't come out of the canyon. These cattle were all together."

"No, she would have gone on through these. She wouldn't have stopped or turned back. She was trotty and leaving the country. I watched her tracks all the way through. At least, I think I had her tracks."

"I didn't see her, Bert," Wilson said.

Sorrells stood up in his stirrups and looked over the flats. He couldn't see far. He rode back across the draw that opened out of Last Chance. He found the pair's tracks in a shallow wash. They were spreading deep tracks and thin manure through the country. Sorrells loped Roller on the tracks a half hour before he caught sight of the pair.

The cow and calf were close together, now and then breaking into a trot and then pacing a few steps to rest. They had not seen Sorrells. He stopped Roller to rest and let the cattle get around a bend, so he could lope ahead of them without being seen.

Cattle in a hurry, when they thought they were getting away, were always intent on their direction and hardly ever looked back. They were also wet. Sorrells marvelled at the wetness that marked the cattle from a distance. If he had not followed this cow and calf the length of Last Chance and had accidentally ridden on them at this time, he would know they had been pressing a long way by their wetness. They had a soggy way about them he could see a quarter mile away. Their hides seemed to slosh as they rolled on their frames. Their tails wrung like pump handles and Sorrells could almost see a mist around them. Their moist heat seemed to hover over them. The cow and calf trotted around the bend.

Sorrells brought the cow and calf back to the herd and he and Wilson penned the cattle in the portable corral. They loaded the calves in the stock truck, tallied the cows, and turned them out of the corral. The cows did not leave. They bawled for their calves. This attracted an old coyote who came and loitered about fifty yards away from the truck. He did not see the distressed calves he had hoped to find, so he lay down in the shade of a joshua to wait in case any little tidbit of any kind fell his way.

Sorrells built a fire and Wilson made coffee. They ate the lunch Charley had packed for them, though it was late afternoon and no longer lunchtime. Porter was nowhere in sight. He had never stayed away this late before. Sorrells lay down on the ground by the fire so he could be near the coffee. Wilson climbed on the truck to watch for Porter.

"You see any dust?" Sorrells asked.

"No. No dust yet, Bert," Wilson said.

"You suppose Dobie's down someplace with his head under him?"

"Maybe so. The Last Chance is full of rough country."

"Well, he better not light any damn fires. He can burn up Last Chance Mountain and I won't go one step to look for him. I'm drinking coffee."

Wilson laughed softly.

"I guess you know it's just gonna be me and you after today, don't you, Wilson?" Sorrells said.

"*I* don't know nothin'," Wilson laughed. "How would *I* know anything?"

"They're going to let the old man go. You know that, don't you?"

"Roy said something about it."

"And you're going to be cow boss," Sorrells said.

Wilson laughed again. "Cow boss, what's that? I don't know what you and Roy are talking about. You are going to be here too, aren't you?"

"Damned if I know," Sorrells said. "I know I ain't wintering on this starve out. I'm going someplace where they know how to sing and dance in the winter time."

"Why would I want to stay here? Everybody will be gone. Why would I want to work alone all winter?"

"So you'll know where the cattle are so you can be cow boss next spring roundup, Wilson."

"Aw, Bert. They're not going to make me cow boss,"

"The hell they're not, Wilson. For one thing, you know the country better than anyone else. For another thing, you belong here. This is your place."

"Oh, no. Not my place. I haven't got no place."

"You should have the job, Wilson. Anyway, you're going to get it, like it or not."

"Aw, Bert. You know how long I'd last as cow boss on this outfit? No longer than anyone else has lasted. How could an Indian cow boss be sure of his job? The son of the Outfit can't even remember my name."

"Make him remember you."

"That don't sound like you, Bert. You don't make people remember you. I'm not going to suck up to anyone to make him remember me either. I don't have to be cow boss."

"Somebody ought to help Roy and Bobby Lang," Sorrells said.

"Bobby Lang will always have plenty of help."

"Well, I'm not staying around. At least not in the winter."

"There's Dobie's dust," Wilson said. The two men rode out to meet Porter. He was driving twenty head.

"You didn't light no fires, so we figured you'd come in sometime before dark," Sorrells said to Porter.

Porter patted a bulging canvas sack tied on the back of his saddle next to his running iron.

"I just found the best mercury samples I ever seen in my whole life," Porter said.

Chapter 28

TIRED MEN, TIRED HORSES, COLD COUNTRY

Al ojo del amo engorda el caballo—*Under the watchful eye of his master the horse will prosper.*

"**W**e've got whiskey, we've got beer, we've got purty little dears. We've got gin, we've got sin, so come on boys and give in," Wanda shouted when Sorrells and Wilson walked into the Rabbit Hutch the night after they had worked Last Chance. She was drunk and didn't recognize the men until they were standing in front of her at the bar.

"Oh ho, my plump and smooth Paiute brave whom never, never has to shave," Wanda said when she recognized Wilson. She looked at Sorrells. "You here too, huh?"

"Come on, Wanda. Give us a poem," Sorrells said.

"Ya want to drink, ya here ta play? Then show me your money or go away. I don't like you anyway," Wanda said belligerently. She wobbled. Her hair was mussed. "Bert," she said: "What are you doing here? I ain't going to like you at all if you are going to cause me trouble."

"Aw, Wanda, lay off and pour us a drink," Wilson said. Wanda grinned at him. "My huggy Bear, my cuddly Bear. For you I care, my Wilson Bear. I do not care for Bert, that's all."

"That breaks my heart, Wanda," Sorrells said. "You still sell whiskey though, don't you?"

"Now, I'm telling you, Bert. If you come here looking for trouble, I'm just the feller to give it to you," Wanda shouted.

Sorrells had never been known as a charming fellow and he knew he could never charm a drunk Wanda. "Whiskey, Wanda. Whiskey. That's all I want. No trouble. I'm skeered of you Wanda," he said.

"I'll give you a drink after you tell me why you're town," Wanda said.

"We came to get Jack Roberts out of the hospital."

"Where is he, then? What have you done, you crumb, with my fine little feller?"

"Cunningham came and got him early this afternoon."

"Hah! So you came to town for nothin'? Fine! Ah, Little Red Man, mine," she crooned to Wilson, patting his cheek. She told the barmaid to pour the whiskey. "Give Sorrells a weak one," she said.

"Why are you so onry tonight, Wanda?" Sorrells asked. "Me and Wilson only came to see you so as not to waste our trip to town."

"Don't want no Big Men comin' around, tryin' to make my girls settle down," Wanda said without looking at him. She began crooning at Wilson again.

Sorrells was ready to leave. Hell, it was all he could do to swallow his gorge and walk into this place any time. Who in the hell could stand a whorehouse, anyway? And then to have the madam downright antagonistic. He wished he was asleep in the bunkhouse. This was, without a doubt, one of the worst whorehouses he'd ever seen. The floor was dirty. The barroom was kept dark to cover the torn cushions on the booths and the sharp, cold edge a sober man felt when he walked in. The barroom stunk of face powder and stale toilet water covered by coats of sweet disinfectant. A man didn't breath air in the Rabbit Hutch. He breathed the odors of women's unwashed, powdered armpits; layers of unbathed short times; unclean feet in dirty, worn high heels that no longer fit; too much singed and unwashed hair; and too many layers of scented makeup. The perfume of the disinfectant permeating the house uplifted all these smells, instead of subduing them and was so penetrating that when a person drank, it invaded the taste and crowded through the nostrils.

More men came to the place and girls began buzzing to them like painted flies. Sorrells quickly ordered a double bourbon and drank it and ordered another. He had always appreciated whores and could take them in friendship or leave them alone. He didn't know why he suddenly only saw the fingernail dirt and the coin-money-smudged, slot machine look of the Rabbit Hutch. Maybe because he realized these were the only women he and Wilson, Porter, Tom, Stacy, and Charley had to talk to anymore. No, not Tom anymore. Roberts had at least been talking to nurses a few days. Sorrells drank and ordered another. After the drink the smell of the place didn't seem so bad. He nursed his next drink awhile. He was waiting for a Chinese girl named Suzie to appear. All the Chinese whores he knew were calling themselves Suzie. He liked talking to Suzie. She could talk Spanish and she seemed to like talking to Sorrells. She didn't walk away if a man didn't want to go to a room right away.

He looked at the mirror behind the bar and it had Christmas wreaths painted on each end with red berries and "Noel" under each wreath and "Merry Xmas" splashed between them with, probably, shaving cream. Sorrells' ugly dark face reflected under the X instead of Christ. He wasn't a praying man, so the X didn't particularly bother him. He smiled to himself, thinking that Merry Sorrellsmas wasn't right either. He saw Suzie in the mirror.

"Suzie!" Sorrells said to her. He automatically looked to her bouncing fanny in the red bikini going away.

"Bert!" she said and kept right on going.

"Come and talk to me," Sorrells said. Suzie did not turn back again. She sat at a back booth with a girl who had already been turned away by a big miner at the end of the bar. The two girls sat across from one another in the booth, not speaking and not looking at one another. Suzie crossed her legs. She had nice, full, ivory, shiny legs. She probably didn't want to risk sitting and talking too long with Sorrells and not making money. Her time was money, she, the harlot, had told him. How the hell could Sorrells blame her? This was her Christmas money coming up. Sorrells had a girl once. Now there was a girl. That Bonnie. One girl, one horse, one pistol at a time. Sorrells' grandfather had said that, and he had never needed a pistol. Don't ever loan your horse or girl and you won't need the pistol, he had said. Find your woman and make a son and don't waste yourself in whorehouses.

He saw the lush, blonde wig piled atop the small, pale head above the blue-white shoulders striped with crimson straps before the girl spoke.

"Wild Man, what you doin' here?" she said.

"*Christ* was a man," Sorrells said and could not say more when he saw the girl was Bonnie.

Bonnie laughed and looked in the mirror to see how she looked laughing by Sorrells in a whorehouse bar.

"What are *you* doin' here?" Sorrells asked, seeing her laugh at herself and noticing again the blue veins through the transparent skin in the tops of her heavy breasts. They were heavy now, her breasts were. The fine skin was tight on them. Seeing the veins pained him. The big eyes in the thin face turned to him, still laughing. They were not mocking him. She looked as happy as a girl who had been hoping her daddy would come in to see her at her new boarding school.

"Grow up, Bert Sorrells," Bonnie said.

"It ain't me who is a toy for the boys," Sorrells said.

"So what? I always told you I was no good. It's time you faced it." She stopped laughing and looked genuinely tough when she said this.

"How long you been here, Bonnie?"

"Hah! Long enough, I'd say, to be called a prostitute. Are you going to buy me a drink or are you going to just sit there like a wart on my nose? If you aren't buying, I'm moving down the bar."

Sorrells called the barmaid and bought Bonnie's mint tea. "I always liked tea better than booze and now I can get it without a fuss," she said, glancing at herself in the mirror. "Now I don't have to guzzle whiskey with any man. . . ."

"Who in the hell wants you to?" Sorrells asked her.

"You do, that's who. So why in the heck don't you just leave me alone?" Bonnie raised her voice.

"Now, goddam it, Bert, I told you not to start any trouble in here. Now, by God, you're going to see what real trouble is," Wanda shouted from down the bar. She came toward them waving a short, black wooden bat. She moved extraordinarily fast. She was plump, not fat. She moved down the boardwalk behind the bar with an extravagance of motion and sound that, at first, made Sorrells believe she was bluffing. He could only believe she was bluffing, because he knew he hadn't done a damn thing to warrant her charging him with a bat. When she stopped in front of Sorrells, he saw that her eyes were wide, the pupils dilated. She was truly on the fight. Sorrells marvelled. Wanda was one female that didn't turn pale and trembly when she went on the prod. Now she was standing back of Sorrells' reach so he couldn't take the bat away from her. If she were really bluffing, she would be up close, waving it at him.

"Get away from him, Bonnie," Wanda said in a steady voice. "I'm going to knock the son of a bitch's head off."

Sorrells reached and held Bonnie on the stool by the back of her neck.

"So that's how it is," Sorrells said through his teeth. "You don't need any man, huh? You've got Wanda for a lover."

"Turn her loose, you God damned son of a bitch!" Wanda shrieked. *"Let her go!"* She came at Sorrells with the same righteous intent any man would have, protecting his woman. She came like a man does who is confident he can handle himself and is used to doing it. Sorrells pushed Bonnie off the stool by his hold on her neck, as he stood up to meet Wanda. Wilson stood up, calmly caught the bat, and carefully, cruelly, twisted it out of Wanda's hand. It took him a while and Wanda, bent over backwards in front of him, did not whimper. When the bat came free in Wilson's hand, she sat down under the bar. When she came back to her feet again, she had a bottle in her hand. She quickly pegged it at Sorrells' head. She missed. She turned and stalked around the corner of the bar. She headed toward Sorrells, picking another bottle off the bar along the way. She paid no attention to Wilson.

"Now, you goddam dirty bastard," Wanda said, coming faster, her chest full of air, her words clipped so she could save her wind for her attack. "I'm going to show you what I do to bastards who choke little girls."

"Now, listen, Wanda. I've had enough of this," Wilson

said and stepped in front of her. "You want trouble, you're going to get it. We'll tear this damned whorehouse to pieces. I ain't fooling. We'll level it."

"I haven't got anything against you, Wilson. It's him I want, but you *get out of my way,*" Wanda yelled, keeping her eyes on Sorrells.

"Let her come, Wilson," Sorrells said quietly. Wanda pushed Wilson and got around him. Sorrells waited until she came into his range. When she started to wind up with the bottle, he slapped her so hard his hand immediately began to swell. Wanda sprawled, sliding on the floor, not nearly far enough after a slap like that, Sorrells thought. She was a solid woman.

"Lock that front door, Wilson," Sorrells said, heading for the only other exit, the door to the rooms. The lock was on the outside. He shut the door and pulled a heavy booth against it. He turned to the room and looked at the four husky men and three whores. Bonnie had joined them at the end of the bar. She was crying on the bosom of another whore. The men had stayed on their stools. They watched him walk toward them. He grabbed Bonnie by the back of her neck and pushed her along, lifting her when she stumbled, to a booth. He let her go into the seat.

"Bonnie, I didn't start this, but I'm finishing it now," Sorrells said. He turned and looked on the four men, seeing the details of none of them. "I don't mean to inconvenience any of you fellers, but I've got business with Wanda and I'd like you to stay here until I'm through," he said to them.

"No. No inconvenience. You go right ahead," the nearest man, the biggest one, said. "You do just exactly as you please, Bert." Sorrells looked at him. He knew the man's face, but couldn't remember where he had seen it before. He walked away. Wanda was sitting on a stool, holding a bar rag on the side of her face. Sorrells took her by the hair of her head, towed her back to the booth, and dumped her beside Bonnie. Wilson was standing by the front door.

"You dirty goddammed sonofabitch," Wanda threatened weakly. "You're in trouble now." Sorrells slapped her on both sides of her head this time.

"Now, Wanda," he said quietly. "I don't like anyone to

call me a son of a bitch, and especially a goddam whoremonger, so, for your own good, don't call me that again."

"Well, what the goddam hell do you want with me then?" Wanda said.

"You understand what I want," Sorrells said softly, almost kindly, to her. "You see, Wanda. You can have any woman in the whole world you want in this place, but you can't have Bonnie."

"Hah! Hah! Hah!" Wanda sneered at him. "How are *you* going to stop it? She's free, white and twenty-one."

"You know how, Wanda? With my own two balls, that's how. Because I'm getting her away from you if I have to burn this whorehouse down."

"Ask *her* what she wants to do. This is a free country. Go ahead ask *her* if she wants to leave here with you, you smart son of a bitch."

"*Crack,*" went Sorrells' open hand on the side of her head.

"And you," he said to Bonnie. "You're the one wrote that letter offering your ass to Bobby Lang, aren't you? You and this old bag of pus."

"You don't know, do you, Big Man?"

"Yes, I do know. I know just as well as if I saw the letter with my own eyes. Even if you didn't, old pus heart here was in on it and you both get the blame. I've heard you whine that same way a hundred times over other miseries, so I know you did it. I'm telling you, Whore, I ain't asking either of you. You get your soured ass out of here and go peddle it someplace else. Tonight, not tomorrow, because tomorrow is going to be too late for the two of you."

"I can't believe it. I never thought I'd see the day you'd talk to me this way," Bonnie said.

"And another thing, while we're on it. You can whore to your black little heart's content, but if I ever catch you doing it around where I am, or calling yourself Bonnie Sorrells while you're doing it, I'll kill you."

"You're going to be sorry, Bert," Bonnie said softly, "Ohhh, you'll be sorry when certain friends of ours hear about this."

"No, I won't be sorry, Bonnie. You know me well enough to know I better have my way about this. If I don't, I'm sure I can get to you and Wanda before anybody gets to me."

Bonnie didn't answer.

"I'll leave you lovebirds alone, now, for tonight. Make it as sweet as you want it for yourselves. *Any* of it tomorrow is going to turn sour and give you both blood poisoning."

Sorrells walked toward the front door, realizing he should know the husky man at the bar, who had called him by name. When he was abreast of the men and they were all watching him, he remembered. He was the slick dick from Vegas, the one who had been escorting Bonnie in and out of the Red Barn. Without breaking stride, Sorrells headed for the slick dick. Dick began to smile at Sorrells.

"You were with Bonnie at the Vegas rodeo, weren't you, Dick?" Sorrells said.

Slick Dick tried to laugh. "My name isn't Dick, but I guess I was, Bert," he said. "You remember? I offered to buy you a drink. The offer still stands."

"I remember. It's funny to me you were with her there and she was busy, and now she's got a full-time job and you are still hanging around."

"That's me, I guess, Bert. Just follering her around, I guess."

"Kinda taking the leftovers, so to speak?"

"Yeah. I guess. Only there ain't much left over after a night here at Wanda's."

"You shouldn't care, though, Dick. It's the work you're getting that counts, ain't it? You brought her here to put her to work, didn't you?"

"Now, wait a minute, Bert. She comes and goes as she pleases."

"But you recruited her for Wanda."

"Well, I drove her up here, if that's what you mean."

"You made a mistake. Bonnie is one you should have stayed away from."

"Well, now. You can tell them two whores what to do, Bert. But not me." He looked for corroboration to the man beside him, but the man's expression did not change. He turned back to Sorrells and said, "You know, you ought to have been a preacher. Then you could have done that kind of sermon in church and been paid for it, but the way things stand, I don't see you are any better a man than I am and shouldn't be reminding me of my mistakes."

"You don't?"

"No sir."

Sorrells hit him with the best straight right hand he knew how to throw, stepped in to hit him again before he bounced off the bar and, as he was falling toward Sorrells' feet, Sorrells hooked him with a left hand that turned him over and landed him on his back. Sorrells was sure the first punch had knocked the man out. The other two, and his head hitting the floor, had been good measure. Sorrells looked to the other men. The whore known as Suzie was staring at him, a stranger.

"If that pimp was your friend, you'd better come on off your stools if you want some of it too," Sorrells said to the men. The man nearest Sorrells looked for a moment as if he might be thinking it over, but he didn't change his position on the stool. The other two weren't even looking at Sorrells. They were all sitting very still.

"No. Christ, no." The man looking at Sorrells said quietly. "That ain't our business. We're working men, here for a good time, is all."

"Have fun," Sorrells said. He turned and he and Wilson left Wanda's. They drove out of Keno, stopping at a bar for two bottles of whiskey. Wilson bought three six-packs of beer. He could drink more beer faster than any man Sorrells had ever seen. He didn't bother to swallow. He just opened his throat and poured it down. Sorrells wondered why he wanted to drink beer that way. Wilson was already drunk. The Indian was griping about the sorry state of his string of horses again. He did not say one word about the Rabbit Hutch. Sorrells drank whiskey and did not say a word about anything. When he had cooled off, he wondered how he was going to back up what he had said he would do if Bonnie didn't get out of Wanda's. He kept drinking and soon he began planning what he was going to do to Wanda and Slick Dick, whether Bonnie left or not.

The lights were still on in the bunkhouse when they got back to headquarters. They carried the whiskey and beer inside. Porter and Charley the cook were playing gin at the table. Jack Roberts, his arm in a sling, was sitting on his bunk and smoking and talking to them. Stacy was camping at the bull and heifer pastures and doing the feeding.

Wilson pounded the whiskey bottles when he set them on the table. He swept his arm over the table and cleaned it of the cards and cups Porter and Charley were using.

"Whiskey!" Wilson shouted. "You're, by God, going to drink fire water now. No more of that goddamned coffee we drink around here every goddamned day."

Sorrells went in the kitchen and brought back glasses and a pitcher of water, thinking Wilson probably figured it was his turn to let off steam. He had to stand and watch the door at the Rabbit Hutch and had not got into any of the action. His blood was up.

"And you, you son of a bitch, Jack. Where in the hell were you when we went all the way in to town to get you?" Wilson demanded.

Roberts smiled at him. "Roy brought me home. I didn't know you guys were coming. Neither did Roy," he said.

"Damn. That Roy never knows nothin'," Wilson turned to the table as though he was sure everyone there knew he had stated a profound truth. "All he does is run around in his four-wheel-drive looking at country we've already killed our horses covering. We're killing our horses, you know that? Now he goes and makes us lose a damn trip to Keno. I mean, that ain't right, is it, Jack?"

"No, I guess not, Wilson," Jack said, smiling at him.

"You're damn right, not," Wilson said, stamping his foot and pounding a fist on his thigh.

"Sit down, Wilson. Have a drink," Sorrells said. Porter and Charley had retrieved their cards and were giving each other looks that said, "See, they're both drunk." Porter wasn't making any cracks, though. He knew when to keep quiet.

"Don't mind me," Wilson said, manhandling the bench and sitting down next to Porter. He snatched a bottle. "I'm just pissed off."

"That's O.K.," Roberts said, still smiling. "Tired men on tired horses in cold country makes a man feel bad sometimes." Sorrells realized he had not asked Roberts how his health was. He had not even said hello to him.

"You guys ain't drinking any whiskey," Wilson growled at Porter and Charley and turned the bottle up to empty it on the cards. Sorrells snatched it from him before the bottle was empty. Wilson grabbed the other bottle and scrambled off the bench, falling to the floor. He balanced for a moment on one buttock, his foot in the air, holding the bottle high, unable to move, hunching his shoulders with the drunken, stalemated effort. He waved the bottle at Roberts.

"Here, Jack," he said. "Drink." Roberts took the bottle and touched Whiskey to his tongue and handed it back. Wilson took another big swallow and tried to give it back to Roberts.

"No," Roberts said, shaking his head. "I better not. I'm too damn sore and I don't want to get drunk. If I fell down right now it would break the last whole egg I'm carrying. Besides that, it don't take much whiskey to hurt my ulcer."

"Drink," Wilson said, stumbling onto Roberts and mauling him while he tried to hold the bottle to Roberts' mouth.

"Aw, let him alone, Wilson," Sorrells said. "He don't want no whiskey. Save it for us who wants it."

"Shit!" Wilson said, straightening up and staring at Sorrells. "Who says I got to let him alone? You?"

"Yes, me, Wilson. Let him alone. Don't waste our whiskey on him."

"Gin," said Charley.

"Oh, yeah? Already?" said Porter.

"You think you're tough enough to make me?" Wilson demanded.

"I didn't think I'd have to make you, Wilson," Sorrells said. "Tough? You don't know what tough is, Bert. You just think you're tough."

"Who's winning?" Sorrells asked Porter when he saw Wilson start stumbling toward him.

"He won that game but I'm still ahead," Porter said.

"You goddam half-breeds, Mexkins, don't know how to fight or love or nothin'. You're nothin'. Mexkin."

"Aw, Wilson, take it easy. Have a cup of coffee or something."

"Don't want no white-man coffee and don't you even talk to me, Mexkin."

"All right, then, Wilson, have it any way you want it."

"I am," Wilson said, weaving and staring at Sorrells.

"Cards," said Charley.

Sorrells drank the last of the whiskey in the bottle

Wilson had spilled. Wilson picked up the empty bottle and threw it into a corner. He knocked Sorrells' hat off and started pouring whiskey over Sorrells' head. Sorrells stood up and Wilson slapped him.

"How do *you* like it?" Wilson said, and Sorrells tapped him hard on the jaw. Wilson's spirit left him and his carcass hit the floor in one, crashing lump. The whiskey bottle skidded across the linoleum. Sorrells picked it up and set it on the table.

"He asked for it," Porter said, looking over his shoulder at Wilson.

Wilson was not breathing. He lay there with his eyes half open, his body twitching.

"God, I killed him," Sorrells said.

"He'll be all right," Porter said. "Give him a little time."

"I don't know how in the hell you guys can go on drinking that stuff," Jack Roberts said. "I really can't see it."

Wilson caught his breath in one big, inward, rushing sigh. His body relaxed and spread out on the floor. Sorrells looked at the broad, blunt toe of the boot he had seen on Wilson every day, all day, for four months, the boot that pushed the gas pedal of the stock truck. Sorrells shook his head. The way that boot had jerked and quivered on the floor had scared hell out of Sorrells. Wilson began to snore. Sorrells dragged him to his bunk and lifted the limp, meaty sections of him onto the bed and then went to his own bed.

He slept heavily, anesthetized by the whiskey for a few hours. He awoke then, instantly awake, his nerves jumping out of his skin, and completely aware of everything he had done on that day that began so long ago in Last Chance Canyon. How long the headlong days of his life were, he thought. He had not meant to include in that day threatening Bonnie, or hitting his friend Wilson, or running into the end of the day like this needing a drink.

He had meant only, that morning, to go into Last Chance and chase the wild bovine. He remembered, suddenly, that when he had pushed Bonnie away at the bar, warm tears had splashed on the back of his hand. He wished to God they had spilled before he pushed Bonnie away. His own tears were running into his ears now. He thought about the funny song about tears in ears and he almost laughed.

Chapter 29

A PLACE TO WINTER

When winter begins and cattle have been located a cow-
puncher feels like finding a place for himself to winter. He
looks forward to wintering in a place where he can fill out his
gaunt spots, keep his broken and healing spots warm, and
where he can get over the edginess and ringiness that too
many days on tired horses in cold country might have caused.
This is part of the thrift a cowpuncher must learn early in his
life if he is to endure as a husbandman. He must look to the
replenishment of his physical well-being like an athlete. This
thrift is sometimes never learned by young men who other-
wise perform their husbandry with great verve. This is one
reason there are not many old cowpunchers around.

Sorrells was unable to move
when Dobie Porter turned on the light to wake him the
morning after he and Wilson had visited Wanda's. The will to
get up and wash again, breakfast and saddle another horse,
load on the stock truck and go to work, was not in him. He
was not sleepy. He was tired of sleep. Sleep had made his
eyes hot. He did not want to stay in bed. The bed made him
tired. He did not want to go back to town and play. He
loathed town. He did not want to close his eyes and the sight
of the ceiling taxed him. He was cramped like an old bull
been run too far. He had no will.

"Time to get up, Bert. Time to go to work," Porter said, looking briefly at Sorrells.

Sorrells did not answer him nor did he move. Porter coughed and choked and stamped his feet, not able to tell if Sorrells was awake because he could not tell if Sorrells' Mongol eyes were open. Sorrells watched Porter, knowing Porter could not see his eyes were open. What a great power to be able to watch closely a man six feet away with that man looking uncertain because he suspected he was being watched unscrupulously.

"Bert?" Porter inquired, and Sorrells couldn't find it in his heart to answer him. Porter went to breakfast. Sorrells lay there trying hard to suspend his animation. He would not move at all and slow his heart down. He would breathe not an excess of air, allowing himself only tiny breaths. Move not an eye. See not through the open eyes. Be not self indulgent with an excess of sight. Close not the eyes. Lack of vigilance might cause sleep. Find a new kind of rest. Become numb. First numb the toes. Now numb up. Go on past the heart numbing and watch the heart, ignored, slow down. Let dry the lips. Glass the eyes and glaze the mind.

Cunningham slammed in through the door. His hat and shoulders were covered with new snow.

"Damn it, Bert, aren't you going to work today? The whole crew is finished breakfast and sitting there waiting for you."

"Tell 'em I ain't coming."

"You're not getting up?"

"No."

"Are you sick?"

"No."

"You're hung over."

"Wore out. Yes, Boss, wore out."

"Dammit, everybody's tired, Bert. You're no better than anybody else around here."

"No, I ain't, but that's what I am. Wore out."

"You damn drunkard. You're hung over, that's all."

Sorrells didn't answer. He tried numbing his toes again.

"Bert, you put me on the spot. How far do you think I'll

go with you getting my crew drunk all the time and not moving out in the morning?"

"Go to hell if you want to. If that is what will make you happy."

Cunningham stood a moment looking down at him. "I don't know," he finally said. "I just don't know how you expect me to back you on deals like this, getting my crew drunk and stalling around in the morning when there's work to be done."

"Go on off to hell, then, or to make money, but leave soon," Sorrells said.

"O.K., then. If that's the way you want it," Cunningham said and went away.

Sorrells tried a while to numb his toes again, but failed. He lifted the great weight of himself, saying he would do this one more time, but not, by God, for long, and he sat up. He located all his clothes with his eyes, without moving his head, before he strove to dress. He looked out the window. Heavy snow was falling. When he was dressed, he stood in his boots and was surprised at how solidly he stood in them, as though it were the first time a pair of boots had supported him. He washed his face without looking in the mirror. He put on his hat and gloves, chaps and spurs, keeping himself moving that long, but had to sit down again before he went out. Cunningham came for him again.

"Come on in and have a cup of coffee," Cunningham said. "We'll talk a while. Wilson's on the prod. Charley told me you had to cool him last night."

Sorrells went to the breakfast table and poured himself a cup of coffee. Wilson had stayed drunk on the whiskey that had been left over. His eyes were red. He was angry. He laughed when Sorrells sat at the table. Sorrells looked at Wilson's face for any marks of the tap he'd given him.

"Any of that whiskey left, Wilson?" Sorrells asked.

Wilson laughed again. "No," he said, and Sorrells saw the small red spot between the corner of his mouth and his chin.

"How are we going to get to work without a little hair of the dog?" Sorrells asked.

"I don't know," Wilson answered. "How would *I* know?

In fact, I don't know if I can afford to go to work. In fact, I might just roll my bed."

"What the hell do you mean by that, Wilson?" Cunningham asked.

"I mean we ain't got no horses to do our work on," Wilson said. "I'm afoot. Worse than that, I've been packing Rabbit and Front Office on *my* back for a month, and I'm going to haul my own little horse home today before I kill him."

"Hell, Wilson, your horses don't look all that bad to me," Cunningham said.

"Maybe not to you. Maybe you don't care about the Outfit's horses, but my horse is not going to work one more day this fall."

Sorrells swallowed hot coffee. She's a-blowin' up, he thought. To hell with it.

"Hell, Bert. Your horses can finish the work, can't they?" Cunningham coaxed.

"Not if I work them on days like this," Sorrells said. "No."

"You can spell your horse with the horses Jack and Stacy were using," Cunningham offered. "You'll have Little Red now. Dobie's leaving out for warmer country today."

Sorrells looked at the old man. Porter sat very still and aloof, coolly looking away from the table.

"What the hell," Sorrells said. "We ain't finished in Last Chance."

"Don't look at me," Cunningham said. "It's his idee."

"That's right," Porter said, nodding decisively. "My belly's been a-hurtin' and my old bones can't go this cold no more. I been a-workin' longer than I intended to. I figure to take my horses and turn them out on the desert for the winter. I may go to Hawaii to that convention." He did not look at anybody. He took out a dirty handkerchief and rubbed the old eyes behind the thick glasses. They had been red and sore from wind, dust, or snow for four months. Sorrells knew a cowpuncher rolled his bed the minute he got out of it when he had decided he was leaving an outfit. He didn't tell his partner it was time to go to work, as Porter had done that morning.

"So you'll have those extra horses," Cunningham was saying. "They're all rested excepting Little Red."

"Horses!" Wilson snorted. "There ain't a horse in the bunch. Stacy damned sure didn't ride good horses and I'm not riding any of Jack's mount in this weather."

"Hell, I can take either one of those strings and finish off what little work is left to be done," Cunningham said.

"Do it. Do it. Do it, Boss," Wilson taunted. "I've been wondering when you were going to saddle a horse."

"Now, wait a minute, Wilson. Do you have some kind of an idea stuck back in your head that I *can't* saddle a horse and get the job done?" Cunningham asked.

"I'd like to see you do *something* instead of yow-yowing all the time about us being too slow."

"I haven't helped because I thought you could do it, and I had other things to do, keeping this ranch going. But that hasn't been any of your damned business. Your business has been to get these cattle gathered and it ain't done yet. I want to know if you are going to finish the work, or are you going to roll your bed. That's all the goddam conversation I want from you. Yes or no, because if it's no, I'm going to go out and get me a new crew."

"I'm going to have to think about it," said Wilson. "I'm going to take my horse home today and think about it."

"You do that, Wilson, but don't blame me if you don't have a job when you come back."

"Oh, I'll be back all right," Wilson said, smiling. "If I don't go to work, I'll still be back to beat your goddam ass for you."

"Don't wait until you come back to try that, Wilson," Cunningham said. "Let's have at 'er right now, if you think you've got 'er in you."

"Well, wait just a minute," Sorrells said. "What kind of a crew is this, anyway? We've stayed together all fall. It ain't time, yet, to start breaking heads."

"I'll whip your goddam ass, Roy," Wilson said, conversationally.

"No you won't, Wilson," Cunningham said mildly.

"Wilson," Sorrells said.

"What, Bert?"

"Will you listen to me?"

"You know I'll listen to you, Bert."

"Let's see how Roy is going to help us gather the rest of the cattle. I know he wants to do right. Let's just face it, Roy. The weather has set in and we're afoot and you know it."

"I know," Cunningham said.

"So let's just stop the Mickey Mouse," Sorrells said. "We've worked four months just as though this outfit couldn't afford good horses. Now that we're afoot, the least the Outfit can do is provide the tools we need to finish. Get us some horses and we'll finish, won't we, Wilson?"

"I'd like to know what for," Wilson said. "I'd just like to know what we are getting out of this deal. Hell, me and Dobie did our hardest work on our own horses. That ain't right."

"I've been doing it for fun. I'd be a fool to do it for the money," Sorrells said. "If we stay, we stay for Roy's stake in this, which is why I came to work in the first place. Let's give him a chance."

"And what about the money? I do it for the money." Wilson was probing a wound that never healed in the crew of the Outfit. "I've been suspending my obligations since August."

"I'll mention it when I call Bobby about buying the horses," Cunningham said. "I can't promise you a raise or more horses, though."

"That's what I thought. You want the job done, but you won't go out on a limb for your crew."

"I know for a fact that Roy has been trying to make it better for us, Wilson," Sorrells lied. He didn't know it, but he knew Cunningham, and hoped he had been talking to the front office for everything the Outfit needed.

"You think he's going to get us a raise and horses to ride with one little phone call, when the Outfit's been run three years without them?" Wilson scoffed. "It would take a better man than Cunningham to get anything for us."

"Roy, it's O.K. to do something for fun for four months," Sorrells said. "It's another horse when a man's profession pays no more for a day's work than fifty cents an hour. I think if a feller had to be out in the weather, he could do better shoveling snow off a sidewalk, and he wouldn't have to saddle a shovel," Sorrells said.

"Bert, I can only promise to do my best. How can I promise any more than that?" Cunningham said desperately.

"That'll have to be good enough for now, I guess. I'll stay and help him," Sorrells said to Wilson.

"It's not O.K. by me," Wilson said. "I can only promise to stay until February. I never quit any man in a storm, but after February I'm going to need a better-paying job. I want a good raise. I want four hundred a month and board and I want a new mount of horses. If I can't get them here, I'll go someplace else."

"Dobie, do you know where we can start looking for some horses?" Cunningham asked.

Porter stood up and brushed the air past his ear toward the crew of the Outfit. "Not me," he said. "It's all you fellers' business. I'm going to roll my bed and get off this cold son of a bitch." He walked out of the room.

Cunningham looked at his watch. "Well, if I'm to catch Bobby Lang by telephone today, I'm going to have to get started," he said. "Wilson, you can take the day off to haul your horse home, if that's what you want to do."

"I am," said Wilson. "But, don't forget. I'll be back to whip your ass if you don't get us a new mount of horses. Remember that."

"All right then, Wilson. You're fired. Don't come back," Cunningham said.

"Wait a minute," Sorrells said. "How the hell are we going to finish without Wilson and Porter?"

"By God, I'll do it alone if I have to," Cunningham said and went out the door.

"Wilson . . . ," Sorrells said.

"Go on after your daddy, you suck-ass son of a bitch," Wilson said.

Sorrells took off his chaps and spurs.

"It's your business, Wilson," Sorrells said quietly. He put his hand on the Indian's shoulder. "Good luck."

"Go on, prick," Wilson said. He took no notice of the hand.

Sorrells caught up to Cunningham at the saddle house.

Stacy had come in with a load of hay. He was standing by the saddle house. He had brought his rope with him and was tossing loops at a bale of hay. He was practicing the hoolie loop he had seen Sorrells use. Sorrells had seen him many times since he had been grounded, and whenever Stacy was not busy bucking bales or driving the truck, he was practicing with his rope.

"The checks in?" he asked Cunningham, grinning. He was wearing a winter cap with the ear flaps tied down by a string under his chin. Snowflakes were sticking to his eyebrows and cheeks.

"Not yet, Stace," Cunningham answered. He was shame-faced about the crew's paychecks after his talk with Wilson and Sorrells. The checks were a week overdue. "Did you already unload the truck?" he asked, looking at the empty truck. "Why didn't you come up and get us to help you? We weren't doing anything but having a bull session."

"How much longer is Famous going to use my money?" Stacy grinned. "I ought to go into the banking business and charge Famous interest."

"I don't know, Stace. I'm going to talk to them today," Cunningham said. "Can I loan you a few dollars? I can let you have twenty."

"Naw. I'll wait, I guess," Stacy kept on grinning. "I just been wondering about it. My car payment is overdue and I'm going to have to pay late charges."

"I'll ask the front office about it," Cunningham said. He walked on. Stacy swung his loop. Sorrells greeted him. He couldn't answer, because he was busy roping and airing his gut lip in the snowstorm.

"Hi, Maudy Jane," Sorrells said in Maudy's kitchen.

"Hi, Bert," Maudy said wearily. She kept looking at the dishes in her sink. She had, for a long time now, been greeting Sorrells like a pack mare would greet her loader. Just the sight of Sorrells seemed to make her swaybacked. She turned the handle of the hot water on and watched it run, while Sorrells and Cunningham walked through the kitchen. She had not turned completely away from Sorrells. She kept the corner of her eye available in case she needed to turn her eye to see him if he came at her, but she was looking away just like an old pack mare does, hoping a packer won't notice her and pick her for some new abuse.

In the office, Cunningham opened a large manila envelope and handed its contents to Sorrells. "I got this in the mail yesterday," he said.

Bobby Lang had sent Cunningham a speed letter from the front office. The letter had no salutation and was signed by the son of the Outfit on a dotted line at the bottom, marked "Sender." The letter contained a list of demands. Bobby demanded to know why the weaner calves the Outfit had sold were fifty pounds lighter than cattle from a neighboring ranch. He had visited with the neighbor at a cattlemen's meeting in Las Vegas and the neighbor had caused Bobby Lang concern that Cunningham was weaning calves too young and too light. He was also dissatisfied with the price the Outfit had received for the calves. He ordered Cunningham to weigh all the Outfit's heifers by age. The tone of the letter indicated the son of the Outfit was disappointed with Cunningham's performance as manager of the Outfit.

"Have you ever seen a letter like that, Bert?" Cunningham asked.

"He talks like he's got a fever. The Bar 22 cattle he is talking about are kept on permanent pasture. Wilson told me the Bar 22 calves stay fat standing still. Our cattle have to rustle to make a living and we've had to wean younger cattle so their mammies could face the winter."

"Bobby sold the first batch of steers. He was in complete accord when I made the deal with the man that took all the rest," Cunningham said. "He was as much a party in the sale as I was."

"He is big-shotting you so you'll know who is boss, that's all."

"It looks like that to me."

"He's greener than I thought if he expects you to cut seven hundred heifers by age and haul them one hundred and twenty miles in the stock truck just so he can know how much they weigh. We should leave those cattle alone until spring now. Working them and hauling them in this cold weather will knock hell out of them."

"I'm just going to have to know why he feels he can run this ranch from the front office. If he is going to do it, he doesn't need me."

"You need to see him in person. Don't try to talk this over with him on the phone. Look him in the eye. You've got plenty you ought to straighten out with him before he gets to running you completely."

"I'd better. He is going to have to know he can't ride my horse from the Boulevard of Dreams."

"Get after him."

"You can go with me. You can answer his questions about the cow work better than I can."

"When do you want to leave?"

"Just as soon as we can pack a bag and gas the pickup."

"I think we ought to help Dobie load his horses and gear."

"We'll see Porter off," Cunningham said. "The old man made it easy for me. I told him I was going to have to lay off one of the crew and he said he would just as soon be the one to go."

"He knew why you were telling him your troubles. He just wanted to save you the trouble of firing him. He wanted to stay. I'm sure of it."

"Hell, Bert, believe me. The old man is seventy years old. He would winter hard on this cold son of a gun. He'll be a lot better off someplace down south."

"That's how he got to be seventy and tough as a boot, I guess. Because he has philanthropists like you and the son of the Outfit to look after him," Sorrells said. He left the office by the back door so as not to scare Maudy Jane again. He saw Wilson leaving headquarters hauling his horse in the back of his pickup.

Porter had rolled his bed and packed his trunk when Sorrells walked into their room. Sorrells loaded the trunk and bed in Porter's old truck for him. He walked down to the corral and caught old Buck and the colt while Porter loaded his saddle and gear. Sorrells led the horses out and loaded them after Porter backed the truck into the dirt bank. Cunningham and Stacy helped. It was time for Porter to go.

A hard veneer had settled on the old man. He did not

see anyone or hear what they said to him as he shook hands.
He kept repeating, "Yeah, well time for me to leave out,
anyway. It's winter," to each man. He looked small and used
up, and the grip in his hand was not strong. He climbed up
into his truck and banged the door shut. He cranked the
window up. He stepped on the starter without stepping on
the clutch and the truck bucked backwards into the bank.
Buck and the colt stumbled and slid to to keep their feet.
Stacy laughed and hollered for Porter to use the clutch.
Porter did not look at him. He started his truck and drove
away.

Chapter 30

RUNNING DOG

Caballo encarrerado, sepultura abierta—*A runaway horse opens a grave.*

Wilson Burns sat with his back to the wall at the end of the bar in the All Hang Out in Keno. He was drunk and mean. He had harassed every person who entered the bar during the past four hours and he had cuffed old Indians who had thought they were his friends. The bartender had given up trying to quiet him. He served Wilson's drinks and got out of the way. He did not call the police. He was afraid of Wilson. Wilson banged his empty glass on the bar. The bartender fixed another strong whiskey and water. Wilson threw them at him if he did not make them strong.

Wilson was thinking he was GONE. He was running mean and nobody was going to stop him. He had busted loose for good. He would never be of service to any man again, because he did not have it in him. People could stand by for a ram from this Indian. All treaties were off. This Indian had been born a warrior and from now on, people had better watch out for him.

His father once told him he was like a dog who chased cars. He chased machines to bite them. He bit at the wheels, as though he could hamstring the machines and stop them. He fought the machines by the old rules, with clean hands, not realizing the machines were invulnerable and would crush out his life without even grunting.

His father told him no one fought barehanded anymore. The battles were all fought with weapons and, because weapons were used, battles could not be fought without vengeance. His father said Wilson would be crushed, as the old ways had been crushed.

In the clan of Wilson's father, the warrior had to fight his first battle with clean hands. If he could not do this, he could not become a warrior. After he had thus proven his bravery and honesty, he could take up the weapons to fight off the cowards who had invented them. In this way, the clan knew that its warriors would never take advantage of a man they had disarmed.

Wilson decided he had fought with clean hands long enough. It was time to take up the weapons of the cowards if he was going to defend himself against them. He was free, now, because he had done his best. He only needed his weapon, his dog, and his horse.

Wilson Burns left the All Hang Out bar and drove up the mountain toward his father's ranch. He stopped at the summit where the road began its descent to the valley to the shack that had housed him as a boy. He got out of his car and stood in the snowstorm. The snow would stand on this summit, now, and this road would soon be closed until spring. He looked around him at the mountains he had known all the days of his life and would now shelter him, cover him, hide him as a warrior. He left his car and walked down the road to the house. His black dog, Scout, met him halfway, and escorted him, hunting in the storm around him.

Wilson went inside and lit the kerosene lamp. His parents were gone. He lay on their comfortable bed, thick with cheap blankets. He found the shoe box in the corner beneath the bed, where he had hidden it. He sat on the edge of the bed and opened the box. He grasped the handle of the .45 pistol and brought it out of the box. He pressed the loaded clip into the handle and felt it click into place. He pulled the action and made sure the first shell slid into the chamber. He put the pistol on safety. He walked out to the corral with Scout and caught his good little sorrel horse. He bridled the horse and led him out to the flat, away from the house. Scout was moving close to Wilson.

Wilson caught Scout's collar and rubbed his ears. He took the pistol out of his belt and shot the dog. When he had quieted the horse, he mounted. He had always loved the horse's short, thick neck. He reached up and rubbed the horse between the ears, under the band of the headstall. He couldn't have ever had a better little horse. He shot the horse down through the poll knot between his ears. The horse dropped to the earth under him and rolled on Wilson's leg, pinning him against the snow without hurting him. Wilson put the pistol to his temple and squeezed the trigger. After a while, clean snow covered his face.

Chapter 31

FRONT OFFICE

Quien tenga hacienda y no la atienda
No tiene hacienda aunque asi lo crea.

A man who owns an outfit and does not husband it, does not have an outfit at all, even though he thinks he does.

Cunningham and Sorrells stopped only for gasoline on their way to Los Angeles. They drove all night. By the time they got on the freeway they were so harried by traffic and sleeplessness they did not feel so formidable about traveling to the Boulevard of Dreams to give Bobby Lang an education in ranching.

To Bert Sorrells, the Los Angeles freeway at eight o'clock on Monday morning was the place Angelinos all must go to have a green-eyed runaway. This was the place their fever to make a living rose on their brows and caused them to stampede ignobly. The stampede let off an odor very much like the odor of terrified cattle running over rock, or recently dynamited rock, but was more like the stench of rushing hot metal mixed with the nervous body sweat of humans rushing out with slaughterous intent.

A stranger on the freeway at that hour, especially a stranger who also was a cowpuncher, felt like a coyote a-gittin'.

A chased coyote. A coyote in that situation constantly watches his backtrail. If he has been chased before, and is a wise coyote, he might also know he is being chased toward hidden traps or relaying enemies waiting to run him to death. He feels he must watch the trail ahead as closely as his backtrail, and his inability to watch all trails and his footing, too, causes his heart to weaken.

A stranger on the freeway also felt like a jackrabbit must feel during a drive in which humans with clubs surround his running ground and slowly stomp forward, closing the circle, clubbing jackrabbits to death.

Sorrells felt exactly as the wild bovine feels when run through a canyon.

"Look at that guy," Cunningham said. He was driving with his head pulled down between his big shoulders, his hands holding the steering wheel in a death grip. "He thinks he's a bullet."

"That guy behind him running him down thinks he's a rocket," Sorrells said, glancing quickly over both shoulders. "Only he's just a misguided missile. Look at him weave! He's liable to swap ends and come right back at us. You'd better watch him."

"I'm watching him. You just watch behind us and tell me when another bullet comes by us on your side."

"I'm watching just like a coyote trying to stop to shit," Sorrells said. "When are we going to break out of this herd? I know how a bunch-quitter feels now."

"Damned if I know. Look at that paper. I wrote down the directions Bobby gave me on the phone," Cunningham said.

"What was that last turnoff?" Sorrells asked. Cunningham told him the name of the exit they had just passed. "Well, the next one is Montenegro and that's where we are quitting them," Sorrells said. "Don't start this way yet. No, no, no. There's another one making deep tracks on my side."

Cunningham turned off the freeway at the Montenegro exit and Sorrells said, "They missed us. Look at 'em go."

Montenegro was not much better, but stop lights kept the livestock from stampeding. Sorrells wondered why the street was called Montenegro. Probably because some poor Mexican by that name had owned this country before he'd been run down and clubbed to death for it.

A half hour later, Cunningham turned off the Boulevard of Dreams onto a parking lot that covered forty acres. He parked the company pickup by a small island of green grass, flowers, and young trees. A Mexican wearing a tightly woven straw hat with a rolled brim and a red tassel dangling off the back was working in the island.

"*Quehúbole, paisano!*" Sorrells greeted him, grinning because he was happy to see someone of his own kind. Sorrells saw him look up, see only the space two inches in front of Sorrells' nose, decide he was only being patronized one more time by somebody practicing his Spanish, and stoop back to his flowers. Sorrells thought he might go over and talk a while with the man, but realized the pace of the Boulevard of Dreams wouldn't allow either of them to enjoy it. He turned away and fell in step with Cunningham. They walked toward a ten-story building, shiny with glass and steel that housed the offices of Famous Enterprises.

The sun on the parking lot was warm and Sorrells felt good to be walking after hours in the pickup. The two men walked out of the sun into the auto lobby of the building. Two healthy, husky, young men in white coveralls were standing there. They faced Sorrells and Cunningham with quiet, courteous, subservient expressions that Sorrells would have hated to have to show to make his daily bread.

Sorrells and Cunningham had walked away about ten yards from the two attendants, when one of them said, not too loudly, "Park your horse, Sir?"

Sorrells grinned happily and wheeled to do battle. They had their backs to him and were sauntering away. Cunningham grabbed Sorrells' arm. "Come on, Bert," he said.

"Now, what kind of a high-headed feller would I be if I didn't accommodate them fellers when they spoke to me?" Sorrells grinned.

"Come on, Bert." Cunningham led him to the elevator. He stopped the elevator on the main floor and looked at the directory in its glass case for the Famous Enterprise offices. He turned to Sorrells.

"Bert, would you mind waiting for me a while?" he asked. "I want to talk to Bobby alone for a few minutes."

"Have at 'er. I know what you mean," Sorrells said.

The elevator closed on Cunningham and Sorrells read the directory a few minutes to see if he knew anybody in the building. He only knew Mr. Bobby Lang, but his name was not on the directory. He was under Famous Enterprises somewhere. Near the elevator was a door marked Executive Club. Sorrells thought of cold beer. He bet he had time for a cold beer if this Executive Club was open. Hell, he could pass for an executive, couldn't he? He tried the door. It was locked.

He walked away on the shiny hard plastic floor. He went around the corner of the elevators to the large, open lobby of the main floor. The whole front of the main floor was tinted glass held by shiny metal. Money banks were on both ends of the lobby. Pretty girls behind the counters in the banks puttered and figured and laughed and talked with one another. They had a damn fine place to work, Sorrells thought.

A small carpet surrounded by easy chairs and ash trays had been placed in the center of the lobby. Sorrells sat in one of the low chairs just to see what it was like. He smoked a cigarette and waited to see what he could see. His long legs stuck up in front of him, out of the chair, and he watched the girls over the tops of his knees in the same way he had watched mustangs over a ridge. The electric light, mixed with the nine o'clock sun strained through the tinted glass, was strange to him. He got up and went out the front door to stand in the sunshine. The long, broad, shallow flight of steps to the street was warm. Across a narrow, quiet business street, were other complex business hives like this one. He could see no saloons.

Standing on the steps with all the people going by, he felt as he had felt when Porter couldn't tell Sorrells was watching him. If he didn't move, the people didn't notice him. They were busy. The girls went along just as busy as the men, their little dresses bouncing along just covering their round behinds, their strides long and quick and full of business. They were all damn fine looking girls and every one of them the same, with the same even features, the same long legs, and, he bet, the same thoughts in their heads. The men tried their damndest to look different. They weren't alike in features or carcasses, but their dress and hair styles showed they carried the same thoughts in their heads. Their expressions confirmed it. It didn't seem to Sorrells this was a good place for men to be. The girls, though, the supple smalls of their backs showing through their smooth, red, green, yellow, blue blouses and dresses, showing their backs were strong, and the sun shining on their bare arms and clean hair, were at home.

Sorrells was glad the sun was shining. The girls weren't all bundled up. He could watch them in their dresses. He was also happy to be away from that windy, snowy, manurey, dusty Ethel weather. If a feller was going to town, he might as well be in the biggest, shiniest town he could find. L.A. was the best he had ever seen, as far as that was concerned.

He decided he had better find someone he knew. The society he had been watching in town brought out the herd instinct in him. He went back into the building to phone a man he knew.

Two girls behind the counters behind the glass doors in one of the banks put their heads together and waved to him, smiling. He waved back at them and walked down the stairs to the auto lobby where he had noticed some pay phones. He was sure the man he knew would remember him. Sorrells had once taken the man and some other L.A. bigshots on a pack trip in the Sierra Madre of Sonora in Mexico, and they had not had fun.

Sorrells was looking for the man's name in the phone book, when Bobby Lang came up behind him and turned him around to shake his hand.

"It *is* you, Bert, I thought you were someone else coming here to pose for a cigarette commercial," Bobby said, smiling. "I didn't know you were coming with Roy."

Sorrells put the phone book back where it belonged. He was glad to see the son of the Outfit. "Have you seen Roy already?" he asked.

"I'm late. I was just going up to the office now." Bobby introduced Sorrells to two men walking with him and led Sorrells along with them to the elevator. He asked Sorrells bright and intelligent questions about the Outfit on their ride in the elevator. The two men quietly stared at Sorrells all the way, one of them from four inches away from Sorrells' ear.

They kept staring when Sorrells and Bobby left them on the elevator. They stared right up until the last crack closed shut on the elevator door. They passed on up into the building to new adventures.

The Famous offices were small, padded with carpeting and soundproofing, too bright with artificial light, and too warm. Cunningham was sitting at a long table in Bobby's office, studying his reports and comparing them with a budget study the front office had made. Bobby greeted Cunningham and immediately rang another office on his intercom. Sorrells started to walk out of the office to a place where he could wait while Cunningham and Bobby talked in private.

"Stay here," Cunningham said. Sorrells took off his jacket and sat at the other end of the table. He looked around the walls of the room, but did not see any framed whores' letters.

"Well, cowboys, how's the ranch?" Bobby asked, smiling. Sorrells could see he was glad for a chance to talk about the Outfit like any hurried businessman is happy to take a few moments off to talk about a hobby he enjoys.

"We're through until the blowing snow lets up," Cunningham said. "But we won't be able to work anymore, no matter what kind of weather we get, unless we get a new remuda of horses."

"What's the matter with the horses we've got?" Bobby asked.

"They're worked down, Bobby. They're too tired."

"I don't think we made any provision for new horses in next year's budget, but we've allotted a hundred thousand dollars to the Outfit. I'm sure we can find money for a few horses," Bobby smiled.

Sorrells was wondering how next year's calf crop was going to get back a hundred thousand, when Bobby said, "I test-ran a new motorcycle I thought would be more practical for our purposes than horses, but I want to tell you, it was a man-killer. A man would be shaken to pieces after one hour working in our kind of terrain on a machine like that."

Sorrells shudder-sighed with relief, no only because he would have to quit the Outfit if he had to ride a bicycle, but because he could see old Sunspot laughing at him if he ever took after the old steer riding a *motor*.

Bobby saw the sigh and laughed. "Worried about your piles, Bert?" he asked. "Don't worry, I wouldn't require anyone to go through that kind of torture."

"No," Sorrells said. "I wasn't worried. I'd hitchlike with my saddle to Argentina before I'd ride one of them things. I was just wondering how we'd catch a dogie calf on one."

"They would be dangerous on the Outfit," Bobby said. "A man could easily get killed on one if they tipped over on him. Then, a man hurt a long way from headquarters could easily die of exposure."

Sorrells shut up. He'd been talking about orphaned calves, not bike riders' piles or long ways from home. What the hell did the son of the Outfit think old Roller could do to a feller if he "tipped over?" Sorrells could understand why Bobby would try absolutely any other conveyance rather than go through another day on Front Office like he had the last time he had ridden with Porter.

Bobby Lang's voice was big, shiny, and loud, not loud in volume so much as it was loud in quick, colorful inflection. The L.A., U.S.A., glass, metal, plastic part of his voice was such that Sorrells could no longer see the Bobby Lang he liked, but only the facade of Television Presence.

Cunningham was stubbornly keeping his head down between his shoulders, his eyes on the reports and studies before him. His hands were still. His whole body was still. He was like a boulder set down in the middle of the freeway. He picked up the blue speed letter he had received from Bobby. He looked at Bobby without smiling.

"The main reason I'm here, Bobby, is to find out what you meant by this letter." Cunningham dropped the letter so it floated to the center of the table.

"What do you mean, what did I mean?" Bobby asked, lightly.

"I took it you don't like the way I'm running the Outfit."

"Well, Roy, I'm sorry. I don't think I implied in any way that I was displeased with your work. I don't even recall what the letter was about." Bobby picked up the letter and read it quickly. "So?" he asked, pleasantly. "How does this mean I was displeased? I've been bragging about you to everyone in Famous Enterprises. That's the way I am. I'm either able to brag about a man or he doesn't work for me. Don't ever worry about what I might be implying when I write you a letter. If I ask you questions, it is only because I need the answers. If I don't think enough of you to ask you a question, I'll notify you of your dismissal."

"The tone you used is not the tone I'd use with a man I trusted," Cunningham said, doggedly. "Where I come from, a boss who catches another man's horse don't need to tell that man he's fired. It's a way to fire a man without arguing or having words with him."

"I don't know what you mean," Bobby said. "How did I catch your horse if that's what I did?"

"You questioned my ability to judge the ages and weights of the calves I sold. You didn't like the price I sold them for. You saddled my horse when you tried to run the ranch from this office. No man can ride two horses at once."

"As for the size and price of the calves, I guess we'll just have to try and get bigger calves and a better price next year. Those were just questions I had in my mind. Just fill out a report about them before you leave. But don't be mistaken, I do like your work. If I didn't, I'd let Bert, here, try his hand at your job." Bobby smiled and winked at Sorrells.

Cunningham wasn't mollified, but he didn't know what else to say to the son of the Outfit. He let his head emerge from between his shoulders.

The phone rang. Bobby picked it up and his eyes smiled at Sorrells and Cunningham.

"Jennifer, Baaaaaaaaaby," he exulted. He winked at Sorrells. He listened. "Yes I think I remember you . . . No, I'm not *exactly* sure." He listened. "I think so, sure. When was it?" He listened. "Yes," he said, doubtfully. "What did you have in mind? . . . Oh, in New York . . . Oh, you're *calling* from New York. O.K., why don't you get in touch with Morrie Goldman in our office there in New York? . . . Sure, Jen . . . That's right Jennie . . . Just tell him I sent you . . . No, he won't have to verify it . . . Don't mention it, Jen. . . . Fine . . . Fine . . . Cool . . . O.K. . . . Bye, bye, Jen." He hung up and winked again at Sorrells. Sorrells crossed his legs and was ashamed of him.

"I had one other question I wanted to ask you, Roy," Bobby said. "I forgot to include it in my speed letter. Do you have this office's copy of the Bar 22's hay bills in front of you?"

Cunningham rearranged the paper. "No," he said. "I don't."

"That's all right," Bobby said. "The gist of what I wanted to say in the letter is that we are missing a stack of hay."

Cunningham leaned back in his chair to relax, but his head went down between his shoulders again. He listened.

"The man at the Bar 22 sent me a bill for five stacks of hay, but your reports only show we have fed four stacks," Bobby said.

"We've fed two or three more stacks since my last report," Cunningham said.

"No," Bobby smiled. "His price for five stacks totaled out the same as your price for four stacks."

"That can't be right," Cunningham said, looking through his papers. "We're buying by the ton, not the stack. He just didn't count his stacks right, or I didn't list the lots right. The tonage is what counts." He began seriously to examine his papers.

"Well, he lists five lots of hay and you list four." Bobby waited while Cunningham hunted for the hay bill. "Well, never mind," Bobby said. "If we are missing a stack of hay, we have lost quite a bit of hay. Never mind, though. You can't hide a stack of hay for very long."

Cunningham studied his papers. He began to write down weights on a piece of scratch paper.

"Who is hauling the hay?" Bobby asked.

"Stacy," Cunningham said.

"And who else? Did you hire another truck?"

"No. Stacy is working alone in the company hay truck."

"Well, I got a bill from another trucking company from over that way. Could Stacy be selling our hay and billing me for the hauling of it?" Bobby smiled.

"Hell, no," Cunningham said.

"Well, it's not important, I guess, but see what you can find out about it. What are we paying Stacy?"

"Two hundred and fifty dollars. Same as everybody."

"You think Stacy would try to augment his salary with a little hay income. Two hundred and fifty dollars might not be enough for him. Maybe he has an expensive girl friend at Wanda's." Bobby winked at Sorrells. Sorrells wondered if Bobby Lang would be a thief if he was only making $250 a month. It was interesting to know Bobby could suspect a man of being a thief because he only paid him $250 a month.

"Nobody is stealing any hay," Cunningham said in a tone that he used with the little smile he didn't want to make. "The discrepancy probably happened because the front office is long overdue paying the bill. The Bar 22 wouldn't even have sent you a bill if it had been paid when I sent you the bill."

"Probably not," Bobby said.

"About wages," Cunningham said, bulling his way along. "Two hundred and fifty dollars a month is the wage you pay. Not getting two hundred and fifty dollars a month is no wage at all. Our checks are a week late. The real truth is, the Outfit owes Stacy money, not Stacy the Outfit."

"I was going to send them yesterday when you called. You can take them back with you and save us the chore of mailing them," Bobby said. He rang the intercom and asked one of his secretaries to bring the payroll for the Outfit. She brought the checks and Bobby handed them to Cunningham. Cunningham looked through them.

"One's missing," Cunningham said.

"They should all be there," Bobby said. He rang for the secretary again.

"There's no check here for Jack Roberts," Cunningham said.

"Isn't he the one who has been sick in the bunkhouse?" Bobby asked. The secretary came in and waited by the door.

"He was injured on the job. He's the one Careful fell on. I explained it to you when I sent in the payroll. I wanted to pay him his full salary. He's a damn fine man and he has worked many extra hours. I owe it to him."

"If he's been working, I'll have a check drawn up for him right this minute," Bobby said.

"No, he ain't been working," Cunningham said, impatiently. "He's just a damn fine man. He can't work with a broken collarbone, can he? How can he stay with us if he doesn't get any money?"

"We'll see he gets Industrial Insurance and Unemployment Compensation. We pay a lot of workmen's benefits. We can't pay it all year and pay him wages, too," Bobby said. "Never mind, Carol," he said to the secretary. She slipped out the door. "How did he get out of the hospital, Roy?"

"He had a little money and I made up the difference. He's going to be broke a long time, waiting for government money."

"He'll have his meals and a place to live. I'm sure there are chores around headquarters he can do to earn that. Is there anything else you want to bring up? I have appointments in a few minutes."

"Yes, I do. I promised what is left of the crew that I'd ask you about a raise in salary," Cunningham said.

"I didn't budget for much of a crew this winter, except for the men fencing and running the heavy equipment," Bobby said quickly. "You can keep two men this winter paying them their present wage. You can raise the wages of the men you keep twenty-five dollars when work begins in the spring and, like I say, your injured man can stay on with room and board."

"I was thinking of paying Bert four hundred dollars starting in February. I want to pay the cook four hundred dollars, too."

"I'll take it under consideration, but right now I can't see how we can pay that much. No one else in the State of Nevada pays it. Actually, I believe the average pay in Nevada is more like two hundred dollars a month for a buckaroo. You better let your cook go until spring, anyway."

"I had a helluva time finding a cook. My crew almost quit in the middle of the work on account of having to work from daylight to dark and cook for themselves. I'll never get that man back if I let him go. Good cooks are too damn scarce."

"We have to let him go, Roy. We can't afford to pay a man for cooking for a crew of two. It's just not good business."

"Business is what I'm talking about. I have to feed a crew in the spring. No cowpuncher minds long hours or small wages or sorry horses as much as he hates cooking for himself. Is two months cooking for two men going to break the Outfit?"

Bobby looked at Cunningham's stubborn face and thought a while.

"I guess not," he finally said. "Let him stay, then. He must be quite a chef to be so precious to you. I don't see Bert putting on much weight, though." He winked at Sorrells again. "Anything else?" he asked Cunningham.

"I want to say this, Bobby. We're not going to be able to keep good hands unless we give them a just wage. We'll always be running transients in and out of the bunkhouse, like you were doing when I came to work for you. Why do you think the Cattlemen's Association is trying to recruit Mexican nationals for cowboys? Why do you think good American cowboys are turning to other jobs that pay more money?"

"Why pay more money for buckaroos? You tell me. Really, now, what does a buckaroo do that makes cattle produce on a ranch? I think all this cowboy stuff is a myth that went out with the longhorn steer and the six-gun." Smiling, he turned to wink at Sorrells again.

"It's a matter of husbandry," Sorrells said. "In all your travels, didn't anyone ever tell you what a husbandman is?" Sorrells knew by the smirk on the son of the Outfit's face that he was not going to listen to any serious statements from Sorrells. Bobby turned away from him.

"I think they went out even before the longhorn did. I think they went out in biblical times, as soon as they found out a man could make more money in the army," Bobby said. He smiled and winked at Cunningham this time.

Sorrells was thinking, if the Outfit only needed two men this winter, it didn't need him. He'd be damned if he would haul hay or fix corrals. His saddle didn't fit on a bale of hay. The Outfit could have Roberts and Stacy. Sorrells knew he would never have had to explain to a real cowman what a husbandman was. A cowman might not recognize the word, but he damn sure knew what a cowpuncher was. There were plenty of good cowmen left. They might not be millionaires like the son of the Outfit, and they might not even pay as much money as Famous did, but they didn't spend $100,000 a year as a throw-away and still make money on their help. Sorrells figured he would just go find himself a cowman as soon as he got his boots off all this pavement.

The phone rang. "Anything else?" Bobby asked, reaching for his phone.

"I guess not," Cunningham said, dropping his papers into his old saddle-leather briefcase. Sorrells picked up his ash tray and looked for a place to dump the butts of his roll-your-own cigarettes. It seemed like an awful mess to leave on the son of the Outfit's table. He didn't see a place for them, so he set the ash tray back on the table. What the hell, Bobby would have another conversation piece to show he was a cowman the next time a conference took place in this office.

"Alligators?" Bobby boomed brightly. "Rassle an alligator?" He laughed. "You are out of your ever loving mind. . . . When? . . . You mean I have time to think about it? . . . I hope not, . . . O.K. . . . We'll see you down there and talk about it then, O.K.? . . . Fine." He hung up.

"That was a fellow down in Florida," he announced. "Wants me to 'rassle' an alligator for a film we are doing on the Everglades next month. How do you like that?"

Sorrells and Cunningham didn't answer. They watched him in much the same way they would if he were being broadcast to them over television.

"Don't leave town," Bobby said. "I'll take you to lunch." He reached for the phone again. He was a busy man.

"No," Cunningham said. "We'll be heading back."

"Take care then," Bobby said. "Send me a summary of your ideas in your next report."

Cunningham stopped the pickup at a light to wait for the arrow to turn onto the Boulevard of Dreams and so to leave town. Sorrells was nodding at two smiling, well-dressed, tanned, pretty brunettes, their teeth extra white and their lips extra red against their tans. In Bobby Lang's office, the telephone rang again.

"Hello. This is Bobby Lang of Famous Enterprises. How do you do?" he said without listening. "Maude Jane Cunningham? . . . Oh, Maudy. Roy just left me a few minutes

ago. How are you, Maudy? How is everyone at the Outfit?...
No, I guess not many minutes ago. Is it freezing at Ethel?
That's what I'd like to know.... Wilson Burns? Do I know
him?... Oh, the Indian boy.... That's too bad, Maudy.... Well,
Roy will be home tonight to take care of anything that has to
be done. I want to get up there soon myself and get out of
this smog.... I really have no idea when, Maudy.... They
just left.... O.K. Good-bye, Maudy." He hung up. He rang
for his secretary. She came in and waited, holding the door
open. "Carol, take Wilson Burns, buckaroo for the Outfit, off
the payroll, will you please?"

"Yes, sir, Mr. Lang," the girl said and slipped out,
closing the door quietly.

Chapter 32

LOOSE WITH THE
SADDLE ON

Sooner or later a cowboy always suffers his horse getting loose with the saddle on. Cowboys get bucked off or their horses get away from them and make them walk.

The first act the horse performs to celebrate his getting loose is usually the retozo, a little running and bucking dance of pure enjoyment. The stirrups flapping emptily at his sides tickle him and bring a more full realization that he has freed himself of the day's work.

A horse accomplished at getting loose with the saddle on will walk along just ahead of the cowboy, his head turned aside so he won't step on his training reins.

Roy Cunningham and Bert Sorrells did not head straight back to Ethel, Nevada. When they broke loose from the Boulevard of Dreams they did not go right home like dependable fellows. They drove to Las Vegas. On the way they did not commiserate with one another over how abused they were, how wronged they were, or how right it was to be a cowpuncher and how wrong the company was. Each had been present at the other's enlightenment on the Boulevard of Dreams and was confident his partner knew what to do about it.

They parked and locked the pickup in the auto lobby of the Horseman's Club. Cunningham registered for their room and went up to bathe. Sorrells went to the barbershop to get streamlined for running and playing. He was the only one getting sheared, so the three barbers and the manicurist had plenty of time for conversation among themselves.

"Jack Clark ain't his real name," the barber at Sorrells' chair said as Sorrells climbed into the seat. Sorrells knew Jack Clark was the man who owned the Horseman's Club. "They say Jack knocked over as many banks as Dillinger." The barber scrupulously kept his eyes off Sorrells. He was performing for the tourist.

"He came here during the Depression in an old souped up Lincoln shot full of holes," the barber in the second chair said. "I know that much, Blacky West and the Indian, Jacques Strongbow, were with him. Jack was all shot up. They doctored him in the old Fremont Hotel. They had the whole back seat of the car stuffed with money." Hah. The money, Sorrells thought. Jack Clark and the gang, real Las Vegas pioneers. Winners of the Old West. Settled here with a real stake, not just peanuts.

The manicurist approached Sorrells. She had been filing her own nails, taking no notice of Sorrells, either. She picked up one of his hands and still had not looked at him. She was very heavy, but she smelled good. Her hands felt very soft and young. She held his hand and brushed the pad of her thumb across Sorrells' fingers lightly. She was very near him, pressing close to his side.

"Can I help you, sir?" she asked.

"No, I guess not," Sorrells said. "What would I do with a manicure?"

"I could put your cuticle in," she said, looking into his eyes.

Sorrells quickly looked down at his lap, exaggerating surprise. "Is that thing out *again*?" he said.

"What?" the manicurist asked.

"No thank you," Sorrells laughed. He was embarrassed by his joke.

The woman turned away and conveyed herself back to her chair, lowered herself so that she made no abrupt contact with it, in much the same way a crane operator, proud of his skill, might lower a ten-ton slab of steel onto a wooden deck, and went back to concentrating on her own hands. She did not think Sorrells was admirable, no pioneer, and not funny. She had her native dignity. Sorrells was just chintzy, like all the others who didn't have to make a living in this town.

"Blacky and Jacques have stayed with Jack ever since," Sorrells' barber said. "I bet they haven't been more'n a block away from him in thirty-five years or more." He did not look at his companions for confirmation of this statement. He was confident of his knowledge of the history and traditions of loyalty in the Green Velvet Jungle.

"Yes, that's true," the barber in the third chair said.

"You're damn right it's true," Sorrells' barber said. Sorrells watched him in the mirror and kept his head very still now that his joke had failed. Not only was the barber an expert on Jack Clark, but he was making the hair fly off Sorrells' head so fast Sorrells was afraid for his ears. This guy probably cut the hair of all manner of bigshots. Sorrells began to feel honored.

"They say Blacky's room is full of tommyguns, pistols, sawed-off shotguns and other artillery," the second barber said. Las Vegas had the true Western tradition of the big, tough law of the gun.

"That's true, I think," the third barber said, looking as though he hoped the first barber would approve his contribution to the conversation. He received no sign from the other barbers so he got up and walked around his chair. He looked sore on his feet. He walked to the end of the big mirror, just out of range of Sorrells' vision.

"Blacky was the trigger man, Jacques was the driver, and Jack was the brains. They never had anyone else in the gang. Jacques still does all the driving when Jack goes anywhere," Sorrells' barber said. The Jack Clark Gang have remained free and independent, just like all great pioneers who made good in our free society.

"Ever notice how neat a dresser that Blacky is?" the second barber asked.

"Neat and natty," Sorrells' barber said authoritatively. He glanced disinterestedly at the reflection of Sorrells head in the mirror. He seemed to approve of his handiwork. He began snipping the scissors on minute hairs above Sorrells' ear. "Quiet and dapper. Don't I trim his hair and mustache twice a week?" Blacky had to look neat and natty so no one would know him and squash him for the bum he was. Keeping guns in his room made him the potential black-hearted force he wanted everyone to believe he was. He would be quickly squashed if he looked like a bum or the other bums found out he had lost his courage.

"That's true," the third barber said, but Sorrells couldn't see him. The first barber had turned the chair around so Sorrells could only see the end of the big mirror out of the corner of his eye and the darkening street outside. He wondered how often the quiet manicurist had been a witness to this same conversation about Jack Clark. "He's a sporty dresser, all right," the third barber volunteered. Sorrells' barber swung his chair around so Sorrells could see all three of them. The third barber was picking up and setting down his combs and brushes and twirling the tonic bottles so their labels could be seen. The labels behind the bottles were reflected in a line along the mirror.

"Quiet and natty," Sorrells' barber said. "Not sporty. Sport is loud. Blacky is neat."

"That's right. That's what I meant to say," the third barber said, trying to be nonchalant about missing the point. Sorrells felt lucky he had not drawn the third barber. The third barber's hands trembled as he arranged scissors and combs on the shelf in front of the bottles.

Sorrells' barber unpinned the cloth and whipped it off his lap. He popped it clean of hair. He put it back, powdered a brush, and cleaned hair off Sorrells' neck and face. He lifted the cloth like a bullfighter caping a bull and showed Sorrells the way off the chair. Sorrells paid. "Good luck," the authoritative barber said as Sorrells went out.

Sorrells found the room he and Cunningham shared. He bathed and changed to clean shirt and Levis Maudy had washed, starched, and ironed for him. He thought about the barbers and their slot-machine values. Las Vegas was just right for somebody like him to run and play in. It was no place likely to miss Bert Sorrells in its framework when he was gone. Sorrells went downstairs and cashed his paycheck. He caught up to Cunningham at the bar. A full drink of whiskey and water was on the bar beside Cunningham. He handed it to Sorrells.

"Well, Roy, here's to you and Maudy and me, work to do and meat in the pot, good horses to ride and country to see, never drunk, sick, or tired, and, Roy, I'll see you in the fall or not at all." Sorrells drank all the whiskey.

"Here's how!" Cunningham said. "You've had a damn good time of it, haven't you, Bert?"

"You bet," Sorrells said. "Let's do it all again sometime."

"Anytime, anyplace I've got a job, you've got a job. There's no reason for you to go now, though. I hope you know that."

"I know it but Stacy and Roberts can handle it until spring. I don't think I could bring myself to climb on old Roller again until then. Maybe you'll get some new horses. I don't believe you ever will. If you do and you are still there in the spring, I'll go out and celebrate, and then I'll come roaring in hung over and chase the wild bovine again with you."

"You know what you're doing, I guess. Don't be mad at Bobby, though. He'll learn."

"Hell, I ain't mad at Bobby. I kinda like him."

"Bert, you're too damned old-fashioned. People just don't work these ranches nowadays like they did when you and I were kids. You've got to learn to keep up with the times."

"You think I'm old-fashioned, Roy?"

"You are. You're old-fashioned."

"Well, I'm not. I'm thankful for stock trucks and better ways to dig a water hole and bunkhouses every night with gas heat. I just don't believe a cowpuncher can keep from taking steps horseback while he's caring for an old cow. I don't believe gasoline will ever replace good hay fed to good horses on a cow ranch. I believe a cowpuncher will be necessary as long as men run livestock for a living."

"Dammit, I believe it too. What I'm saying is that quitting the Outfit ain't showing Bobby Lang how it should be run. He's green but he ain't unreasonable."

"The hell he ain't."

"Well, he ain't, Bert."

"It ain't reasonable to run an old cow so she'll be sure to lose money. He's doing it for the fun of it and to spend money. He doesn't do it for a living. That's his business and I don't blame him. I'm just saying it ain't my business."

"What do you care why he owns the Outfit? Don't tell me you didn't love every minute of the cowboying you did this fall."

"I also believe cowboying is a useful occupation. I do it for the old-fashioned reason, to raise beefsteak. Bobby's reasons don't make him a bad feller. He just don't need me, that's all. I can't see any reason for working for a man when my work ain't worth anything to him. Deep inside that boy is the idea a cowpuncher is some kind of a retard who rides around playing cowboy with real horses and cattle and all Bobby has to do to keep a cowboy is smile at him, call him by his given name, and give him enough to buy a bottle of whiskey to suck on once in a while."

"Hell, Bert, I never heard you say you needed more money. I'd give you part of my own salary if I couldn't get you money any other way."

"Money ain't what I'm talking about. I'll work for any man as long as he believes a cowpuncher does a man's work."

"Well, Bert, like I say, you know your business," Cunningham said.

"If that is settled, let's run and play and forget about any other business. Is that all right with you?"

"Let's have at 'er,"Cunningham said and smiled. "Let's do 'er up Wild Man style."

"Let's blow the lid off," Sorrells said and squalled like a wild man.

Cunningham, embarrassed that Sorrells was starting an early turmoil, said, "I hope, you drunken son of a gun, you spend your whole paycheck. You'll *have* to go back to work when you're broke and hung over."

"Well, by God, if you hope that, I hope it too," Sorrells said.

At midnight, they were out on the Strip drinking whiskey, watching the shows, and gambling. Sorrells and Cunningham separated in a casino. Sorrells walked across deep red carpet and sat down at the spotless green felt of a blackjack table. He bet a dollar and won, let his winnings ride, vowing he would see how far his dollar would go. When his dollar had become thirty-two dollars in five hands, he took a deep breath and bet it. Thirty-two dollars were almost four days' work on the Outfit. He drew a Jack of Diamonds and a Queen of Spades. The dealer hit his own sixteen with a King of Spades and Sorrells' dollar had earned him sixty-three. He knew he would not have to wait for another Famous Enterprise check to go on his own way. He gave three dollars to the dealer and went to cash his chips.

He walked by the door of a piano bar and looked in, searching for Cunningham. Sitting at the edge of the spotlight on the piano, wearing a red wig, her face pale and tight, Sorrells saw Bonnie Sorrells. He went on and cashed in his chips. He spent another thirty minutes making a big circle, looking for Cunningham. He went back into the bar where Bonnie was and found Cunningham down at the farthest, darkest end of it. He sat down with Cunningham.

"Where you been?" Cunningham asked him, grinning. "Been looking for somebody?"

"Been looking for you," Sorrells said, looking at him.

"You been goin' awful slow, ain't you? I been here waiting for you to lose your money. How much did they get?"

"I'm way ahead of them."

"You been sandbagging. I know how you play. You won't get rich just playing to stay in the game."

"Don't need to get rich. Just need a night on the town."

"Have you snuck off to try and locate Bonnie yet?" Cunningham laughed.

"Now what the hell would I want with Bonnie?"

"You mean to tell me you wouldn't light up like a burning barn at high noon if Bonnie came up and rubbed against you right now?"

"I damn sure wouldn't."

"You wouldn't even snort in her flank and bite her on the neck?"

"Hell no. I don't bite poison meat."

"Well, pard, you're going to get another chance."

Sorrells didn't answer. Cunningham grinned.

"See that redhead over by the piano?"

"I already seen her."

"Well, it *is* Bonnie, ain't it?"

"It's the old thing, all right." Sorrells took a good look at her. She was so pale she looked faceless in the spotlight. He wondered how he had recognized her at all. Her face was just another label lined up beside a thousand others just like her in this town. Just another jade, was Bonnie. Green Jade Tonic, to make out-of-towners' manly hair grow. She was now waiting on the shelf to be poured. Watching, bored, waiting for a salesman from a place like the Boulevard of Dreams to get drunk enough to reach for her, tip her up, and pour out her green contents. Sorrells laughed to himself. Boy, how he knew she hated waiting to be tapped at the end of a drunk. She never had been much of a drinker, and, by the looks of her green grasshopper drink, she still wasn't. She used to have more fun on one grasshopper than Sorrells could have with a whole bottle of whiskey. Now she had to wait on two sop faces, and Sorrells laughed because she looked tough enough to do it.

He laughed out loud, knowing she would recognize his laugh any time, any place. She had experience in locating his laugh in a crowd. She looked up to another part of the dark room and only for a moment searched it. She looked at the pianist's hands as though interested in them, sipped her green drink, and acted like she was laughing at one of the sops she was supposed to be attending. It was a damn cinch Sorrells had never bored her.

"Well, get after her, cowboy," Cunningham said. "You ain't worrying about that drunk with her, are ya? Go on. You might do some good."

"All right. You take the black-headed gal sitting next to her and we'll all go out and get loose with the saddle on."

"Oh, no. Not me. Maudy Jane ain't big, but she's sharp. After she cut my throat, she'd cut me off my feed. I ain't having anything to do with any old scags tonight."

"Hell, that black-headed gal ain't no scag. Take a good look at her. She's just right. I'll tell you what . . . you get after Bonnie and I'll take the black-headed one."

"Naw. I've had enough night life. I'm going to buy the biggest steak in this hotel. Come on, let's go get a steak."

"You go. I think I'll stay."

"Come on, Bert. Bonnie'll be here when you get back."

"I ain't got room for steak and whiskey, too. I'm still digesting the last piece of Famous Enterprises' beef I took on."

"O.K. If you ain't here when I get back, I'll see you back at the room."

"Fine, pard," Sorrells said. Cunningham left, walking straight and smooth as an Indian on the tracks of a deer he knows is headed for one of his snares. Bonnie looked up and watched him. When she recognized him, she searched the end of the bar for Sorrells until she found him. The spotlight went off, and she went back to attending her out-of-towner, while the pianist stood up from his piano and talked with them.

Bonnie said something to the brunette and drank the last of her green syrup. The brunette looked at Sorrells and then prodded the sop sitting next to her. They all got up and the sops shook hands with the pianist. Bonnie and the brunette laughed and talked with him while they started walking out. The sop with the brunette stopped her halfway to the door, mauled her, and said something to her. She laughed and pushed him toward the door.

"No tricks, hey?" the brunette's sop said loudly. "You *are* tricky, aren't you, baby? Let's just not have any trickiness about your tricks."

People at the tables in the bar ignored them when he looked around to see if they were paying attention to him. He saw Sorrells watching him. An audience. "How's tricks, cowboy?" he shouted across the room. "I got mine, where's yours?" Sorrells sipped his whiskey. Bonnie did not look at him. She hurried her sop out the door. "Wahoo," the sop with the brunette said weakly. His voice was drowned down by his own rising drunkenness.

While Bonnie walked away, Sorrells wondered why, with all the thousands of green tonics in this town, he still liked the label that wasn't good for him. Just the sight of Sorrells made her mad enough to run out and stick her head into a bush and wring her tail. He felt like going over to her stool and putting his hand on the seat of it to see if she had left it warm. It couldn't be warm, the way she looked. Brittle and greedy, that's how she looked. Besides that, she was either very sick, or exhausted, or both.

Sorrells settled down to drinking whiskey. Cunningham came to see him and left him again to go to bed. Hours later, too many full hours for any man to wait and still have any doubt his woman had spoiled on him, Bonnie sat on the stool next to him. She didn't look as pale as she had hours before. She didn't have her red hair on, now. Her thick blonde hair was cut short and lying on her head like a child's who had been out to play. Her face was very clean and childlike.

"What happened to that red mane you were sporting?" Sorrells asked her. "I thought you were old Sorrel Sorrells, runaway mare who used to belong to Bert Sorrells."

"I'm no sorrel and no Sorrells. I've changed my name to Sorel," Bonnie said.

"Congratulations. It fits you better. Short and sweet. You must not have much time to bother about names in this town."

"Not any damn names and not any damn, unnecessary, drunken cowboys. So what the damn hell do you want with me at this time?"

"Nothing. Not a damn thing. *Ninguna cosa. No mas nada*, as the Mexican says." Sorrells ordered a grasshopper for Bonnie.

"I'd just like to get it settled. How long are you going to keep popping up in my life? I'm getting just damn sick and tired of it," she said.

"Hell, I just came in to run and play. How did I know I was going to be stomping up your running ground? I thought you'd gone higher class and taken off to Los Angeles or Chicago or New York or someplace like that. Miami is nice for girls this time of year, I hear."

"Hah! Don't make me laugh. For some damn reason, every time I look around nowadays, I see your ugly face making sad-dog yellow eyes at me."

"Go on, then. Get the hell out of my sight. I didn't ask you to pull up your socks and girdle and look me up. Go on and have your damn fun and leave me to mine."

"I came here to face up to you. I was afraid of you after

what you did at Wanda's. Now, dammit, I've stopped being afraid and I'm here to tell you to leave me alone."

"Leave you alone to what? Not that I give a damn about you, but what in the hell is so great about this graveyard of derelicts? You remind me of an old mare that ran off through a barbwire fence and is still running, thinking somebody wants her. Who wants an old runnin' off wire-cut mare? The flies are blowing you, you're sagging in the carcass, and besides that, you run off. You'll just keep on running off until you're sure nobody wants you. Ever wonder why everybody's been dropping you lately?"

"I wish to God you'd join the crowd."

"Good. Consider yourself dropped by me, too, in case you've been doubting it."

Sorrells stood up to leave. He stood behind Bonnie's stool. Bonnie's head bent closer over her hands on her drink. She did not look back at Sorrells. He put his hand on Bonnie's shoulder. The shoulder was warm under a nice brown sweater. "Hell, Babe, there ain't any use in us picking at each other any more. I guess we're both doing the best we know how. I love you a lot, Bonnie. I hope you do good. I'll tell you one sure thing. I'm quitting the Outfit and getting the hell out of the country. I'm turning it over 'em . . . to you, the millionaires, the whoremongers, the bartenders, the mechanics, and the government workers. So have at 'er, Bonnie, for she never was, or will be, mine."

"What will you do, Bert?" Bonnie asked, looking down at the drink she had not tasted.

Sorrells laughed. "Well, Babe, without you. I'll do without you before I do anything else."

"Thank God for small favors," Bonnie said, and started to cry. Her shoulder jerked quickly, smally, under Sorrells' hand, like a new life coming to the surface. He said to himself, you self-righteous son of a bitch. Who are you to think you can go around accusing people and then forgiving them so you can walk away and leave them in a place like this? He sat down again and softly rocked Bonnie by the shoulder.

"Well, don't bawl, Babe," he said. She stopped him from rocking her, so he began patting her. All she needed was a little attention once in a while. She stopped crying. She sat there, holding it back. She moaned, and the sound of it made her laugh.

"You sonofabitch, you've made me bawl every chance you got ever since I was a little squirt," she said, without looking at him. "You big bully."

"You looked so damn bad, it made me mad. Then, I've never been nice to you when I should."

"Yes you have. You were always good to me. That's why I can't take it when you look at me as though you'd like to kill me."

"Well, I'd like to wear out the seat of your pants, maybe. Honestly, Bonnie, sometimes I think you'd wear your own rear out biting on it if you could reach it."

Bonnie didn't seem able to hold her head up and look at people's faces. She looked away from anything that moved. "Will you ask him to bring me a straight shot?" she said.

When the bartender brought her the whiskey and Sorrells had paid for it, she said, "I'll have to owe you. I didn't bring my purse."

"You never in your life had to pay for your own whiskey when you were around me," Sorrells said.

"I know, but I thought I ought to start, since I told you to let me alone."

"Where is your purse?"

"I never carry one around these places."

"Where do you put your money?"

"In my pocket, when I get any."

"Didn't old sophead pay you anything?"

"No."

"Didn't you go off with him for money, for hell's sake?"

"Yes, but he was too drunk."

"Come on, Bonnie. Don't give me that. You were gone long enough to sober up an ambulance case."

"He told me to come back tomorrow night."

"Yeah, and he'll be gone, bragging at his favorite bar that he got you free."

"I know it."

"Are you broke?"

"Broke? I can't remember what money even looks like."

"Well, I've got money."

"That's all right. I'll get by until I get a job. I've got a place to stay."

"Where?"

"With that girl you saw sitting by me at the piano."

"Friend of yours?"

"Well... I guess so."

"Well, dammit, what kind of a friend?"

"Well... like Wanda."

"Jesus Christ, I love you!" Sorrells muttered. He got all his money out and counted it. He had $140 dollars and some change. He handed seventy dollars of it to Bonnie.

"No. You work too hard for your money," she said tiredly.

"Look, I ain't going to give you any more. Take it." He stuffed it inside the neck of her sweater.

"I'll pay it back."

"I don't want it back. Hang on to it. Don't show it to anybody. Let's just say you're partners with me in our old business."

"Can you take me home now, Bert? I'm almost ready to fall down and die, I'm so tired."

The bartender called a taxi for them. Walking with Bonnie, in the light of the casino, Sorrells saw and felt how much like a child she was. She acted like a little girl caught by her daddy out too late. She walked like such a little girl would walk when she was too tired to remember how to walk in high heels. She let Sorrells lead her along, but somebody else had broken her to lead.

When the taxi driver found the duplex Bonnie wanted, Sorrells walked her to the door. Head down, she rang the doorbell and when no one answered, she pulled open the screen door and knocked softly. A light came on in the house and she raised her head enough to notice it. She kept her head down for another moment and then took Sorrells' hand and looked sideways at him.

"Bert, do you think you might be able to come and see me now and then?"

"Yes," Sorrells said, only to confirm the insurance she was asking for. The door opened and the black-headed woman pushed the screen door open wide enough for Bonnie. She had on a man's terrycloth robe too big for her, and was barefooted. Cunningham sure knew a scag when he saw one.

"Hon, how did you make out?" the black-headed woman asked and caught Bonnie around the neck to rub cheeks with her. Bonnie looked back at Sorrells like a little dog being overly fondled, but knowing she would never get away. She was resigned to be at hand for that petting. The woman looked at Bonnie's face, stroked her hair, pulled her into the room, glanced angrily at Sorrells, and shut the door in his face.

Chapter 33

TURNED OUT

Most outfits turn their saddle horses out when they are not being used. Horses rest better and stay in better condition if they can run free and easy, away from man. They keep active rustling for their own feed and water. Their feet do not grow long and soft. They do not grow unhealthily fat. They get over being petty and ill-tempered from having to depend on man for their sustenance. They rest and get over a peevishness caused by too many long, hard-working hours close to man. They enjoy a vacation in the elements natural to their own society.

Sorrells knew he was not going to stay on the Outfit when he saw headquarters again. Cunningham let him out at the bunkhouse and drove on to his own house. Maudy was alone on the Outfit. Sorrells stood in the cold wind and snow a moment and looked around. The place was a graveyard. To Sorrells, it had the aspect of an open grave with unfathomable capacity. He did not want to be a new corpse to fill it.

Whoever had decided the headquarters and living spaces for the Outfit should be here at Ethel, should have thought better of it, because of the example of the old buildings. Hardier souls had long since abandoned Ethel, Nevada. A man might endure eating and sleeping here if he loved the work he was doing. He could never spend a restful winter here, because he would not be able to hope or laugh or sing and dance here.

Sorrells went into the bunkhouse to change his clothes. The bunkhouse was deserted and cold. Sorrells wondered how he had managed being corralled to his eating and sleeping here for four months. He was dressing hurriedly, shivering after his bare feet had been on the linoleum, when he heard the front door of the bunkhouse open and close. He was afraid, listening to the footsteps of someone coming through the rooms toward him. He was ready to fight when Cunningham came into his room. Cunningham leaned against the doorjam. Sorrells hurried to finish dressing.

"Bad news, Bert," Cunningham said.

Sorrells sat on his bed. "Now what?" he asked.

"Wilson went home and killed his dog, his horse, and himself."

"No," Sorrells said. "Is this damned place going to get us all?"

"I believe it will," Cunningham said.

"How did you find out about Wilson?"

"The sheriff came out and told Maudy. I guess he didn't know Wilson had been fired."

"When did he do it?"

"I don't know. Stacy, Charley, and Jack went to the burial yesterday. They haven't been back."

Sorrells rolled his bed and packed his grip.

"What are you fixing to do now?" Cunningham asked.

"I'm going to pull the shoes off my horses and then I want to turn the little horse loose with the wild bunch."

"I'll help you," Cunningham said. He walked with Sorrells to the corrals. They caught Big Red, Baldy, and Roller, Cunningham held them while Sorrells pulled the shoes and trimmed and smoothed their hooves.

When Sorrells led the last horse up the alley to turn him loose, he felt he was a stranger to the corrals, as if he were only a visitor there for a moment, doing someone else's chore as a favor. He had no reason of his own to be there any longer. During the work he had thought he belonged there with Wilson, Porter, and the rest of the crew. Now he felt impersonal to the place because he was finding out it had always been impersonal to him and to his partners. The only personal place Sorrells was sure of was his grave, and he would have to endure too many impersonal days on the Outfit to wait to be buried there. He did not want one more hour of it.

Sorrells and Cunningham loaded the pickup with hay, and Cunningham drove through the horse pasture while Sorrells stood in the back and cut wires and rolled blocks of hay to the remuda. He did not begrudge the chore. He felt it just wasn't his business to be doing it and never had been.

Sorrells loaded Little Barney in the stock truck and he and Cunningham drove out to the joshua tree where Sorrells had tied the colt the day he and Porter had caught him. Low clouds rushed densely close overhead imposing their lack of color on the country and closing around the truck. Sorrells led the colt away from the truck. Barney raised his head, searched the country, and nickered. Sorrells removed the halter and the little horse moved off without looking back. Sorrells looked him over again. He was not sorry to be letting him go. The horse Sorrells might have called Barney was going to be a small horse. His little velvet nostrils, sniffing for a sign of his own kind, seemed toylike now.

"Look, Bert," Cunningham said and pointed. A band of horses was lining out through mist on the skyline across a high ridge about a mile away. They were leaving, but Sorrells thought he recognized the sorrel stud, sire of the colt's band. The colt saw them and ran after them. He ran surely, lightly, without looking down, calling to them.

While the men watched the colt running to catch up, a young blue stud appeared on the slope under the ridge where the band had disappeared.

"That looks like a stud we saw on Montezuma Mountain last fall," Sorrells said. "He'd been whipped off a band that was running over there. He's come this far looking for a friend."

"He's like old Wilson, isn't he?" Cunningham said.

"Yes, he is," Sorrells said.

Later, after Sorrells said good-bye to Maudy and loaded his outfit in Carlotta, he stood a moment to be sure he had forgotten nothing. He saw the saddle horses lined up on the blocks of hay in the horse pasture. He saw old Roller, lean from the work he had given Sorrells.

"Good-bye, Roller," Sorrells said. The wind had died. The place was still. The man's voice was thick. "Reeolah, good-bye," he called. Roller raised his head and looked toward the man. When he looked down at his hay and lowered his head to it, the man drove away.

MAVERICK

A maverick is a full-grown bovine owned by no man. He carries no brand or earmark. He is free and uncounted and untallied on any bookkeeper's books. He is not a member of the beef industry. He is to the cattle breeder what the mustang is to the horse breeder. An abomination. The older he gets the wilier he gets and the harder he is to get out of the way to make room for gentler, more domestic, more productive members of his species.

J. P. S. BROWN

has been one of the most respected writers of the American Southwest for the past two decades. If you enjoyed *The Outfit*, you'll want to read the all-new Arizona Saga. In April, Bantam Books will publish the first volume in this exciting new series by J. P. S. Brown:

The Arizona Sage #1:

THE BLOODED STOCK

Turn the page for a dynamic preview from *The Blooded Stock*, on sale April 1, 1990, wherever Bantam Books are sold!

The Cowden brothers were prowling the southern edge of their home range. They rode onto the tracks of a group of riders driving a bunch of their cattle toward Mexico and hurried after them.

Ben Cowden was glad he and his brothers were riding fresh horses. The Cowdens raised good horses so they would be well mounted in situations such as this. They often extended their prowling for days into unfriendly country. The Cowden horses would not quit on a man in a tight spot.

At noon Ben left the tracks and climbed a hill to look across the main draw of the Buena Vista range into Mexico. He stopped his horse so that only his hat and his eyes cleared the top of the hill, and he saw the dust of the cattle. Mexican riders were moving them.

"Well, there they are," Ben said, after returning. "No use hurrying. We'll catch them in the Santa Barbara foothills. They must be vaqueros from the Maria Macarena Ranch. They'll stop to water at La Acequia."

"Good, now we can go straight to them and quit this tracking," said Les, the second oldest brother. "I don't want any more *tracking*. It makes me *tired*."

"How can anybody complain about tracking a herd this big?" asked Mark, the youngest brother. "Paula Mary could do it." He was laughing at his brother.

"You ought to have the kink in your neck that I do. I've been the one had to do all the looking down for tracks."

That was the end of the fun for Mark. Les was serious. Mark looked away after the cattle and forgot about tracks and discussions.

Ben had been surprised when Mark opened his mouth to talk. He usually did not say much. Always at the right place at the right time in his work, Mark was usually quiet and reserved. He followed his brothers along with quiet good humor and did whatever they decided to do, but every once in a while Les brought an argument out of him. Les's judgments amused Mark. Les was extremely hot tempered and quick to attack anything that made him angry. Mark knew he was lucky Les was gentle with his family. Sometimes Mark just could not help laughing at him, though.

Ben and Mark were seldom angry with Les. He ran himself with his feelings, but he had good reasons for being emotional. He was only nineteen and he was out trying to retrieve cattle. He did his work looking over his shoulder for Apaches who might run a wooden shaft through him and cattle thieves who might shoot him and cut off his ears so his mama would not know him.

Mark was only seventeen, but he gave each task a lot of thought before he took hold of it and he was as good a cowboy as Les. Ben was twenty-one. The brothers were born after the Civil War and in the middle of the Apache War. They went horseback before they could walk and had never known a time without conflict. Their mother and father taught them to find peace inside their family.

"What'll we do when we catch them, Ben?" Les asked. "Can we teach them a lesson this time?"

Ben laughed softly. "What can we teach them? They own the school today. We'll own it tomorrow. They tracked some of their cattle over here and are driving some of ours back with them. We'll get ours back if we can and might have to bring some of theirs home. Where's the lesson in that?"

"Well, we should make them sorry for taking our cattle."

"Papa says we'd have to do something sorry to make them sorry."

"Well, let's at least bring back some of their horses and leave them afoot for a while."

"No, we won't take anybody's horses. Take a man's horse, or shoot his dog, or steal his wife, and he never lets you live it down. Anyway, what would we do with those dinks the Maria Macarena vaqueros ride?"

"Fatten them up and sell them, I guess. That's what I'd do."

"We have too many *good* horses to feed. What could we do by stealing a few dinks, except cause a hardship on the Mexicans by putting them afoot and on ourselves by having to pour a lot of feed into them? How would we explain to Papa when somebody told him Les went crazy and tried to sell someone a Maria Macarena dink? We'd have to sell them. Which one of us would want to be seen riding one?"

"I sure wouldn't let Papa know. I'd keep them in Temporal Canyon until they looked good and the brands haired over. Then I'd sell them to the army at Fort Bowie. No horsemen from this county would ever see them."

Ben was leading the way around the crest of the hill so

he would not be silhouetted against the sky. A horseman might not live long after he showed himself on top a hill in Arizona. The only time the Cowdens ever saw the silhouette of a horseman was when somebody drew a pretty picture of one and published it back East for all the world to see.

The Cowden brothers rode south through cedar, piñon, and white oak beside the open draws of the Buena Vista and across the Mexican border. They did not talk. They kept their horses at a high trot a good distance apart and concentrated on seeing what they had to see. They watched the ground for tracks, even though they were keeping the dust of the cattle in sight. They looked closely at any shape that was within range of a rifle or a pistol, or the flight of an arrow.

They saw the spring grass was better on the Mexican side of the Buena Vista because not many cattle were running there. Apaches liked to take Mexican beef with them when they returned to their haunts in the Sierra Madre. They were decimating the herds of Maria Macarena cattle. They did not take many Cowden cattle. The Cowdens stayed on the prowl to keep their stock from drifting south.

All humans and warm-blooded animals were prey to the Apache, but when an Apache thought about his enemies, he thought about Mexicans. His hate for Mexicans was in his blood. Mexicans had taught the Apaches awful ways of getting even with enemies. They gave the Apaches back what the Apaches gave them with more imagination and pleasure than Americans ever did.

Ben Cowden looked down and saw the smooth print of a *tegua*, the Apache footwear. He slowed his horse and coursed away from the trail looking for more. He found the tracks of five Apaches. He looked to the other side of the trail and saw that Les was holding up four fingers. Nine Indians had walked across the cattle tracks, then split up to overtake the herd. They probably planned to hook in and attack the vaqueros from both flanks and be in position to hold the cattle.

The brothers heard the shots then, four or five pops that sounded harmless with no echo in the open distance. They climbed the side of the Santa Barbara hills so they could study the camp at La Acequia a mile away. The dust of the herd was going on past the camp.

"Now, that's not right. The vaqueros should have rested the cattle there." Ben watched the dust. "Look, those cattle are being hurried."

The cattle were crossing an open rise.

"I don't see horsemen with them," Les said.

"We better get ourselves down to that camp," Ben said.

The brothers split apart, drew their pistols, and made a run across the side of a hill above the camp for a good look at it. They ran off the hill through the camp and stopped at a stream beyond it to let their horses blow. Ben and Les looked into each others' faces. They had ridden so close by the bodies of two vaqueros that their horses had shied from them.

"I only saw two carcasses," said Les. "We've been following three vaqueros, haven't we?"

The brothers rode back to the bodies and examined them a moment without dismounting. Both men had been shot with arrows, stripped and lanced. The sight of them made the brothers look around at the hills for Apaches again. They felt they might be taking their last look at their mother earth. The staring eyes of the vaqueros had certainly not enjoyed their last sight of God's creatures.

Ben said, "This one's going to raise a wail. He's Pedro Elias, Don Juan Pedro's son. I wonder why he rode all the way to our side of the Buena Vista and then slowed himself with cattle on the way home. He must have known Apaches might get him. I guess he felt like taking chances today. I know one thing, he was a working son of a gun."

"This one over here is Jose Romero," Mark said quietly. "He and I pardnered playing fiddles at the last Patagonia dance. Nice feller. He's married to Margarita, Don Juan Pedro's daughter. He sure could sing."

"Well, we better hush up and keep our eyes open. Don't relax," Ben said. Then he saw the track of small bare feet by the body of Pedro Elias. "Here's our other vaquero." He followed the track away.

"I guess we'd better move them out of the sun," said Les. He rode to look inside the camp's adobe house.

A ramada shaded the front of the house. Ben followed the barefoot tracks to the back of the adobe and saw that the child had climbed to the roof.

"Bajate. Somos amigos. No te vamos a lastimac." Ben said, quietly. "Come down, we're friends. We won't hurt you."

Someone on top of the roof gave voice to his tears then.

"Bring yourself down," Ben said.

The top of a small, black head showed above the parapet on the roof. "Let me see you, *buqui*," said Ben. "Come on."

A pale face, muddy with dirt and tears showed over the parapet.

"Ai, poor little fellow," Ben said.

"Tengo miedo," the boy said. "I'm afraid. It's too high."

Ben moved his horse against the building, stood on top of his saddle, and offered his arms for the child. The boy stepped off the roof into his arms. Ben rode to show him to his brothers. He was about twelve.

Ben handed him down and Les sat him in the shade while Mark brought him water in a gourd.

"Como te llamas?" asked Les. "How are you called?"

"His name is Pepe." Ben said. "He's Jose Romero's son. We know each other, don't we, boy?"

"Si," the boy whispered with an intake of his breath.

"This is the boy who worked the roundup on the Buena Vista with us last fall and made such a good hand." Ben said. "He's grown so big I didn't know him."

Les and Mark picked up one of the bodies to carry it into the house and the boy started to cry. "My father," he said. His grief pressed a squeak out of him when he tried to speak again.

Ben gripped the boy's bare toes in both his hands to steady him. "It's all right. We'll put your people in the house and take you home to your mother."

The boy made himself stop crying, but he looked away from Ben miserably. *"Gracias."*

"Drink water so you can tell me what happened," Ben said. "How did you escape the Apaches?"

"They didn't see me."

"Tell me. Where were you when they attacked your people?"

"I don't know. The *partida* we were driving was on the stream. A cow had stopped in the mesquite thicket when we passed through. I missed her at the stream and went back for her. She faced me in the thicket and armed herself to fight. I went in after her afoot. She broke out and trotted toward the other cattle, and I remounted my horse.

"I was still riding in the cover of the *mesquital* when I heard the shots and the Apaches screaming. My horse ducked back from the noise and threw me. I was riding bareback and as I flew over his head I snatched my bridle off. The horse jumped over the top of me and trampled my ankle.

"He ran away, and I crawled into the thicket and hid. My uncle Pedro was screaming, but my father never made a sound. After my uncle was quiet, I heard the Apaches move away with the *partida*. When they were gone, I went out and found my father's body."

"What did they take, besides the cattle?" asked Les.

"All the cattle and horses, the clothing, arms, and provisions."

"Didn't they look for you?"

"No, they would have found me. I did not have a good place to hide. They could have tracked me."

"I wonder why they didn't look for you," said Les. He smiled. "Was your guardian angel with you?"

"Maybe they didn't realize my horse was carrying a rider. I left no saddle marks on him, and he carried no bridle."

"It's a good thing you didn't run after him," Les said.

"I tried, but my ankle hurt so bad I sat down, and then my uncle started to scream. He suffered an agony with those screams. I couldn't go any closer."

The boy bowed his head and began to cry.

"You're a brave boy," Ben said.

The boy controlled himself again. "I didn't cry until I saw my father's dead eyes."

Ben watched him another minute, then shook the boy's feet gently and said, "We'll hurry to the Maria Macarena now so you can be with your mother and so your grandfather can send someone for the people."

Ben picked the boy up and sat him behind his saddle. Mark had watered the horses at the stream. The brothers rode for the Maria Macarena and reached a hill above the hacienda at dusk.

The main building was built like a fort, in a square with an open patio in the center. All doors opened indoors on the patio except the front entrance. Four horsemen could enter abreast through this archway. It was high enough to accommodate a wagon and team and was secured by an iron gate and a heavy wooden door.

Aged cottonwood and mesquite trees shaded the hacienda. The only windows on the outside of the main building were long, narrow slits high in the walls that served as rifle ports. Ben gave out a cowboy call so the hacienda would hear them coming and have time to recognize them.

Juan Pedro Elias, the elderly don who owned the Maria Macarena, came out the front archway to greet them. He recognized the boy riding behind Ben and did not smile. Ben looked over his head and saw Margarita, the boy's mother, lean against a wall, stricken with fear to see her son return without her husband and brother.

"*Hola*, Benjamin," said Don Juan Pedro. "What happened?"

"Bad news, Don Juan," Ben said. "Your son and your *hierno* were attacked by Apaches. Your little grandson only escaped by chance and the intercession of his patron saint."

Ben gave the boy his arm and swung him off the horse to Don Juan, but waited for an invitation to dismount. Everyone in the community had come to the front of the main building. When Margarita fainted against the wall, another woman hurried to catch her. Ben had danced at fiestas with Margarita before she married.

"Dismount, please, gentlemen," Don Juan said.

The Cowden brothers stepped off their horses. They were ready to sit in the shade with a drink of water.

"Please, hand your reins to these boys. Let my people put up your horses. Please come inside." Don Juan was embracing Pepe with one arm. He took Mark's arm and escorted them both toward his front door. His daughter was lying with her head in the lap of the woman who had caught her. He turned to his workers and family. "Here, you, men, you, Genoveva, you, Chata, help this poor woman. Carry her inside."

Pepe stopped beside his mother. The Cowden brothers passed through the wide, cool archway to the open patio inside the hacienda. Lamps and candles were lit and the place smelled of fresh flowers and moist earth. The floor of the enclosure was worn adobe brick newly swept and sprinkled with water to cool it and settle the dust.

Don Juan asked that chairs be brought for the brothers. Les did not wait to be served water. He stepped up to an *olla*, a pot sweating with cool water that was hanging under the ramada. He scooped out a drink with a gourd that was floating inside. He quickly sucked all the water out of the gourd. He drank another gourdful. He scooped out another and held it a moment. "I'll tell you," he said. "I dry up like a corncob every time I even smell an Apache." He sipped half of that water, scattered the rest over the patio brick, then gently floated the gourd in the *olla*.

"Here, Chata, you women," Don Juan ordered. "Bring clean cups so these men can drink water. Bring them coffee. You, *muchachita*." He pointed to a young *gata de casa*, a girl employed in his household. "Bring my *demajuana* of mescal. These men have come a long way under great stress. They're tired and hungry. Here, Chata, see to their supper and then tend to their bedding in the guest room. They'll want to be together in the same room when they sleep."

Ben was amused. Don Juan was always good to the Cowden brothers when they came to his house. The usual reason they were there was to retrieve cattle Don Juan's vaqueros had driven away from the Buena Vista range. The only sign the old don ever showed that he might have differences with the brothers was to give them the same room so they could be sure they would not be separated and betrayed.

Mark was smiling for the same reason, but Les was not. Les was busy accepting a cup of coffee and spooning sugar into it from a bowl held for him by a servant. He took a small cup of mescal when it was offered him, swallowed the stuff quickly, and looked around for more. He uttered no sound of appreciation even though he heard his brothers thank the servant softly and politely. He was seldom polite unless he suspected A.B. or his mother was watching.

Don Juan was busy attending to the grief of his household and the care of his grandson. His wife had been sick in bed for many months, and after a while he went into her room and quietly shut the door. For a few moments no sound came through the thick walls. Then all of a sudden a long, high, wail of agony came through as if nothing would ever silence the woman's grief. Ben wondered how long Sonora and Arizona women had been screaming with sorrow because of the Apaches. The cry was not weakening.

The brothers walked to relax their legs while they sipped mescal from Don Juan's clay demijohn and waited for him to come back. Cow's horns were mortared into the walls so horses could be tied to them inside the enclosure. The hacienda's tack was kept under the ramada that sheltered the walls and doorways.

During the day, the *talabartero* who tanned and finished the ranch's hides did his leather work at a table in the patio. The saddles were astraddle individual stands in a line against a wall with every braided horsehair cinch neatly caught up to a keeper by the horn. Every *reata* was tallowed and coiled and hanging on the near side of each saddle below the cantle. A tallowed quirt of braided rawhide hung from each saddle horn.

No more sounds were coming from the mother's bedroom, and after a while Don Juan came out and went straight to the demijohn. He poured stout measures of mescal for himself and the Cowden brothers.

"Doña Tili will never survive this illness now," Don Juan said. His eyes were red. "No one completely survives the loss of a son. And to lose a son to the knives and lances of murderers..."

Ben could see the man was cornering most of his grief inside himself, but part was escaping and having great effect on his eyes. He was about fifty years old, straight and physically strong like A.B., dressed plainly as people did who lived hundreds of miles across desert from a store. "We are fortunate that you and your brothers did not catch up to my son sooner, I suppose," Don Juan was saying. "You might also have been killed."

"I'm sorry we didn't catch up before they reached La Acequia. We'd have been honored to help them in the fight," Ben said.

"It's true the Apaches might never have attacked if you had been with my people." Don Juan smiled. "But then, you and my son might have argued over your reason for coming after him."

"We expected no argument from Pedro. Our errands to the Maria Macarena are always friendly. We have never been shown anything but friendship on this ranch."

"Ah, gentlemen must be kind, must they not?"

"Our father wants us to be good neighbors."

"The world is full of evil, Benjamin. We have to fight the savage. Let's not bring harm to a neighbor. What made you follow my son?"

"He crossed the Buena Vista and picked up cattle on the edge of our Harshaw range. He cleaned out an area where your cattle and ours share a spring. That spring is a long way from the Maria Macarena. We wanted to help him separate our cattle from his and bring them home. We're always ready to help you round up stock on range we share in common."

"As any neighbor should," said Don Juan. "I'm glad you're here. Your friendship is a comfort to me. Ah, now see, your supper is ready."

Don Juan led the way into the candlelight of his dining room. The floor was worn brick, like the patio, but every other surface in the room was shining with polish. Thick, ax-hewn mesquite beams spanned the ceiling, their old hardness reflecting the fire of the candles. A white linen tablecloth covered the table. Napkins and old silver were laid by old chinaware.

The meal was simple. Stewed corn, broiled beef loin, beans whipped and fried with cheese, and white sheets of flour tortilla were served. The black coffee had been ground at home and the sugar roasted on an open fire. The dessert was wild honey and butter on hot tortillas.

After supper Don Juan left his guests and went to look after his household. The brothers sat quietly in the darkness of the patio, smoking. Two vaqueros came in with a priest from Santa Cruz. One of the women showed him into Doña Tili's bedchamber. He was in the room a few moments when the brothers heard the mother's scream, *"Aaayyy!"* once again, and then no more.

The brothers were ready to sleep by then, and they trooped to their room. Their beds had been formally turned down, their *tendidos*, the places for their resting, prepared according to the strict and generous rules of Sonoran hospitality. The beds were laid on heavy sailcloth cots with Yaqui blankets and flannel sheets over cotton mattresses. The cots were large and easily accommodated the tall Cowdens. Each cot was against a wall with its own bedstand and lamp. A pitcher of water with a clay cup was placed under each stand. Without conversation the brothers undressed and lay down to sleep.

In the morning they went out to saddle their horses and found them inside the patio tied to the cows' horns. The horses had been bathed with yucca soap and brushed from their foretops to their hocks. They were feeding at mangers full of fresh sacaton hay. Don Juan had given orders that they be fed corn at dawn so the brothers could leave early if they wanted to.

Don Juan stood by while the brothers were saddling. Les and Mark mounted their horses as Ben turned to say good-bye.

"We know you won't be celebrating your saint's day tomorrow, but we wish you happiness on all your future San Juan days," Ben said, and he embraced Don Juan. Then he mounted and turned his horse toward home with his brothers.

ABOUT THE AUTHOR

Born in Nogales, Arizona, JOSEPH PAUL SUMMERS BROWN
—J.P.S. to readers of his books and Joe to his friends—was raised
on a sprawling 185-acre ranch and is a fifth generation Arizona
cattleman. While attending Notre Dame University and majoring
in journalism, he also enlisted in the U.S. Marine Corps Reserve.
At Notre Dame he claimed the middleweight boxing championship
in 1951; the following year, he won the light-heavyweight
championship.

After college Brown returned to the family ranch and began a
career in journalism, working as a general assignment reporter on
two weekly newspapers, *The Apache County Independent News*
and *The Holbrook Tribune News*, where he wrote a popular
column called "Highway 66." He later went to work for the *El
Paso Herald-Post*, winning the Scripps-Howard Award for best
farm reporting in 1954.

That same year, Brown enrolled in the U.S. Marine Corps
Officer Candidate School in Quantico, Virginia, and he was
commissioned a year later. Released from active duty in 1958, he
returned to the cattle business in Mexico and Arizona, and
continued to run the family cattle ranch in Arizona.

It wasn't until 1965, during a bout with hepatitis, that Brown
began to write. His first novel, published to critical acclaim, was
Jim Kane. In 1971 it became the basis for the movie, *Pocket
Money*, which starred Paul Newman and the late Lee Marvin.

A stint as a cowboy gathering maverick cattle provided the
inspiration for his second novel, *The Outfit*, which is considered a
southwestern classic. Bitten by the show-biz bug, Brown began
furnishing livestock for the motion picture industry, eventually
supplying four-legged supporting casts for some seventy-seven
movies.

In 1974 his third novel, *Forests of the Night*, was published;
1986 saw the publication of the novel *Steeldust*, as well as the
short story "Butterfly Dog," which appeared in *City Magazine*. In
1990 Bantam Books will publish *The Blooded Stock*, the first
volume of his original series, The Arizona Saga.

The author and his wife currently make their home in Tucson,
Arizona.

ELMER KELTON

THE MAN WHO RODE MIDNIGHT

☐ 27713 $3.50

Bantam is pleased to offer these exciting Western adventures by ELMER KELTON, one of the great Western storytellers with a special talent for capturing the fiercely independent spirit of the West:

☐ 25658	**AFTER THE BUGLES**	$2.95
☐ 27351	**HORSEHEAD CROSSING**	$2.95
☐ 27119	**LLANO RIVER**	$2.95
☐ 27218	**MANHUNTERS**	$2.95
☐ 27620	**HANGING JUDGE**	$2.95
☐ 27467	**WAGONTONGUE**	$2.95

"An American original."
—*The New York Times Book Review*

ELMORE LEONARD

For rugged stories of the American frontier, there is no writer quite like Elmore Leonard. Pick up these exciting westerns at your local bookstore—or use the handy coupon below for ordering.

☐ ESCAPE FROM FIVE SHADOWS (27202 • $2.95)
_____

☐ FORTY LASHES LESS ONE (27625 • $2.95)
_____

☐ THE BOUNTY HUNTERS (27099 • $2.95)
_____

☐ GUNSIGHTS (27337 • $2.95)
_____

☐ VALDEZ IS COMING (27098 • $2.95)
_____

☐ LAST STAND AT SABER RIVER (27097 • $2.95)
_____

☐ THE LAW AT RANDADO (27201 • $2.95)
_____

TERRY C. JOHNSTON

Winner of the prestigious Western Writer's award for the best first novel, Terry C. Johnston brings you two volumes of his award-winning saga of mountain men Josiah Paddock and Titus Bass who strive together to meet the challenges of the western wilderness in the 1830's.

☐ 25572 **CARRY THE WIND** $4.95

Having killed a wealthy young Frenchman in a duel, Josiah Paddock flees St. Louis in 1831. He heads west to the fierce and beautiful Rocky Mountains, to become a free trapper far from the entanglements of civilization. Hot-headed and impetuous, young Josiah finds his romantic image of life in the mountains giving way to a harsh struggle for survival—against wild animals, fierce Indians, and nature's own cruelty. Half-dead of cold and starvation, he encounters Titus Bass, a solitary old trapper who takes the youth under his wing and teaches him the ways of the mountains. So begins a magnificent historical novel, remarkable for its wealth of authentic mountain lore and wisdom.

☐ 26224 **BORDERLORDS** $4.95

Here is a swirling, powerful drama of the early American wilderness, filled with fascinating scenes of tribal Indian life depicted with passion and detail unequaled in American literature, and all of it leading up to a terrifying climax at the fabled 1833 Green River Rendezvous.

Look for these books wherever Bantam books are sold, or use this handy coupon for ordering: